Baramulla Bomber

Svastik Trilogy-Eka

Clark Prasad

NIYOGI
BOOKS

Published by
NIYOGI BOOKS
D-78, Okhla Industrial Area, Phase-I
New Delhi-110 020, INDIA
Tel: 91-11-26816301, 49327000
Fax: 91-11-26810483, 26813830
email: niyogibooks@gmail.com
website: www.niyogibooksindia.com

Editor: Gita Rajan
Cover Design: Damonza
Layout: Nabanita Das/Niyogi Books

ISBN: 978-93-81523-97-1
Publication: 2013

Printed at: Niyogi Offset Pvt. Ltd., New Delhi, India

Praise for Baramulla Bomber

"Intelligent and comprehensive with enough narrative to support another instalment."

Kirkus Review, International acclaimed book review agency

"A genre on its own, with an inquisitive writing style. Mythology, history and politics take life within the parameters of science. A well needed dialogue and Clark Prasad is our pioneer."

Rheea Mukherjee, writer, co-founder BWW,
www.bangalorewriters.com

"Have built up the element of suspense very well."

Anuradha Goyal, author, blogger and book reviewer,
www.anureviews.com

"The book forces a person to think and connect the dots. His way of writing makes the reader feel as if they are witnessing the events as they happen. It's a must read for anyone who likes espionage stories."

Anupama Sensharma, Delhi

"The head popping POV that the author has given to its characters made me love the book even more. For what I want to give Mr. Prasad a standing ovation is the brilliantly extensive and extensively brilliant research work which he has done for the book. It told me of the facts about Kashmir that I, even after being a Kashmiri, didn't know about my land. In the age when the authors do not even bother to look up a dictionary while writing a book, Mr. Prasad has proved that if you work harder you'll have a piece of gold in your hands in the form of the book. Hats off!"

Jassi Mir, Srinagar

"Action packed and riveting! A smart, immersive piece of writing that just sucks you in. Can't wait to read the next book in the series!"

Hemant Galagali, Mysore

"The story will keep you engaged throughout. It is a thrilling read and my recommendation would be to go grab your copy. The book is worth it!!!"

Shweta Sharma, Bangalore

"Watch this space! A genre of writing not seen in India and the novel never overwhelms or bores."

Naveen Khurana, Bangalore

For my parents, sisters,
roomies, friends and her....

WARNING

There are images and illustrations in this book. In order to avoid plot-spoilers please do not flip through the pages or read mid sections.

A REQUEST

Reviewers are requested not to give away the details of the plot in blogs, social media sites or other media channels which may act as plot-spoilers for others.

"The religion of the future will be a cosmic religion. It should transcend personal God and avoid dogma and theology. Covering both the natural and the spiritual, it should be based on a religious sense arising from the experience of all things natural and spiritual as a meaningful unity. Buddhism answers this description. If there is any religion that could cope with modern scientific needs it would be Buddhism."

Albert Einstein

FACT

India's Ironman and the first Home Minister of Independent India, Sardar Vallabh Bhai Patel wrote a letter to Prime Minister Jawahar Lal Nehru, on 7 November 1950, warning him about India's lack of foresightedness with respect to China. He apprised him of the danger China posed to the Union, and requested a meeting to discuss the steps that he had listed out, to tackle the situation.

Sardar Patel died on 15 December 1950, and the situation with China continues to remain tense.

All the departments, associations and organisations in this novel exist or existed in somewhat similar structure.

All the past reportage, news or events mentioned have occurred or are believed to have happened.

All the presented science facts are true, and experiments have been conducted to test related hypotheses.

All the locations and streets exist or existed, somewhat similar in description.

'In the beginning was the Word, and the Word was with God, and the Word was God'

John 1:1(50-100 AD)

'Prajapati vai idam agre asit tasya vak dvitiya asit vak vai param brahma'

Rig Veda(3000 BC)

In the beginning was Prajapati, the Brahman (one supreme) with whom was the Word/Vak (AUM) and the Word was verily the Supreme Brahman.

Prologue

Si vis pacem, para bellum

If you wish for peace, prepare for war

T-MINUS 1 HOUR TO EVENT

Present Day
Somewhere in Nordic Region Airspace

December 11, 18:30 CET

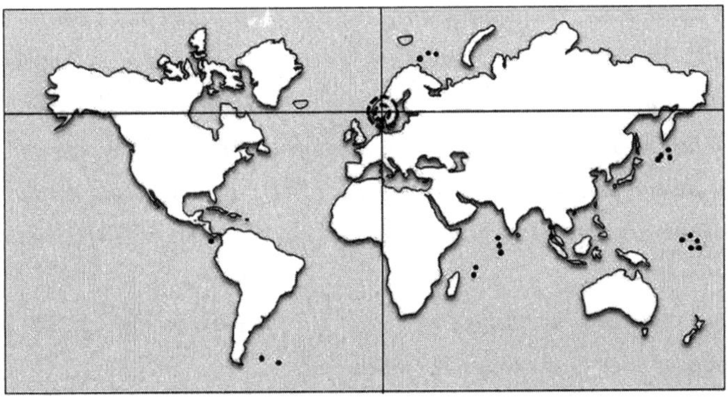

'**Lady, if you** were a guy I would have said that you have some balls!' yelled Adolf, raising his voice to be heard above the surrounding noise of the military jet and gusty wind, thousands of metres above the ground.

'Darling, we do have balls. The difference is that ours are a bit closer to our head, so they work better,' shouted Aahana as she winked at him, putting on her oxygen mask, and jumped off the bomber plane, but not before chanting a sacred set of words *Aum Mani Padme Hum* in her mind.

Adolf watched her rapidly drop out of sight, her skydiving form perfect. *Mansur Haider is one lucky guy to have a girl like her.*

Next to exit the bomber jet was the Indian Home Minister, Agastya Rathore, strapped to a commando. Finally it would be Adolf's turn to jump, accompanied by a British commando who completed the team.

Agastya took out his mobile phone and looked longingly at a photo of himself and his wife. He glanced back at his partner who was ready to take him down. Placing his mobile back in the zipper pocket, adjusting his gloves once again, and putting on the oxygen mask, he breathed in, feeling the pure air rushing into his lungs. Agastya prepared to make the jump as the bomber plane flew in a curve around the designated drop zone, his legs getting a tingling sensation.

As they took the flight and jumped out, he could feel the instant rush of blood and the cold wind assaulting his face. His mind was a battlefield raging with questions:

'GOD! *Here we are on the way down to destroy the Ancient Biblical-Vedic weapon tested at the Shaksgam Valley and here I am feeling that I am too old for this stuff. And to think of it, I would not be here if there had been no Partition or if the first war with Pakistan had not been stopped in 1948. If Lal Bahadur Shastri had not died in Tashkent or if Indira Gandhi had stuck to her decision and rolled into the western part of Pakistan during the 1971 war,* WE *would not have been in this grave situation.* IF *only there was a chance to roll back* TIME *and change the past.*

When could have we changed it? Could it be it back in 1947 on the 2nd of November or when God's power was unleashed!

GOD'S POWER UNLEASHED

Jornadadel Muerto Desert, Los Alamos
New Mexico, United States of America

July 16,1945,05:35 MWT

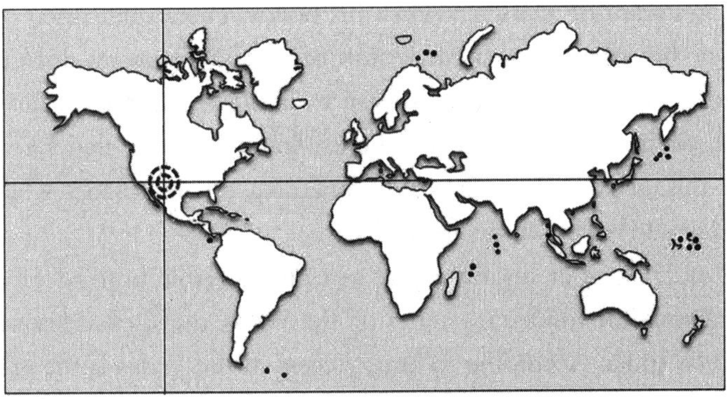

It was a brilliant sight, as though the gods had unleashed their power in the burning of a thousand suns. God seemed to have been tamed, and power lay at man's fingertips. The rumblings of the loud blast ten miles away could be heard across the base camp. Men in dark glasses at the base camp, many miles away, watched as the first atomic explosion, aptly titled 'Trinity' took over. Many of them cheered and laughed, others cried in excitement. For these men, this weapon signified the end of war. But a small group stood silent, the men who knew they had unleashed heaven's wrath from the past. One of the silent men, watching the spectacle and the commotion around him, hung his head as he turned to walk away from the room. His shoulders drooped as if with the weight of the universe, a burden he would not die with, only carry in his soul, crying for what he had created. He was J.R. Oppenheimer, the leading theoretical physicist of the world.

Oppenheimer recalled lines from the *Bhagwad Gita* wherein Vishnu in his avatar as Krishna, exhorts Arjuna to do his duty and not worry about the result. During this interaction, Vishnu, a part of the Holy Trinity of Hinduism, grew into his large, majestic multi-arm form and announced to the awed Arjuna—'Now I have become Death, the destroyer of worlds.'

What have we done? We have used the forbidden knowledge of our lost ancestors to bring wrath in our world. The knowledge died for a reason, we are not worthy enough to exploit it.

Feeling despondent, he walked away from the group of cheering men. A stream of tears ran down his hollow cheeks but dried out by the time he entered a small makeshift office to pick up his documents. The area of Los Alamos was special to him as he had spent his early childhood in a boarding school here. Now it seemed that he would dread this place as he unleashed something on this planet which he hoped would never see the light of day.

Pondering over his future, he got an insatiable urge to carry on investigating the hidden mysteries of the Vedas, the ancient knowledge books of India. According to him, 'Access to the Vedas is the greatest privilege this century may claim over all previous centuries,' and he expressed his feeling openly, wanting to teach, but worried about its implication in the world.

My life is finite, the universe infinite. To whom do I entrust my knowledge? Should I allow it to die with me? The notes of Kaul, on those tablets of Shaksgam Valley, seem impossible to believe. But Kashmir does hold secrets, secrets more ancient than Philistines or Israelite people, secrets which only a Kashmiri may know.

The year "it" began: 1947

14th August: Pakistan is born
15th August: India gains Independence
WAR FOR KASHMIR BEGINS

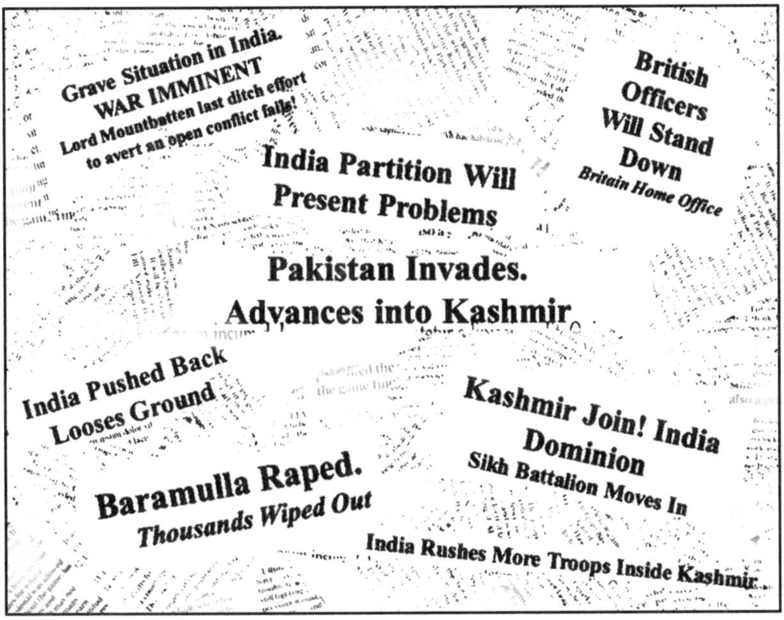

'We have declared that the fate of Kashmir is ultimately to be decided by the people. That pledge we have given, and the Maharaja has supported, is not only to the people of Kashmir but to the world. We will not, and cannot back out of it. We are prepared when peace and law and order have been established to have a referendum held under international auspices like the United Nations. We want it to be a fair and just reference to the people, and we shall accept their verdict. I can imagine no more fair and just offer.'

Pandit Nehru,
Prime Minister of India,
2nd November, 1947,
Broadcast to the nation over All India Radio.

MEETING OF THE CHOS SKYONG

Stone Cave Near Kintraw,
Scotland, United Kingdom

November 6,1947,23:10 GMT

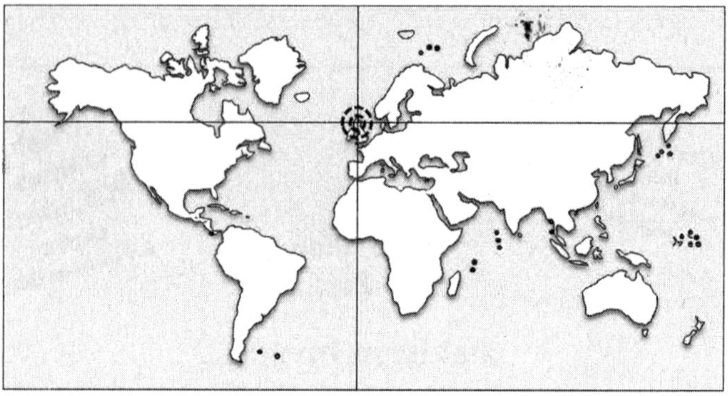

James 4:14: *Why, you do not even know what will happen tomorrow. What is your life? You are a mist that appears for a little while and then vanishes.*

Mist has many connotations from enchanting to sinister, as it creates an aura of imagination and mystery. It appears for a period, dimming the visibility around the area it envelopes, till it vanishes. But till that time the aura builds and stories are born sometimes taking the form of myths. Myths built upon legendary personalities, groups and folklore. Celtic land is not new to such folklore. Known for its ancient monoliths, Norse history and scenic beauty, the village had its own secrets—secrets known to many and secrets known to few. Its forest protected such a mystery.

Deep in this forest was a series of caves, majestic and murky, the meeting place of the Guardians, a secret few were aware of. The caves were a sanctum to the Guardians, a location where they assembled to discuss ways to control free-will in the world. The Guardians had the power and influence to do so; they belonged to ancient Royalties.

The stage was set for a showdown inside the caves, remodelled more than a century ago during Queen Victoria's rule by the Guardians who had at that time helped her gain control over the throne, ensuring that it was done independently enough. Thousands of years ago, this ancient Council of Royalties was established at a time when kings were considered the descendants of Gods. There were twelve families, twelve royalties tied together by their royal bloodline. Each family represented a constellation in the celestial sphere. After a few centuries each constellation got a zodiac name which each family took up as their identity. An identity which brought them together to this cave near this small Scottish village.

Fresh wind from the countryside blew into the cave's small opening and gushed out again into the open air through a network of underground channels. Eleven nobly dressed figures had already arrived inside the cave at the duly appointed time to meet their leader. As they assembled around the table, they could sense all was not well with their leader. They greeted each other with the sacred primordial sound *Ogham* in a similar deep baritone and looked at their leader to start the proceeding.

'DAMN the Indian Leadership…plausible deniability…that is exactly what they will hear from these Pakistanis for years to come,' boomed a heavily accented Welsh voice as his fist sporting large rings banged on a round mahogany table. The towering dark-haired figure was breathing heavily, his body trembling, red nostrils dilating. His hands were spread out on the table, his head bowed. Slowly, he raised his head and swept his deep blue eyes around the table, glancing at eleven middle-aged figures looking at him.

'Sir Trimble, we tried to pass the message and make our moves, but it was of no avail,' cried out a voice from one corner of the table. All eyes were on him, staring with displeasure. Sir Trimble looked at the elegantly designed ring which the Guardian, who replied, was wearing and noticed the green coloured stone. *Emerald stone—he is from the Cancer constellation, one of my father's challengers.*

Sir Trimble looked at his ring, and the greenish-yellow coloured Topaz stone.

Each of the Guardians wore a ring with a stone representing their constellation. The ring was handed down to the descendants since its creation centuries ago. Each ring stone was tri-decagon-shaped or thirteen sided, and rested on gold and platinum based metal. The rim of the ring had twelve constellation signs engraved on it, with one constellation showcasing the wearer's zodiac star, highlighted in gold and larger than others. The head Guardian moved his left index finger on top of the shiny stone of his ring. He raised his head, looking at the engraved Swastika inside a six sided star on the archaic wooden round table. He then shifted his gaze towards the group.

'Fellow Guardians, fifth of November is a date that Great Britain will never forget. Likewise second of November will be for India, a date filled with regret. Something they could have changed, if only they had realised its importance.'

A British royal family member and a veteran of many anti-Nazi operations, Sir Trimble was not new to stressful situations. He continued loudly, 'Standing down and not taking sides was not a favourable option but Sir Auchinleck was right in issuing the stand-down order to British officers, instructing them not to fight if war broke out between India and Pakistan.'

The guardians inside the cave were silent. It seemed they were heading towards another crisis which promised to spiral out of control. The tall aristocrat calmed down and regained his composure.

He looked towards a wheatish skinned fellow guardian Vishvanath Rathore, code name Leolus, after the constellation Leo, and spoke sternly, 'We needed to ensure that the Pakistanis were pushed out of Kashmir. Why could we not stop the Indian Prime Minister from reaching All India Radio and announcing the statement four days back?'

'The Home Ministry was clueless, and that's where things got murky,' replied Guardian Leolus. 'Not to mention the pressure from Mr Baker, the Secretary of State, and his cronies in the Commonwealth Relations Office. He is the mouthpiece for Pakistanis during all Security Council meetings at the UN.'

Sir Trimble was still breathing heavily but it had a rhythm to it now, 'Nehru did not need to do it but we can do nothing about it.' He folded his hands and watched as his peers nodded in agreement. 'Pakistan's main objective will be to ensure that the Indian border is as far as possible, from Rawalpindi.

He stood in silence now. The immense responsibility of leading this ancient council had been handed over to him five weeks earlier. His mind was struggling to comprehend the next steps.

Nine years ago we made our biggest mistake. We could have stopped that young Jewish student in Paris, from killing the Nazi diplomat. Who knows then Kristallnacht, would not have happened and Hitler would not have established his stranglehold. Hitler was a mistake, and then the Jewish student and now Kashmir. Everything is going out of hand, and if Oppenheimer connects more dots like the power of God he unleashed, we will be doomed. Take control of yourself! We can still manipulate this planet.

Sir Trimble was now calm. He spoke up, 'Remember our motto is always universal determinism and that there are no coincidences in life, only perceptions and illusions of coincidences. And, my fellow Guardians, we, members of *Chos Skyong* have failed in doing our sacred duty. We should not brood over what has happened. Everyone makes mistakes. We did what we thought then was in the best interest of the world.'

He looked around the table for some reaction, but got none. He continued, 'It does not matter now. It is a thing of the past, and we need to think about the future and get ready to take some level of control in Shaksgam Valley, for that will be their destination when they return. We will need to find a roadmap to take control of Shaksgam Valley which is now in Pakistan's control. India still has Baramulla. How is the region now?' Sir Trimble looked at Leolus.

'Well, fellow Guardians, the Baramulla region was totally ravaged and plundered by the Pakistani troopers and the Kabali tribal people. In fact…' He stopped for a moment, looked at the group, took a deep breath and continued, 'Hardly 1,000 inhabitants were left alive out of a total population of 14,000.' The room reverberated with a collective gasp. 'They spared no one. They attacked the St Joseph's Franciscan Convent compound and stormed the hospital and the small chapel inside it. They raped and killed the nuns, the patients, the doctors and even pregnant women were murdered in cold blood.'

'And your cable mentioned that there is only one survivor from the Haider family.' Sir Trimble's tone was heavy with concern.

'Yes, the Haider family baby was just born. The Mother Superior, the colonel and many others died saving him.'

Sir Trimble looked relieved. Standing up, he walked towards the other end of the room and addressed the group again, 'What plans do we have for him? Where is he now? He needs to be…'

BOOM!

A blast ripped from below the table. Sir Trimble, who was standing near the edge of the south side of the room, was flung up to the ceiling. As he came crashing down he saw the bodies of his compatriots splattered around the room. His chest was warm with blood. He tried to focus his fractured vision around the room. One of the council members was trying to drag himself up and fell in front of him.

'I am sorry…' he said and breathed his last.

'Leolus…don't…Oh lord…GOOD GOD, *mea culpa*…protect the Haider family. We have failed…We…we…' Sir Trimble took a ragged breath. 'We have…to protect Shaksgam Valley *our sanctum sanctorum*…' The frail voice faded in the smoke-filled room.

The mist begins to clear outside the cave where a tall and lanky figure hiding behind the trees raises his head on hearing the blast. Abhimanyu Kashyapa's young teen face is plastered with a worried look, his feet begin to tremble and he clutches the bark of the tree not removing his brown-eyed gaze from the entrance. The horses jump around feeling the vibration of the shockwaves, but settle gradually after a few moments. The tall teen stands up and begins walking towards the cave entrance. He begins to pray as he strides slowly ahead; his face shows a sense of calm as he thinks of the words from the Gita.

Kyon Vyarth Chinta Karte Ho? Kis Se Vyarth Darte Ho? Kaun Tumhe Maar Sakta Hai? Aatma Na Paida Hotee Hai, Na Marti Hai.

How true. Our soul is like this mist, only present for some time in this finite body and then returns into the universe. Leolus, Rathore Sir, was right. Something was going to happen. I just have to help whosoever is alive in the cave and pass on the legend of the Guardians to Leolus' descendant whenever he or she will be ready, and protect Baramulla's Haider family.

1947 TO 1965

1947: Oppenheimer becomes Director of Princeton's institute.

1948: India-Pakistan ceasefire, Kashmir and Indian border frontlines changed.

1950: Abhimanyu Kashyapa loses track of Haider family of Baramulla. Rathore family (Royal family of Rajasthan) joins active politics after merging with the Indian Union.

1953: Abhimanyu Kashyapa joins the Indian Army.

1960: Formation of World Academy of Art and Science by eminent scientists like Albert Einstein and Oppenheimer; (official) aim was to make aware to humanity the dangers inherent in scientific discoveries.

1961: Indo-China War, Captain Abhimanyu Kashyapa captured as POW. Loses 90 per cent of the men under his command. Gets released later.

1965: Indo-Pak War, Major Abhimanyu Kashyapa leads charge into various combat operations. Wins medal for unmatched valour in battle.

1965: Oppenheimer diagnosed with malignant throat cancer.

THE APPRENTICE JOINS

The Institute for Advanced Study,
Princeton, United States of America

October 3,1965,15:45 EST

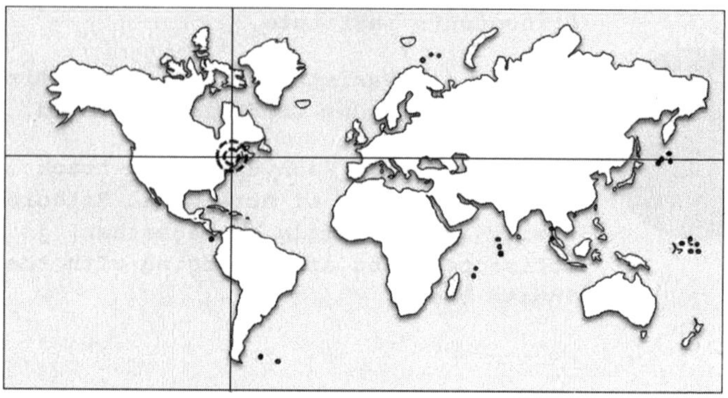

The six hundred plus capacity Alexander Hall was sparsely packed with doctoral students awestruck at what they had just heard and seen. Two hours into the lecture, the blackboard was chalked out with multiple formulae and illustrative diagrams which were elaborated by the senior professor of theoretical physics. Now with a broken and feeble voice, the professor was taking his last lecture in this position, a position once held by Albert Einstein. The lecture was not part of the curriculum, but the doctoral students' attendance was ensured via word-of-mouth around the dormitories, classrooms, lanes and parks in this institute.

Smoking a half-lit cigarette hanging by his mouth, Robert Oppenheimer studied the students as he concluded his session on his theories around primordial elements and primordial sound. Knowing that this was the academic home of great scientists like Albert Einstein, John von Neumann, and Kurt Gödel, he expected a lot of scepticism to set in among the students. The father of the atom bomb was expecting this to be reflected by a potential barrage of questions fired at him. But the expressions of his students did not change—he sensed a mix of disbelief, sarcasm and awe in their body language.

'Professor!' A voice rang out from the first set of students sitting to his right. Oppenheimer adjusted his grey suit as he turned his gaze towards that corner, and nodded to the student to go ahead.

Finally someone breaks the ice.

'Professor, we get the concept of primordial nuclides as elements which were left over from when the universe was created, but how do we take that there is a concept of primordial sound attached to it?'

'Yes, sir, it sounds absurd…space is a vacuum,' other voices spoke out in his support.

Now in his sixties, the seasoned professor still got excited with the challenges thrown at him, especially from sceptics.

'Class, we all agree that the earth was formed more than four billion years ago, and the universe which was formed with the big bang concept is much older than that.' The professor waited for a moment to take in his breath as the class nodded in unison. 'So one of the theories is that the universe is ever expanding…but what if we take this argument a little further. This ever expanding universe before was a dot, a void and the primordial sound is a force expanding it.'

Looking at the puzzled faces, he thought of simplifying the explanation.

'In a flute, the air inside gets compressed and rarefied by the sound waves, thus creating music for some and noise for others, like me.' The class broke out into a small spontaneous laughter.

'So I have your attention now,' the professor smiled. 'The sound waves or the primordial sound in this case in the universe is due to compression and rarefaction of matter and light. One may think that a force is pushing the universe out, creating something like a ripple effect. Now the universe is expanding, but a limit will be reached sometime in the future. After that two things may happen. Either it will begin to contract or snap depending on who controls it.' Oppenheimer snapped his finger, still trying to create an impression among his audience, hoping for someone who would pick his thoughts and continue his studies into the Vedas. He was looking for an apprentice.

In the last row a lanky Asian-looking bearded doctoral student with a prominent parrot nose watched him carefully. He felt a sense of urgency to jump in and support the professor. He raised his left hand and as soon as he got the professor's attention, spoke in his deep baritone, 'You are saying this is based on an ancient *Vedic* book from India.'

'Books. There are four Vedas–Rigveda, Yajurveda, Samaveda and Atharvaveda,' said the professor, indicating the number with the fingers of his right hand. 'Each denotes a separate set of knowledge. Knowledge we still need to understand but are now in a position to decipher.'

'Professor, is it true that you believe that the 1945 atom bomb explosions—those in Hiroshima and Nagasaki were not the first ones to be done on this planet?'

'Yes. Nuclear weapons have been used in the past by our ancestors.' The professor keenly observed the young bearded student. 'You seem to have inputs for this discussion. What is it you want to add?'

The lanky student stood up, walked briskly down the aisle, took his place at the mike and slowly turned to face the lecture hall. He elaborated on the theory of how the old civilisations of Harappa and Mohenjo-Daro were hit by a calamity 5,000 years ago. Families were buried alive together as seen in the skeletons found holding hands or embracing each other. Food was being cooked during the time and grains preserved in the vessels were dug out from the sites.

'And to top it, these skeletons, grains and the area have signs of radiation, ancient radioactivity. The impact though is not like the extinction event aka the Shiva Hypothesis,' he spoke in a hushed tone and then raised his voice to a considerable pitch, 'It appears as though a nuclear explosion had descended on them!' He banged the table in front of him.

As soon as he thumped the table, the vibration resounded around the hall, and the bell outside the hall rang signalling the end of the lecture. The students stood up thanking the professor for the insightful (for some) and thought-provoking lecture. Oppenheimer thanked everybody and bade goodbye. The lanky Asian standing on the floor rushed up to get his books and bag. Turning around he saw Oppenheimer walking out.

I have got to meet him; I am close to the solution to my masla, *my problem.*

Oppenheimer walked out into the open ground in the beautiful and sprawling campus. The eight-hundred-acre area of buildings, rows of pine trees, wetlands and farm fields was the perfect place to theorise.

'Professor…Professor Oppenheimer!' called out a voice loudly.

Holding on to his hat in the wind, Oppenheimer turned around on hearing his name. It was the lanky parrot-nosed, bearded Asian student.

'Professor, a moment, I need to share more.' Oppenheimer waited for him to continue. 'I have completed a doctorate in electromagnetism where I have assisted, Dr Joseph Rotblat, your colleague from the World Academy of Art and Science. I also worked with Mohammad Abdus Salam in the past.'

'Aha…Joseph, my Polish friend, and Salam, he is one of the most intelligent minds from the East. How can I help you, young man?'

The lanky bearded man blurted out in a hushed tone, 'In the beginning was the Word, and the Word was with God, and the Word was God…I would like to work under you professor.' Oppenheimer stood silent as he studied this interesting young student.

'And what is this *word*?'

'It's the primordial sound, the sound which was there during the creation, during the big bang…and is always present around us. Even now when we talk its sonic vibration is around us.'

Oppenheimer did not show any reaction in his face. The wind picked up pace as Oppenheimer held on to his hat, and kept his left hand on it as he continued. 'So you have heard of my research in the sonic vibration around the Hindu chant of "AUM" in the universe…I did not speak about it openly.'

The student looked on and smiled, and gave a gentle nod. Oppenheimer, using his right hand, took out a small spiral notepad from his inner coat pocket. He turned the pages using his right thumb, as the student's gaze turned towards the notepad in expectation that the professor was going to show him something.

'See these drawings, do they make any sense to you?' asked Oppenheimer as he passed on the notepad to the inquisitive student. The student smiled as he saw the three drawings.

'This is from Talim, our secret language of Kashmir.'

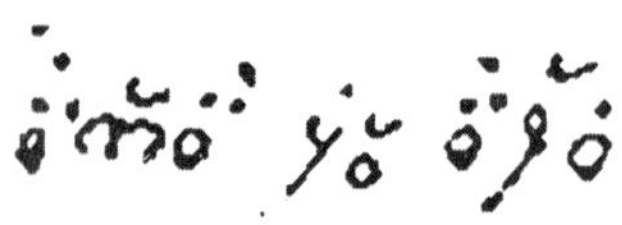

Oppenheimer heaved a sigh of relief

Maybe, just maybe…I found a person who can build me the weapon of universal sound which brought down the walls of Jericho from the book of Joshua in 1400 BC. The words…yes I remember…and seven priests shall bear seven rams' horns before the ark; and the seventh day ye shall compass the city seven times, and the priests shall blow with the horns.

'And Joshua commanded the people, saying: Ye shall not shout, nor let your voice be heard, neither shall any word proceed out of your mouth, until the day I bid you shout; then shall ye shout,' mumbled Oppenheimer, keeping his eyes closed as the young student gazed at him confused.

'What professor?'

'Come to my beachside property in the island of St John in the Virgin Islands. We can continue working there…and I did not get your name.'

'Dr Nasir Abiad Raja.'

'India or Pakistan?' asked Oppenheimer, taking a fifty-fifty guess.

'Neither, professor, Kashmiri,' He sounded proud of his origin.

1965 TO PRESENT DAY

1967:Birth of Agastya Rathore, grandson of Vishvanath Rathore, and son of international test player Dileep Rathore. Major Abhimanyu Kashyapa becomes godfather to young Agastya.

1967: J. Robert Oppenheimer dies, post a coma in Princeton. His protégée Dr Nasir takes over Oppenheimer's research files from his house in the island of St John in the Virgin Islands.

1971: Indo-Pak War, for Bangladesh's freedom. Brigadier Kashyapa prepares for attack on Western Pakistan towards Rawalpindi under special directive from the Prime Minister. The attack called off due to backroom negotiations by the global community.

1980: General Kashyapa retires from Indian Army, and joins active politics along with Rathore family.

1988: Agastya Rathore passes out of Cambridge, along with Aditya Khurana, son of then Prime Minister of India.

2005: Agastya Rathore joins active politics.

2009: Dr Nasir receives Nobel Prize in physics with his ground breaking work in acoustic physics.

2010: Agastya Rathore's party wins elections. Aditya Khurana becomes the Prime Minister of India, Agastya the new Home Minister, and General Kashyapa, the Defence Minister.

2011: Dr Nasir moves to Pakistan and works under General Pervez Musa Hussein. Sets up a laboratory in Shaksgam Valley.

One year before Present Day: Haider family tracked by General Kashyapa.

PRESENT DAY BEGINS

218 DAYS TO EVENT

Lutyens Road,
Delhi, India

May 07,15:30 IST

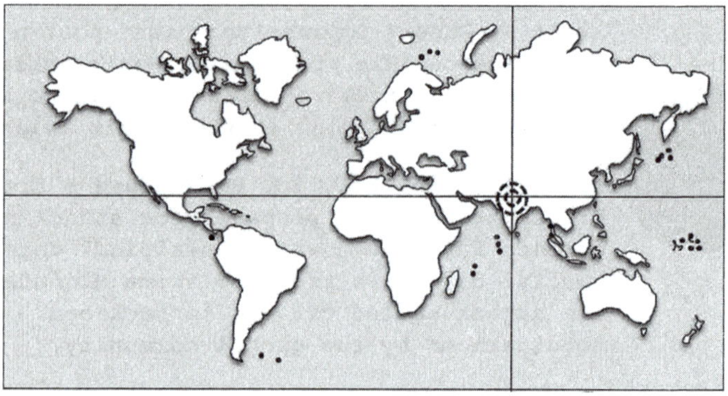

A **fifteen feet** long portrait of the twelfth century Greater Arabian Peninsula Islamic caliphate political map was spread magnificently across the light turquoise coloured wall in the hallway. Framed in a metal colour, the portrait showed the kingdom of Saladin, the famous King who ruled Arabia from 1174 to 1193, defeating the Christian Crusaders. The portrait was part of the grand royalty showcasing around the politically significant bungalow. The main design built on a principle of French architecture, with Kashmiri and Iranian carpets laid out in several rooms, was a reflection of its owner's taste. He was blue-blooded, a descendant from one of India's ancient royal clans, with not only many family secrets but a great national responsibility. Agastya Harshvardhan Rathore was India's Home Minister, at forty-five, the youngest in history.

Agastya thought of his Cambridge days and the strong bond he shared with his Prime Minister; he thought of how they met their life partners and of his infatuation with Carina, the Swedish blonde, his course mate for Archaeo-Astronomy.

Those stars have so many secrets, and we have so much to learn. We can only learn if we are at peace with ourselves. And peace can come only by war.

Agastya Rathore looked up. He stroked his light chin strapped beard, which sat smug around his oval, tanned face. He had thick jet black hair combed back to reveal his large forehead. A small cut from an old injury was visible below his lips. At five feet eight inches, he had a lean physique and deep blue eyes.

Agastya called in his private secretary and told him to hold all calls until 6:00 pm, unless it was from the Prime Minister's Office (PMO) or from Central Counter Terrorist Command (CCTC); he wanted to rest. The secretary duly noted his request.

He got up and walked towards the bookshelf mounted on the wall. The books reflected his eclectic reading, but the ones in this section of the shelf focused on Pakistan, China, terrorism, and covert operations. Agastya picked up *Chinese Strategic Culture and Foreign Policy Decision-Making: Confucianism, Leadership and War*, a book by Huiyun Feng. With the book in hand he walked to his bed. Lying down, he started thumbing through the book, reviewing the mental maps that formed in his mind.

For thousands of years no war with China; the communists took over sixty years ago, and everything went downhill. They attacked Tibet to liberate it, liberation from what?…and with reports that Shaksgam Valley is getting active with Chinese troops and Pakistan ISI, some serious weapon testing may be happening there… India would need to move ahead quickly. Time is running out, and peace can come only by war, a war which can be manipulated and controlled.

The Indian Home Minister turned his gaze to his right index finger and its gold-platinum embroidered ring studded with onyx locked in by thirteen titanium clips.

The ancestral ring protects me. Thanks to my mentor General Abhimanyu Kashyapa, I now know about my link to the ancient order of the Guardians. His story about the Scotland blast of the guardians was unbelievable, but he did carry my grandfather's body back to India…and the Kashmir issue was left unresolved in that meeting. Hope all goes according to plan for Kashmir now.

SECRET VAULT

VOL 3, ISSUE - II MAY

Shaksgam Valley (Kashmir) Back in the News with Tunguska-like Event

By Our Correspondent Lyon Picard

Paris: An earthquake occurred in the northern part of Kashmir and China at around 7:17am local time, May 7. The quake was measured at 3.4 on the Richter Scale, with the epicentre located around the Shaksgam Valley (area ceded to China by Pakistan) in the Kashmir region. What has confused the various Meteorological Offices is the jarring of all seismographs in the region. The area is now closed to visitors, and cordoned off by the Chinese Army.

There are reports of a group of Norwegian mountaineers, Nordic Rockers, en route to Mount K2 from Shaksgam Valley getting stranded in the area. Chinese and Pakistan armies are coordinating the rescue effort. Satellite pictures from NASA's 'Lincoln Near Earth Object Observation Programme' have shown large tracts of trees flattened over a hundred square km, near Shaksgam River. An asteroid hit is ruled out by Canadian satellite NEOSSat.

Shaksgam Valley had been also in the news a month back, with Roscosmos (Russian Federal Space Agency) satellites monitoring the area for Unidentified Flying Objects (UFOs) reported by certain amateur astronomers, and spiral shaped sky phenomena similar to that which hit Norway's sky in 2009, a day before US President Obama was going to receive the Nobel Peace Prize.

A similar mysterious flattening of trees was seen over 2,000 square km (800 square miles) near the Tunguska River back on 30 June, 1908, in Czarist Russia. *More details from Shaksgam Valley are awaited.*

CABLE: US EMBASSY ISLAMABAD TO CIA LANGLEY

VZCZCXRO3157
DE RUEHIL #0768 0120352
ZNY SSSSS ZZH
P 120352Z JUN 12
FM AMEMBASSY ISLAMABAD
RUEHBJ/AMEMBASSY BEIJING PRIORITY 4879
RUEHBUL/AMEMBASSY KABUL PRIORITY 6679
RUEHNE/AMEMBASSY NEW DELHI PRIORITY 0078
RUEHKP/AMCONSUL KARACHI PRIORITY 4188
RUEAIIA/CIA WASHDC PRIORITY
RUEKJCS/JOINT STAFF WASHINGTON DC PRIORITY
RUEKJCS/SECDEF WASHINGTON DC PRIORITY
RHEHNSC/NSC WASHDC PRIORITY

Monday, 12 June, 03:52
S E C R E T SECTION 01 OF 01 ISLAMABAD 000065
SIPDIS
EO 12958 DECL: 06/12/2062
TAGS CHN, EAID, MOPS, PK, PREL,SKV
SUBJECT: REPORT ON SHAKSGAM VALLEY INCIDENT
Classified By: Ambassador Rudolph Burgan, Reasons 5

1. (S) Summary and introduction: In his June 11 meeting with Ambassador Rudolph Burgan, ISI Chief General Shaqukat Patuadi spoke about the Shaksgam Valley Incident. The reference was to a mining accident flattening a part of the region, and suspected ufos in the area. Following the meeting ISI Chief General Shaqukat Patuadi spoke privately with Ambassador Burgan. End summary.

2. (C) Meeting Participants: U.S. Assistant Secretary Ryan D. Willy, Bureau of South and Central Asian Affairs Ambassador Rudolph Burgan, Lieutenant General Ken Monger, Defence Representative to Pakistan Ms Naomi Woods, Senior Advisor, Bureau of South and Central Asian Affairs Embassy note taker.

Pakistan, ISI Chief Shaqukat Patuadi, Ministry of Foreign Affairs Brigadier General Ramiz Ahmed.

3. (S), ISI Chief General Shaqukat Patuadi refuted all allegations that Pakistan establishment is trying to cover up a military experiment conducted in Shaksgam Valley, with the help of the Chinese. He showed photographs of the area which were matching the ones taken by our satellites and those shared by India's DIPAC (Defence Imagery Processing and Analysis Centre). Accusations that Al Qaeda was present there were decried, calling it preposterous for the Indian government to think that way. He had some choicest words for the RAW, and their new anti-terror department CCTC. According to him a mining accident caused the flattening.

4. (S), The U.S. Ambassador reiterated that the US government believed them. On being asked for details of eye-witnesses from a four member mountaineering team, they showed their ignorance. In private conversation, the ISI chief told the Ambassador that General Pervez Musa Hussein would be taking over his position after six months.

COMMENT

5. (S) The Chinese maintain the mining accident story and Indians mention some impact seen in Kashmir with a minute seismic activity recorded at the same time. New Delhi Embassy would need to dig some more.

The incident indicates a Tunguska-like event but needs confirmation at the ground level at Shaksgam Valley. Covert action recommended by non-US assets.

Based on 09STOCKHOLM552 secret cable with Swedish Government indicating that they would be coming out of neutrality, usage of Särskilda Operationsgruppen—SOG, the Swedish secret service arm would be fruitful. The task can also include locating the missing mountaineering team *Nordic Rockers* from Norway.

129 DAYS TO EVENT

C.I.A. Safe House,
Islamabad, Pakistan

August 4,15:30 PST

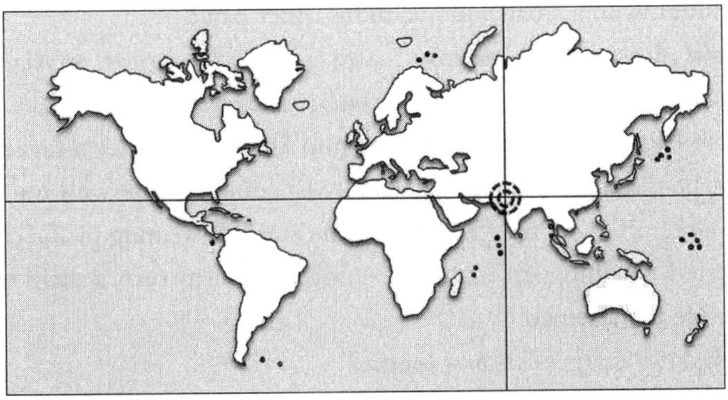

The humid atmosphere inside the small room began to change with the strong gust of wind blowing through the open windows and rattling them. The room, part of an insignificant looking flat, began to get wet as the gusty wind also brought in a gentle drizzle. The drizzle gradually picked up speed; the water trickling into the room formed small puddles that grew into tiny streams across the faint yellow coloured tiled floor and flowed where a six feet tall bearded man lay spreadeagled on the floor. The water drenched him; his legs jerked in response. He opened his eyes slowly and moved his head from side to side. He arched his back and lifted his body off the floor, turning suddenly as the window rattled again. His lungs felt overburdened. *Am I poisoned? Why am I shivering and nauseated?*

He checked his watch.

Forty minutes but looks like hours since I fell. My bones are hurting…what was I doing…I was listening to the CD! The music sent in the package.

Increasingly disoriented, the tall Swedish intelligence covert agent scanned the room, trying to locate the CD-Player, and dragged himself towards the corner where the red coloured pint sized player had fallen. The window banged one more time. He looked out. From the second floor he could see a medium built person in a black kurta standing outside, looking directly at him. Picking up a monocle lying on the table beside the window, he placed it in front of his right eye to identify the man; he looked familiar. The man's heavily bearded face broke into a sadistic smile as he waved one hand holding some sort of a radio transmitter, with a small antenna in his other hand.

Jalal Afridi…now I remember…Shaksgam Valley, he took me there…my guide to the place, the music CD package was given by him.

Just back from a covert operation in Shaksgam Valley a few hours earlier, he did not have an opportunity to communicate with the base. His chest hurt as he tried to breathe; he started sweating profusely. As he started coughing up blood, he noticed his arm turn a dirty bluish green. He felt alarmed.

My throat is dry. I have been poisoned!

Inside his body, a losing battle raged on with every passing second. His organs were collapsing, he was becoming delirious. He rushed towards a grey wall cupboard holding the silver cross hanging from his neck tightly with his left hand. Praying hard, he tried to reach his communicator. Sweeping the gadget from the shelf, he slumped on the floor with his back against the wall. Sliding open the device, he did the iris scan to operate the device. Nothing happened.

What the fuck! My iris is changing. This is the weapon the terrorists are going to use. Will a phone ring now?

He jerked his fragile body as he felt his phone vibrate inside his loose pyjama pockets. Taking out the sea blue coloured phone, he saw the same area code from Dharamshala India which the Nordic Rocker mountaineers received shortly before their untimely death in Islamabad after returning from Shaksgam Valley.

The Nordic Rocker climber Linda's details were right…I am not answering. Damn it! I did not pass all the information from Shaksgam Valley, especially around the Chos Skyong tablets.

He dropped the ringing mobile and brought his communicator close to his eye to try the iris scan again. The device beeped and became operational. Letting out a long puff of air, the Swede pressed an app linking him directly to his base. He did not want to miss anything important about his assignment that began two weeks back. He would have to send the message heavily coded.

The Chos Skyong tablet inscription in the cave wall in Shaksgam Valley, there are more superior powers in play here. I should have reported it to headquarters. Now I don't have time…my body, rigor mortis is setting in my legs. Apophenia, that's the only way I can get the message across safely.

As soon as he finished, he began punching the message quickly, with trembling fingers he removed a marker from his pocket and struggled to draw a pattern of crisscrossed lines and geometric shapes on the wall. He stopped every few seconds trying to breathe deep as he gasped for air. He turned the communicator towards the wall and took photos, attached them to his message and sent it across to his headquarters.

Cannot take a chance by leaving the images like this…

Pulling out his service gun now he raised it with his limited strength and fired at the communicator and on the walls where the illustration was scratched. The background music of the market was getting louder and blood started trickling out of his mouth.

Mansur Haider is going to be involved and I hope we get him. Adolf your job is to complete the task now.

'In nomine Patris, et Filii, et Spiritus Sancti,' he cried out aloud. His voice died down and he slumped sideways as rigor mortis set in across his body. But before he shut his eyes, he took one long last look at the wall where his illustrations of the Star of David and the Swastika were now wiped out.

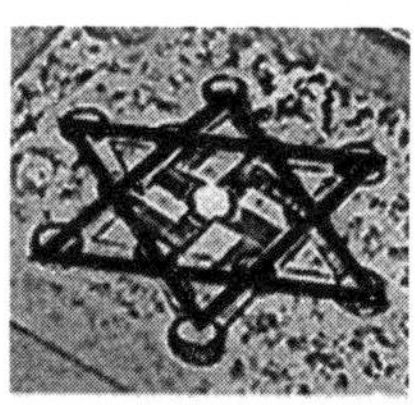

119 DAYS TO EVENT

Affarwat Peak, Gulmarg/Baramulla, Jammu and Kashmir, India.

August 14,11:00 IST

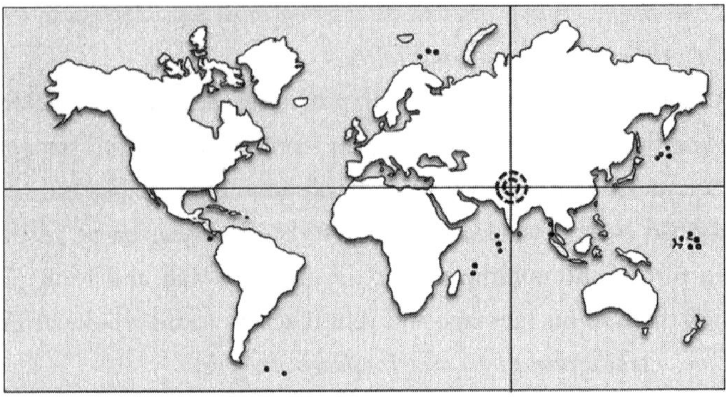

'**Ya Allah! Kheencho!** Ya Allah! Kheencho!' The shouts reverberated from the top of Mt Affarwat. Local boys chanted the call as they pulled sledges, with tourists, up the barely snowy slope. The visitors were filled with the anticipation of the thrill of sliding downhill from the peak. One could sense the lack of oxygen not only in the air but also in the flushed faces of the few tourists who made it to the summit.

Mansur Haider looked around and felt a gush of emotion. Fifteen years earlier he used to come here almost every day during the tourist season and do the same thing these boys were doing now. Standing six and a half feet tall, his height and broad build got him a lot of attention. His unshaven stubble, long hair, and green eyes attracted a few flirtatious smiles from the ladies nearby. This was not new to him, and he had learnt to ignore it for the most part.

Taking in the scene around him, he reflected that things were different now. The sledges were made of metal, a far cry from the ramshackle wooden crates he had used in his teens. Even the cost of a ride had doubled to a hundred rupees. But one thing remained the same, the joy of seeing snow. The air was charged with the infectious excitement of people screaming with delight as they saw the snow at a distance and braved the last few hundred feet to walk to the top after reaching the base camp by cable car. Though the snow at this point was found only at the top, leaving the rest of the area a rocky landscape, adults could still be seen behaving like kids. Mansur smiled and knelt down to pray.

It was over five years since his last visit, and in making the trip to the top he was reassured that he could still climb it from ground zero. This visit had taken on added meaning for him as he had promised his father that he would one day pray for his soul from this peak.

His father, Mustafa, died two years ago in their ancestral village in Baramulla. Working as a caretaker on a houseboat, he received a word from home that Abba was unwell. On reaching his village, he encountered a pall of gloom and silence. At home, he found his mother crying. It was a strange sight for him—he had always seen her as an iron woman who held his world together. Not like this.

His twin sisters ran out to him, hugged him and started sobbing. Mansur knew all was not well. As a man and the only brother, he had to control his emotions and hold back his tears.

'Mansur, come in,' came the voice of the village doctor.

'How is he, Chacha?' asked Mansur, hoping against hope that he would hear something positive.

'Well, Mansur, I do not want to lie…the condition of his heart was already bad due to heavy smoking and this fever has made him feeble over the last few days.'

'Why did you not take him to a hospital?' Mansur demanded as he entered the room where his father lay. The ailing man had smiled on seeing his son.

'Because if my time has come, it has come, my Sher-e-Kashmir,' said Mansur's father, Mustafa, who frequently called his son the Lion of Kashmir.

'Abbu, why?' Mansur held his father's hand with his six-fingered right hand. He could not hold back the tears any longer.

'My son, my only son, it is over. Allah's wish is that I go to him. He told me so,' he said, now speaking in a feeble voice. 'But he promised that he would take care of all of you and said my Sher-e-Kashmir will not only make me, but also the whole *jahan* proud.'

'Abbu, I don't care for the world, I only care for you and my family.' Sobbing, he put his head on his father's chest.

'Shhh…my son…no…no, you may not understand now, but in time you will. Allah wishes it and he will not disappoint me, and don't you worry, I will see the *kainaat*, the universe, through your eyes. Promise me you will pray for my soul on Affarwat Mountain, and you will follow whatever I told you there. Promise me…'

'I pro…,' It was over. Mansur did not finish what he wanted to say.

Now back on Affarwat hilltop, Mansur closed his eyes and knelt at the very place where he and his father used to visit regularly. Mustafa used to bring his son here to search and prepare him for his so-called destiny. Mansur had never understood what that was all about.

He always said I will, as the time draws near…back to prayers now.

After a few moments he finished his prayers and knelt to make some marks on the ground. Mansur began drawing two reverse triangles and formed a sign his father wanted him to understand; it was related to his family history. But he did not know about the link.

'Mansur…Man, you made it!' bellowed a voice a few feet away from where he knelt. Mansur looked up and saw his best friend Samir romping up the slope towards him.

Samir Ansari was as similar to Mansur as he was different from him. He was Mansur's childhood friend and loved him as a brother. He was not quite as tall as Mansur, but at almost six feet, his crew cut and black eyes still made a lot of hearts skip a beat. Mansur felt Samir was probably the most flirtatious person in Srinagar, if not the whole of Kashmir. He was born with a silver spoon; his father a powerful politician and a businessman ran a profitable hospitality business.

They greeted each other in their unique way, shaking hands, then drawing the hand backwards and clicking the fingers of the same hand near their heads—strange for those who were watching, but it had been their signature salutation since childhood.

'So you finally did it!' exclaimed Samir, draping his arm across Mansur's shoulders.

'Yes! Samir, I did pray as my father wanted.'

Samir shrugged his shoulder and removed his Aviator sunglasses to look straight into his friend's eye.

'But I still feel it's incomplete as I never got a chance to say yes to my father that day, and I don't know if he can hear me now.' Mansur looked far into the distance, across the peak in the direction of the LoC, or Line of Control, the border with Pakistan-occupied Kashmir.

'Well, you know what he used to call you, Sher-e-Kashmir and he believed in you…believed you would change the hostile environment in Kashmir.' Samir then saw the illustration Mansur had made on the ground. His gloved right hand with the Aviators tightened and his mood suddenly altered into concern. His mouth was slightly open as he looked quizzically towards his friend.

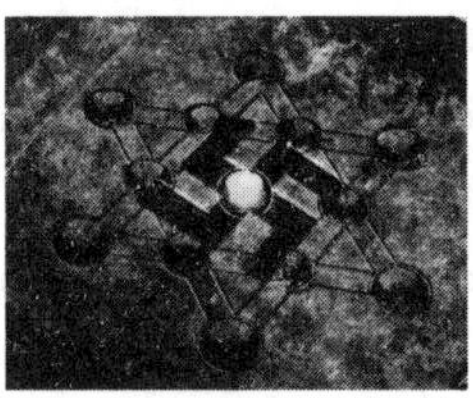

'It is not what you think.'

'What do you mean? Isn't it the star we should not draw? This is for those Jews.'

'Patience my brother, this is not the *Star of David,* though it looks like that, all I can tell is that my father wanted me to draw this here when I prayed for him today. It's a family thing he said, and see that each point and intersection here has a circle drawn, and also lines connecting in between…so it is different.' Waiting for a response which he did not get, Mansur continued in a reassuring tone, 'I am a Muslim, a Kashmiri and a human, Samir. I will never bring disrepute to my religion but will also not disrespect another religion. These signs are in my ancestral prayer rug also.'

'Well, the lines in between form a Swastika…but your Abbu was also an amateur astronomer into Zodiac signs,' said Samir as he put on his Aviators again and smiled, craning forward towards Mansur. 'And he grew up after your grandparents were killed in the St Joseph's Franciscan massacre back in 1947. You should think you and your family are blessed,' he whispered softly as they started walking down the slope.

'Hmm, maybe you're right. He always said that I would know the secrets, of stars and my family, in time,' replied Mansur as he carefully balanced himself on the steep slope.

Suddenly, Samir called up to Mansur with a smile on his face and a wink of an eye. Mansur knew what he was up to, and he winked back, pointing towards the cable car holding area.

'Are you thinking what I'm thinking?'

'Yup…and NOW!' shouted Samir, and they both dashed downhill.

Taking care that they didn't fall, struggling to keep their balance, the run was more a series of hops and jumps with the wind blowing on their faces. While Mansur's hair flopped around and his smile dazzled, Samir had an intense look in his eyes. The tourists looked on in amazement. Although they both enjoyed competition, each looked at it differently. While Samir was drawn to competing with others in order to feel superior, Mansur was content to compete with himself. He owed this attitude to his father who kept telling him, '*Always compete with yourself and your own weaknesses! Magic will happen and you will emerge stronger.*'

The slope was uneven, covered with rocks and loose soil, and in some areas there were bluebells, forget-me-nots, and buttercups. All this would be covered with snow in the next few months, but the flowers always returned with the onset of spring. *Such is the resilience of nature,* thought Mansur, jumping and now racing towards the spot, still a little behind Samir. Mansur caught up with Samir and overtook him as they approached the stairs to the entry point. But even as Mansur reached the first step, Samir stretched out, put one of his gloved hands on the platform stairway, grabbed the railing with the other, hoisted himself over it with a grimace and lunged forward to the doorway shouting, 'Wooo-hooo…Samir is king!'

'Yes, you did it and only because you used your head for the first time,' joked Mansur.

'What the fuck, Mansur! It's fair and square. You should try it. Sometimes a bit of grey is okay; all is not black and white.' Mansur just looked at him with his hands on his knees, and they burst out laughing.

It was a panoramic view from the peak, and the cable car ride, connecting Gulmarg Valley to Affarwat Peak made the journey more memorable. As they rode down the peak in the cable car, Mansur thought of how his life had changed in the last two years since his father's death. He had become the head of the house and taken charge of the family. His sisters were still studying and his mother had returned to the village to take care of the saffron farm. This decision meant sacrifices, and he had to set aside his dream to play cricket. Mansur felt the idea was farfetched.

Kashmiris cannot dream; other Indians will not support our rise and we will always be looked at with suspicion. Father thought otherwise—if one does not dream, one cannot achieve, he used to say.

'Look, Mansur. The hill people are still there,' Samir said, pointing to the huts below.

These so-called hill people have produced great fast bowlers from Pakistan, but not here in India. It was nice to see them bowl…their rhythm, their pace…

'Where did you go?' called Samir, slapping the window of the cable car. Mansur jolted to attention and looked at him. Samir smiled.

'Lost in history again, right?'

Mansur nodded.

'Well, whatever makes you happy...only you know what is in your dreams.' Samir took a sharp intake of breath, and continued speaking as he let out the air, 'But I wanted to meet you urgently…on some other business…well, sort of news actually…I am getting married.'

Mansur jumped up, causing the cable car to swivel. Samir's eyes were wide open. He hadn't expected such a strong reaction. 'Cool down. What happened?'

'I never expected you to tie the knot so soon. So who is the lucky girl?' Mansur was now smiling.

'Well, there's always a first time! I'll tell you about her, but there's something else, something more important I wanted to discuss with you.'

'What can be more important?' said Mansur, looking at Samir with surprise.

'Well, it's something very important I want you to do for me. I can't tell you about it here. I'll tell you on our ride to Srinagar.'

Mansur was now more perplexed.

It's better if I wait and let him speak when he wants. Probably it's one of his pranks.

Reaching Gulmarg Valley, Mansur and Samir moved out of the cable car and headed for the souvenir shop near the entrance. They had to cross a garden to reach the shop. The area was bustling with activity—families on holiday, children playing, and scores of college students milling about. It had not been like this a decade ago. Starting with a trickle, the tourist flow to the region had risen to close to a million in a year.

'Salam valekum,' the smiling, chubby souvenir shopkeeper greeted Mansur and Samir as they entered the shop.

'Valekum Salam,' replied Mansur. Samir was looking at a few posters that had been selling as a rage among tourists, but his eye was caught by something else…a papier mache sculpture.

'You remember this,' said Samir, picking up a cat-shaped form and dangling it in front of Mansur. 'Hey…did you forget?' he smirked, putting down the object.

'No, I did not.' Mansia's reply was quiet in tone, almost cryptic.

'Well I still remember it…ahem, buttercup flowers, Juliet houseboat. The cat papier mache,' Mansur was not smiling at Samir's comments.

'Stop it, Samir. It's not funny.'

'See, brother? It was just a fling in the mountains and she returned to Mumbai. You know that…she said it herself…"Only Companionship." Why do you still remember her? Aahana Yajurvedi is gone…Move on brother move on.'

'Probably I am cursed and it's not easy—you know how things changed suddenly. Call it a fear of losing.'

Samir sensed Mansur's withdrawal. They started walking towards the car park. As they passed the golf course, Mansur looked closely and saw work being done on it. He stopped and gazed at the lush green fields.

Samir looked at Mansur and felt a twinge of doubt in his mind.

Will he be able to do it? How do I convince him? Better still, as per the plan I won't tell him anything and ensure that things happen.

Mansur turned and continued walking with Samir. The silence was deafening now as the two friends approached Samir's car, a black coloured sedan.

'So you haven't told me your story, how did you meet. When did you propose? And most important, who is she?' joked Mansur, trying to break the stifling silence.

'Jump inside first and I will give you everything, even the good stuff,' said Samir with a wink.

Both started laughing and were happy that the tension bubble had popped. They got inside the car. Samir started the engine and it roared to life. The journey towards Srinagar would last two hours along a picturesque path. Everything about the journey brought back memories of his childhood days with his father. Mansur began to stare at Samir, and he raised his eyebrows questioningly when Samir looked at him.

'Okay, okay…Her name is Shaza…from Mumbai. She works for a media agency.'

'That's all? You talk a mile a minute. And speaking of that, I would like you to slow down a little bit,' said Mansur. Glancing at the dashboard, Samir saw that he was driving at around 80 kmh. Not fast for him, but probably fast for Mansur.

'You ran the 100m dash back in college under twelve seconds, and were the fastest bowler we had…and you are scared of this speed.'

Mansur gave a disapproving look towards his buddy.

'I will slow down, don't worry. We are stopping at a nearby apple farm anyway.'

'Why? And Shaza…'

'I just want to have some tea and discuss something important with you. Shaza, hmm…well, you can ask her yourself. She is coming next month. And yes, she knows a little about you.'

Mansur felt sure this was no prank, but he would need to wait to hear what he had to say.

Strange, Samir is more excited about speaking on something else, other than his Miss Mysterious.

Samir parked his car on the roadside near one of the apple farms. As they got out, they could see an overview of a village on one side of the road. On the other side was the apple farm. The landscape was magnificent, with a bird's eye view of the village and farms. Samir had parked the car near a small tea and snacks shop.

'That's the place for your tea?'

'Yes,' said Samir as he took out his Four Square cigarettes. 'Cigarettes are not like women,' was Samir's cheeky standby whenever his friends asked him why he never changed his brand.

'Salam Bhai. Two teas, please,' said Mansur to the tea vendor.

'Where have you been the last three months?'

'Before that I want to ask if you remember the Allan Border Game?' said Samir as they made their way up to the apple orchards.

'You mean the last game, right?'

Samir nodded.

'The last game in the valley and the only international cricket match I saw, September 9, can't forget that date, my birthday and Abbu was there.'

Mansur faintly remembered the game, but what remained unforgettable were Allan Border's eyes as he walked back into the dressing room after the game. They were filled with utter determination. Mansur's interest in cricket began on that day, and he decided that this was the place he wanted to be. The sound, the roar, and the atmosphere had completely enchanted him.

'What about that game?' said Mansur while staring at Samir. He sat down on the ground near one of the apple trees. Samir took a deep drag from his cigarette and blew smoke circles from his mouth.

'I am speaking about your dream. You still remember it, don't you?'

'Well…yes, but I have a different one now, which is to take care of my mother and get my sisters married,' said Mansur, watching a few children trying to jump up to pluck the apples.

Samir turned to where Mansur was looking and started walking towards the apple tree and continued speaking, 'And if that happens…I mean, if your mother does not need to work and your sisters get settled, will you…'

'Stop. Don't do it,' shouted Mansur, getting up suddenly and running towards Samir and grabbing his hand.

'Let the kids try to pluck the apples themselves.'

'Eh...what do you mean?'

'Well, they didn't ask for it, right? And if you pluck the apples for them they will not learn how to do it and thus never experience for themselves the joy of plucking.'

'Hmmm...you have a point there,' said Samir, now looking at the kids and patting one of them on the head. One girl gripped a vine and raised herself to pluck an apple. Seeing this, the other two boys did the same on other trees and got their apples. Another boy used a stick to bring a few apples down. The orchard reverberated with the children's loud, boisterous laughter as they jumped around, showing off their apples to one another and then to their parents.

'See? If I hadn't stopped you we wouldn't have seen this moment. That's the way I always learnt.' Mansur smiled and felt a sense of tenderness watching the kids. He continued, 'So, where did you disappear for so long? Was it for your fiancé Shaza?

Samir removed his jacket and pulled up his grey coloured sweat shirt. There was a deep scar running across his shoulder. Mansur gasped and appeared shocked.

'That's not all,' said Samir, removing his right leather glove and raising it in front of Mansur's eyes; half of his index finger was missing.

'Climbing accident in Ladakh, brother. Could have been worse.'

They looked into each other's eyes, Mansur widening his eyes, crinkling his brow, and gasping out a puff of air. Samir winked, smiled and put his arm around Mansur's shoulder.

'Shit happens! And all things happen for a reason...the philosophy of Karma. But the thing I want to discuss with you is the good news.'

'What good news?'

'Well, my friend, I managed to arrange a job for you at the cricket stadium in Srinagar, and you are not going to refuse.'

Mansur stood there not knowing how to react. He was appreciative of the concern that his best friend had for him and nodded in agreement.

They both turned their heads as a boy came to deliver the tea in plastic cups. They drank the tea.

Mansur has fallen for it. Sorry my friend. I was not in Ladakh but in Shaksgam Valley in China…but what you will be doing is for the greater good of our land. First step taken. Now Janab will have to make his move to twist other arms and manipulate the system.

118 DAYS TO EVENT

Suburban Islamabad, Pakistan

August 15,05:45 PST

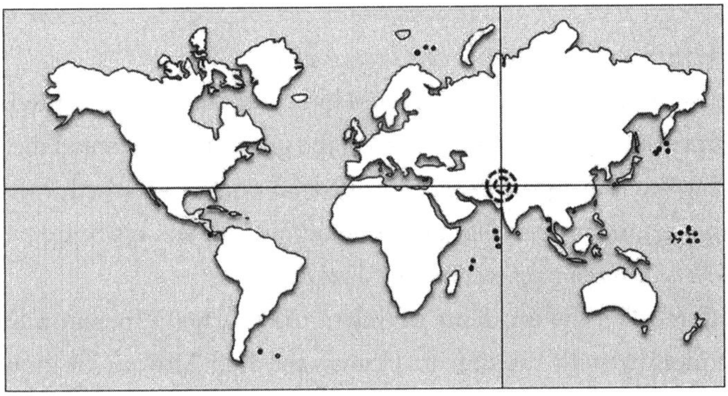

'**Don't kill me**, don't kill me...'

Bang...bang! Two gunshots rang out, followed by a loud explosion. Smoke engulfed the Jamia Hafsa Madrassa Complex. The operation was successful. Brigadier Pervez stood at the site with a Sig Sauer pistol in his right hand, watching the ongoing operation across the compound at the Red Mosque locally known as Lal Masjid. He knew he would never ever forget the eyes of the child into whom he had just pumped bullets; tears started to stream from his eyes.

Pervez Musa Hussein woke up with a jerk, breathing heavily and sweating. The air conditioning was on and he could feel the cold air against his wet forehead.

The nightmare is back, he thought. But it had seemed so real, as if it were something happening now and not something he had done five years back when he was part of the operation involved in the siege of the Red Mosque.

Why did the students of the Red Mosque have to kidnap those Chinese masseurs? We can never be hostile to the Chinese.

Pervez Musa Hussein raised his five-foot-five-inches physique from the bed and walked out of his room to the courtyard. Every stone and brick here reminded him of his lost family. This was the house where he grew up and where he met his recently deceased wife. His only son, who was martyred in the Kargil operation against India, in Kashmir in 1999, was born here. He gazed at an *Olea europea* tree in the middle of courtyard.

This tree is as holy as it is mentioned in our holy book, my son…my son how much I miss you. Wish the tree could bring back life.

His servant approached, greeted him, and asked if he wanted some tea. Pervez nodded his head, knelt on the ground, and opened the water tap near the flowerpots. The water gushed out, he splashed it over his face, noting the water's slight metallic odour, and wet his beard.

This recurring nightmare will never leave me.

He recalled the incidents of July 3, 2007, when Operation Sunrise got underway with the aim to cleanse the Red Mosque of non-state elements. He did not expect a young fourteen-year-old boy to come in front of him, and he did not expect he could ever shoot such a boy at point blank range, but he did. Picking up the injured boy, he had raced outside, hoping to save his life, when a loud explosion took place in the basement area where the final shootout was happening. Standing above the site of the blast, he fell down and lost consciousness, only to wake up in a military hospital.

Pervez Hussein thought highly of the students in the Mosque. They were well trained and had good equipment. He remembered the onslaught of smoke grenades, incendiary grenades, and fragmentation grenades that had met them as they entered the complex.

The encounter could have stretched on, although it still would have ended in their deaths.

The servants entered the courtyard. One was carrying the tea along with refreshments and the other a huge bundle of newspapers. The servants greeted their master, and Pervez nodded his head as he took a seat on the rocking chair. The servant placed the papers on the small round crystal table beside the chair. The papers included the local *Daily Times*, *Nawa-i-Waqt* and *Pakistan Observer* along with others from around the world. There were Indian newspapers along with the *Washington Post*, *New York Times,* as well as the *Shanghai Daily*. Pervez liked reading multiple newspapers. His mentor had told him to listen to all sources and come to understand them; only then would you know how to manipulate them, he had tutored, and the pupil religiously adhered to the coaching.

He is right, and with his blessing I managed to save two boys from Lal Masjid...my twins, my two sons–Jalal and Altaf Afridi. How lucky I am, two boys, twins...one in Pakistan and one in India. Jalal took care of the CIA agent Kurt. Now Altaf should take care of the situation in India and should find more about Mansur Haider.

'*Janab Chai.*'

Pervez looked at his servant, and directed him to pour the tea into his cup. He started reading an editorial about the five years that had elapsed since the Red Mosque incident.

This independent media was not there in the thick of battle...our respect is going down...and the impotent civilian government is more worried about its ten percent commissions than the country.

Today he had to meet his President and Prime Minister for a national briefing to see how the Army was performing against the Mujahideens and the action being taken against the Haqqani network.

Everyone has changed. The Chief of Army and the head of ISI are also stooges for the Americans. Even India is stronger now...and I need to bring balance back in the favour of Allah. With Dr Nasir's weapon successfully tested in Shaksgam Valley, the kafirs will not hear it, but will die a dog's death. The foreign agent Kurt came close but Jalal took care of him using Dr Nasir's weapon.

The General smiled and began getting ready for his meetings. First was an inspection in NESCOM, the National Engineering and Scientific Commission, the premier research agency of Pakistan. The second was with his loyal ally, the Chinese politburo General Zeng Chan, who was visiting Islamabad after inspecting his troops in *Azad Kashmir.*

Two hours later he was walking inside the research agency, where three years ago he met Dr Nasir Abiad Raja, a theoretical physicist and a second generation American citizen of Pakistani descent. This scientist who studied under another esteemed physicist, J. Robert Oppenheimer, 'father of the atomic bomb', was extremely popular and respected among his peers. He was also awarded the Nobel Prize in Physics. His current work around atmospheric winds and its impact on anechoic chambers was widely publicised. General Pervez looked at the sea of scientists in front of him. Using this esteemed group of scientists for his personal project, in the name of the state, had been beneficial for him.

Project Babylon…our name of the Shaksgam Valley weapon. Some work still remains but with the blessing of mighty Allah, the Caliphate will rise up with the sound of Allah! Who would have thought Dr Nasir will use the ancient Biblical Jericho weapon, revived with Vedas and quantum physics. He says it's by the Hindu's primordial sound that the weapon works, for me it is the sound of Allah!

After the inspection, he moved towards ISI's office, to meet General Chan. He let the window down, much to the surprise of his driver. Eyes closed, the warm wind began hitting hard and his white hair began to lose shape. The car slowed down.

'Don't slow down! Keep the same speed.'

The driver dutifully agreed. Pervez closed the window and took out his iPad from his black briefcase. Switching it on, he tapped on an application, and entered a password. The application made the screen blank. He took out his sunglasses, wore them and smiled.

Damn Dr Nasir and his brains, creating this encrypted application which can only be read by me, using these customised sunglasses. The success of Project Babylon will depend on him. Allah should give him the strength to finish testing of the weapon and everything will go as planned.

Pervez looked at the visibly blank iPad screen, began tapping the screen and read the contents, sent by General Chan.

December 9 and 10: Strike in Heart of India

Phase 0: *Look at an opportune moment and use the Dr Nasir Abiad Raja sonic weapon on the Indian cricket team using a human carrier.*

December 11: Global confusion aka The EVENT!
Phase One: *Put India on the defensive. China tables a bill on Kashmir independence in UN.*
Phase Two: *Blow up the Nobel Peace Prize Concert party.*

December 12: Get hold of military assets
Phase Three: *Military Coup to take over Pakistan.*

December 13-15: Indian government in chaos
Phase Four: *Multiple terrorist strikes across Indian cities with gunmen resorting to hit and run tactics.*

December 17-19: Force India into submission
Phase Five: *Stage a revolt in Kashmir against India.*

December 17-20: Create environment for military take-over in China
Phase Six: *General Zeng Chan will overthrow the new politburo.*

December 21: Total dominance by China
Phase Seven: *GhostNet-like action to be resorted to, but this time to bring down cyber systems across the world, unlike the last time when it was used by Chinese hackers for surveillance purposes only.*

December 31: Establishment of Islamic Caliphate

I will declare Pakistan a military state with a Communist agenda. The Pakistani people will accept the change, a belligerent attitude towards India and a few capital punishments to politicians will make them happy. Dr Nasir's sonic weapon will remove all military resistance. If the Caliphate cannot be raised from Kashmir to Greater Arabia, nothing in the world will remain.

Pervez removed his glasses, shut the iPad and kept it back in his briefcase. The ISI headquarters was now around the corner, and Pervez took in a deep breath and slowly exhaled.

118 DAYS TO EVENT

ISI Headquarters,
Islamabad, Pakistan

August 15,15:10 PST

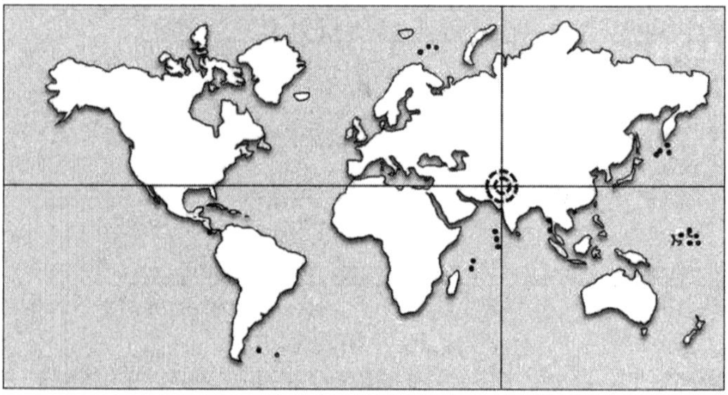

Two pairs of four-stars were shining on two different military shoulders in the well-decorated office, in Joint Intelligence Bureau section of the ISI headquarters. One pair of four stars was over the pine green colour uniform of General Zeng Chan, Vice Chairman of the Central Military Commission of Chinese armed forces, who was comfortably seated on a plush black leather sofa. Seated along with him was the head of India operations for Joint Intelligence Bureau in his green uniform, General Pervez Musa Hussein.

'So my friend you have your chess pieces in place all over this country against the wishes of your incompetent Prime Minister', said the Chinese General giving a slight chuckle.

'Yes, very well, three Corps commanders are supporting me. The X Corps based in Rawalpindi and Azad Kashmir and the V Corps based out of Karachi are also going to be in soon.'

'That's around 150,000 men, but do bring in the 30,000 combat men stationed at Pansi and Jacobabad. You know why?' said the Chinese general giving a slight wink at his compatriot.

'Yes, they surrounded the airport and gave protection to U.S. Air Force personnel in that base.'

'And Air-Force?'

'Air Force Commander at the Masroor Airbase at Karachi, with eight attack squadrons is in.'

'That's over 150 of the US Fighting Falcons, the F-16C/D and the Chinese JF-17, and half of transport squadrons.'

'Yes…supply chain is always important…and the Naval Commander at Karachi Naval Base is my boy from his first day as the chief there.'

'And India's Coldstart strategy.'

'Fuck India's COLDSTART strategy; even after 26/11 Mumbai attack they were pussy-footed to make any show. And your army, my friend, will teach them a permanent lesson.'

Both Generals laughed, giving some choicest words to India. They stopped as the door opened, and Dr Nasir entered. Both men waited patiently as he set up a presentation on his laptop to show his progress to the two sponsors. Over seventy and still a bachelor, his silver hair matching his fair face, the Nobel Prize winning scientist walked with a slight limp but without any discomfort. He looked at both of them.

'Thank you for your patience till now, and letting me work on my own terms,' began Dr Nasir as the two Generals nodded gently.

'As you understand the basic principle of our weapon focuses on sound waves killing the subject, but the subject is unaware of the sound. A mixture of frequencies will cause bio-effect on various internal organs and the CNS killing him slowly.'

'Yes but you still have not explained how it works on the frequency,' said General Pervez.

'It is customised to the location and situation and that is my limit for now. Creating a universal working mass weapon is still far-away.'

'I get it, I did go through your complete report on the Shaksgam Valley experiment…a mass weapon can be hidden to achieve surprise but both living and non-living elements get destroyed by it. No wonder it worked for the Nazis and you too got some early lead with the old research provided to you.'

'Dr Nasir, what about the new mini version of the sonic weapon… that directed sound energy without a projectile that you've been working on?' General Pervez looked directly at him.

'Yes, it can impact at short distance and be directed at the person…only advantage is that it works quicker now…much quicker than the version Jalal used on the C.I.A agent in Islamabad earlier in the year.'

The Generals nodded as they listened to the passionate scientist continue in front of them.

'Can you tell us at least what was the basis of your weapon, how did you develop the blueprint?' asked General Chan.

'The ancient Indian texts called the Vedas, the Yajurveda, specifically, along with my mentor Robert Oppenheimer's notes. He was in possession of certain Buddhist scrolls also.'

'What was so special about these scrolls,' asked General Pervez.

'It had the secret of power of the sound and sound wave. It is said that the ancient Buddhist monks used to manipulate sound waves using metallic singing bowls to travel to other dimensions and worlds.'

Both Generals looked on with a straight face, and let the silver haired scientist continue his talk.

'In fact, Generals, these singing bowls were made from seven known metals and planets of that time. And iron in the bowls was from the Himalayas. One such weapon has been documented in the Bible, "the fall of the walls of Jericho".'

'Hmmm…the Old Testament story when Joshua's Israelite army fights their first battle during the conquest of Canan and brings down the walls of Jericho using a sound weapon.'

'Yes General Chan you are right! So for me the work had already started…I just completed his incomplete studies. The power is now mine…I mean, ours!' said Dr Nasir, changing at the last moment and speaking in an apologetic tone.

General Pervez frowned, and General Chan raised his eyebrows and spoke, 'Well it is our weapon, and without the Chinese Army's help in providing you the access to various Tibetan scrolls, you would not have completed this.'

'General I apologise, for my fellow countryman's gesture…he is passionate about our cause.'

The three men were silent for a minute, but it looked like an eternal period. General Chan cleared his throat, 'Gentleman I would also like to discuss about the extra-terrestrial impact that the sonic weapon testing had done. It brings in unusual visitors,' said General Chan taking out a file from his brown briefcase kept on the side table. He continued, 'our astronomers have got photographs of these triangular shaped unidentified flying objects flying over Shaksgam Valley.'

The General opened the file and placed six black and white photographs on the table. General Pervez and Dr Nasir saw the photos; Dr Nasir smiled.

'Five of the photos are magnified and these objects looked triangular, but they may be some other high level flying objects…the Americans and Russians have such vehicles, and so do you. Right?'

General Chan gave a small smile, but his concerned look returned as he turned towards General Pervez. 'We can confirm no American, Russian or our spy crafts were involved, so we need to assume these can be extra terrestrial in nature…and the sixth photograph gives that impression.'

Dr Nasir gave a gentle laugh, as all three looked at the triangular shaped flying object leaving behind a faint light stream.

'Well we cannot do anything about it, I leave a response to this "phenomenon" to you Chan, we have a time-table to follow for now,' said Pervez and looked towards Dr Nasir.

General Pervez looked sceptical; his wrinkled brow rose as he stroked his hair and stood up.

'Why do you believe in the Vedas so much?'

'They contain knowledge which cannot be corrupted as it is the best way the knowledge was received.'

'What do you mean?'

'There are four ways of receiving knowledge elaborated in the Vedas…by direct perception—*pratyaksa*, by induction or analysis—*anumana*, next is by receiving it from another source or apparent authority and, the final way by which I got my real knowledge is by scriptures, the process known as *sabda*—that of descending knowledge.'

There was a brief silence before Dr Nasir continued.

'So, my *not-so*-respectful friends, the only perfect way is by the final way—descending knowledge. Let me quote...*tadevam sarvatah srestha sabdasya sthitetattva-nirnayakastu sroti-laksana eva na tvarsalaksanopi.'*

Dr Nasir took a moment and looked at the military generals, salivated his throat before continuing, 'And to end this discussion the only reason that this is the best way of transferring knowledge is that it does not suffer from any of the material defects which the humans also suffer from; *bhram*, confusion-illusion or *pramada*, imperfect senses and negligence, or *karanapatava*, imprecision and *vipralipsa* which is the tendency to cheat, to deceive.'

'Doctor, do you mean to say that Vedic knowledge is out of this world?' growled back the Chinese General.

'Yes...the Vedas are divine in nature and it is said to be *apauruseya* in nature, which means something which is not touched by mankind...so it has come from the gods themselves.'

The two generals looked on, and burst out laughing, slapping the elderly physicist on his back. Dr Nasir did not react and just nodded as he left the room.

Let them laugh, as of now I have no choice but to work with them to make my experiments a reality. The UFOs are my new concern now, we shake up things to tap into the power of the universe and they show up. The Vedas mentioned it and so did Oppenheimer...ancient archaeo-astronomers mapped them around the world. Only time will tell if they are returning for good and the side they are playing for.

After a few hours Pervez was inside his room, alone. He was looking at the photograph of Mansur Haider. Also certain satellite intercepts of movement and the radio transcripts of Indian intelligence agencies talking about him.

Mansur Haider, this Baramulla kid can be of help to us...but got to be sure why the Indians are discussing about him. My primary headache is the Indian Home Minister Agastya Rathore, he is covertly aggressive with his anti terror cell CCTC... but I don't have orders to kill him. Will listen to what he's got to say in tonight's interview with Malini Basu.

118 DAYS TO EVENT

Lutyens Road,
Delhi, India

August 15,20:45 IST

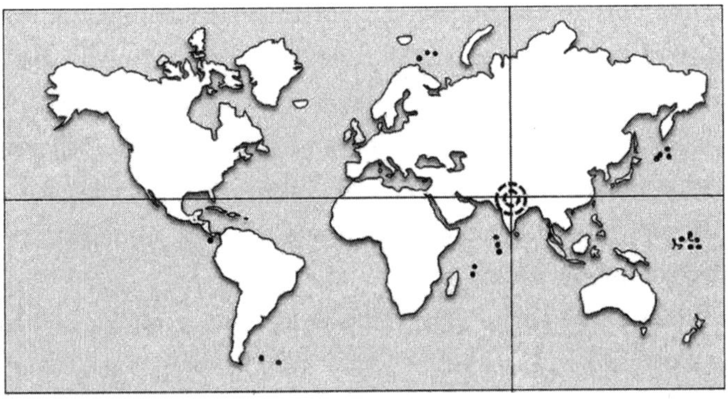

Malini Basu, Newsgate reporter and Arthur L. Carter Journalism Institute post graduate, was ready as she waited for the Home Minister. Thirty years old, she wore a blue satin shirt along with a white medium length skirt, which went well with her bronze skin and short-cropped corporate haircut.

The hall had been set up for the interview. With four cameras in place, three stationary and one roving, the Newsgate team had prepared well, as always taking the smallest details into account including the general ambience, the positioning of furniture, accessorising the room for the interview and the like.

The Home Minister came from a royal lineage of Rajputs—India's royal warrior class. Some historians also believed the Home Minister's family to be descendants of the Suryavanshi clan. After the British left the country, his elders answered the call of Sardar Vallabh Bhai Patel, India's first Home Minister, to join the Indian Union. There was opposition from some quarters in his kingdom, notably from the royal cabinet, but the family was firm in its decision.

As Malini waited, she looked around appreciatively at the tastefully done up interiors.

Agastya was a family man, with two children studying in a boarding school and his wife, Vitasta, a Kashmiri…

JJ, the Newsgate cameraman, tapped Malini on her back to remind her that the minister would be entering the room soon. She nodded, and almost immediately saw the minister entering. He wore a grey kurta with jeans and black leather sandals. She couldn't help noticing the Kashmiri carpets on which he was walking; designed by his wife, she thought.

'Hello, Malini, good to see you again,' said the minister cheerfully.

'Yes, Minister, nice to see you too,' she got up to shake his hand. The Minister took her hand; his grip was firm and confident, not the case twelve months earlier.

'So when do we begin?' The minister asked as someone helped him put on a wireless collar mike.

'2100 hours following the headlines, we will go live directly,' Malini's briefing was short and crisp. JJ raised his left hand marking the countdown to go live. 5, 4, 3, 2, 1…thumbs up. They were on.

'Good evening, India! It's a lovely day here,' Malini smiled into the camera. 'On the occasion of India's sixty-fifth Independence Day, I am happy to be here with our Home Minister, Agastya Harshvardhan Rathore, a man for all seasons, India's man of the people.'

'Thank you…Fire away,' boomed Agastya.

'The top news of today…What is your view of the Prime Minister's Red Fort Speech?' She had decided to get directly to the point. The minister smiled.

'Well, what he said is what we mean,' the minister's reply was sharp and quick. Malini moved her head forward a little and gave him a questioning look, anticipating more. 'Times have changed, and we need to change to keep up with them. We cannot cling to the past,' continued Agastya. 'Not only the Prime Minister but the entire cabinet and government wants to move ahead on this road where we want the entire world to see us differently…in a more proactive way.'

'Can you elaborate what you mean by *proactive*?'

'India is one of the largest economies in the world, with the potential to become *the* largest in the future. For UN peacekeeping missions, we have been providing support not only in terms of logistics, but also the largest manpower forces. With a population of over a billion, we want to be engaged in a global way. Our time has come…and we want to be heard.' Agastya leaned back with a confident smile.

Malini pondered over ways to get an exclusive comment on a controversial subject. It would be good for ratings, like the time she got the Pakistani foreign minister to admit that someone in the Pakistani administration was supporting Osama Bin Laden. There were then rumours in Pakistan's defence circles that General Pervez Musa Hussein from ISI was the man in question, but nothing came of the subsequent investigation apart from the Americans and Indians keeping their eyes trained on him.

'Sir, does this mean that we are open for direct involvement in Afghanistan and Iraq, or would you say this is this more for the upcoming Security Council expansion?'

'Well, as far as our stand is concerned, if things do not begin moving we will have to start making them move. The world has to know we exist. Ours is a culture of love and hospitality, and that is known throughout the world. Our intelligence and economic skills are widely appreciated.' He gave a slight pause before continuing. 'Now we need the world to know that we are a responsible power, a power with not only democratic values but also humanistic ones,' he said, smiling curtly.

He's *referring to China. Old story…let me shift focus to the Mumbai terror.*

'Sir, we are approaching the anniversary of the 26/11 Mumbai terror attacks in a few months and yet the terrorist leader is still to be captured.' said Malini in a sarcastic tone.

She stopped and noticed Agastya fidgeting slightly. Taking a deep breath, she spoke more loudly, her voice filling with emotion. 'Sir… the people of India have one question: Why can't we take direct action? Action like the Americans did to take down the mastermind of 9/11?' She raised her pitch only to tone it down.

Agastya knew that what he felt and wanted to say in the open would not go down well with his party. He was the Home Minister, and sanity above all else was needed amidst all the mayhem across the subcontinent.

Most of the media believed that taking decisive action was better than following the diplomatic channel. In Agastya's mind, any action taken could result in a *domino* effect, whose outcome was not predictable.

He looked straight into her brown eyes and said, 'Malini, I will answer your question with a question. Are we as a society ready to make tough decisions and bear the consequences?' She was taken aback for a moment and prepared to reply, but he continued.

'Do you remember the 2004 Beslan incident in Russia?'

She knew it well. It had happened while she was enrolled in her journalism course at Columbia. It involved Chechnyan separatists who held a school hostage. The rescue attempt had led to the deaths of more than 400 people, mostly young children.

'I support the stand the Russian government took then and has maintained in tackling terrorism in their country. However, as a society, we cannot take such stern action because the risk of extreme collateral damage is too high. It's easy to say, but when the time comes, we have to ask ourselves just how much we would be…willing to sacrifice.' Agastya gave a long pause, looked down.

For the next fifteen minutes they took questions from the audience. It was the usual mudslinging—questions asking for reasons for the lapses, to which the minister responded with poise. They ended the interview, and the anchor thanked the audience and the minister. Looking at the curvy young lady who had begun packing up he smiled, giving her a clear view of his famous dimple.

'Well, I have got a cricket match to catch,' said the Home Minister, getting up from the chair and removing the collar mike.

'So you like cricket, Minister?' Malini queried as she walked with him towards the hallway door.

'Who doesn't…who doesn't in India?' boomed the Home Minister. 'Even when they were not doing well in the recent past, there was still hope, and where there is hope there is life.'

Agastya smiled as he bade her good luck and asked her to send him the feedback the channel received on the interview. While the minister was busy talking to Malini, his secretary was trying to get his attention.

He finally managed to catch his eye as Agastya put his hand on Malini's shoulder and walked her out. They shook hands at the door and the minister approached his secretary.

'What's happened? Did Dykes slip the radar again?' he enquired, motioning for his secretary to move to the adjoining chamber. *Dykes* was used as an internal communication code for General Pervez Musa Hussein, the next ISI chief and Agastya's main headache.

'Yes sir and...just received this communication from CCTC,' said the secretary, handing him a sealed envelope.

The message read: *'Pakistani ISI project Babylon, reaches next level. Mansur Haider name been discussed by them. First contact carried out successfully.'*

Reading the communication from his counter terrorism department he smiled. The Minister asked his secretary to go to the communication room and tell them to keep him updated on the situation.

Well they are predictable, and will definitely dig more. A weapon has been developed by Dr Nasir that I am sure, but I don't know what it is or how it works. Need more help, but don't trust the CIA on it...YES! I can bring Carina and her Swedish intelligence service in for this. Let me take one step at a time and initiate formal contact with her.

117 DAYS TO EVENT

Tulegatan,
Stockholm, Sweden,

August 16,19:30 CET

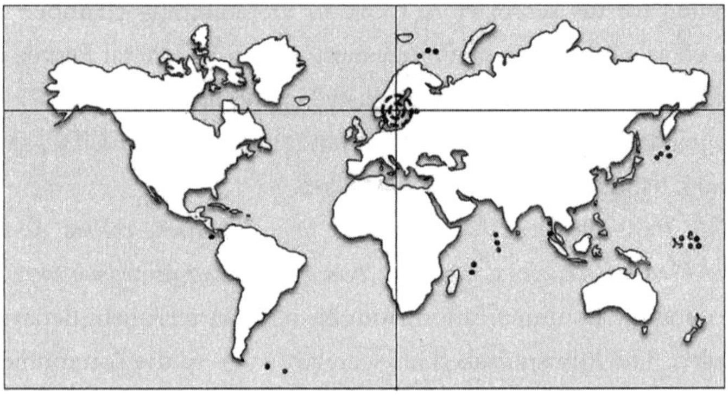

Italian classical music was playing in the background along with the dim lighting which engulfed the therapy room of Nifolki Zuch Spa. This was one of the premium spas of the city where the rich and famous went for top-dollar, state-of-the-art therapy sessions.

Lying on her back in a private room with a towel draped over her was Carina Leijonhufvud. She was a regular here. At forty-two, she had an hourglass figure and young radiant skin which made her look ten years younger than her age.

'More pressure, madam?' asked the masseur, a seven footer who weighed three hundred pounds.

'Yes, Erik…more. And use the elbow on my back.'

'Sure,' replied the masseur.

The masseur continued his treatment with precision, moving the towel onto each area as he worked it and kneading and rolling his way up her body. The ninety-minute treatment was a weekly regimen for Carina. It was one of the few indulgences she allowed herself. She was single and had not had a steady boyfriend for many years. It had finally dawned on her that it was better to be single than to be saddled with emotional baggage. *Total control*, that's what she liked. And at the moment she definitely liked the pressure being applied to her back.

'Can you turn around, madam,' said the masseur, lifting and holding the towel at one end so that she could turn over. From the corner, he saw her body and felt his heart jump. *She did have a sense of authority to her, but she only works for the government. What a pity*, he thought.

Little did the masseur know that the woman at his fingertips was no ordinary woman. She did not work for just any government agency. She was the head of *Särskilda Operationsgruppen,* SOG, the covert intelligence agency of his country. Not just that, she could take down three guys of his size in a few seconds with her bare hands.

She gazed at her right ring finger. The embroidered ring made out of gold-platinum alloy was studded with a shiny, light blue, polished gem-stone, Agate, locked in by thirteen titanium clips. Each clip had a grey-green coloured moonstone gem embedded like minute drops.

The order of the Guardians needs to be restored. The world is falling apart and with the Shaksgam Valley incident, someone has found a new power. Kurt Edberg, my best agent is dead, but has identified his killer...that two timing Jalal Afridi. Something sinister is happening as per Kurt's earlier inputs of a potential terror strike in December, and even the Indians know about it. My old pal Agastya has contacted me to help him out.

The massage once over, she slid out of the massage table, and walked towards the shower in full view of the masseur. The masseur continued to arrange the room, helping himself to glances in the shower cubicle which was now getting steamed up. Carina, with her hands spread across wide against the walls and legs slightly apart, faced the full force of the hot shower. The water guzzled out as sparkles into her face. Carina was now deep in thought.

Kurt's replacement and my new agent Adolf Silfverskiöld would need to get up-to speed soon. Tonight Adolf is with his god-fearing girlfriend. What a combination, he does not believe in God and she is an ardent Church-goer.

116 DAYS TO EVENT

Byälvsvägen Road,
Stockholm, Sweden

August 17,05:29 CET

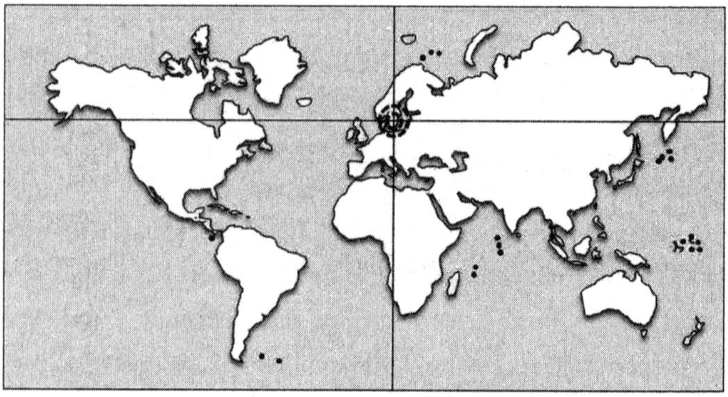

A loud ring and Adolf Silfverskiöld was on his feet. It was 5:30 am. Adolf heard a loud moan from his girlfriend, Mikaela, who was in bed with him.

'It's Sunday, for God's sake, Adolf,' she bellowed at him, sitting up and then falling back, staring at him with tired eyes, biting her lip. Adolf looked at her and smiled. In the dim green light of the room he could still make out Mikaela's contours under the sheet. One of her lovely bare legs poked out from beneath the Ekelund-design Nordic bed linen.

Adolf bent down and whispered, 'You really look like something special right now. Gives me a lot of ideas.'

'Don't you…not now. Aren't you tired?' said Mikaela, nudging Adolf away.

'If I was tired you wouldn't be coming here,' said Adolf in a low voice. Mikaela shook her head, smiled, and planted a kiss on Adolf's cheek. 'And going to be an important week for you, Dolfy, going to work for a new boss.'

'Yes, I know.'

'Tell me all about it when you return.'

'*Ja.*' He walked into the bathroom and splashed his face with water. Examining his six and half feet muscular body in front of the full length mirror, Adolf could see a couple of bullet scars, one on his right chest and the other on his left hand. *Permanent love bites*—that's what Mikaela used to call them, and they were her favourite places to sink her teeth in.

After a few moments he stepped out and did some stretching and on the wall shelf noticed his NATO Meritorious Service Medal and Sweden's Armed Forces Medal in bronze for International Service, awarded to him the previous year for his heroic actions on the battlefield.

Adolf dressed in his track suit and prepared to go jogging.

The sun will be up soon enough.

He stretched on the roadside outside his house and started running. Five miles to go, and then he would hit the gym.

This week he would be working for a new boss. At 29, Adolf would be one of the youngest agents to be assigned directly to the chief of SOG, the covert intelligence agency of Sweden. It was exciting as the identity of his new boss remained a closely guarded secret.

Funny, he thought. *I don't even know who I'm going to work for…literally.*

His had been a meteoric rise since being commissioned to the Swedish Air Force nine years ago. His potential came into prominence during his stint with the European Council Nordic battle group, a military force whose chief aim was rapid deployment in times of crisis. Adolf was ranked *Överstelöjtnant Kommendörkapten*, or Lieutenant Colonel, when he was transferred to *Fallskärmsjägarna*, an elite paratrooper regiment, two years ago. This unit specialised in elite military operations, and he saw action in Goz Beida, Chad as part of the *European Marines* for EUFOR and Kabul, Afghanistan as part of ISAF. These postings did have one effect: he got a good tan that Mikaela liked.

One more mile to go. I hope Mikaela wakes up by the time I am through at the gym. Of course she will. I promised her that I would hear her Nyckelharpa music recitation... so good to know she will be playing for Nobel ceremony concert in December; she has come a long way from the club shows. But she will still drag me to the Church for praying to something I don't believe in!

Four hours later, Adolf and Mikaela were in the Saint Eric's Cathedral. Rows of wooden benches were filled with worshippers. The congregation was singing a prayer song. While Mikaela was singing her heart out, Adolf was silent, admiring her. She nudged him, expanding her big round blue eyes at him. He smiled back and winked at her. Mikaela gave a look of disapproval and turned her head away from Adolf giving a small smile.

Ahhh...there she smiled again. I may not believe in her Lord but I believe in her. If angels exist, they would have her voice.

The prayers continued in the nineteenth-century cathedral. The hymns from the singers were enhanced with the enveloping rhythmic sound from the pipe organ. The Father began speaking 'All open the book to Psalm 137, By the rivers of Babylon'. After twenty minutes he gave the final prayers and all members stood up and said 'Amen' in unison. Well, almost all members. Adolf was silent. Mikaela glared at him again, and he smiled back at her.

The prayers closed and the congregation began to walk out slowly. Adolf increased his pace as he neared the large wooden oak doors. Mikaela then extended her left hand to hold on to his elbow and tug him back. Adolf felt the jerk, looked back, pressed his lips tightly and raised his eyebrows. Mikaela nodded her head sideways.

'Don't rush, let's walk out slowly.'

'Yes my love. Anything for you.'

Both walked out slowly to the car park, where Mikaela's car was parked. Adolf took out the keys and sat in the driver's seat. Mikaela sat down slowly, patting her dress as she adjusted herself.

'Adolf, I need to talk to you.'

Adolf gulped. He understood the tone.

That time and again 'why don't I believe in the lord'...JESUS...why doesn't Jesus leave me alone.

'I understand you don't believe in God and I appreciate you coming down here with me, just for me.'

Adolf looked on with a blank expression, not wanting to react.

'At least for my sake say "Amen" at the end of the prayer.'

Adolf tried to smile.

'No…don't do that…NO!' said Mikaela raising her pitch slightly. Adolf turned his gaze down. Mikaela suddenly felt guilty.

'I did not mean it that way…'

'Shhh…you have every right over me, and I promise I will repeat "Amen" next time *whenever it is required.*'

Mikaela smiled and ran her hand over Adolf's golden-blonde hair. Adolf smiled and whispered 'Amen', softly.

'You know, Dolfy, chanting "Amen" provides positive vibrations to the mind, so say it at least for science, if not for the Lord.'

Adolf was silent, then he nodded slowly and smiled. Mikaela also smiled back at him.

'"Amen" is pure and has evolved from other prayers. In fact another prayer word "Ogham" from the Celtics in ancient England has a similar impact on the human mind.'

'Ok…Amen and Ogham may be brothers in arms,' quipped Adolf.

'Well Amen and Ogham are related, but there is the "Aum" from Hinduism also. Some say "Amen" is derived from "Aum".'

'Hmmm...'

'I don't know much, but came across these theories during a research I am doing for a paper. When I know more I will tell you about it.'

'Well I don't need to learn these things…you are there for me right,' whispered Adolf.

'God will find a way into your heart…and when he does you will remember me first', said Mikaela as she strapped on her seat belt.

Adolf bent towards her and planted a soft kiss on her lips. He then undid her seat belt, to free her. She reciprocated and moved her arms around him, gently pressing herself against him.

Three days later, Adolf was getting ready for work.

Mikaela talks a lot, yes, but it only makes up for my lack of being verbose.

Adolf gave a short laugh.

My Mickey.

It had been over three years since they had first met, but their romance had only grown stronger, despite Adolf's frequent trips across the globe in the course of his national military duties. He still vividly remembered how he got to know her during a local music show, in which he saw her playing the Nyckelharpa or the Swedish harp, with her group.

Her involvement in keeping alive old Swedish music kept her busy. She ran a grassroots campaign to establish a strong community for local musicians and with a few thousand people playing the instrument in Sweden, she had managed to drum up interest in it, across the entire Nordic region.

Now she would be playing music in Oslo this December in front of royalty and would fulfil a lifelong ambition.

Adolf came out of his house and walked towards his car, noticing that the garage door was tight and squeaky. *More oil,* he thought as he pushed open the door and entered the garage.

What a squeaky noise! Well, after the lecture on music, notes and the human mind from Mikaela, any sound will make me think…imagine manipulating sound to create orgasmic and euphoric feeling, she says it's done regularly to unsuspecting listeners. Wow! Sound creating psycho physiological effects! To create distortion of the mind and body! Her sexy voice has that kind of effect on me; one does not need to manipulate music for it.

Adolf was smiling now as he admired his custom-made Volvo, which the agency had delivered to him yesterday. A new set of wheels got Adolf's adrenalin flowing. He opened the door of the car and got in, appreciating the interior and its leatherwork. It would take him thirty minutes to drive over to the Defence Ministry. From there he would be flown by chopper to the headquarters at Karlsborg, for three days of induction training before his first meeting with the boss.

I will propose to Mikaela soon. I don't know when. Got to get the ring first as it might be a spur-of-the-moment decision. She will say yes…I know she is not happy that I don't believe in God, but with so many dead bodies falling across you…who would? But she is my lady, conventional and soft…In less than a week a new boss. Who could it be?

113 DAYS TO EVENT

SOG HQ, Karlsborg, Västergötland, Sweden

August 20,09:30 CET

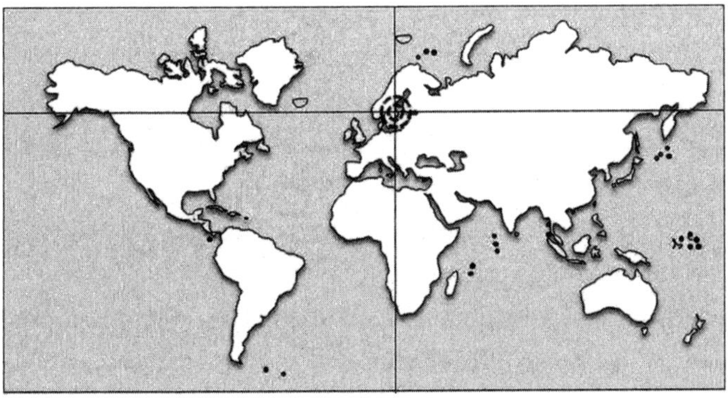

Carina Leijonhufvud was in the SOG office, looking at files that had been placed on her desk by her executive secretary, Lovisa. Fifteen minutes passed before her intercom rang and Lovisa was on the line. 'Madame, Adolf is here.'

'Okay, I will buzz you and then you can send him in,' said Carina.

Adolf was waiting outside. Lovisa was trying to engage him in conversation, but Adolf kept it short, just chit-chat. The phone rang. Lovisa answered the call. She looked up with the phone in her hand and gestured to Adolf that it was time.

As he entered, he noticed the impressive office design.

Not bad for an Intel office, he thought.

Adolf headed towards the end of the room where Carina was sitting looking at a file, which he presumed was his. Behind her was a painting, a replica set in the 15th-16th century. Portraying a church setting, it depicted a knight with a sword and many other religious figures. They all seemed to focus on an old man with a white beard in the middle of the canvas.

I have seen this somewhere before, can't recall where. One thing for sure...the old man in the centre is someone important.

Adolf's attention returned to his meeting. They greeted each other, and she began speaking while he stood there.

'Based on our assessment you are our strongest resource on Humint (Human Intelligence),' said Carina. 'Your assignments in Afghanistan included the Khandar raid and the undercover job to prevent the assassination of the entire Afghan cabinet—all very impressive.'

Adolf thanked her with a straight face.

'What do you know about Project Babylon?' asked Carina with an air of authority.

'What would you like to know—the origin, the inventor of the gun, the scandal...' Adolf paused, waiting for her response.

Carina signalled for Adolf to sit, which he did, pushing the chair closer to the table facing Carina.

'Adolf, assume for a minute that I don't know anything about it and summarise it for me in a few lines.'

Adolf closed his eyes and took a deep breath, and as he exhaled, he opened his eyes and looked up at the ceiling. He noticed in the large design overhead something resembling a star system.

She must be into astronomy, he thought. He gathered his thoughts and then looked at Carina and smiled.

'Well, Ma'am, let me begin by giving a summary in two sentences, and then I can elaborate if you want more details.'

Adolf got up, put both his hands on the back of the chair, looked at Carina, and said, 'Project Babylon was a failed weapons program project to build super artillery guns commissioned by Saddam Hussein during the late 1980s. The project was cut short when its supposed project manager, Gerald Bull, a Canadian, was assassinated in 1990.'

'Continue,' said Carina.

'It was a good idea, Ma'am, maybe too good. Otherwise Bull would not have been assassinated. Still, it needed some tweaking. The aim was to build a gun with a large cannon and a bore with high muzzle velocity to fire projectiles great distances,' said Adolf, gesturing with his hands as he talked.

Carina sat still, moving only her eyes to try and maintain eye contact with him as much as possible.

'So who killed Bull?' said Carina as she got up, and walked to the drinks cabinet. She removed two crystal glasses and a bottle half-filled with Mackmyra Preludium 02.

Isn't it a little early for that?

Adolf's thoughts interrupted his words momentarily but he quickly resumed the conversation.

'Who didn't want to silence him? In all probability it was Mossad, but it could have been the CIA, MI6, or even the KGB.'

Carina offered a glass to Adolf. He politely refused.

'I insist,' said Carina in a stern voice.

Adolf caught his breath.

Fifteen minutes and, she is acting bossy. How difficult it was going to be working with her.

With his thumb and index finger Adolf indicated only a splash. Carina poured a small drink in his glass and asked him to take ice or water as he wished. While he poured water into his drink he saw Carina filling her glass halfway and heard the ice making a clucking noise in the glass as she dropped in two cubes.

She lifted her glass, Adolf responded, and both took a sip.

'That's a good overview of Project Babylon. I am sure that you know all the technical details as well,' said Carina.

Adolf nodded.

'Very good, Adolf. Excellent,' she said emphatically, watching his face to gauge how he reacted to praise. No change.

'It's just generic info, Ma'am, and I said this earlier, the concept was good, but it had its flaws.'

'What about the Safari Club and its relations with BCCI?' said Carina, shifting the discussion to another tangent.

Adolf was well acquainted with the Safari Club and BCCI. He began by explaining that the Safari Club was an alleged cabal of intelligence agencies which was formed secretly in the mid 1970s. This organisation was formed by nations which differed on more points than they had in common. Nations like Egypt, Iran, Saudi Arabia, and even France were a part of it. There were indications that it had the patronage of the CIA. Its main agenda was to counter the KGB of the erstwhile Soviet Union.

Nice way this kid is elaborating the facts, and his body language…excellent, Carina mused.

Adolf paused to make sure Carina was with him. She told him to continue.

'In order to run this show they needed finances. This requirement resulted in the CIA and other friendly agencies supporting a small Pakistani bank, BCCI—Bank of Credit and Commercial International—which became a major international bank within a few years. BCCI became a money-laundering machine, in which not only black money turned into official white money, but the funds were used for various clandestine operations. A U.S. Congressional inquiry also took place in the 1990s after which the bank was asked to wrap up its operations.'

'You have put forward good points, you do know your history…but what do you think in retrospect about this whole thing?'

'Well this was responsible for many governments being toppled and multiple covert activities taking place. In fact, in retrospect, the seeds of current world terrorism were initially funded via these channels. Cause and effect, it's that simple,' said Adolf.

He looked deeply into Carina's eyes as if implying that the Western world shared much of the responsibility for the gestation of terrorist activity. It was like during the Cold War, when both sides wanted to be one-up on the other, and neither could stop.

Carina raised her hand, indicating him to stop. She walked up, opened a file, removed a piece of paper, and held it out.

'You should see this.'

As she handed him the paper, Adolf asked what it was.

'This is the last communication from your predecessor, who was stationed in Pakistan as part of SIC group; I'm sure you know what it is. We in the SIC group were investigating the Shaksgam Valley incident. We had sent him to work undercover with an aid agency to follow on some leads shared by CIA.'

'Yes I know the SIC group, Shared Intelligence Club of US, British and our intelligence set up after Abbottabad raid,' said Adolf as he took the paper and saw his chief nod in agreement.

He read the paper…

'Project Babylon Operational, New Safari Involved. Potential BCCI Support'

Adolf felt his stomach tighten. He looked over the paper, with a tense face.

'Ma'am, are you *sure* that this is the same Project Babylon?'

Precisely, Adolf…Precisely, thought Carina.

'Well, Adolf, the Intel is that something has been activated in Pakistan. After the Shaksgam Valley incident, which we are still not sure about, I don't want to take any chances. I don't trust Pakistan or China one bit; the Indians are also not telling what they know about what happened in that valley.' Carina's voice was not only serious but also intense. 'Sometime in the first week of May, an explosion took place in Shaksgam Valley. The official version was that it was a mining accident with the Chinese exploring rare elements there. However, sketchy reports from a team of surviving international mountaineers present there gave a different version and the area was locked out to the outside world since then.' She continued, 'Our agent Kurt Edberg is dead! Ring a bell, does it?'

'*Ja*, I think. Was he by any chance with NATO forces in Afghanistan?'

Carina nodded, satisfied at his ability to connect the dots quickly. 'Yes both of you served together, and he recommended you by sending your serial number and details a day before he died.'

Adolf's face registered his surprise.

'And that was not the only message he sent that day with your name, he also sent the following quote from the Bible.' Carina looked up at her computer screen and then turned her face slowly towards Adolf. Her voice had a slightly higher pitch as she repeated the words, 'In the beginning was the Word, and the Word was with God, and the Word was God.'

'That's John 1:1. Why did Kurt send that?'

'Hmmm…. Good! You are a Sabbath visitor or may I say an escort to your girlfriend, to meet the lord.'

Adolf was slightly uncomfortable with the conversation as he fidgeted with his hands towards his right pocket to feel for his small Bible, which his girlfriend Mikaela insisted he carry.

'Look Adolf, a lot of things have happened quickly and in this sea of information you would need to find the answer. And you are going to be working on *getting* to the bottom of this information or misinformation. And if you have to go to Pakistan, India or China, go!' She turned her back on him and looked at the magnificent portrait on the wall.

Adolf thought, *Pakistan! Does she really expect me to go there? I am supposed to get married at the end of this year. I am supposed to propose to Mikaela soon.*

Adolf stood up and saluted Carina, and she instructed Lovisa from her desk to give him further details and guide him to his operational desk. As he walked out he pondered over the magnificent portrait, trying to place it. Pope, Church setting, and knight with sword, all looking at the old man with a white beard in the centre.

Lovisa was standing outside the door holding a file which she handed over to Adolf as he came out. Adolf smiled at her, and she winked back and said, 'How was the inquisition?'

Adolf stopped walking as he realised what the painting was. The old man was Galileo, and that painting was *Galileo before the Holy Office*. The painting depicted the inquisition conducted by the Catholic Church to stop Galileo's books on the theory of heliocentricity.

An **hour passed** as Adolf sat at his desk and pored over the material given to him. Three hours had passed when he heard the clicking sound of heels.

It's Lovisa. More CDs and files on the way.

'So how is the young baby doing?' Lovisa stood by the door with one hand on her hips. Adolf smiled subtly. 'You bored? Ma'am sent you this,' said Lovisa, handing over a memory drive. 'She will be calling you soon.'

Adolf took the data storage drive, inserted it into his laptop, and then heard the beep from the fixed phone on the table. He lifted the receiver and heard Carina's voice on the other end. 'Settled in and comfortable?'

'Comfortable, but trying to read up and decipher different facets of the material shared till now,' replied Adolf shuffling papers and photos across from the files kept in front of him.

'It's a lot, I understand, but I know you can do it Adolf…take it from the most recent reports received.'

'Right Ma'am, thanks for the support…looking at the last photos sent by Kurt before his death.'

'So any thoughts on the Star of David, Swastika or the geometric shaped photo sketches Kurt sent from Islamabad?'

Adolf stared at the black and white novel size blow ups of the two illustrations. One blow up had multiple geometric shaped drawings and a weird script. The other had a Swastika and Star of David illustration. 'Only thing for now, it can be an ancient language and may be a Nazi connection.'

'Nazi?' Carina asked surprisingly.

'The Nazis did spend quite a lot of resources searching for ancient weapons and tried to develop them. They had theories around a space weapon…and they even had trips to Tibet and Kashmir…this may be an angle worth going through,' said Adolf confidently.

'Hmmm...run it through the Thor database.'

'Yes Ma'am.'

'Now see the memory drive I sent. Its password is *daivata*,' said Carina as Adolf typed it in. 'Brief me on your thoughts regarding the photos from Kurt before you leave for the night.'

The flash drive powered ahead with a pop up appearing which Adolf clicked as Carina was speaking. A photograph came up listing his bio details on the side. There was also a Safari Club tab.

Adolf was about to speak when Carina continued. 'The Safari Club tab is mentioned. Not the old one which you described, but a new one according to recent intelligence inputs—a suspected alliance between the intelligence arms of certain countries along with terror groups.'

'Sounds like a lot! How did they stay hidden for so long?' asked Adolf with a cold tone.

'Some sketchy report was present, but Abbottabad Intel gives us more. One more thing, the green-eyed guy, he is your bunny, the target for observation. His name is Mansur, Mansur Haider, location Kashmir, India.'

'Why India and not Pakistan, when the original intercept came from Pakistan?' asked Adolf, a little puzzled by this sudden development.

'Kurt's passed on a photo of this man. There was a lot of Intel passing through various agencies, and his name specifically came up in various online chatters between India, Pakistan and London,' she said in a single flow, and then continued in a concerned tone. 'MI-6 and CIA are not considering him important, but I have a hunch that something is heating up. We need to find out. They will have their operative on the ground so I would not like to use them directly.'

Adolf liked the way Carina mentioned her hunch, as this was the way he himself liked to work. The brief silence was intruded with Lovisa connecting in between.

'Sorry to disturb you Ma'am, but the President is on the line.'

'OK, a minute, Lovisa, keep him on hold.'

'Sure Ma'am.'

'Adolf, you will go to India. We have to find an appropriate route for you.'

'Okay Ma'am, got it. I will get my head around the operational requirements and get started today.'

'Not today…Now! I need to push off, not nice to keep the President waiting; we are a democracy after all.' He heard her chuckle.

Adolf gazed at the photograph directly into Mansur's green eyes.

A bunny, to be watched. Why are you so important? What are you hiding? Speak to me. What kind of weapon are you going to use…something which the Nazis wanted?

CABLE: US EMBASSY DELHI TO CIA LANGLEY

VZCZCXRO3157
DE RUEHIL #0351 0120352
ZNY SSSSS ZZH
P 120852Z AUG 22
FM AMEMBASSY DELHI
RUEAIIA/CIA WASHDC PRIORITY
RUEKJCS/JOINT STAFF WASHINGTON DC PRIORITY
RUEKJCS/SECDEF WASHINGTON DC PRIORITY
RHEHNSC/NSC WASHDC PRIORITY

Monday, 22August, 18:21
S E C R E T SECTION 01 OF 01 Delhi 000056
SIPDIS
EO 12958 DECL: 03/12/2062
TAGS WAR,PK,CHN,EAID,PK,SKV
SUBJECT: REPORT ON INDIA WAR CABINET MEETING
Classified By: Ambassador Yitzhak Herzog's, Reasons 2

1. Summary: Indian war cabinet met and discussed scenarios of China string of pearl strategy. To be shared with cabinet tomorrow. Mansur Haider still neutral.

COMMENT

2. India's home minister Agastya Rathore has prepared a presentation to be shared with India's cabinet soon. This is after getting inputs from Defence Minister General Abhimanyu Kashyapa. They expect China's string of pearl expansionist strategy will limit India's defences. Details of counter plan not available, which will be shared later by Minister X.

3. Mansur Haider of Srinagar, his status is still neutral. Advice to increase surveillance on him.

110 DAYS TO EVENT

Prime Minister's Office,
Delhi, India

August 23,08:30 IST

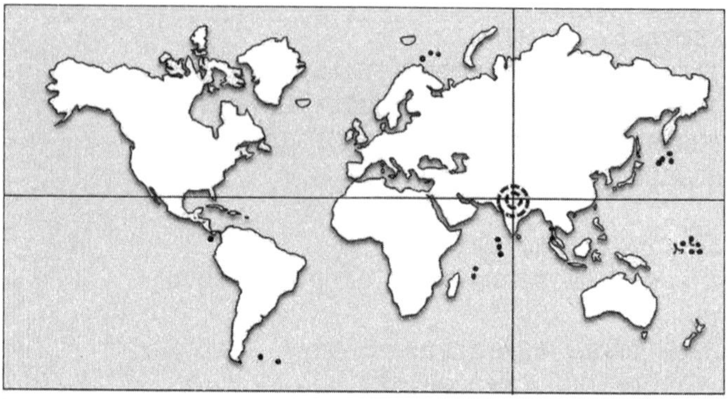

'**This can't be** possible, Mr Prime Minister,' said the Minister of Agriculture, visibly upset over the message (China's threat to India) that had just been delivered during the last hour. He continued. 'Do you really expect us to believe that this is possible?'

Agastya saw how unhappy the Prime Minister was at that comment. *Jeez, give the guy a break, time to pitch in.*

'I am sure most of you know something about the game of chess. Either you have played it or you know the basic rules,' said Agastya, standing up and walking towards the white board on which the power point slide was being projected.

'The objective of chess is to capture the king. It can be done in three moves when playing with an amateur or many more moves when playing with an expert,' he began in a low tone before raising his voice.

'However, in both cases the game proceeds with set moves before going in for the kill…do the castling step, protect the king. Move forward with the rook, pawns, queen and other pieces to take out the opponent's pieces. Make him feel vulnerable, make him feel the threat to his king—a check—make him run and fight for survival. Finally finish him off with checkmate,' exploded Agastya.

'I don't get where you are heading with this,' said the Minister for Environment. A few others also wore puzzled looks.

'China has us surrounded, and there is no stopping them. Primarily it's the so-called "string of pearls" strategy of surrounding us.'

'What does string of pearl mean?' asked one of the ministers.

'The port and airfield construction projects across South East Asia by the Chinese supposedly to protect their energy supply from other countries...but that's only a cover for military expansion,' replied the Minister for External Affairs, Smriti Rao.

'Thank you Smriti. Most of these ports were financed by a Chinese state owned corporation with a hidden agenda of supporting the Chinese Navy.'

'Now gentlemen, picture the map of South East Asia, silent beautiful and all is well. But slowly the thing changes,' Agastya stops, raises his clenched right hand, starts to open the fingers one by one.

'Pakistan port in Gwadar, Sri Lanka, Hambantota and Colombo, Bangladesh, container shipping facility in Chittagong, Burma, a deep-water port in Sittwe and Kyaukpyu, and new supply facilities, Vietnam, airstrip on one of the islands in Paracel archipelago.'

Agastya took a deep breath, feeling the cold conditioned air going in. He continued, 'and new military bases, bordering in Kashmir and Nepal. Air force facilities Tibet…list goes on and on. We are getting surrounded.'

'My friends the map then looks like this.' Agastya stepped aside and the screen showed the map of India surrounded by Chinese supported bases and ports. There was an eerie silence around the room with ministers' ashen faces looking on.

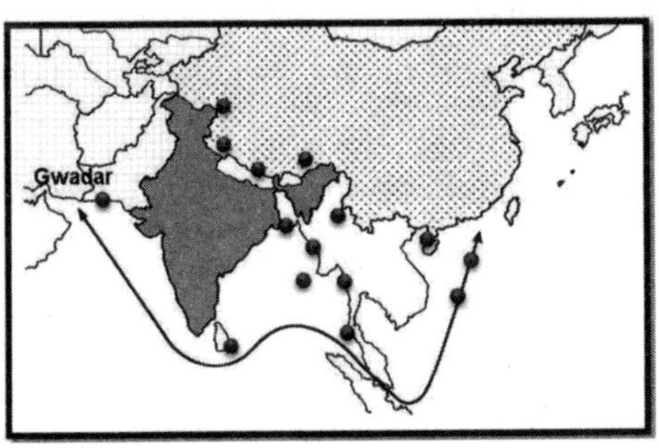

'CHECK…comes in from the enemy, another CHECK,' said Agastya loudly, pressing his hand on the table and stooping to face his colleagues. 'And then we keep running and running. The Americans will not come as they are too busy fixing their economy and becoming embroiled in election showdown as if it were World War III. Britain will provide only moral support, Russia may engage in discussions but it may be too late,' said Agastya.

The room was now humming with positive energy, and it seemed as if he had woken up everyone. The prime minister looked at his friend and raised his hand, indicating him to stop.

'No, Mr Prime Minister, they need to know,' said Agastya, lowering his voice again and trembling in anger.

'My friends, we are on our own. We will receive only lip service. Remember fifty years ago, the war of '62 with China? Only two countries—yes, only two countries—Ethiopia and Malaysia, spoke openly against the Chinese attack,' said Agastya, holding up two fingers, in a V-sign.

'I expect this time, too, no one will talk. Then later it will come... CHECKMATE, and then all will be over. But we shall not let it happen again, certainly not like this.'

'So you want us to continue with our work and act like nothing has happened, sort of like when the so-called Shaksgam Valley incident happened?' queried another minister.

'Let me be clear: We hope nothing happens. But we will not be under-prepared as we were five decades back...and the Shaksgam Valley incident is a not a verifiable fact, just a hearsay,' elaborated Agastya, walking back and sitting in his chair.

The prime minister, who was listening to the ongoing discussion, nodded his head and looked around at the others as he lifted the yellow file on the table before him.

'Please read the contents of "Operation Vajra" file very carefully. It is customised for each one of your departments and includes the action that you will need to take when this operation begins.'

The yellow, unremarkable-looking files were circulated among the ministers.

'I know that you all are aware of this, but it bears repeating: The contents of the file are highly confidential. Please take the next four hours to read it over...memorising the contents and passwords.'

The prime minister walked towards a grey door which connected the conference room to a chamber. He pressed an orange button on an electronic contraption at the side of the door. The red LED light on top of the door turned green, indicating the door could be opened from inside.

'Please leave your mobile phones and other electronic devices on the table,' said the man who came through the door. Everyone knew the man, the prime minister's security chief. The ministers were a little taken aback and started questioning why they needed to spend the next four hours inside the adjoining chamber without any communication with the outside world. They were told that they would be shown a thirty-minute film on the subject at hand.

'Why is this necessary, Mr Prime Minister? Don't you trust us... and what about the defence minister?' said one of the cabinet members.

The prime minister had an urge to utter the famous Reagan dictum, *trust but verify*, but it could create more issues instead of the bonhomie he wanted from his team.

'It's a security protocol, my friends,' said the prime minister. He continued after a brief pause. 'As far as the defence minister is concerned, he is one of the architects of this file along with the Home, Finance and Foreign Ministries.'

Heads started turning towards Agastya Rathore, Smriti Rao, and the finance minister, Mohammed Abu-Bakr. The prime minister looked at the faces of his cabinet colleagues. He understood their surprise and said, 'This was prepared as part of CCS, my friends, and they will be joining you inside.' The CCS or Cabinet Committee on Security included a political and executive council.

The ministers removed their communication devices and set them on the table, muttering disapprovingly as they walked towards the inner chamber. One of the veterans looked at the prime minister and said, 'This never happened during Indira Gandhi's time.'

'Well, I am not Indira Gandhi and this is a different era,' said the prime minister, recollecting that there was once a time when everyone followed verbatim, the dictum of leaders such as Nehru,

Shastri and Indira. How times have changed, leaving him to rely on arm twisting.

Agastya knew the phones could be tapped. He himself knew, along with the prime minister and defence minister, that there could be a potential CIA mole among them, and there was a history to it. As per the CIA's declassified papers, it was alleged that there was a CIA mole in Indira Gandhi's cabinet who gave away the war's ultimate objective. The plan involved taking over a strategic zone in Pakistan Occupied Kashmir and striking down the capability of the Pakistan Armed Forces to attack. The action was stopped on December 16, 1971, when Richard Nixon, then the U.S. president, convinced Nikolai Podgorny, Chairman of the Presidium of the Supreme Soviet of the USSR, that unless they overwhelmed India diplomatically and stopped their movement into western Pakistan, they would face a major confrontation with them. The superpowers then colluded with China to halt India's march into western Pakistan.

It won't be like 1971, thought Agastya.

This time we will complete our objective, no matter what the cost! I will get clandestine help and Carina has promised to send whatever information she has on General Pervez. She did mention about a potential December strike...but what does she want in return?

109 DAYS TO EVENT

**SOG HQ, Karlsborg,
Västergötland, Sweden**

August 24,02:30 CET

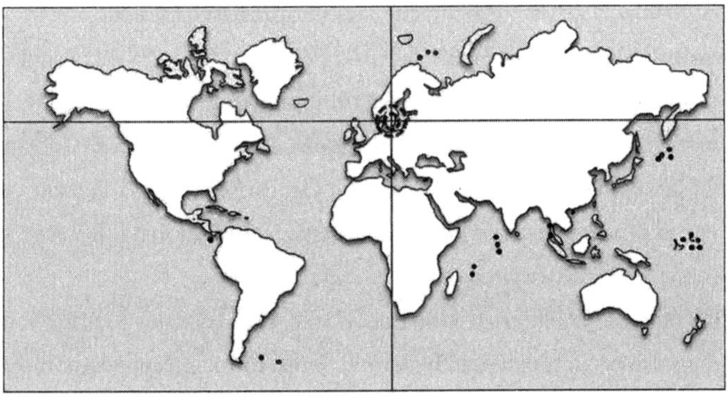

The day turned to evening and the evening turned to night, but the silence enveloping Adolf's cubicle persisted. The only noise interrupting this quiet was that of the file pages being turned and the gentle hum of the air-conditioner.

Gosh, I feel irritated. A few moments of this silence is ok, but now it's haunting and irritating.

He dropped the files on the desk and rubbed his sleepy eyes. He swivelled his chair one eighty degrees.

This case is more than what it seems. Kurt requesting me to be present, something which he knows I don't...what could it be?

Gathering his thoughts on how to pace his first report in a direction contributing to the team on this case, Adolf began indexing the issues and placing them in mental buckets with tags.

Subject line...Nazi link cannot be ruled out, right.

Swivelling his chair back towards the laptop screen, Adolf shuffled his hand on the screen. The milky-way galaxy screensaver changed, and the password request came up. Once Adolf entered it, the desktop was visible and he tapped on an icon shaped in the form of a gloved hand holding a silver coloured hammer. The icon activated the encrypted email service used internally by SOG. Adolf began typing.

Subject line: Nazi link in Shaksgam Valley incident

Dear Ma'am,

Looking at the different pieces of information, I have developed theories around it. I would like to highlight two areas based on a historical perspective, my thoughts on Jalal, his local attaché and our primary suspect.

Symbols: The Swastika and Star of David, symbols of Nazi period—This line of thought will not hold if we take other religions into account.

- Swastika is present in various religions like Hinduism, Buddhism and civilisations like the Indus Valley, the Greek period, and Persian culture. Even in our neighbouring Finland it is used in traditional folk art products. The symbol is associated with well-being.
- The Star of David also consists of the two triangles representing the ruling tribes of Judah and Benjamin. This, in turn, represents the twelve tribes. This sign is seen in pagan practices and across different regions, like India. The symbol in this case is associated with balance between male and female energy. The female triangle, the downward one, is associated with giving birth, menstruation and keeping focus on earthly matters. And the upward triangle signifying the male showcases prowess of imagination and the surge of seed.

Shaksgam Valley Incident: Nazis were known to believe not only the element of fringe science, but also in trying to locate and commandeer such items from around the world. If they came to know of such items or stories, they sent it to various teams. The Nazis did send search teams into Tibet and presumably Kashmir. So there is a level of interest for us to understand what they found.

The satellite photos of the areas and scans of the upper atmosphere show an event similar to Tunguska. A similar reading was observed albeit on a much lower scale in Nazi Germany just before World War II.

I would like to suggest an alternative thought—**the 1936 crash in Schwarzwald (Black Forest), near Freiburg, Breisgau—Germany**. This was the suspected crash of an **alien ship** allowing Nazis to gain a technological advantage by reverse engineering of the alien craft. The aircraft was powered by anti-matter, symbolised by a black sun. This symbol can be found in places of worship in ancient Babylonia and Assyria. 'Project Babylon' in the message may be related to this reference of a new weapon linking it up with the 'Super-Gun' theory. With Higgs Boson particle found, the next step would be anti-matter and anti-gravity weapons for some. I suggest the following hypothesis:

A weapon system has been developed with the help of a technology which the Nazis were looking for in Tibet and Kashmir. Mansur's family may have a connection; so a background check is needed on the history of the family.

The hypothesis is subject to finding how Kurt was murdered by the assassin, as the autopsy reports a zero gravity body damage. The questions are, is there a new weapon being created which took him out? If so, who controls it? Who is/are Jalal's handlers?

On the mode of operation, I need to do more digging on Mansur Haider to see the best way to get a cover story and reach close to him. I would need to have CIA inputs from their operative inside Srinagar.

Will update more on any new developments that I think or find out.

Signing Off,
Adolf Silfverskiöld
Överstelöjtnant Kommendörkapten

Adolf read the mail one more time, clicked the send button, and then shut down his laptop.

I hope she does not think I am crazy. I need to develop open options as the autopsy report of Kurt does not make sense.

Few minutes passed as Adolf stared at a photo of Mikaela and himself, pinned in his cubicle. He shut the laptop and slipped it into the black leather case, slung the case across his shoulder in one swift motion. Going down in the lift towards the lobby, Adolf was thinking about Mansur when his mobile started buzzing.

Carina! Doesn't she sleep?

He took the call and walked out into the lobby as the lift door opened. 'Yes Ma'am. Good Morning!'

'Long night or early morning, Adolf? Nice start.'

'Yes, only the beginning, but we need to act fast; if my fears are right, we are looking at a new weapon system.'

'I agree, it would have been helpful if Kurt sent direct references instead of a cryptic message.'

'The situation may have demanded it.'

'Yes, and I still think that his recommending you has to have a link, so do keep that factor in.'

'Yes Ma'am. I need to get more on Mansur Haider, his family, background...'

'Bjorn and Stephanie have already started; I have instructed them to set up satellite surveillance and get a file ready soon.'

'That's sounds good, so we will watch him from the sky, and know more in detail what he is like...before a potential ground surveillance.'

'Yes correct...so prepare for Srinagar. Till then, let's find out more about his story, his daily routine and his girlfriend,' said Carina.

'Girlfriend?'

'Yes, Aahana. Aahana Yajurvedi. I've sent some public details of her to you, read it after the call.'

'OK Ma'am.'

'Good night.'

'Good night.'

Adolf, saw the mail download in his mobile and opened the attachment in it. He raised his eyebrow as he read:

Graduation in Physics, Oslo University

B.Com from LSR, Delhi University

Business Management from Colombia

Relationship status: Unknown, but known to be in relationship with Mansur Haider, Rohan Kumar and Naveen David Talpade.

Other Points: Gold medal and distinction in academic studies, speaks four languages, and avid rock-climber. Interests in mythology, Buddhism, Vedas.

Man she does a wide range of topics.

The next page, Aahana's photograph comes up. Adolf gazed into the brown eyes.

Beauty and brains, it will be interesting crossing paths with her.

108 DAYS TO EVENT

Bandra Kurla Complex,
Mumbai, India

August 25,09:40 IST

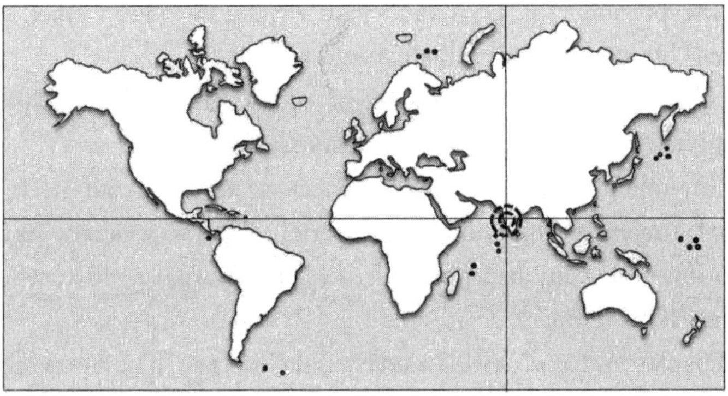

There was extreme tension on the 20th floor of the Magneta Building, where Zrotriya Intelligence Ltd. was located. The white room was well illuminated, and preparations were in full swing for the presentation as people shuttled in and out. Written notes were passed around and last-minute checks were run on laptops to make sure all had been finalised and was ready. This division of Zrotriya Global was an investment banking firm that dealt with raising capital, trading various kinds of securities, and managing mergers and acquisitions of a corporate nature.

Aahana Yajurvedi stood calmly in the midst of the noise and bustle. Dressed in a purple shirt and white business suit, her gaze was focused on the white flashcards, with their extensive notes on the project, in her hand. Aahana flicked back her loose, shoulder-length hair as she sat down. At five feet three inches she loved wearing high heels. She was born in England and raised around the world, travelling with her father, a career diplomat with the Indian Foreign Service.

Rohan, Aahana's colleague and ex-boyfriend, sitting across her was amazed at her calm. They had broken up by mutual agreement about three months ago; she cited mental and social incompatibility. He thought it was a joke and still believed that she would come running to him.

A short, lean figure entered the room. It was Mathew Keckley, also known as MK to his colleagues, the firm's managing partner. MK had been working in the industry for over forty years and was renowned for his global connections. Some said that he could connect with anyone—even the president of USA or British royalty or even a chief in the Kalahari Desert; he knew which strings to pull.

'How much longer to start?' his deep baritone voice boomed through the room. There was a hush across the floor.

'Ten minutes, Mathew, that's a neat tie around your neck,' said Aahana, smiling at him and raising her right hand to welcome him into the room. Not many had the guts to speak like that to MK, who was known for his temper.

'Thanks, Aahana,' MK looked her in the eye. They exchanged a nod. MK took his seat at the head of the table and the rest of the group found their seats around the table. MK respected both her intellect and her guts. The video conference equipment showed up the conference room in Rio. As the clients in Brazil assembled, the tension kept rising and all eyes were on Aahana as everyone waited to see if she could sway the client.

'Good evening, gentlemen,' said Aahana, her voice crisp and clear, with a smile on her face and her left dimple showing.

'Good evening, Aahana. So we finally meet!' The lead speaker from the client's side smiled at her.

About two hours later the presentation was concluding and the client had agreed to send the contract for long-term engagement. Calm was not the case about an hour back when the client was firing questions about findings and analysis of the project, as well as its hypothesis. But Aahana was not fazed. She had been in similar situations before—several times—and remained patient through the questions.

If you keep calm, solutions will come. The issues are never the problem, but how your mind reacts to them. One loses not by lack of knowledge, but by lack of application of the knowledge at the appropriate time, thought Aahana.

After the meeting concluded all members in the room applauded its success. They shook hands with one another with broad smiles. MK was the last to shake Aahana's hand. He put his left hand beside her right arm.

'Good. Meet me in my office later...say about 4:00 p.m. I need to discuss something important—your next career move,' said MK, walking out and flashing a thumbs-up sign.

Aahana was now walking up to her cabin, which was five floors above the conference room. As she walked up the stairs her heels made a click-clack noise on the Moroccan marble stairway.

It seems the whole world is at my feet, and now MK probably wants me to go to Oslo, perhaps in a leadership position. Why am I not happy? Why do I feel like something is missing?

As Aahana walked up the stairs, she did not hear her Blackberry. The beeping stopped for a moment, and then started again. Someone was trying to reach her desperately.

Aahana opened the door of her cabin, her control centre. She walked past the certificates and awards prominently displayed on the walls. The green certificate stood out from the others. It certified her as an advanced mountain trekker, and she had received it for climbing the highest peak in Norway along with her university buddies and climbing group *The Nordic Rockers*. She looked out of the window and gazed at the Mumbai skyline.

My friends from Nordic Rockers also gone, three dead and Linda Choy missing...and I was not there to support them. Why did they have to go ahead with the climb in Shaksgam Valley despite the warning? And here all these feelings of invincibility, fame and money...But what have I actually achieved, or have I achieved anything at all?

Aahana was leaning forward with both hands on the window sill when she heard something.

My Blackberry...I had it set on vibrate.

She removed her Blackberry, which despite the name had a green covering, one of the minor design innovations she applied to the items in her life.

*Seven missed calls from Shaza and Sharon...*Aahana was a little perplexed as she wondered what had happened to them.

The three of them had been college buddies. They were known as the 'Super Queens,' which was the name of their rock band in college. Though Aahana was the oldest of the trio by four years, they shared all their secrets. *Well, almost,* thought Aahana.

It's been some time since we got together. I wonder what's on their minds. For the first time that day Aahana felt an inner sense of joy as she called Shaza.

"*All the single ladies...All the single ladies...All the single ladies...*"

Wow…now that's my song.

'Hello,' said Aahana, looking up at the curtains and sinking into her black leather armchair.

'Hello, girl…Guess what?' said Shaza in a drawn out, flirty tone.

'No…No…' said Aahana in surprise.

'When did this happen?'

'Wait ten minutes…We are almost there.'

'You are coming *here*…Now?' said Aahana in an excited voice.

'Yeah, girl…Sharon is with me.'

'Great. I am off till tonight. Come straight to my cabin. I will inform security.'

Shaza has definitely snapped her man. Could it be Samir…Mansur's friend? The last time she sounded like this was when she was hooked the first time.

It's Queens time again, and about time too…I know what I want to do now, thought Aahana, while removing her jacket and hanging it on the coat hanger nailed on the wall. *I need a break and a long one at that. Got to find Mansur and get hold of him in Srinagar.*

A couple of hours later Aahana stood before MK. Her friends had brought her up to date about Samir and Shaza and while they waited in the lobby, she met up with MK. She needed to take an indefinite leave of absence. MK listened to her patiently; he was surprised to hear her in this mood. She called it a hiatus, but MK knew better.

She is lost inside, searching for something...most likely love. I let mine go for this, and I only think I am happy.

'MK? I hope you are not disappointed.'

Keckley waited for a few moments to respond. He kept looking at her and gradually started to smile. 'Well, shouldn't I be?' he said, shrugging his small shoulders as he walked towards her. He placed his left hand on her head and continued, 'Search for what you want, and find it! Don't let regret ruin your future,' his tone was soft and fatherly. 'You know you are always welcome here. So if you ever need any help, don't hesitate to reach out.'

They started walking towards the door. '*Aum Mani Padme Hum*,' said Keckley reciting the Tibetan prayer. He knew of Aahana's interests in Tibetan culture and also of her ancestral links to the ancient Vedas; her being a Yajurvedi meant she belonged to a race that has the knowledge of the Yajurveda, the second book in the Vedas.

'*Aum Mani Padme Hum*,' replied back Aahana as she smiled, shook hands with her mentor, and left the room.

On the ground floor, Aahana was standing with her friends. Rohan came running to her as the news of her quitting spread.

'How can you just drop everything and go away?' he asked.

'It's my life and I can do whatever I please.'

'What about us...I...I was your boy!' He raised his voice in an intimidating manner. The people in the lobby started staring at them.

'Us? There never was any "us".' Aahana was perfectly composed. 'You are not my boy. You are only mama's boy.' The girls tried to control their laughter, but Sharon could not help laughing.

Aahana opened the box she was carrying and showed a papier-mache cat to the ladies. 'Wow!' exclaimed Shaza. 'It's customised with your name written in Urdu. Who...tell us...tell us,' Sharon pestered Aahana.

'Stop it,' said Aahana, smiling now from ear to ear. 'Let's first reach Srinagar. I'll tell you on the way. Mansur is there...'

'What...You have been a bad...very bad lady keeping such a secret from us. He is Samir's friend,' said Shaza hands on her hips. Shaza could see the spark of happiness in her best friend's eyes.

100 DAYS TO EVENT

Suburban Srinagar,
Jammu and Kashmir, India

September 2,04:15 IST

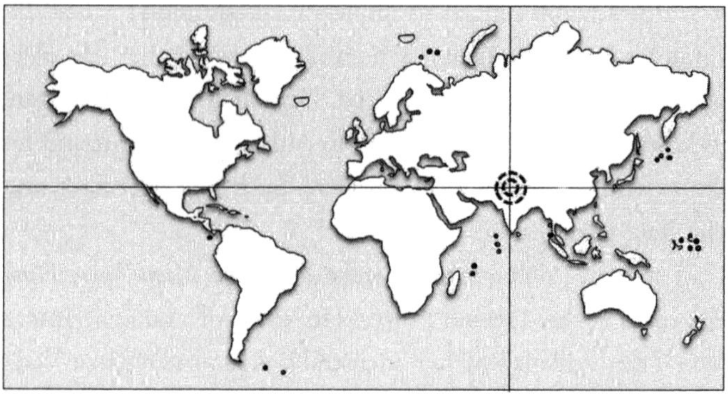

It was a windy and misty morning in Srinagar after the night's rain. Mansur got up and sat on the edge of his bed, the green light from the night bulb casting a ghostly light in the room. His toes brushed against the elegant wood flooring. He got up, took a broom, and went outside to sweep his veranda. Mansur was preparing to perform his *salah*—prayers—as in a few minutes the time of *fajr*—dawn prayer—would begin. Then he went inside to change his clothes and perform the ritual ablution using water from the tap in the corner. He picked up the highly decorated prayer rug rolled up and kept in his wall cupboard. The rug was adorned with geometric, landscape, and floral motifs. It was a family heirloom that he guarded well.

Abba told me this rug was made by ancient Persian artisans, and gifted to our Haider family centuries ago for some work done by one of our ancestors. So many centuries and it is still surprisingly strong. Abba, at least praying here connects me to you.

As he walked out onto the small veranda again, his mind raced but he forced himself to concentrate on the prayers.

Standing tall and facing west, towards holy Mecca, he started reciting *Al-Fatiha* and then chanted *Bismillah Ar Rahman Ar Rahim*, In the name of Allah, the most gracious, the most merciful.

After the ritual bowing, prostrating and recitation, he finished his prayers and got up, folded the rug, and carried it inside under his right arm.

Two weeks...How life can change in just two weeks. Samir was right...It was god sent. Now I am chasing a dream...my dream.

Over the last two weeks, things had changed dramatically for Mansur. He now had a permanent job with the Cricket Association of the State, assisting in the daily functioning of the cricket stadium. This was a unique opportunity for him as he would not only get a stable income and growth opportunity, but he would also be able to train and practice in the same stadium. He would be able to realise his dream to bowl, to bowl fast as the wind without worrying about setbacks in life.

All thanks to Samir, thought Mansur as he changed again inside his room, preparing for his morning exercise routine.

Mansur dressed in his rugged grey shirt and blue track pants and put on a thin windcheater. He walked out slowly, taking care not to disturb his mother and sisters. It was 5:15 in the morning and the sun was not out yet. Stepping out, Mansur took a deep breath to enjoy the fresh air. All was still. The air was fresh with the fragrance of wet soil. The smooth gurgle of the Jhelum vibrated in the atmosphere. Morning prayers could be heard at a distance. The pure sound always raised Mansur's concentration level.

Mansur started stretching and warming up as he reached the road, bending sideways and touching his legs with his hands. Jogging down the rocky road, which shone from the light cast by the street lamps, he increased his pace before hitting the main road. Mansur reached Abdullah Bridge, one of the new bridges over Jhelum.

The guard standing outside the tourist reception centre near the bridge waved his hands, and Mansur reciprocated. He stopped near the holy Hazratbal Mosque and bowed in front of it before moving on. Mansur also ran by the Yuz Asaf tomb, which some believed to be the tomb of Jesus of Nazareth, who had come to India after rising again from the dead.

Throughout history, mankind had always been in conflict. This could be avoided by finding peace within oneself and moving forward. All one needs is to understand the message of any messiah as they all preach love and not hatred...and love is so beautiful with Aahana now coming to Srinagar soon. And to imagine that Shaza, Aahana's friend is getting engaged to my best friend Samir...divine intervention.

Mansur reached the foothills of Shankaracharya temple, said to be over two thousand years old and built by the mythical Pandavas. The security personnel frisked him before he proceeded. He continued his jog up the steps. Now his body was aching and he began to slow down.

It is better than when I started. Weeks ago I could not even reach this place. Now, at least the pace and stamina has improved.

Mansur reached the top and climbed the last few steps which led to the sanctum sanctorum of the holy Shivalingam. He bowed again, but did not enter. He went behind the structure and fell on his knees, now totally exhausted and breathing heavily. The son of the temple priest came around and offered him water. Mansur looked at him.

'You have arrived earlier today...you are improving,' said the boy.

Mansur was now thousands of metres above sea level. He smiled at the boy and put his hand on his head. He looked into the child's brown eyes.

'The earlier the better,' said Mansur as he stood up slowly with his hands on his knees. 'But you know what? I really enjoy coming here, and the water you give me is no less than a life saver.'

Now standing upright, Mansur could see from his vantage point at the top, the entire city of Srinagar in one stroke. He took in a deep breath and moved his eyes from left to right while slowly turning his neck as he let the air out. Seeing the city in its full glory in the morning as the sun rose, Mansur felt humbled by the awesome sight he witnessed every day.

Srinagar is heaven on earth, and some day...some day it will be free. Will I play a part in it? Abbu always said I was going to do great things in life. The time has come for me, now I need to fight for my freedom.

99 DAYS TO EVENT

Sher-e-Kashmir Stadium, Srinagar,
Jammu and Kashmir, India

September 3,10:15 IST

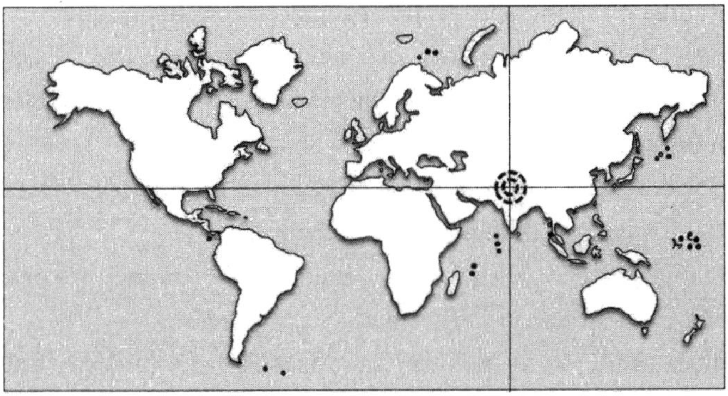

The morning practice session was taking place, with all three practice pitches busy with players. On two pitches there were bowlers who were bowling, and in the third, an automatic ball machine was installed. The bowling machine had been donated by one of the national cricket board members, Aziz Abubaker.

Mansur was sitting in the office when he heard a loud blast from the direction of the field. Jumping to his feet, he moved out, and saw most of the staff running onto the field. There was smoke billowing from the area of the practice pitches. A couple of players were lying on the ground.

Oh my god! Was it a bomb?

As they reached the practice pitch, they suddenly heard and saw the players laughing. The security personnel moved in, aggressively pushed the players behind and told the people to move back.

'It's the bowling machine…short circuit, just some smoke, so no worries, all's well,' said Amir Bhatt.

Amir Bhatt was the team coach and a strong motivating factor in getting the game back on its feet across the state since taking control over ten months ago. He was not a tall man, standing at five and a half feet, with a slight paunch and broad forehead. His face was pockmarked, a legacy from his childhood affair with smallpox. Despite being over fifty years of age, he had an infectious energy which was complemented by a deep baritone.

Two of the bowlers who had been standing next to the machine were injured by splinters from the machine and were bleeding.

'First Bashir, then Nasir, and now these two,' said Bhatt in a concerned tone. 'If it goes on like this then we will have no bowlers left on the team.'

'It will be fine. These two will be ready in a couple of days, as the doctor informed,' said Mansur's boss, Farooqh.

'The machine is also gone now, friend. How will they get practice? Our first game begins in a few days.'

'Bhatt sahib, see if you can use Mansur,' said Farooqh, pointing towards Mansur and signalling him to come over.

'Farooqh, this is serious. It is cricket.'

'When did I say we were playing football here?' said Farooqh, smiling. 'This guy will be good. Trust me…I have seen him bowl; he is a good pace bowler.'

'Really!' said Bhatt in a slightly sarcastic tone. 'Son, what do you know about bowling?'

Bhatt tossed a ball at Mansur towards his lower left side. Mansur instinctively bent towards his left, moving both his hands and cupping the catch, going on one knee and then getting up in a jiffy. Bhatt raised his eyebrows.

'Sir, what I know about bowling is that it takes one ball to finish a batsman's career and also that it takes only twenty balls, twenty good ones, to win a test match.'

'You have shoes for running,' said Bhatt, looking down at Mansur's feet, which were covered by semi-worn out sneakers.

'Yes.'

'Okay! Show me what you've got,' said Bhatt. He signalled the batsman to get ready to face Mansur. A little crowd formed as players on the other practice pitches came and stood along the side of the net to see Mansur bowl.

Rafiq Khan was the batsman standing at the other end of the pitch. Rafiq was a hard-hitting youngster, returned recently from UK and one of the rising stars on the J&K cricket team. He was also a likely candidate for selection to the national team with a string of good performances over the last twelve months.

Mansur, who was standing at the bowling end with the cherry-coloured ball, started moving towards the pitch step by step to count for his run-up. As he walked back, he could see that all the eyes were on him. His mind was calculating what ball to bowl to him—yorker, bouncer, slower, or a swinging delivery. Rafiq on the other end was thinking that it was another bloke again. Rafiq knew what was coming; the bloke would run fast and throw the ball with all his strength.

Eighty percent probability was that it will be chest high if not a bouncer, assuming it is a legal delivery; otherwise it will be a wide.

Rafiq moved slightly behind the crease line to position for a pull or hook on the back foot. Mansur stood at the end of the bowling crease. He smiled. He knew what he was going to bowl. Bhatt watched Mansur standing with both hands holding the five and a half ounce red cherry loosely, his feet together and his top half leaning forward. A normal run-up for a fast bowler was 35-45 metres; Mansur was standing almost 60 metres from the pitch crease.

Mansur started running slowly, first ten metres down at a medium pace, the next twenty with a slight pace and board, leaning forward with the ball in his right hand, the next twenty with a quick pace and longer strides. Rafiq was getting ready for a bouncer as he saw Mansur's large frame coming closer. The last ten metres of the stride before the delivery was to be bowled and Mansur was now coming on very fast.

He jumped high in the air, his right hand holding the ball in a skewed grip. With a side-on action like Akram's, he released the ball. It was let go from a height of more than eleven feet due to his height, hand length, and jump.

Rafiq braced for a fast one, and his mind stopped for a few milliseconds as he saw the ball coming towards him.

DAMN IT! It's not a fast ball; it's a slob, directly at my legs. Got to adjust…

Rafiq knew the ball was a slob resulting in a slow delivery, but he presumed a fast one would come and was already on his back foot when the ball was hurled at him. The trajectory of the ball bowled by Mansur was like a beamer, but it started going down quickly. He tried to compensate by moving his left leg forward, but it was too late. The ball landed directly between his legs, below the knee rolls, and he squared up completely, plumb leg-before-wicket or LBW.

After releasing the ball Mansur followed on his stride towards the side of the crease till he reached the middle of the pitch. Seeing the ball hit the pads, he turned around to appeal to a fictional umpire. He stopped suddenly midway, realising that there was no umpire. Looking at the coach directly, he waited for an answer, eyes aglow with hope.

Bhatt was standing with his arms folded on the side and saw this.

Oh, my Almighty God! A perfect slow ball, terrific jump, side on action, and impressive follow through…Where had this guy been?

The coach did not want to show any reaction when Mansur looked at him, but when the ball hit the pads his eyes widened of their own accord.

'Okay, now give me three balls, all different.'

Bhatt started walking towards his assistant coach and told him to stand as the umpire.

With the umpire in position and Mansur ready to bowl again, Rafiq felt a little embarrassed.

Three balls now. Got to strike it out. Let me wait for the ball now and tackle it by the merit. This bloke is no pushover; his action was perfect.

Mansur was now a little more nervous. He wetted his lips with his tongue and gulped saliva to wet his throat.

First it was just a ball, now three balls. These may be the only three balls I get. Got to make them count. Let me see how Rafiq moves and plays the first ball and then see what to do with the next two.

Mansur ran down again over the wicket, this time bending his back more, and let go the old ball with all his might. The ball was going towards good length area, hit the pitch, and climbed up quickly to Rafiq's right and zipped away, barely missing his nose.

'OHHHH!' went up collectively from all around.

Bhatt now stood upright. He liked what he was seeing. Mansur now looked Rafiq in the eye. Rafiq, too, kept his gaze steady.

'Next ball,' said Bhatt to break the tension.

Mansur was walking back towards his run-up at a fast pace, and a ball was thrown to him by the coach. It was a shiny ball, a brand new one. Mansur bowled the second ball. The second ball was an out swinger, and Rafiq tried to play a cover drive and got an edge.

'Keeper's catch,' said one of the other batsmen standing outside the nets.

Rafiq frowned and closed his eyes to regain concentration. Mansur looked a little ahead and knew he was doing perfectly, irrespective of new ball or old ball. Another ball was given to him as he walked back. This time it was an old ball probably, used for fifty or sixty overs.

Bhatt was testing Mansur with different balls.

The bowler was ready again. Standing with both hands on the cherry, Mansur's mind was hearing voices from the 1986 game. Twenty-six years had passed, and the gaze in Border's eye crystallised before him.

Australia became world champion in 1987 and remained in that position for a long time and is still feared. Abbu, I wish you could see me now.

Mansur started his run, now holding the ball tightly with both hands. He continued to run fast, his grip steady. He held this grip till the last five metres. Bhatt was watching closely and he knew a *yorker* was coming.

Mansur jumped and released the ball at the last moment while dropping his right hand. The ball headed straight towards the wickets. He saw Rafiq, who was now holding the bat in a low position expecting a *yorker*, then the ball started dipping inwards suddenly from the right side.

The ball moved quickly and hit the middle stump with Rafiq not able to bring his bat down quickly. He looked back to find his timber shattered. He knew what was coming, but the speed and angle did him in. Mansur jumped up and so did a few of the players around him. Mansur jogged up to Rafiq to apologise. Rafiq removed his gloves and shook hands with Mansur and said, 'You only did what you were supposed to do, so there is no need to say you're sorry.'

As they both started walking out of the nets, the coach had his hands on his hips and signalled for them to stop. 'Mansur, why are you coming back? Continue bowling for the next fifteen minutes and then give me thirty minutes of field run. If you have any strength left then bowl again for fifteen minutes.'

Both looked up and started walking back. Bhatt seemed unflustered by what had happened, unlike the others around. But the fact was that he never liked showing emotions. He now wanted to check Mansur's stamina and bowling pattern, before and after the field run.

Samir stood outside the field knowing that he should have been on it but for the freak accident that damaged his bowling arm. He looked at the finger on his right hand and felt a sense of sorrow, but he was happy that Mansur seemed on the brink of finding a place on the team.

He removed his mobile phone, tapped on an app to make the line encrypted and secure and pressed the pads to dial a number.

'Salam Valekum Janab,' said Samir, looking around to make sure that no one was nearby to listen to him.

The other person returned his greeting and asked Samir why he had called when he was instructed not to ring up in the afternoon.

'Janab, you wanted a bomber, I have got you one.'

'So he is on the team now?'

'Looks like it, and if things go well he will be around the national team and then…' Samir's tone died down slowly.

'Don't get your hopes up, we still have long way to go,' said the other voice harshly.

'Insha Allah we will have our victory and Mansur will bring us freedom, dead or alive.'

'But don't tell him anything he does not need to know.'

'Don't worry; he will not know what he has done until the last moment, the very last one.'

'He may not need to know at all, I hope you understand.'

'Ji, Janab.'

'I sent you a memory chip at the dead-drop location, did you analyse it?'

'Yes, I took it in the morning before the casing was destroyed, will be going through it in a short while.'

'Good, send me your thoughts. We need to understand how the weapon works. Nasir is not sharing much in the open for us.'

'Will do Janab.'

'Khuda Hafiz Samir.'

'Khuda Hafiz Janab.' Samir disconnected the call and looked around for signs. All he could see were people on the field and his unsuspecting friend bowling at the practice nets.

So our Operation Babylon has started. Wonder what India will look like after three months. Only mighty Allah knows.

'M**ansur, don't dream** and don't think about the future…we are Kashmiris,' she said, her eyes brimming with tears. She placed her hands over her eyes. Her three children stood around her, unable to grasp why she was crying. Mansur had just informed his family of the turn of the day's events on the cricket field and how he could be drafted into the side.

'Ammi, what happened? I don't get it. Why are you spoiling such a nice day?' Mansur was disappointed at her response.

'Son, dreams are not for us; we should not dream, not be allowed to dream.' Her reply came a little too quickly as she started to wipe her face with a small cloth kept on the table.

'What is wrong with dreaming, Ammi?'

'It's not our destiny, we can't do what others are doing,' she said sternly.

Mansur stood silent for a moment, thinking about the times his father told him stories of invincibility, heroism and predestination. His father often spoke about how humans are connected with one another through God. 'All religions have this connection with him up there' and he would point to the sky. Mansur's father, an orphan, was looked after by a family friend.

'Your father was a noble man; his biggest strength was his biggest enemy. He always believed, and it is this belief that always sparked disappointment in him,' she said, signalling for the girls to sit down.

'It is this belief that I am carrying within me and moving ahead. And what's happened to you, Ammi? You always used to say that I could do whatever I wanted in the world, and the only important thing was to believe in myself and build hope inside me.'

'Yes, I did, and somewhere in my heart it is still there. The power of hope, but since his death I am shattered inside.'

Mansur understood his mother's dilemma. They could not dream that they were their own masters rather than the Indian or Pakistani government, local political groups, or the Western world. No one considered the normal Kashmiri on the street who was simply manipulated and tossed around at the whims of a larger world. Most youths in the Valley had a vague sense that they were used and abused by events and circumstances they had no say in or control over.

'Ammi, I understand...but if we don't dream and act on our dreams we will never come to know our destiny,' said Mansur, looking into his mother's moist eyes.

'The only difference in me since the last year is the understanding I have developed that if I don't do it, no one will. I am the only one capable of making that change happen. Only then will Almighty God help me.'

'But son, remember that some things are destined...'

'Yes, some things are destined...and probably there are no coincidences in life, but mother, I just cannot help thinking of father's last words–"what if". What if I dream of making it big, what if I believe I can make it happen, WHAT IF I do it...and am successful?'

Mansur's mother hugged him, and his sisters too came in close. Mansur put his arms around all three of them. Standing tall, he looked like a shepherd holding his little flock of sheep together.

'Mother, the motivation of "what if" is so strong that it can work magic, and we will only know if we walk that path. If that is our chosen destiny, we will only know if we walk it; the choice is ours.'

'Yes, Mansur, you are right. Probably age has made me weak and circumstances have confused me. I forgot. It seems like a dream, and all dreams have to end someday.'

'Mother, remember the story of signs told by Kasha,' said Sana, looking at Zoon. Kasha was a local oracle famous for reading one's destiny through coffee grounds. She was dismissed by many as a rambling old woman who merely said what people wanted to hear. But she had a lot of followers who swore by her.

Zoon said, 'Yes, Mother, remember what she said about *Bhai jaan*?'

The Haider family had gone to see her about six months ago. The visit was by accident as Kasha called out from the window and told them to come up. They were hesitant at first but went into the two-room wooden structure.

Inside, the room was lavishly decorated with Persian design curtains and various Buddhist wall fixtures. Her face was freckled and lined with age, but her eyes shone brightly. She looked at Mansur who could not avoid her deep gaze. Her gleaming blue eyes met his green eyes and a connection was made.

She told Mansur to drink the coffee as she felt that she needed to tell him something. Mansur followed her instructions and drank from a small porcelain cup. After a few minutes Kasha looked at the cup. She closely examined the inside and smiled. The sediments of the coffee had formed a pattern, and it was from this pattern that she was able to read the past and get a glimpse into the future.

At first Mansur played along, but then his stomach started churning as he anticipated his life was about to turn a corner. After all, who can resist the temptation of knowing what lies in one's future?

Kasha began by saying that Mansur was unclear in his mind but not in his heart as it was strong and beat with honesty. As she rambled on with pointers on Mansur's life, she surprised the family with what she knew about him. She impressed upon him his history of lost opportunities and how he let himself down. Kasha's main message then changed to how to understand signs and interpret the same.

She said, 'There are signs all around us, and we need to understand them if we want to interpret them. Some signs show the direction and means needed to reach our destiny. At the same time, there are many signs to stop us and force us to change direction. Identifying these negative signs is the most important thing as they always come at a crucial time when, by just overcoming them one last time, we can move into our promised land.'

By now she was in a deep trance, her mouth slightly open, with the tongue dangling out. Her pupil and iris turned up with only the white sclera visible. Looking like a possessed woman, she started jerking in a rhythmic circular fashion.

'Remember Mansur, the sound of the *kainaat* (universe) was created billions of billions of years ago and it is still out there. Everything is in harmony and perfect balance. Find this balance with your surroundings.' She stopped suddenly, her body steady for a while before she started the circular motion again, this time in the opposite direction. 'Haider, when the bird lands on your shoulder and chirps, you will find your destiny. Go forth and fulfil it for all of us.'

Mansur and his family heard her out and a sense of hope took root within them. She finished by telling him that he will know when the time is right. She approached him and whispered in his ear while handing him a piece of paper.

Mansur and his family thanked Kasha, and he gave her some token money. She accepted it, saying she would keep it and not use it. She then took a card, and scribbled on it before handing it over to him, telling him to read it whenever he had questions about his role and place in life.

Mansur's mother thought of that day, and it seemed like it happened only yesterday.

'She said a lot of things, but I do remember the part about how we need to learn to see the signs and make a choice,' she said, her voice now more in control. 'My son will always make the right choices.'

'Yes, mother, always remember, as father said, "What if".'

Saying this, he told his mother not to cry anymore as their troubled days would soon be over. 'We can and only if we will, and I will—be more than determined—from now on. We are being watched and protected from above,' said Mansur, comforting and embracing his mother. 'I will turn my dream into a vision, and this vision into my mission. This will turn into a reality one day, and we will get our freedom, *amin.*'

'Yes my son…*amin.*'

98 DAYS TO EVENT

SOG HQ, Karlsborg,
Västergötland, Sweden

September 4,01:15 CET

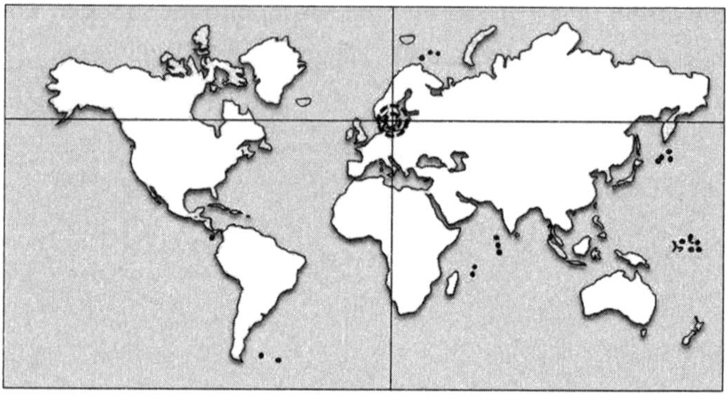

As Mansur jogged in the morning, thousands of miles away, the SOG operations team kept their eyes glued on him. Late into the night, the investigation was in live mode with emphasis on structuring and taking ahead the threads and hypotheses collected till date. The room had a few more technical operatives sitting at their terminals and monitoring their screens. Adolf sat behind an oval shaped operational desk and stared into the screen.

'Thank you for joining us. For our presentation today, we will take you through two things. First is our hypothesis to decipher the language type illustration sent by Kurt. And second our latest report on Mansur Haider,' said Stephanie.

'OK, continue.'

Stephanie turned towards the screen as Bjorn changed the presentation file in his laptop. All eyes were on the screen now. The dark screen turned to a white background, as three pairs of letters came up.

'What you have on your screen along with Kurt's symbols is the Jewish Hebrew language and the ancient Angelic signs…which is said to be given by the Angels directly. We still can't identify the language, but there is some similarity between them.'

Shaksgam Valley Illustration | **Hebrew Alphabet** | **Angelic Illustration**

'Some pattern may exist…and do check other ancient and dead languages', added Adolf, clasping his hands on the table and supporting his chin now.

'Yes we will prepare algorithm and run it through Thorsystem and see if we decipher it,' replied Stephanie.

'It is a start, and I like that you all arc thinking. But how did you come to this theory?' asked Carina.

Stephanie moved closer to the screen, breathed in deep and spoke, 'The angles, slants and design of these images which Kurt sent look like a language. Every language has a start—a parent language, or a sub-parent language. For example, the current English language has a sub-parent language from Celts. French, sub-parent language is Latin and Roman languages. All of them however have come from the Proto-Indo-European as a parent language.'

Interesting, thought Adolf, as he raised his eyebrows and spoke up, 'What about Hebrew…it is said to be a much more ancient language.'

'Yes it is, and so is Sanskrit from India. Kurt was investigating the Shaksgam Valley incident in Kashmir, and came across these inscriptions which he sent across to us. The Kashmiri language is from Indo-Iranian source and on further investigation, some research suggests that it has other sub-parent language sources like Persian, Arabic, Sanskrit and even Hebrew.'

'Very interesting hypothesis you all are working on. I get it now, like the Big Bang theory started the universe, every language must have had a beginning. If we identify its parent or sub-parent's source we can decipher it.'

The team nodded in unison, and broke into a small smile as they saw Carina smile at them.

'In that case, continue to its logical end, and get the results. Do you have anything new on Mansur?' said Carina, turning her gaze from Stephanie and Bjorn towards the screen where the satellite image showed Mansur running.

'On the topic of this Kashmiri suspect, we have more details.' Bjorn waited for Stephanie to place the related dossier in front of everyone in the room, 'He has not travelled out of Kashmir and does not have any Indian police record on him.'

'He was never charged by the Indian law enforcement agencies? This is interesting.' Adolf spoke up, surprised.

'What gets interesting is his family name Haider and his father's name—Mustafa. Mustafa, who is dead now, was a farmer by profession and grew up as an orphan; his parents and most of his extended family members died during the Partition of India.'

'So what is interesting in that?' Carina was not impressed.

'The interesting part is that Mustafa's place of birth is St Joseph's Franciscan Convent, Baramulla,' said Bjorn, adjusting his oval shaped spectacles as he read from Mansur's dossier.

Carina straightened her head and looked directly towards Bjorn, eyebrows raised in surprise. Bjorn was taken aback and looked towards Stephanie for support.

'Yes ma'am, the same massacre in which British citizens were killed, the one you requested to check upon when you joined.'

'Yes, I remember, Stephanie. Four years back on 31st October, around 11am.'

'Yes! That time we did not get any details as records were not available with our Indian counterparts. Just about an year back the record became active...may be someone from Mansur's family provided the details.'

Or someone who wanted to keep his identity a secret no more.

'Really interesting,' said Carina pensively and thought again.

Looks as-if another half a century plus year loop of the Guardians (Chos-Skyong) is going to close. We may have located the Haider family finally. Sir Trimble, Scorpus, will be really interested in this information.

Carina had a serious tone now, 'Continue.'

'Yes Ma'am. Mansur's love interest…Aahana Yajurvedi, her transactions and communications indicate that she may be travelling to Kashmir,' said Bjorn. He sniffed adjusting his spectacles again and added 'more details are there in the dossier.'

Carina's eyes shone as she turned towards Adolf who was looking at the live image of Mansur running along Srinagar's streets.

'Link up with Aahana in India, Adolf, and use your persuasive skills to come close to her. We know Chinese have tested a weapon in Shaksgam valley, and if Kurt believes that this guy "Mansur" is linked, we would need to come as close to him as possible. And this girl may be the only way to come close to him.'

Adolf smiled and scratched his nose.

'You don't need to worry about that, will plan out with Bjorn and Stephanie, on the plan of action.'

'Keep me posted…and, "God Speed" Adolf. Amen!'

Carina watched Adolf get up, salute and leave, her mind thinking of the next steps to follow up on Mansur.

God Speed to me also. Need to connect with Sir Trimble, Scorpus, the head Guardian and update him on the development. We have located the Haider family.

98 DAYS TO EVENT

Buckingham Palace,
London, United Kingdom

September 4,11:30 GMT

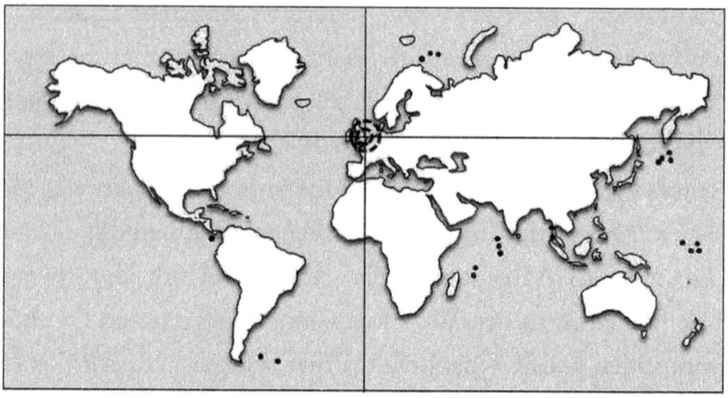

The sea-blue coloured push button phone was situated in a corner of the heavily engraved oak table. There were two push buttons on the phone, a blue one for activation and a red one to disconnect. The unique thing about this phone was that it was activated by biometrics—fingerprint and voice, and a password. Only a limited pool of people around the world could communicate via this phone.

Sitting beside this table was an elderly figure. He seemed perfectly relaxed as he sat on the chair with his legs crossed. The radiant face and the ceremonial dressing indicated his royal lineage. The room was small and had minimal furnishing. He looked at his watch and then at the phone. The LED around the buttons changed from white to blue and flickered again after two seconds. He used his thumb to press the blue button, which instantly recognised his thumb print. A light shone from the middle of the dial towards his face. He picked up the phone receiver for the penultimate security and final identification, which took the password and voice identification simultaneously.

'Scorpus,' he said, waiting for two to three seconds to pass before saying the password—*Omnimodus Determinism,* universal determinism. The LED around the dial stopped flickering and the blue light remained shining.

Carina spoke from the other end. She said, 'We have a GO!'

'Is it positive this time?'

'Intel suggests the same. We have a name, Mansur. I have placed my agent Adolf behind him.'

'Good! But I am afraid I have more bad news,' said the old man.

There was a slight pause.

'My source in China indicates that if we fail, there is a chance we will see the rise of a green dragon—Pakistan is turning communist, it will not be far when China takes control of Kashmir. First Tibet and now Kashmir.'

'We will have to take things as they come; such a situation will not arise. I assure you,' Carina on the other end spoke reassuringly. 'We have to organise ourselves step by step, progress steadily; but I need your permission to revive Leolus.'

'It's been over seventy years now, since the bomb blast and the track is lost. Will Agastya believe you? After his grandfather died in the blast in Scotland which almost incapacitated me.'

'We have to take this chance. I will find a way.'

'Okay, go ahead Gemini, but you know the consequences if you don't succeed…we may have to ensure that he is not alive.'

'Losing is not an option I grew up with,' said Carina, now in an authoritative tone. 'And I would like to add this: losing my position is nothing as long as we serve the good lord. Like you always said, we have been here for more than ten millennia and will continue to be so in some form or the other. No going back!'

The old man thought for a while, and stretched his legs. Now in his eighties, he knew his time was coming to an end. The baton had to be passed, and it had all to be done for the sake of balance in the world.

'One more issue, the Haider family, has most likely been located,' said the female voice breaking the short silence.

'Yes I read what you sent me, stroke of luck or destiny playing games. The one who we may need to protect is the one we are spying upon, Mansur Haider.'

'We all have to do our duty.'

'You are right…and speaking of duty, are you wearing your ring more often now? Will you show the ring to Leolus?'

'I do wear it now, but will not show it to Leolus for now, as he is still Agastya Harshvardhan Rathore, India's Home Minister, and I am assuming he is not informed of the Guardian order.'

'Well, someone has to show him the light.'

'I will do that, with the help of the book of the Guardians. Each family has one; he has to locate his. I am sure that it will be in the safe-keeping of his mentor General Abhimanyu Kashyapa.'

'Yes, thanks to him I am alive, he pulled me out alive from that cave, Agastya's grandfather did not mention he had brought an orderly along with him…and the same boy is India's Defence Minister now.'

'All is part of a greater plan, I hope, from the gods.'

'Yes but we have to take back control of the world, so find what Operation or Project Babylon is. Confirm if the Shaksgam Valley incident was due to an ancient Jericho sound weapon which the Guardian book has mentioned.'

'Don't worry…we will solve it! I am not sure about the sonic factor but will try to focus investigation using that angle also.'

'Good...Then we can call it a day, Gemini. Hope to connect with you again.'

'*Ogham*! *Aum Mani Padme Hum*.'

'*Ogham*! *Aum Mani Padme Hum*.' The female replied the ancient greeting giving a deep baritone pitch to the sound.

The old man pushed the red button to end the call. He removed a protruding black plastic dongle attached to the phone to make the phone inoperative. The old man unlocked the room, and limping out, entered the long, carpeted hallway. He could see tourists around the corner engaged in their usual chit-chat. This was not unusual in Buckingham Palace. Seeing them, Sir Trimble smiled.

The truth should not come out. Our royal lineage from Alfred the great should continue to rule the world incognito.

Sir Trimble was not a direct descendent of Alfred the great, but carried the responsibilities handed down to Anglo-Saxons from the

Celtics and from ashore from the East and South. The Guardian Council has always taken control directly or indirectly of all notable activities of the British Empire; they have failed and fallen sometimes but right now, at its frailest point, Sir Trimble was making another attempt to revive and regain control. Kingdoms had changed and dynasties wiped out, but the ancient council predated Christianity and ran on the credo of universal determinism.

On the other side of the phone, Carina took on a different name. Gemini, the family name the Guardian Council had bestowed upon her ancestors many centuries ago. She now looked forward to getting in touch with the Leolus family, whose torchbearer was Agastya Harshvardhan Rathore.

Controlling Kashmir with all its secrets is the key and my fellow classmate Agastya should help me with it. Adolf should link up with Mansur, using Aahana and it would be then easy to monitor Mansur Haider. Haider, is he really part of the lost family?

91 DAYS TO EVENT

Jogibara Road, McLeodganj,
Dharamshala, India

September 11,11:30 IST

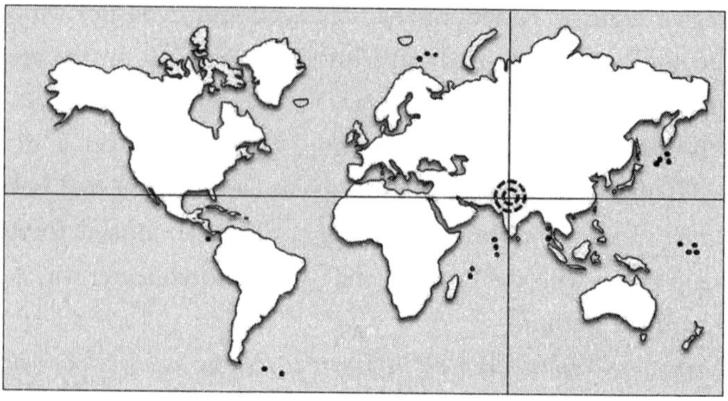

McLeodganj is the little Lhasa of India; situated about 10 kilometres from Dharamshala, it is the seat of the exiled Tibetan government. The tiny Buddhist town is always awash with worshippers, tourists, and nirvana seekers from various places. A short, bald man was sitting in a bamboo shack opposite the Dharamshala Community Library. He sat on his haunches along with a group of men, sipping occasionally from a cup of tea he held with both hands. A pair of eyes was watching him closely from across the library. Adolf stared at his adversary, finding him to be familiar.

Jalal in India? In this place? Kurt's files referred to Dharamshala, but not to Jalal. They concerned the mysterious call from this place to the Nordic Rockers mountaineers' team in Shaksgam Valley before they began to die.

Adolf was four days into India as a tourist and carried a green book, a book which proved that he was Tibetan in origin, his mother—in this case—was a Tibetan born in exile. He travelled to Chandigarh where he befriended Aahana and her friends using his intimate knowledge of mountaineering (he knew Aahana was passionate about it) and showcased his thirst for knowing more about Kashmir. While in Dharamshala, he investigated the addresses of three calls made and found them non-existent, the latest being a fictitious room number from a hostel beside the library.

As Adolf concentrated on his suspect, little was he aware that two pairs of hands were moving towards him. Sensing trouble, he jerked and turned around, twisted his body like a viper's, slanted one knee on the ground and caught hold of the assumed assailant's hands. He was mistaken. His new-found friends stood before him.

'Ewvvvv....Adolf!' cried out Shaza, visibly in pain, with Adolf's muscular hands holding both her hands interlocked tightly in a criss-cross fashion. He loosened his grip, stood up with an apologetic grin.

'Lucky you did not stop me, I would have used my taekwondo on you,' said Aahana, as she rubbed her friend's flushed hands.

'Sorry ladies.' Their third friend arrived on the scene to ask what had happened as readers sitting inside the library looked at them, bewildered; for most of them, this was a big piece of action, piece not seen in their sleepy town. Adolf explained to her and profusely apologised again, and sensing that his suspect may have moved, he swivelled his head towards the shack. Gone!

'It seems you are busy, looking for your friends; we will meet up at the hotel,' said Aahana. Adolf nodded and apologised yet again for putting Shaza in such pain.

'At least we know now we are protected by a superior Tibetan-Nordic hunk, who will guard us and take care of us when evil forces attack,' Aahana teased.

Adolf broke into a smile as they parted, but decided he needed more information about his suspect. Picking up a book randomly from a rack on his side, he briskly walked towards the librarian. Flashing his green book as an identity along with his hotel details, he took the book and rushed out. His suspect had vanished. He went to the tea shack and tried to chat up the shack owner who seemed completely disinterested. Adolf looked around again as he strode out slowly from the bamboo shack, bending his head first to avoid the low opening and raising it to scan both ends of the road again.

Missed him by a fraction.

Adolf went and enquired with the tea-stall owner. He did not get a favourable response. Adolf thanked the stall owner and walked away.

Got to be Jalal but perhaps he is visiting or is not so familiar with the shack owner. The guy did not seem to know him. Maybe his familiar looking face simply confused me. Something to report back…the analysts can scan satellite photos or engage the Indian intelligence to check him out.

On his way to the hotel, he hailed an auto rickshaw coming his way. After waving away a sequence of autos carrying multiple passengers, Adolf finally waved down one in which he could travel alone. He bargained for the price at fifty rupees over and above the meter fare.

Well, till I reach the hotel at least I have a book to keep me company. Glancing down at his book he saw the title, *Anahata Nada: The Unmade Sound of the Universe* by Dr Gomin Tamang.

How appropriate, something about music and sound which Mikaela may not know. I will try to read some and brag about it to her.

Back in the tea-shack, the owner dialled a number to call his customer and friend. On the other side the bald man, Altaf, listened attentively, all the while keeping an eye on the tall foreigner from a distance. As a covert operative of a clandestine ISI cell in India, Altaf Afridi worked hand in glove with a Chinese intelligence cell in Dharamshala. He saw his enquirer board a rickshaw and instructed one of his henchmen to follow him on a bike.

Can he be linked to the CIA agent my twin brother Jalal Afridi took care of, a few months back? If so, he will meet the same fate. Till then I have to reach Delhi to meet my political contact and then Srinagar, to check on Mansur, General Sahib is worried about him.

After an hour, back in SOG's headquarters in Stockholm, Carina received a status update e-mail from Adolf. She finished reading the report on a suspect who resembled Jalal and got worried.

This may go out of hand. We are cooperating with the Indian Intelligence but I need to pass this information and some detail around Mansur to Agastya 'off the record'. I will meet him in person, privately. This way I can also check if he is ready to know about the Guardians.

88 DAYS TO EVENT

Gotland Island,
Sweden

September 14,17:15 IST

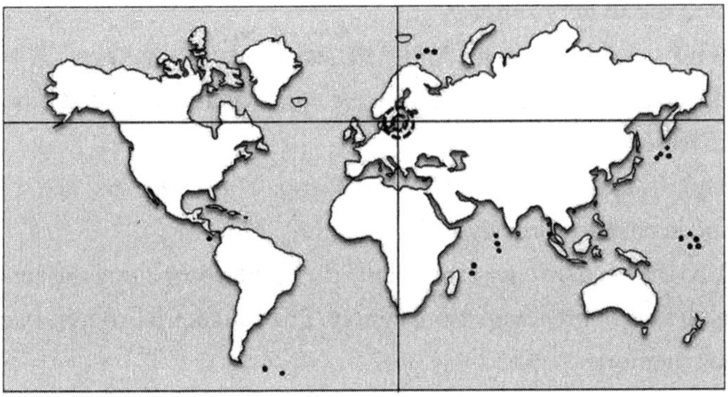

Agastya Rathore was standing next to an ancient stone structure from the Viking age, which was marked with multiple grooves. He was wearing a zipped up black jacket and a dark blue baseball cap. With the sunglasses and stubble, he looked like any tourist. He adjusted his small backpack, put his hand inside the left pocket of his stone-coloured jeans to take out his phone, and started to take photographs.

These grooves…over three thousand of them, evenly spread around this island. My, my...the power of the ancients! They have placed them to follow the celestial bodies for cosmological calculations.

He was visiting to meet a classmate from his Cambridge days, Carina. Both took an extra research diploma in Archaeoastronomy studies. Archaeoastronomy dealt with the subject of how people of the ancient times studied and understood the various astronomical phenomena.

Carina always had a knack for surprises. She was always ambitious, but I never expected her to wind up in the intelligence services of Sweden. Good for her… and she chose this place for the meeting, definitely for the love of the stars.

'It's almost precise, isn't it? But not like your Jaipur Jantar Mantar,' came the familiar voice, which Agastya was hearing after a long time. As he turned around, he saw Carina, looking exactly as she did ten years ago.

'You are like vintage Mackmyra, getting better with age,' said Agastya, extending his right hand as he took her in from head to toe.

Carina's long blonde hair bounced in the breeze, the razor cut finish spreading over her shoulder. She wore a long black skirt and a white buttoned top in zebra stripes.

'Who said I was aging? And Augi, stop your roving eyes. That sort of behaviour is not becoming at your age. You'll give yourself a heart attack,' teased Carina.

'Ahh, I just can't take my eyes off you. You know me, like a horse with the license to thrill and…'

'Also the license to go for the kill,' they said, completing the sentence in unison before breaking into laughter. The statement brought back old campus memories.

'Good to hear your cheerful voice. I thought all the work and tension may have taken your soul away,' said Carina, lowering her voice.

'Yeah, one needs to keep one's sense of humour in times of crisis, just like Professor Wallander told us during the Nordic Mythology lectures.'

Agastya paused to appreciate the nostalgic moment.

'So what do you have for me that I had to fly here to get it? I hope you have not come with that *archaeoastronomy* passion of yours,' said Agastya, gesturing expansively with his hands towards the sky.

Carina smiled and shook her head.

'Not today, don't worry…' *but in time you will see for yourself my fellow Guardian,* she thought as she noticed his gemstone ring on his right finger, but did not react.

'I wanted to meet to pass on some sensitive information to you in person. It may be a related part of the Shaksgam Valley incident, whose Intel we are already sharing. Hope the Intel is useful.'

'Yes, it is. Thanks for sharing the details you have. We also believe the Chinese and Pakistanis have a weapon system. The Americans should do more to stop them; speaking of which, how are the Yanks and Pakistanis holding up?' asked Agastya.

'Well, in a nutshell, they are friends by day, contentious in the evening, and enemies by night. Next day the cycle repeats.'

'So it's a question of not *if* but *when* they will break up and the US attacks Pakistan, not covertly but overtly.'

Carina nodded as they walked around the open field now, the breeze gently hitting them. She also gazed towards Agastya's right index finger with more intent now to focus on the ring and recognised the stone.

He may know, about the Guardians, Chos-Skyong order.

Carina, not showing any expression on her face, took out a small blue coloured box from her right pocket. She handed it over to Agastya, who saw a clipped memory card in it. He tossed it up gently and caught it again, and turned his gaze towards Carina.

'The password.'

'Grooves@Jantarmantar.'

Agastya gave a gentle laugh.

'So what is in it?'

'Two things, first details of a suspect who may be connected to the Shaksgam Valley weapon. His name, Mansur Haider from Baramulla.'

Agastya's lips parted and his eyebrows were raised for a moment before he composed himself again, and looked directly into Carina's eyes.

'Ok, anything special about him.'

'The details are in...he may be a bomber—Baramulla Bomber.'

'Is it about the expected December attack which your intelligence team shared with my team?'

'Yes, most likely. We are following him. Hope you understand.'

'Yes I do. I will do the same, and if need be, eliminate him.'

'Let us be certain first, before taking any pre-emptive action.'

'Sure, and what about the other fact.'

'A suspected Pakistani agent, his name is Jalal Afridi and we tracked him to Dharamshala in India.'

'Really? We do suspect a Chinese cell there, but Pakistan?'

'Well a lot of new things have come up and I will share them. But remember Agastya, this is for "your eyes only", I am not sharing this officially,' said Carina in a serious tone.

Agastya nodded and smiled reassuringly.

'So Augi, how do you plan to tackle the Chinese?'

Agastya shrugged his shoulders and looked at Carina with concern writ large in his eyes.

'See, Carina, we cannot predict what can happen, only make plans… prepare for the worst and hope for the best…*Si Vis Pacem, Para Bellum.*'

'So you are preparing for war in order to have peace.'

'Yes, but I fear if things go bad and we cannot control them, it will be like crossing the Rubicon! After that, only god will know how to put things right.'

'There is always hope, and we will not abandon you…this is a promise.'

Agastya felt relieved on hearing that. After twenty minutes of exchange, they agreed to wind up the meeting. Both walked towards their cars.

'Next time I would like to meet General Kashyapa.'

'Well, of course, once we get this situation out of our way…I will bring General Kashyapa with me,' he said.

'Speaking of your mentor, where is the old man now?'

'He is in Tajikistan, trying to strengthen our defence ties.'

'Aah! A backward defence line against Pakistan,' said Carina. They kissed on the cheeks, bid goodbye and walked out towards their cars.

Agastya, it seems now you know about the Guardians, thought Carina as she got inside her Volvo S80 sedan.

He was wearing the Leolus ring…he does know. General Abhimanyu Kashyapa must have educated him only if he thought he was ready. One more bloodline regained, but got to deal with Project Babylon first, and find out where the attack is going to take place in December.

Sitting in his car, Agastya watched Carina drive off the village road, behind the background of the setting sun. He took out his laptop from his backpack, turned it on and inserted the memory card. Going through the details, Agastya's face changed from neutral to concern.

So they know about Mansur. Carina's agent is following Mansur. I need to get a report on him. First, I need to put one of my agents behind this Jalal Afridi. Good that General Kashyapa is coming in tomorrow. We can take our plan to the next level now…Baramulla Bomber...nice tune to it, can use it.

86 DAYS TO EVENT

Farkhor Air Base,
Tajikistan

September 16,17:15 TST

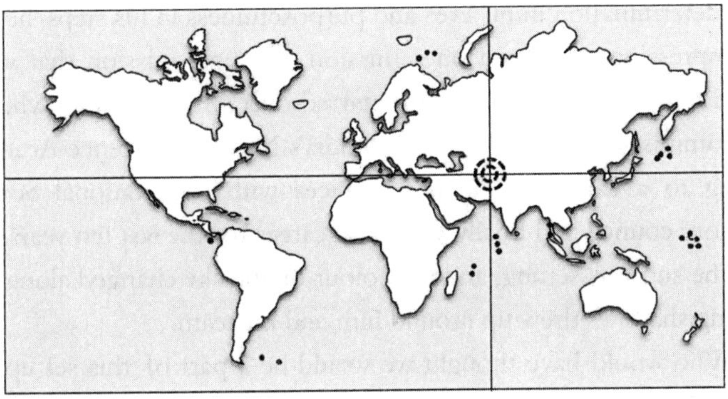

The Gulfstream G550 military jet of the Indian Air Force was getting ready for departure from Farkhor Air Base located about a mile and a half from the Tajik-Afghan border and eighty miles southeast of the Tajikistan capital of Dushanbe. It began in the late-1990s as a military field hospital and had developed into a fully fledged Indian Air Force base. The unique history of the base went back to its field hospital days, when on September 9, 2001, the leader of the Northern Alliance, Ahmad Shah Massoud, who was engaged in fighting Taliban in Afghanistan, died after he was targeted by assassins in his command centre in the northern part of the country. Ahmad Shah Massoud, also known as the Lion of Panjshir, had told his friends in the CIA that if he died, America could be assured that something bad was going to happen to them.

Sitting in a pensive mood, was General Abhimanyu Kashyapa, India's Defence Minister. He was present at the hospital that ill-fated day when Massoud died, and he felt that something powerful would be taking place in the world…although he didn't know what. Two days later, on 9/11, his suspicions were confirmed.

If Massoud had been alive then he could have passed on vital information and potentially averted the tragedy.

'All ready, sir,' the uniformed co-pilot who was flying the aircraft said to the Defence Minister. He got up and started walking towards the waiting aircraft. Despite being around eighty years old, neither the gait of the retired Army General nor his energy had diminished. With determination in his eyes and purposefulness in his steps, he gave the impression of a man on a mission, the final mission that would crown a glorious career that had started over fifty years ago when he was commissioned as an officer in India's National Defence Academy, leading to a career in defence services with the National Security Advisory council and finally a political career for the last ten years.

The sun was setting, and the colour of the sky changed along with it. Long shadows drew up around him and his team.

'Who would have thought we would be a part of this set up, two hundred years after the "Great Game" started, Sir,' said Abhimanyu's assistant while walking with him towards the jet.

'We are in it, thick and fast now…no turning back, my son. And I hope you have learnt valuable lessons in the last two years of working with me on how to conduct one,' said Abhimanyu in a stern, emotionless voice to the young pretender.

The visiting party boarded the flight and Abhimanyu took the seat in the front row which he always preferred. His small three-member team also boarded, along with two defence personnel from the Air Force. General Kashyapa had seen it all; from having been a prisoner of war during the 1962 China conflict as a junior officer to leading a battalion in the 1971 war against Pakistan. As the jet taxied on the runway, General Kashyapa gazed at the evening sun setting over the base. He put his hand over his French beard, deep in thought.

83 DAYS TO EVENT

Prime Minister's Office,
Delhi, India

September 19,09:25 IST

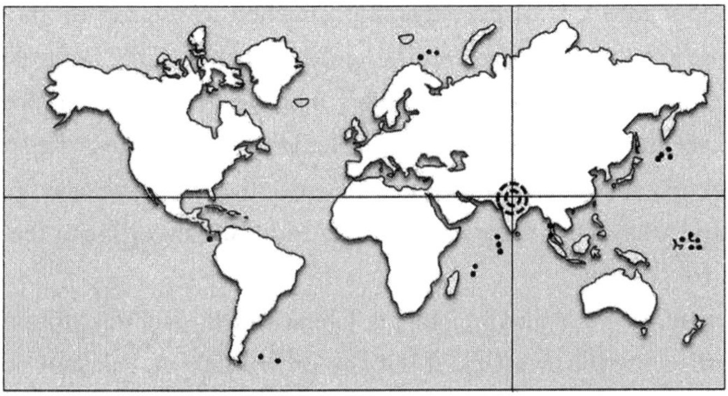

A black SUV entered the PMO. The security guard at the gate did the customary checks despite the high profile occupant in the car. General Kashyapa sat inside the car, still thinking about the emotional ride of the previous night when a tirade of memories of those horrid seven months as POW in the '62 war with China had flooded his head. He looked at the security officials doing the checks and smiled at them. The defence personnel saluted the minister as he moved inside, and he nodded in acknowledgment. Once a soldier, always a soldier, that's what General Kashyapa believed. Moreover, a soldier never questions.

Inside the PMO meeting room, the Cabinet Committee on Security, chaired by the Prime Minister, was sitting along with India's internal agency, the Intelligence Bureau, or IB, and the external intelligence agency, the Research Analysis Wing, aka RAW. Also present were the panel of Armed Forces Chiefs with all three service chiefs.

They were waiting for the Defence Minister's report of the current national security situation. The door opened and the Defence Minister entered in his usual swift stride. He greeted everyone in the room, and then shook hands with them. In his other hand he held a stack of files, which he started handing out to each one of them.

'Please do open the files and go through them as I give the references during my discussion,' said the Defence Minister as he sat down in his chair.

He then removed the data storage device from his top pocket and plugged it into a USB port that was attached to the top of the table. The presentation appeared on the screen in front of the table. All eyes were on him. Agastya looked at his mentor, General Kashyapa, and could see that despite the hectic travel and late-night arrival, he still had the energy and enthusiasm to chair this meeting. Agastya knew time was of essence as things were closing in on India and everyone in the room had a role to play.

'The news is not encouraging. If China attacks us today, not only the eastern front will be attacked but the probability of Pakistan pushing in on the western front is strong, especially in the Jammu and Kashmir and Gujarat regions.'

'I can understand Jammu and Kashmir, but why Gujarat?' asked Smriti Rao.

'For economic reasons, my dear. They can't attack Mumbai directly so they will attack Vadinar, and we all know why that location is important to India. Intel had suggested that the attack on Mumbai in November was only a test run. They can do the same at multiple cities and towns, and Vadinar can be one of them.'

Vadinar is one of India's well known hotzones for terror attacks. Though only a small coastal town in the Jamnagar district of the state of Gujarat, it is, strategically speaking, the jugular vein of India's oil-refining facilities. The town has three oil refineries with a capacity to store over two million tons of oil, and an operating capacity of 99 million tons. Its destruction would have a decapitating effect on India as it would devastate it economically. Defences in the area have been strengthened with the Coast Guard having established a new North West Command there. However in times of war, it remains within striking distance of cruise missiles fired from ships or land-based missiles fired from Pakistan.

'Babur cruise missiles from Pakistan will most likely be used for attacking this port either via sea or land, however Ghazani or other medium-range missiles can be used from a longer distance,' said the Defence Minister.

'So what are the chances that we can handle war on two fronts?' asked the Prime Minister, looking towards the Armed Forces chiefs.

'Under basic conventional warfare we can hold China and Pakistan off for a couple of weeks, but that depends on the escalation factor,' said the Army Chief, who was also the head of the current panel.

'Can you elaborate on the escalation factor for the audience?'

The Army Chief looked at the Defence Minister, who then double-clicked on a video file titled 'Operation Saw.'

A global map came up, the shot zoomed in on to the Indian subcontinent with emphasis on north-eastern India along the China border displayed prominently.

'This video will show the escalation factor scenario and resultant outputs,' said the Army Chief.

'Phase one is limited to border skirmishes.'

Arrows came up on the map to indicate flashpoints. At first there were three arrows on the eastern front from the Chinese side. This was indicated as day one; later, on day two, a few more red flashes appeared.

This time there was one flash on the northern front on the Ladakh side and one flash each at the border of Uttaranchal state.

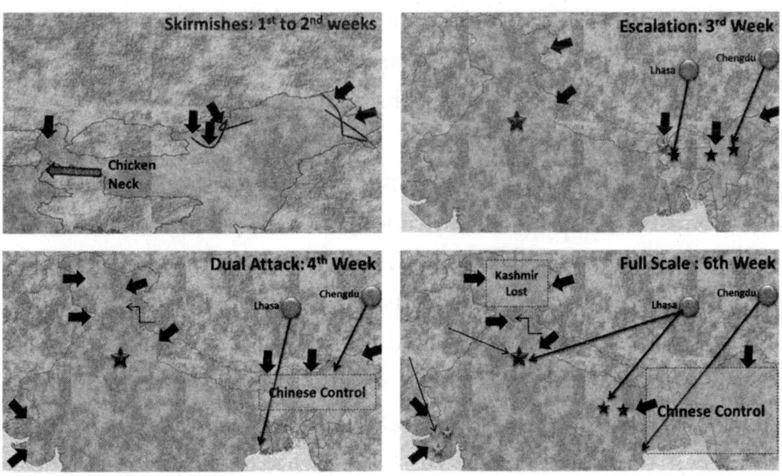

The video played on till the sixth week where the end result was India facing battlefronts from Pakistan and China at the same time. Both Kashmir and East India were lost to China.

The Army Chief continued. 'We expect to move into brigade-level engagement after four or five days if diplomacy and external pressure fail to stop it.'

'Smriti, what's your opinion on the international community's reaction if this breaks out?' enquired the Prime Minister, leaning back in the chair with his hands behind his head.

'There will be a lot of lip service, but that's all it will be,' said Smriti, who then took a deep breath and closed her eyes. Exhaling, she opened her eyes and continued. 'In a best-case scenario, Russia will intervene. I fully trust the leadership there.'

General Kashyapa chuckled and shook his head; all eyes in the room turned towards him. The Prime Minister planted both hands on the table before him and looked at Abhimanyu questioningly.

'It's the same old story. We were alone before and we are alone now. No one will want a war or engage negatively with China. As far as I am concerned, the only people who will come to our aid are the Chinese!'

Abhimanyu punctuated the word 'Chinese' by making the double quote gesture with his hands. 'Our National Security Advisor will have something to say about this scenario.'

The National Security Advisor addressed his colleagues, knowing fully well that what he was saying was merely hypothetical and was based on his calculations on what could happen if a war broke out and went on for more than a week.

'By "Chinese" the Defence Minister meant non-Hans. As you know, there is growing disillusionment among Chinese people of all fifty-five different communities. The common man is facing the brunt. The only thing that keeps them together is the government propaganda machine along with stringent censorship and an iron fist.'

Most of the members in the room nodded their heads. Agastya did not like what he was hearing. There has to be a way…a way to get through to the Chinese leadership. Changes had occurred this year since the new leadership had taken charge. Hawks still remained, but which country does not have a problem with hawks in the government?

The NSA continued. 'And it's strongly believed that a war is needed to bring the nation together but a war can also tear it apart.'

'What do you mean?' asked the Finance Minister, bewildered.

'There are nationalist sentiments of self-rule in at least three regions, i.e., the Tibetan Autonomous Region, the Mongol Autonomous Region, and especially in Xinjiang, which was the erstwhile East Turkmenistan.'

The NSA continued to talk about East Turkmenistan or Xinjiang, how it was the biggest point of concern for the Chinese leadership. There had been lots of riotous activity there due to feelings of ill will among the ethnic people towards the Han settlers which rose from 6% in 1949 to nearly fifty percent.

The NSA continued with his monologue for the next ten minutes.

'Thus a war may unite the Hans, but it would also create an opportunity for others to act, so I strongly doubt if the Chinese leadership will support a long war, which could lead them to act on two fronts, both internal and external,' said the NSA, winding up his presentation.

'Tell me, General, after the first phase, will heavier conventional forces be used?' The Home Minister spoke up in a concerned voice. Agastya didn't care for war. It was never a solution for him. According to him, war was created by people, and if people could be won over, then wars could be prevented.

However, on the other side, General Kashyapa always felt war was the best solution for peace and he always gave as an example, the peace that had ensued in Europe following the two World Wars in the first half of the twentieth century. War also made the West more sincere and responsible as nations in terms of security and strategic affairs.

'Well, it will, unless we as usual take the higher moral ground and do nothing,' replied the Army Chief curtly.

'This means the introduction of Air Force and missiles systems, both offensive and defensive, right?' The Foreign Minister spoke up in a serious tone.

'Yes, ma'am. At this time we do not expect a naval war due to the maritime distance with China. This is where we believe Pakistan comes in, to attack our coastal cities using sea-based Jihadi elements again. Only this time the Pakistani Navy will be used officially, as the likelihood of a military coup will increase.'

'How do you foresee this situation?' asked the Prime Minister.

The NSA interjected here to say they were expecting a military coup in Pakistan by Jihadi elements in its armed forces. On being asked the reason for the expectation, he said that the agencies had certain intercepts and a couple of human intelligence sources following the arrest and interrogation of a few Jihadi elements from the states of Kerala and Karnataka.

'They will again say that these are non-state actors. It's been three years and their behaviour has not changed. We should take some kind of military action, a pre-emptive strike. Soft diplomacy will not work,' said the Finance Minister, agitated, as he looked at his Cabinet colleagues.

'A lot remains unchanged from the past. In the past, they used to operate in the open and the only difference now is that the terror elements have been driven underground…but America is trying its best,' said Agastya.

'America is a golden goose for the Pakistanis; they receive aid upon aid, and yet America has learnt no lesson. Instead of tapering off the aid slowly and making them independent, they have made them more dependent on America than the Pakistani Army,' said the Finance Minister.

'Yes…it used to be said that Pakistan is run by three As – Allah, Army, and America. It looks like it's the reverse now,' said the Defence Minister in a low tone, now standing and leaning both hands on the big oak table, his breathing slightly accelerated. Agastya looked at his colleagues and smiled, trying to inject a reassuring atmosphere into the room. Despite the expression, Agastya's face registered his worry. No one could predict what would happen, now that the ball had been set in motion.

'Folks, America is going to do what it has to do. They believe Tibet is a part of China and yet they say that the Chinese government should talk to the Dalai Lama,' interjected the Prime Minister.

He continued after a brief pause. 'America and the other countries will not tackle China directly, only soft diplomacy will be used. We will do the same, but if the need arises, we all know how to defend this country!' The Prime Minister slammed his hand on the table. 'I have full faith in our people that when the time comes we will rise. We have been here for more than 5,000 years and will continue to do so in some form or another. And it is my responsibility!' His voice reverberated in the room.

Everyone in the room was surprised to see the Prime Minister's vehemence. A man of few words, he was known to have a calming influence on those around him. There was silence in the room. By his standards, Khurana had overreacted. But it was a plan, a plan to show the buck stops with him. To send home the message that he was the leader and willing to accept responsibility, a rarity in the country's political circles where everybody wanted to shirk responsibility rather than take the flak. He had jumped into the muck, and now it was up to him to clean it up. If not him, then who?

The discussions went on for another couple of hours, but the participants did not tire; instead they seemed to energise one another with their talk. There was the usual tea and coffee break, but discussions continued on the side even then.

The group was slowly inching towards an understanding each side trying to outdo the other to achieve their strategic objectives. For China it would be to reach India's Siliguri corridor, also known as India's Chicken Neck, thus cutting off India's eastern half from its western side; for India it would be to enter Lhasa, the capital of Tibet, and announce its liberation, hoping that internal civil unrest in other autonomous regions would reach its peak during that time.

A highly optimistic assumption, thought the Defence Minister. He knew that in an all-out conventional war, India would have to rely more on external factors for success if it played by the traditional rules. He had a solution in mind, and it involved not only swift tactical manoeuvres, the objectives of which he expected to complete in three days, but also use of non-conventional weapons, despite India's stand on NFU, i.e. No First Use of Nuclear Weapons.

Time will decide who will be the last man standing.

No one wanted to mention the 'N' word, but before the meeting ended, it came up at the discussion table. The Prime Minister cut short the discussion, saying that it would take them on an irrelevant tangent and they needed to concentrate on the plans they had shared with the cabinet earlier in the month. By that time the Army Chief had shared details of two regions in China where silo targets were present—the city of Luoning and the Hainan islands—both of which housed both ICBMs and medium-range missiles.

As the marathon meeting came to an end, the Prime Minister lightened the mood by saying, 'Now we have a lot of missed calls to attend to!' Everyone gave a slight laugh, despite being aware of the serious implications of what they had discussed.

'So most of us should meet up again at U.S. Ambassador Yitzhak Herzog's party,' said Smriti Rao as she stood up. Everyone nodded and ascertained that they would be attending the dinner meeting scheduled for that evening.

Agastya, Prime Minister Khurana, and General Kashyapa remained seated at the meeting table. Agastya had his usual pensive look, while Khurana relaxed in his chair, leaning back into it. The retired General motioned for the others to leave as he felt the need to have a word or two with the Prime Minister and Home Minister.

With the room to themselves, General Kashyapa looked at the two young men before him. He knew there was much to do and felt good that they were at the helm as they had time on their hands, unlike him, who knew he was at the twilight of his active political life.

'It will take great courage to tackle things if they get out of hand,' said the Defence Minister.

'Yes, it will, but if it gets out of hand you realise we may need to launch *Operation Vajra*.' asked Agastya.

'Don't worry about the consequences, I will handle all that, political and social. After all, it's my call. And remember, Pakistan has nothing to lose by attacking us, their leadership does not care if the military takes over their decisions. We, on the other hand, have everything to lose. So a pre-emptive strike is important. Let them give us one reason and we will blow the living daylights out of them,' said the PM in a soft but serious tone.

'You make it sound so easy,' said Abhimanyu, thinking that after many years there was finally someone in the political circle who had the courage to push the button.

'If I don't take the call, who will? We need to take our country back to where it belongs, and if not us, then who?'

'The shining light of the east, the golden bird from the golden era,' Agastya said, now standing up.

'Agastya, my friend, it will be back to the future again,' said Aditya Khurana in a high note of optimism. He looked at Agastya, smiled, and put a hand on his shoulder.

'Hey, buddy, we will make it, with your support and the blessings of Kashyapa Sir, we will achieve everything.'

'Just like the eighties, right?'

'Yes, just like the eighties, Agastya. As you recall, there was so much hope and optimism around the world. Yes, there was the Cold War, but there was also more hope that things would get better,' said Aditya.

'You are right, back to the future again, or let me put it like this, Adi: We have to trust our destiny, build hope among the people, and then things will happen,' said Agastya in a confident tone.

'Nice saying…I can use it in the next elections.'

The three of them laughed. This line had been mentioned by a local seer *Kasha* whom Agastya had met in Srinagar when he was there for his honeymoon. The PM and Defence Minister walked out, as Agastya stayed behind. Ten minutes passed.

Kasha has been right till now. Vitasta, my lovely wife…Let me call her, he thought, taking out his mobile.

Agastya dialled Vitasta's number, a pre-recorded voice mail answered. 'Hiiiii! You have reached me, that is, Vitasta. If you want to talk to me call me again or message me after the beep.' The sexy, husky voice brought a smile to his face.

A new message. Nice…I'll call her later.

Agastya walked out and entered one of the adjoining empty rooms. Closing the door behind him, he walked towards the glazed windows. Looking outside he could see the garden, where a lawnmower was being put to noisy use.

He took a deep breath and then let out a loud scream as he turned his eyes up. The scream lasted for five or six seconds before he fell to his knees. His eyes had become moist after the effort.

A couple of attendees rushed in. Agastya told them all was well and he was just a little tired so he had fallen on the ground. He stood up and walked out of the carpeted room.

No time for past emotions. Time is running out, but now we have a lead with Carina's suspect Jalal, the bald man, seen in Delhi. One of my agents is behind him and we shall know more.

79 DAYS TO EVENT

Railway Station, Defence Cantonment, Delhi, India

September 23,20:00 IST

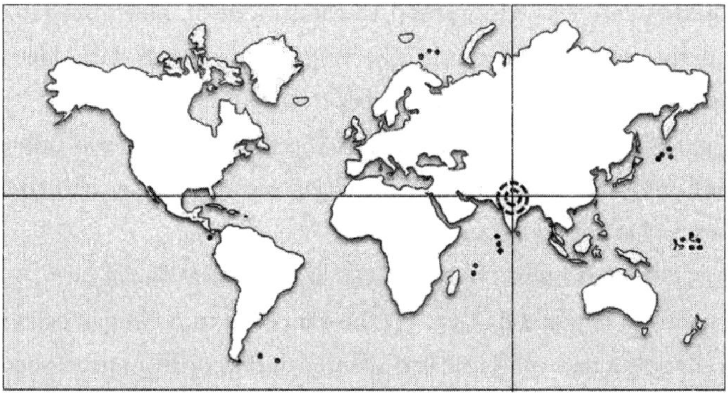

The atmosphere at the Delhi Cantonment railway station had an eerie quality. The station was located on a lonely stretch and was quiet during the night. There were more dogs milling about the station than people. Walking towards the station was a tall, clean-shaven, bald man. He wore trendy black jeans with a loose-fitting dark T-shirt and high-end sports shoes; he looked like any ordinary college boy. He was Altaf Afridi, twin brother of Jalal Afridi and adopted son of General Pervez.

He tried to adjust his small black backpack, trying to catch a glimpse of the person following him.

Damn! A tail. Got to lose him.

He knew that his only chance was to keep walking and get over the skywalk-bridge. It was normally empty at this time and suffered from a chronic case of under-lighting.

Will need to take him off, he thought as he calculated his best options.

In two to three minutes I will reach the bridge.

The two men entered the almost deserted station. The man at the rear was a CCTC agent, assigned by his boss Agastya to follow Jalal. He kept looking at his target, wondering what he would do next. The tail thought he would finally be able to catch him in the act; he had re-sighted him just thirty minutes ago after losing him an hour back. But he had not been able to catch the person whom he had met in the Defence Colony area. His pace increased as he saw his target now running on top of the sky bridge. He wondered if he had been spotted, but couldn't care less. He wanted to catch hold of him now. He raced towards the skywalk and ran up the steps. It was pitch dark. He pulled out his standard issue Glock 17C pistol.

The bald man was now ready. The top of the bridge was unlit, with only faint moonlight penetrating the cloud cover. His eyes had adjusted, and he saw his tail racing up the stairs.

Poor sod, he thought. *This will be his last run before his fall.*

As the tail reached halfway up the stairs, his mind began calculating how to handle a face off. If he was spotted and a confrontation occurred, then he would have to knock his opponent down and take him alive. His only worry was that his opponent did not share this concern.

Altaf crouched on the floor of the sky bridge, his stance that of someone prepared in equal parts to stand his ground or pounce. Both his hands were on the ground. The right hand was poised over a bag, ready to throw it at his adversary. The other hand behind his back held his faithful stiletto with a reinforced grip. The stiletto had a clip point blade and was double-edged, with one side smooth and the other having a saw blade feature. It was also laced with a neurotoxic to promptly incapacitate the victim. He knew he had an advantage—it was dark and he was dressed all in black…and god was on his side against the infidel.

As the CCTC officer came up the stairs, little did he expect an object to come flying towards his face. The bald man lunged forward the instant he hurled the bag. He picked up speed, and as he approached he slid into his target, using his strong legs to trip his adversary.

The CCTC officer turned and fell on his back; the gun fell away from his hand into the darkness. He tried to compensate for the fall by changing position, expecting his target to jump over him. But this was of no use. The stiletto pierced him on his right leg near his groin and he felt the sharp pain paralyse his body. The stiletto was then twisted and he groaned loudly, but the sound was drowned out in the loud barking of dogs under and on the sky bridge.

Altaf used his left hand to wound his adversary before jumping on top of him for the penultimate act. He then used both his hands to hold down his tail and head-butted him hard. With the incapacitating wound on his leg and the concussion from the head butt, the tail began to pass out. Altaf took out the stiletto and brought it close to his victim and sliced it.

Altaf slowly turned his head and smiled. If it had not been for that day in 2007 in Red Mosque in Islamabad, when he and his twin brother were picked up by a then unknown officer, he would have died. The officer raised them, educated them, and trained them. Altaf Afridi, the assassin, an operative of General Pervez. He looked at the dead body and bent down to search the dead man's pockets. Running his hands inside his jacket, he removed a clump of paper.

Restaurant bill.

Irritated, he threw it away and emptied out the pockets. He found a wallet with an ID card in it. "Captain Sunil Kochar," CCTC, special wing. He searched the remaining pockets, found nothing, and searched the victim's shoes. *Nothing.*

He got up and walked away from the body. He slipped the wallet inside his bag and walked down the stairs towards the empty platform.

CCTC, special wing. Hope he has not communicated with anyone in the last hour. First were the male and female snoopers in Dharamshala. We may have been compromised; hope General sahib takes care of it.

Few kilometres away, the United States Embassy complex located at Chanakyapuri was bustling with activity. The new U.S. Ambassador, Yitzhak Herzog, was hosting a dinner party.

As the group moved towards the dinner tables Agastya's mobile beeped. He picked it up to hear a trusted voice at the other end. After exchanging a few words with the caller his face grew ashen. He slipped the Nokia back into his pocket. He closed his eyes tightly for a moment and walked towards the area where dinner was being served.

After the dinner, the group dispersed, with the women and men forming separate groups. Agastya felt this was the best time to share the information that he had received with the PM and Defence Minister. 'Aditya, a Dolphin has been sunk,' said Agastya in a low, serious tone as they walked. The Prime Minister paused for a moment and started walking again, now more slowly. Abhimanyu simply shook his head.

'How long?'

'About an hour back, just fifteen miles from here,' said Agastya, who waited a moment and cleared his throat. 'I picked him personally, was just a kid.'

The three walked silently towards the main complex. The Prime Minister stopped suddenly, turned, and looked up at his colleagues. 'So does this mean what I think it does…he was following Dyke's man, whose track we keep losing?'

'The same whose name was shared with you by your unnamed source,' asked General Kashyapa.

'Yes Sir', replied back Agastya, nodding his head slowly. General Kashyapa nodded back with a slight smile knowing the source was Carina. Agastya continued, 'Another piece of news is that more frontline Chinese troops have been seen at our borders. We know what that means.'

'Operation Vajra has to start now,' said General Kashyapa with both his hands on his hips, as he knew he would need to lead this operation now.

'OK initiate it, only Phase one.'

'Good. So this means, gentlemen, I will have to make my move now. I will contact Yitzhak and thank him for the evening.'

'Yes, you carry on and I will inform the NCA that we may go on Double Take, if required!' said the PM to the retired general. 'Double Take' was India's Nuclear Command Authority code authorisation for Stage Four preparation. Under this code, the army went on full alert and some of the nuclear cores were made ready in conjunction with the warheads in preparation for the next level of authorisation.

As both of them saw the tall figure of Abhimanyu Kashyapa move towards the lawn in search of Yitzhak, they started moving again towards the complex.

'We are taking a big risk Adi. But if we focus on the risks, then the returns will always remain stuck in the middle, neither here nor there.'

'Yes Agastya, there are controlled risks and non-controlled risks. Like my relationship with Saloni, that's a non-controlled risk for you and a controlled risk for me, and speaking of it…Saloni is getting expensive. Do something.'

Agastya was not amused; he did not like what he heard.

'Don't bring up the name. This is not the time or place—and don't forget you lapped it up. The political fallout can be terrible if the media gets wind of this.'

'Like you said, it's a matter of the heart, Agastya, my friend. It's about a human connection.'

'I trust we will not bring up the name again.'

The Prime Minister, Aditya Khurana, nodded as they entered the steadfast structure of the embassy. Little did they know that Yitzhak had instructed one of the internal security personnel to activate his short-distance listening (SDL) device and follow them at a distance.

With an SDL, one could hear nearby conversation at greater clarity from the control room. A remote sensing robot that resembles an insect can be flown or a human tail can be kept behind the target. Yitzhak could clearly hear what passed between the two. By the time the mini operation was activated, however, Abhimanyu had left the discussion, so he missed the initial part of the discussion.

Saloni. That's interesting; wonder who she is. Is it something we can leverage with the Indians?

Yitzhak knew that the Prime Minister's marriage was on the rocks with the constant pressure of balancing political life with personal life.

I think someone will be interested to know about this development. India's own sex-scandal, very good. The Indian government is surely going to have its hands full, especially with the instability coming up in China. SALONI, hmm.

74 DAYS TO EVENT

Dal Lake, Srinagar,
Jammu and Kashmir, India

September 28,09:15 IST

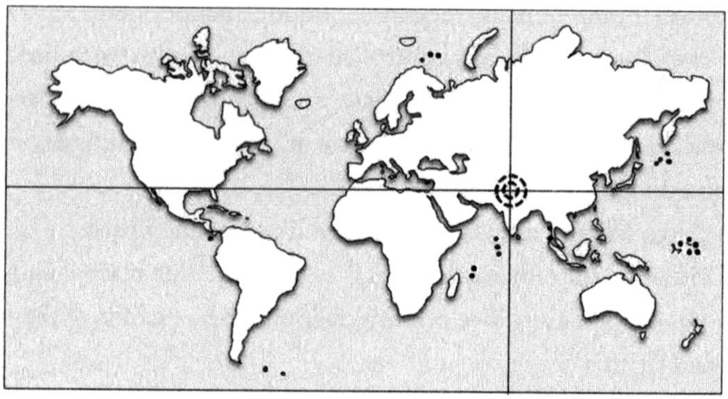

Romance was in the air, and Adolf could feel it. He was miles away from his sweetheart, but chatting away. Mikaela had just informed Adolf that her abstract for an essay titled – "Acoustic Designs in Physical World' was accepted to be published in a leading physics journal. They continued to chat.

Adolf: Congrats...another feather in your cap.

Mikaela: Ja☺ it took me sometime to write but I finally managed to finish it.

Adolf: You and your music! Good, good...so what's the essay about?

Mikaela: Relation between sound and the physical world. I have recreated the experiment of Ernst Chladni.

Adolf: Ernst who?

Mikaela: He was a 17th century musician and physicist, who used a violin bow to create geometric patterns to prove that sound, affects physical matter.

Adolf: Wow, science I like it. Send me a copy...so that I can read.

Mikaela: Sure, will do, love. Give me a few weeks, I will finish the essay and send it. Miss you ☹

They chat for a few moments and later sign off.

Well, so much for romance. At least her music is keeping her busy, and I am here in Kashmir. Still, I don't get why am I here observing Mansur. What could we possibly need from him? Mansur is a straightforward bloke, and nothing new has come up related to Kurt's death.

Adolf mailed back to Carina on the situation in detail.

The only new thing I have learnt is cricket...and the only question which comes to my mind is to find out how this man reached the state level when he had not played much competitive cricket before this. Is someone manipulating the system?

Before signing off on the laptop, Adolf received a message from HQ about a rental car used by a Pakistani during his visit to Oslo.

The car was used near the town of Karlstad on E18 highway. He was travelling from Oslo. A King James Bible with the first line of Psalm 137.1 marked and highlighted was found in the car. Some illustration similar to Kurt's signs was present on the same page. Oslo address and the name provided was invalid. Investigation is on.

Adolf removed the Bible, which Mikaela insisted that he must carry, and checked for section 137.1.

Psalm 137.1 words are "By the rivers of Babylon, there we sat down, yea, we wept, when we remembered Zion."

Is this related to Project Babylon? The injuries sound familiar to Kurt's.

Adolf typed back requesting for more details. Raising his reading glasses, he looked at his watch and saw that it was time for him to get ready to catch the *shikara,* or the local boat transport, towards the mainland for some local sightseeing.

Watching him with long-distance binoculars from a far-off houseboat was Samir.

Who is this guy? I don't like him, but his background check came clean. Need to tell Janab to find out more about him. We will not fail. The second phase of Operation Babylon would begin tomorrow with Mansur playing the Services team.

Two hours later, Adolf walked alone through the old part of the town, trying to assimilate the surroundings. Most of the people did not show any particular interest in him apart from the children who ran around him or took a glance and moved back into their houses.

Rows of wooden houses were across the lanes painted with multiple colours, predominantly green. He regularly took out his Nikon camera from the black leather pouch around his waist and took shots.

I should get some souvenir for Mikaela here. So beautiful! It could be our honeymoon destination.

'White man with camera, missing someone, your love?' Adolf turned around in circles to see who had passed the comment. 'Answers lie at the top. Look in the direction of your God. Up! Up!'

Adolf looked up and saw an old lady with silvery, unkempt hair, pointing at him. She told him to take the stairs and climb up. A few children who had been following Adolf started laughing and shouted.

'You have been selected...you have been selected.'

Adolf could not understand the game. The children urged him to go up, and a few passersby saw the old lady and then gave a faint smile as they looked at him.

'Sir you can go up, no problem. Her name is Kasha, a sort of seer or oracle,' said one passerby. Adolf exchanged a few more words with him about Kasha.

So she doled out free advice based on her reading of coffee leftovers. Let me see this, India...land of palmistry and astrology...let me experience a piece of it.

Adolf walked up the stairs, each step creaking under his feet. 'Ahh! May the Lord Jesus bless you!' Kasha spoke in an inimitable style, gesticulating wildly and rocking her face side to side while talking.

'I don't believe much in God,' said Adolf as he scanned the small room. No table, just things strewn around.

'Ahh! Interesting! Interesting! I also don't believe in God, but I believe in God's messengers,' she said and started laughing hysterically. 'They were all there, and all came here or have a part of them here.'

Adolf did not stop her from ranting. She gave him a small cup and poured coffee into it. Adolf went through the process of drinking, breathing in the cup and waiting for it to dry. Kasha was rambling about things in the local language. Some minutes later, she picked up the dry cup and started reading.

'You have come from a cold country from very far on a very important mission.'

Adolf was not impressed and said that was too generic for a soothsayer. On hearing this she sat down holding her knees together and twisted her head parallel to the floor. She stopped and froze, not moving a muscle for some time and looked as if she was not breathing. She was like a statue and the breeze just moved her hair; she fixed her gaze on Adolf.

'You have a deep relationship with sound…with music…she brings colour in your life, and rhythm.'

Is she speaking about Mikaela? Still generic.

Her head was still positioned parallel to the ground but her frown slowly gave way to a smile.

'You seek an answer relating to sound…an ancient sound…too ancient even for God's messengers.'

Adolf did not show any reaction on his face, as he felt he would hurt the old lady. She stopped for a moment and turned her head straight now and started looking around through bulging eyes. She looked into the coffee cup, turned it around slowly with her wrinkled hand and dropped it. She moved forward till she was only a feet away from his face. Adolf was now slightly disturbed seeing her eyes bulge that way. It was not normal or rational.

'You are following someone, but someone is also following you. The one who follows you, she is close and stronger than you, very close and much more beautiful than you. Both of you will find the answer together, you are searching to understand the universe, the sound of the universe.'

Adolf thought this was enough for him for a day. He got up, removed a five hundred rupee note and gave it to her, so that she could eat something nourishing. She told him to put it inside the box at the corner of the room. Adolf went to the wooden box which had fungus growing on it, and opened it using two fingers. To his astonishment, he saw a stash of gold and money in it.

This hag is not poor, why doesn't she use this money? He turned around and did a Namaste.

'You will find the answers you are looking for…you will find your destiny…and then you will feel small,' she said as he went out of the room.

Wow! What an experience! She is right though. I am following someone...but about the sound... He walked down the stairs and came out to the lane, the kids were still there.

Someone following me, that a "she" who is beautiful and more powerful than me.

Adolf walked some fifty metres ahead to a tea shop and asked for *kahwa.* He began sipping it, when he heard a familiar voice from inside the shop.

'Hey Mr Swede, looks like you are following me.'

Adolf stopped sipping, and glanced inside the small shop. Sitting a couple of benches behind a rack was Aahana. She stood up and walked out, paying for the refreshment she had had. They exchanged a few words, and Adolf was surprised to see her here, especially after what the old woman had said. They stepped out and heard a loud shrill voice tearing through the lane.

'In the beginning was the WORD, and the WORD was with God, and the WORD was God.' Kasha leant forward out of her window as she uttered the words. As soon as she uttered the word, she threw a crumpled paper in their direction, which was caught by a young boy and she disappeared inside. Aahana stared at Adolf with a quizzical look. Adolf stood stunned.

Did she know something or was this a fluke? It's her fascination with sound and knowledge of the Bible. Nothing more than a coincidence…she cannot know that was also one of Kurt's messages.

Adolf called the boy, who came dutifully smiling. Adolf moved his arm forward towards the boy asking him to show the paper. The boy was hesitant, but gave the paper to Adolf when Aahana handed a chocolate to him. Aahana winked at Adolf, who shrugged his shoulders and took the crumpled paper. He opened it slowly, as Aahana moved her head closer to Adolf to get a view of the uncurled page. Adolf showed no reaction on his face, but Aahana raised her thin eyebrows.

'Adolf it's the sign of Aum, and the word Amen. Why will she send you this?'

Adolf folded the paper, and put it inside his right jacket pocket.

'No idea, but will keep it for respect. Well so much for today dear…tomorrow is another day,' said Adolf.

'Tomorrow's is not another day. Tomorrow is my Mansur's game,' spoke back Aahana ecstatically.

73 DAYS TO EVENT

Sher-e-Kashmir Stadium, Srinagar,
Jammu and Kashmir, India

September 29,15:55 IST

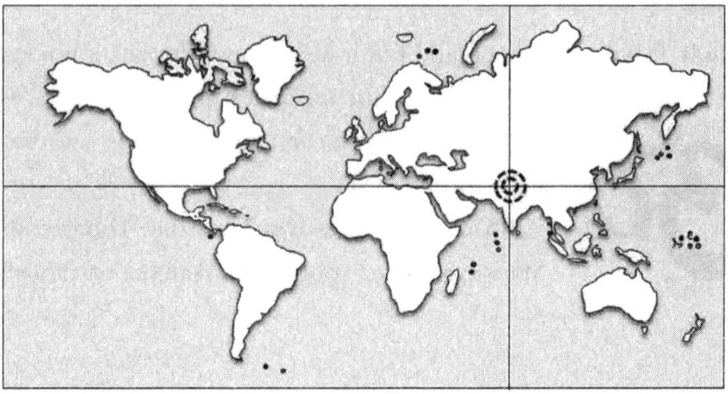

'Howzzat! **The bowler**, wicket keeper and close-in fielder appealed simultaneously. Their hands were raised in unison as they faced the umpire, expectantly. The umpire stood in front of the wickets and then slowly started raising the dreaded finger for the fourth time that day.

'It's OUT,' the umpire growled, and the fielding side jumped with joy. The batsman was not happy and stood his ground for a while, but eventually he turned and started his walk back to the pavilion. He muttered something at both the bowler and the umpire as he moved quickly towards the east end of the field where the batting side's stands were located. The bowler remained unfazed despite the batsman gesturing something to him. He had won the battle and there was no need to continue to charge the atmosphere any more than necessary. Plus he had taken his seventh wicket, out of the nine that had fallen that day.

For the bowler, Mansur Haider from Jammu and Kashmir state team, it was his debut game. The whole stadium was echoing his name, 'Mansur...Mansur...Mansur...' the place vibrated with energy.

It was a turn of events for the state team—a rookie bowler had provided them with a solid foundation for winning the game.

The Services team, which comprised players from the Indian Armed Forces, was in tatters. Coming into the game as firm favourites, to control day one of this four-day game, they had no answer to the pace barrage being thrown at them.

'Aahana you lucky girl, he is sooo fast!' Shaza screamed as she tried to pull Aahana down.

'Yes and they gave him only two overs before lunch, how bad…see, he has taken all but one wicket now,' Aahana shouted back.

Shaza was more animated now and hugged Samir. 'Samir, how lucky he is…Mansur getting this chance, it's like the devil possessing him when he is bowling.'

'His deliveries are now coming over 150 km,' said Sharon as she saw the electronic scoreboard displaying the ball speed.

'Sharon you are right. This kind of speed has not been seen in domestic circles and definitely not in India. This was the pace of Australians, Pakistanis, and even the old West Indies team of the late 1970s.'

Aahana, Sharon, and Shaza were on their feet jumping up and down with joy. The stadium was packed to capacity, the crowd evenly divided between the local populace and the visiting Services team supporters. Adolf was sitting through the commotion, and despite having some knowledge of the game, he still could not understand the LBW (Leg before Wicket) decisions. Aahana explained it to him twice, but it did not stick. Samir was also there for some time before he moved to another side of the ground, stating that he had to do some operational work. As a patron of the grounds and ex-player he had full access to the grounds, and he also had to see that the game went on smoothly.

A couple of more performances like this would strengthen his case for a chance on the national stage. That's Janab's job. He will handle that part. And then our mission will continue to the next level.

Mansur was now ready to bowl the last ball of his ninth over and forty of the first innings. In his mind he recollected that in the first two overs, the only thing he wanted to do was to put the ball in the right place. At lunch time the coach told him that if he bowled like that, there would be no place for him in the team.

At first Mansur was shocked, but then the coach added, 'Just go out and make it happen—bowl as fast as you can and let the ball do its magic.'

How right he was! Mansur had started his run, standing before him was the eleventh batsman.

While reaching the final leg of the run, Mansur sent in a dipping yorker which uprooted the leg stump. The Services team was all out for one hundred and twenty runs. The fielders rushed in and lifted Mansur on their shoulders. The crowd went wild with joy. Yes, they were happy that their team was enjoying the upper hand, but they were happier that the Services team was at the receiving end. It was poetic justice for them.

Mansur's first innings match figures were: 9-5-9-8, nine overs, five maidens, nine runs, eight wickets, a dream debut by any standard. He searched the stands for his sister and mother who had come to see him perform. He saw them and raised his hands. He also saw Aahana and her friends and waved to them.

Wish Abbu was here. I am sure he will be happy in heaven now.

Roy from the Newsgate channel could not believe what he saw. He thought Malini and JJ had missed a great bowling performance, as they wanted to investigate a political sex scandal arising in Delhi with the name of some Saloni being thrown around. His focus returned to cricket. He turned towards another reporter in the stands.

'What is the best debut by any bowler in history? Did Mansur beat it today?'

The other reporter was also dumbfounded.

'I don't know, let's check the cricket online staff, maybe they will have stats,' said the other reporter, equally impressed by what he had seen.

'This is news!' Roy took out his phone to inform Malini about the performance.

The crowd was ecstatic and noisy. Even the Services team supporters were applauding Mansur's brilliant performance.

A couple of spectators watched silently.

'We need to get to him, Afridi sahib. Do we know what we have to do now?' Gulfam hunched over as he spoke. A local Kashmiri and strong sympathiser of Pakistan, he was watching the game with a bald man, who had entered India four weeks earlier, via the Nepal border and moved to his base in Dharamshala.

'We need to make sure this is his last game, and the last one for Adolf and Aahana,' His tone was cold and sadistic.

'Are you sure?'

'Yes. There are other people watching him, probably some of our brothers also. We need to reach him first and take credit.'

'Is that necessary?'

'Yes, otherwise how will the funds come? Without funding, our movement is dead.'

'Right.'

'So how will we do it?'

'Create an accident, we will follow them and kill him…not now and not here, at the appropriate time.'

55 DAYS TO EVENT

Monkey Hill, Tanmarg,
Jammu and Kashmir, India

October 17,08:15 IST

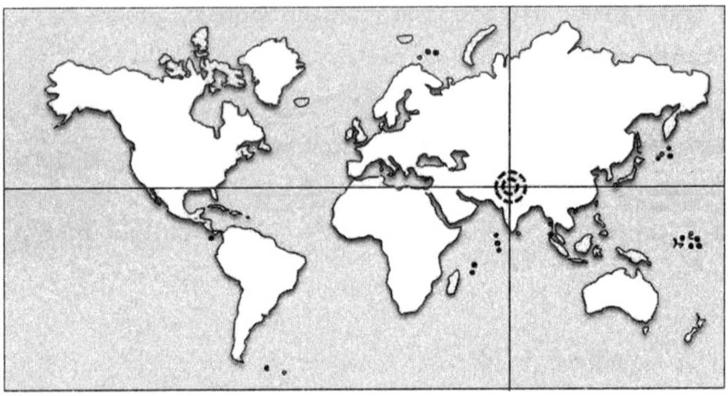

The landscape above Monkey Hill was pure white. Winter had set in early by almost a month. Such apparent climate shifts were usually attributed to global warming, but be that as it may, an extra month of snow gave a bigger boost to the region's tourist economy. This was one of the best places in the country for snowboarding and skiing. To reach the area, you had to move from Gulmarg to Tanmarg and then hike for half an hour to Monkey Hill. As the name indicated, monkeys were in greater abundance than their biped cousins. The view from the five-thousand-metre peak was majestic and serene. Downhill was the sparsely populated village of Drang; to any skier the thousand-metre descent was breathtaking. With the sun beaming over the snow-clad hill and the snowflakes swirling in the air, the notion of "paradise on earth" took on a new meaning.

Mansur stood once again on his favourite peak. Seeing the snow all around made him happy, and he was happier still because he was with Aahana, who, apart from being an ardent mountaineer, was also a ski champion. Her forte was freestyle skiing, an acrobatic, aerial form.

Aahana and Mansur had first met on Monkey Hill more than a year ago, during one of her ski trips. This time, she expected to spend a lovely day with him and her friends, and she was dressed for the occasion in a red and black one-piece ski suit. On her head she wore a black cap, and dark ski goggles protected her eyes from the glare. She smiled at Mansur, who was also wearing a ski suit but seemed slightly uncomfortable in it.

Mansur was at peace. Few days ago the cricket game had finished with a day to spare and he'd had a match tally of fifteen wickets, his effort lauded as one of the best debuts seen in many seasons. He had been declared the man of the match and had received praise from all quarters, even his opponents. There was talk of him breaking into the national side quickly, the only sore point being that media coverage had been depleted by the political sex scandal in Delhi. Some were saying that the Prime Minister was directly involved with a woman named Saloni, a personal assistant working in the PMO.

Now the three girls were standing on the peak with Mansur, Samir, and Adolf. The six had taken off from Srinagar to stay at one of the hotels near the base camp in Gulmarg, reaching their destination early in the morning. The only troubling aspect so far, especially for the girls, had been the monkeys, which continually hopped around and beat their chests as the group hiked up the hill. Samir and Mansur told the others not to be bothered, they were quite safe.

'I still say you should try it, Shaza,' said Samir, trying to goad her into joining them for the downhill plunge.

'If God had wanted me to go plunging downwards through snow he would have given me wings,' replied Shaza. Her hands were crossed, trembling, on her chest. The fear of the height, the cold, and the monkeys was pushing her to her limit.

'You're scared of the monkeys? Wait till you see the snow leopards and the avalanches,' said Mansur in a cocky tone, grinning.

Aahana hit him across the back with her ski pole and he gave his usual 'ouch', more drama than real pain. But now Shaza and Sharon were in no mood to move.

Samir looked at Shaza, then Aahana. But it was Adolf who came to the rescue with the suggestion that he could stay behind with Shaza and Sharon while the others continued. On hearing this, Samir said that he would stay behind and the rest should go ahead. Shaza apologised to Samir and he hugged her, 'Don't worry.' They decided to go down the Monkey Hill trail after approaching the area via another route. This would give them more time on the slope to enjoy both the open ground and the Alpine trees crowning it.

Mansur, Aahana, and Adolf were getting ready to start their run, with a total skiing time of five to six minutes.

They were being watched from another hillside.

Altaf kept his eyes trained on them through his rangefinder binoculars. By his side were Gulfam and a couple of other extremists, all of them trained by General Pervez Musa Hussein. They were well equipped, with combat assault gloves, tactical knee pads, turbo-fan military goggles to see even during fog or low visibility, and the latest warfare ski paraphernalia, supplied courtesy the Americans to the Pakistan government. The equipment, originally earmarked to fight the Taliban, had instead ended up in their hands.

Altaf put down his hi-tech rangefinder. His job had become easier. It was now no longer a single-target exercise; collateral damage was allowed. The instructions from the General were to kill anyone around Mansur, period.

'They're starting their descent…Let's get ready.' Altaf got the men on line. They checked their Crimson Trace SPEC laser-tipped handguns, which they'd need to use with their ski poles when the time came.

'We will intercept them in a little over a minute if they're moving towards the village, leaving us with additional time to do our job,' said Altaf coldly.

When they saw three of their targets take off and the other three stay on top of the hill, Altaf needed to take a quick decision. Looking at his men, he instructed Gulfam to stay there and use the rifle to take down the targets on the hilltop while he and the others would go after the three who were skiing. They then pushed off and headed down towards their targets.

Samir, Shaza, and Sharon watched as their friends disappeared. They saw how elegantly Aahana and Adolf moved, with Mansur trying to catch up with them after a slow start.

Aahana was enjoying her downhill slide and teasing Mansur and Adolf by slowing down and cutting across them with sudden twists, showering them with snow.

'Aahana is really enjoying out there,' said Samir holding his gloved hand over his eyebrows.

'Yes, she is and look at the way she is teasing Mansur…aha…she is showering them with snow. She does know how to ski, my girl,' said Shaza as she took both her gloved hands together close to her mouth and shouted, 'Go, Aahana, Go!'

'Yeah…go Aahana go,' said Samir quietly.

Samir looked on with a sombre expression. Seeing this, Shaza hugged him from behind with her head resting on top of his shoulder.

'Yes, you both forget about me…I should have joined Adolf,' said Sharon sarcastically. All the three started laughing. Samir hugged Shaza gently and planted a kiss on her lips as he turned her around. He noticed something in the distance and halted the wet kiss.

'What happened…why did you stop?' said Shaza as she also turned around to see what he was watching.

'That other group is closing in on them,' said Samir with concern as he pointed towards his friends and the other group of skiers.

Another set of eyes was watching all three parties with *Steiner* class Commander XP military binoculars, standard issue for the U.S. Army. He was closer to the Altaf group but hidden behind some nearby rocks. He was clad in all white for camouflage. He too was equipped with U.S. Army instruments, but was from the Pakistani Special Forces. Major Emraan, now deep into his operation, had been following his target, Mansur, for the last week, and had had nothing special to report…till now.

He put down his white binoculars, knowing that there was going to be a flashpoint. From the looks of things he understood that the group that started their ski run in the direction of Mansur was actually on the intercept course as he saw them with handguns. Judging by the equipment they were carrying Emraan felt that they were probably his comrades, but he was certain he would have been advised if other operatives were present.

Either these are freelancers or I have been told a lie. Samir is there and may be in danger. Time to return a favour.

Lies were not unusual, with the lines of communication intentionally smeared with the ever-changing chain of command within the middle and higher ranks of the Pakistani armed forces. It was like a game of ping-pong that had been going on for the last twelve months, and this was bound to create ripple effects, what with various power centres trying to gain control. All Major Emraan knew was that he had to observe, report, and do nothing.

Wrrr! Thud! A sudden vibration. Even when using a silencer with a long-range rifle, a substantial noise is made. Major Emraan, who was prone on the ground, got up on one knee and held his handgun poised in his right hand. Using his left hand to hold the binoculars, he saw that the person who had not descended with his suspected colleagues was firing at the two girls and Samir was on the other side.

Wrrr! Wrrr! Thud! Two more shots were fired in quick succession, and Emraan saw one of the girls go down with the other crouching beside her.

'Shit! Shit! Samir, what's happening?' shrieked Shaza, holding Sharon's bleeding hand. Her white coat was quickly drenched in blood. Sharon had collapsed and started trembling from the aftermath of the shock and the excruciating pain.

Samir immediately swung into action and dragged the three large backpacks in front of the girls, blocking the direction from which the first bullet had come.

'Stay down, flat...spread out! Don't lift yourself,' Samir shouted as he rolled over. Samir unzipped one of his jacket pockets and in a single motion removed a Glock 17C model pistol. Shaza was shocked to see a gun in Samir's hand, and her mouth dropped open. She saw a red light coming up on it, part of the GTL 51/52 tactical marker. Samir now stretched out his body on the ground, raised his hands in front of him, and pointed the semi automatic to the sky and fired two rounds. He then rolled for a distance till he reached a collection of rock and boulders and fired a couple of more rounds.

Four rounds of the seventeen used, but two more magazines with me...I can hang on.

He looked at Shaza eye-to-eye, mouthed, '*I love you...Trust me,*' and fired two more rounds, this time in the direction of the shots. He saw the firing now clearly as the bullets hit the bags. He fired another two shots from his pistol and in doing so, drew the shooter's attention. He indicated for Shaza to lie flat and grind into the snow along with Sharon. Shaza blindly followed his instructions and was crying now, totally confused.

The shots are being fired from the east...a sniper rifle. It's no use my being here with the girls in danger. I need to expose myself and move towards the shooter. Damn!

Wrrr! *Wrrr*!

A few seconds passed.

Wrrr!!

Now I am sure a semi-automatic rifle, two shots at a time. Seven rounds from the shooter. My 9x19 calibre should bring him down once I hit him! Or them! I have to act fast...awww!

Samir touched his left shoulder; it felt warm and painful.

I have been hit! Allah! Now only one option is left...got to move forward and draw the shooters away from the girls. If Shaza sees me bleeding she will come here... can't be close to them.

I hope Mansur and the others are safe, he thought. He couldn't have been more wrong.

Aahana slowed down a little to let Mansur catch up. Adolf seemed to be a swift mover, which came as no surprise; after all, he was an adventure sports instructor. She could see three other skiers coming in their direction. One of them was bald, the sun reflecting off his head. Adolf and Mansur were closing in on Aahana, and Adolf, wanting to impress with his skills, started kneeling and jerked his body upwards when he rode over a small snow-covered rise. This raised him slightly, which turned out to be lucky for Mansur as he came in front of him.

Shoosh! Crack! Tck!

The lower quarter of Adolf's right ski snapped in mid air. The broken piece flew across Aahana's face as she leaned her body backward to duck while controlling her ski run with the poles.

Adolf landed; all three moved as one without stopping. They knew something was wrong.

'That's a shot! Those guys are firing,' shouted Adolf, 'Keep moving, don't stop! They have hand-guns.'

They saw the three skiers all dressed in white closing in on them with two of them holding in their hands what looked like handguns.

Not wanting to take any chances, they increased their speed, but by this time the three skiers following them had removed their guns and were firing in their direction. At the last minute they made a sudden turn into a small Alpine patch. Mansur, the least experienced skier of the three, was not as fast as the others.

'Mansur, just follow my lead, hit harder…bend your knees Mansurrrr…. Bend your knees!' Aahana shouted.

'I am trying.'

'Don't try, keep moving you both, I will tackle these gunners,' shouted Adolf as he slowed down to let Mansur pass him and break up the group.

Altaf Afridi saw Adolf break away and shouted 'Follow…the white-man Jafar, and I will take care of Aahana.' The two groups went in opposite directions.

Damn! They're not following me, I am not the target. Got to take care of the tail first before getting to the bald man….He does look like Jalal…he must be Jalal.

He crouched, reducing his body exposure, then he used his ski turn to stop suddenly and surprise his tail, who banged into Adolf's ski poles which he held in front of him. As they fell, Adolf came down on his adversary's throat with his elbow and used his other hand to hold out his gun. One jab from the strong Swede was enough to crush the would-be assailant's windpipe, and blood spilt out of the victim's mouth. Adolf did not waste a moment. He picked up the attacker's fallen weapon, not removing the one he carried and started his slide to join the other two.

Time and momentum lost, got to reach them fast…they are also the target… it does not make sense! Adolf got a glimpse of Aahana and Mansur along with the assassins closing in on them.

Aahana and Mansur were now better positioned, making zigzag patterns and sudden jumps to avoid the bullets which were coming more frequently.

'Don't keep firing; we will be out of bullets. Get closer and fire…,' shouted Altaf as he thought, *my brother Jalal you did your job in Pakistan killing Kurt. I will do my job and kill everyone here. No one can stop operation Babylon.*

As the two assassins began to gain speed and close the distance, Adolf suddenly soared above them, taking a shot at one of them. The clean hit brought down Altaf's partner. The playing field was level. Altaf shouted in rage and plunged forward with increased ferocity. Adolf was now moving with greater momentum and saw Altaf move sideways to avoid him and gain on Mansur. As they careened downhill they fired at each other with the trees between them. The cottages in the villages were now visible and the slope would soon be over. Before that there was a slight elevated point, and ahead of them they saw Mansur and Aahana jump over it.

They moved in that direction and hit their poles harder, hitting the elevated slope together. They jumped, turned, and swivelled around, like ballet dancers in the air. Shots were coming on continuously. While landing, Adolf lost control as he tried to balance his half-broken right ski on the ground. He fell with a loud thud, his hand still clutching his gun.

'Ahhh!' Adolf shouted as he felt the fresh wound on his left arm. He looked towards his assassin, now on the ground on all fours and sliding slowly as they hit the plains.

I must have got him, Adolf got up and fell down. He had sprained his ankle.

At the top of the hill Samir approached the sniper, firing at moments towards the shooter. As he gained from one end, from the other direction, Emraan ran at full speed towards Gulfam. Samir was hit once more but now knew the shooter's location and took cover behind one of the trees, firing several rounds.

Damn! My vision is blurring...got to keep moving, thought Samir as he moved forward again.

Wrrr! *Thud*! Samir fell flat on his stomach where he was hit. The shooter now came closer to him pointing a hand-held gun towards him and the rifle hanging on his shoulders. Samir slowly tried to raise his right hand.

Both had their guns pointing at each other. The Glock pistol versus another Glock, both of them believed one shot would take care of the other person.

As Samir was about to fire, a shot was fired.

This is it! My end has come...Shaza...Allah!

Samir then saw his assailant stoop and fall down as another shot was heard. He lay back against the tree.

Down the hill, Mansur and Aahana stopped, removed their skis, and ran towards Adolf. Both knelt down as they tried to lift him. Adolf sat up with Mansur's support.

'The bald man is dead, I think he skied forward and fell,' said Mansur, balancing Adolf's weight.

'How are you holding up?'

'Well how will one feel when shot at...but not new to me, have been fired at before as a kid...more worried for Aahana here.'

'Mansur!' said Aahana and held his hand. She turned her gaze towards Adolf, 'Where did you learn to shoot like that?' Aahana spoke up through her laboured breathing.

He looked at her and smiled. 'You'll never guess. We first need to contact Samir on top and make sure things are fine there. Any law enforcement people around?' asked Adolf slowly.

Mansur helped Adolf get up, and they walked towards the cottage in the near distance as Aahana ran ahead to get help. As Adolf passed the bald man, he bent down and checked for IDs, but came up empty.

Funny, he is smiling. He is Jalal just bald, the same person I saw in Dharamshala.

On top of the hill, Samir wanted to reach out to Shaza but lacked the strength to move. A small figure appeared from behind, and Samir relaxed his grip on his gun as soon he saw Emraan, a familiar face.

'*Kyun Janab, how are you?*' Emraan greeted him as he opened a side pouch on his pants and removed a single-shot injection and punched into Samir's neck. Samir's eye widened as he felt his heart beat faster.

'This adrenalin shot will help your body cope with the stress till your guys come and take care of you.' said Major Emraan. Shaza was seen running towards them.

'*Begum ko salam bolna.*' said Emraan, conveying his cheerful greetings to Samir's beloved. 'Now we are even.' As he got up, he placed beside Samir, a couple of iodine bottles to be used as antiseptic.

Samir closed his eyes, surprised at the turn of events.

Probably fate. What goes around comes around. I saved his life in Shaksgam Valley and here he saved mine. Now we are quits.

48 DAYS TO EVENT

Central Hospital, Srinagar,
Jammu and Kashmir, India,

October 24,11:05 IST

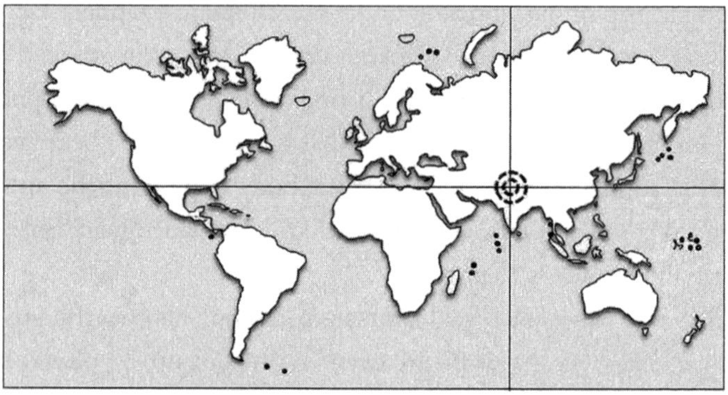

Despite the fairly chilly weather outside, the air-conditioning in the private recovery room in Central Hospital was on. Two security guards were stationed outside the door, with more in the hallway monitoring the movement of staff, patients, and visitors alike. Most of the security was courtesy the local constabulary, but there were a couple of CCTC, (Central Counter Terrorist Command), agents placed outside in the hallway and one sitting inside the room. Samir and Sharon were convalescing inside, and extra precaution was being taken. Inside, the private room looked like a hotel suite. Aahana, Shaza, and Mansur were in the room visiting their friends. Samir was in the ICU for three days, before he stabilised and was moved into this private ward.

'So Mansur, you did it again, and I missed your game again,' said Samir with high energy, getting back to his old self.

'It just clicked. That plus the fact that the opposition team was short of good batsmen,' said Mansur.

'You should thank me, man. If I had not insisted, you would have sat around here doing nothing at all–apart from spending quality time with Aahana.'

Hearing him say this, Aahana held up her purse and mock hit Samir on his bandaged arm. Samir made a face and grimaced as if in pain.

Following the incident at Monkey Hill last week, activity increased around the region. The army, which had pulled out its main units from various towns, was getting back inside, not in large numbers but with small security detachments. They were scouting the area for any other suspected extremist elements who might be related to the incident. Given the vicious nature of the attack, an inquiry was ordered by the State government.

Mansur had another game to play, this one an away game against the team from Delhi. The game ended in three days with the Jammu and Kashmir team winning by ten wickets. The star performer was once again Mansur, who took fourteen wickets–five wickets in the first innings and nine wickets in the second. He had been nicknamed "ENT specialist" by his teammates. ENT stood for *Ear, Nose, and Throat*, which were the areas of the batsmen hit or followed by balls from Mansur. He got off to an unremarkable start despite having the new ball in the first innings, and went wicketless during his first spell. But post-tea he came back strong with the old ball and even contributed to the batting order with a half century in the first innings. Mansur came back as a hero having defeated the Goliaths—the Delhi team led by none other than the captain of the national team.

The local papers from Kashmir had a field day writing about Mansur, but the performance did not receive national coverage and only a token reference was published. The national news was still covering a suspected sex scandal involving a personal assistant named Saloni in the PMO office as well as the Chinese troop movements near the eastern front. The Monkey Hill incident was hushed up by Delhi and mentioned only as an infiltration bid.

Mansur did not mind that he had not been covered, as he was playing for the love of the game, and was chasing his father's dream. He smiled at Samir. 'Well, brother, you surely did. It was like magic, and seeing you recover is making me feel better.'

'Aha! Me? Don't worry. I have God's hand over me.'

Shaza then put her hand over him, posing theatrically. Everyone in the room started laughing.

Mansur looked at Aahana and winked, and she winked back. In his mind, though, he was worried about Samir, as the government agencies believed that the attack was an attempt to kidnap or murder him as his father was a famous local politician.

The CCTC investigator got a call on his headset, and he opened the door. An agent dressed in a blue suit entered the room, and to Mansur he looked familiar.

He is Nikhil Srivastava, my first wicket.

Major Nikhil Srivastava from the Services team was the CCTC agent heading the investigation team. The tall, lanky figure looked different, now that he had exchanged cricket gear for a smart-looking suit. His holster was just visible, a silver glint coming off the handgun handle. He acknowledged Mansur with a smile and a warm handshake. It was unlike the last time, when Mansur had pointed him in the direction of the dressing room after taking his wicket.

Samir's mood turned serious as soon as he saw the Major. The Major indicated that he needed to talk to Samir alone. Almost simultaneously, a medical team entered to shift Sharon to another room, as she would be discharged in a few hours. Sharon was happy to be leaving the hospital, saying that she wanted to take the first flight back to Mumbai.

'Why Mumbai? Adolf is in Delhi,' said Shaza, giggling. The girls laughed, with everyone looking at them wondering what could be so amusing. Adolf had moved to Delhi one day after the incident as his Embassy wanted to debrief him on the incident and assist him in any way possible.

Everyone cleared out, leaving Major Nikhil and a couple of other CCTC agents with Samir in the room. They wanted to plug some holes in the story. Samir knew in his mind that he had to answer in such a fashion that nothing about *Project Babylon* leaked out to the others. He was a master at deception, and it would not be difficult.

48 DAYS TO EVENT

Sher-e-Kashmir Stadium, Srinagar
Jammu and Kashmir, India

October 24,15:15 IST

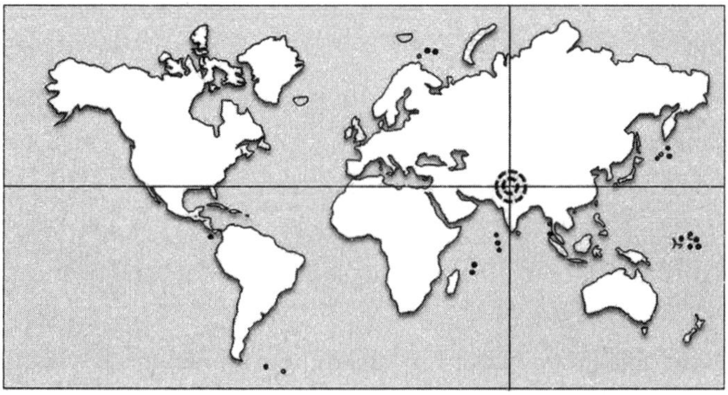

Still shaken by the shooting, Aahana and Shaza wanted to forget what happened and were lying down on the lush green grass outside the playing field and watching the proceedings during practice on the ground. Though the sun was brighter today, it was also windy, and Aahana was having trouble keeping her hair out of her eyes. Both girls went with Mansur to the stadium to watch him practice. The team was preparing for the next game against Mumbai, which was an away match, set to begin next week.

'We better move up to the stands, I am already wet from the dew,' said Shaza as she stood up and checked her clothes.

'So soon! You are too delicate, my princess,' said Aahana as she turned to get on her knees. And with arms on her waist she looked at her friend. Shaza shook her head and extended her arms to Aahana, who took hold of them and sprang up. They walked to the nearest seating area. One of the boys rushed to them holding a couple of glasses of hot *kahwa*. The girls loved the local drink, made up of saffron, cardamom, and green tea leaves.

They sipped from their cups, holding them as is the wont, with both hands, and talked over the past day's events. Shaza asked about Aahana's father's reaction and his subsequent trip, which resulted in a guarded escort being assigned to them. Shaza was worried for Samir, but had also been surprised to see him in action. She knew his interest in shooting but never dreamt that he carried a gun. Aahana calmed Shaza down and said that it was okay, and as soon as Sharon was discharged that evening, she would take her Dad's help to move to Delhi.

'So have you and Mansur talked about that?' Shaza was calmer now.

'About what?'

'You know, you and him…him and you'.

'Nope, we didn't.'

With a frown on her face Shaza placed her right hand over Aahana's left arm.

'Some things are better left unsaid, and sometimes it's better that nothing is said,' said Aahana in a reassuring tone. They both looked at Mansur, who was now bowling at the nets.

Mansur had bowled for over thirty minutes and was now on the trot without a break, looking slightly jaded. The coach was calling out to him to take a break. Mansur said he wanted to keep bowling. Bhatt raised his voice and said, 'Come here…Now! I don't want you to risk getting injured.'

People around the grounds looked at Bhatt. It was not often that Bhatt lost his cool, especially not over urging a player *not* to practice hard. Mansur chugged along towards Bhatt and indicated he wanted to do twenty push-ups. Mansur saw him nodding his head, smiled, and went to the ground and started his push-ups, which he completed in less than half a minute.

'So, you don't think this sort of activity is too risky, do you…eh, coach…eh?' said Mansur, rising and jumping up and down. Bhatt raised his hand and told him to stop. He placed his hand on Mansur's shoulder and started walking. From afar, it looked as if he was walking with the support of Mansur.

'You know how fast you are, right?'

'Yes, coach, speed gun suggests that I'm in the 150 km/hr range,' said Mansur without a sense of pride.

'Right. And what happens to the batsmen when they see you coming at them at that speed?'

'I don't know. Either they hit me out or play defensively.'

'At your speed, Mansur, the batsman's reaction time to play a shot decreases, and so does his ability to think about which shot to play. And as long as you are coming at them quicker they will have to concentrate more,' said Bhatt, trying to emphasise the importance of speed. 'But don't get carried away by speed, as it is also important to maintain line and length.'

'But so far I am doing well in that department,' said Mansur.

'Don't be defensive. The last thing I want on my team is a defensive-minded fast bowler,' said Bhatt, addressing Mansur as if he were his father. 'You are special and you have a gift, a gift every fast bowler wants…to be the quickest and most dangerous. And the fact is you can do it.'

Mansur stopped and bowed down as the coach was now virtually talking into his ear.

'Son, you have a good attitude, one I hope you'll continue to maintain.'

Mansur and Bhatt continued talking for another thirty minutes. Suddenly there was a commotion in the direction of the stadium's administration block. Aahana and Shaza stood up to see what was happening. A couple of personnel ran onto the grounds shouting at the top of their voice. Aahana and Shaza held hands and made their way down onto the grounds. People started converging around Bhatt and Mansur and cheering. Mansur stood frozen for a moment and appeared visibly shocked. Bhatt had his hands in the air, and patted Mansur. As the girls neared the group they saw Mansur and a few other people getting down on the ground and praying.

Aahana thought, *they are thanking God for something.*

Mansur got up and was lifted by the group, with Bhatt now laughing in a peculiar way. Mansur told his friends to put him down as he saw the girls approach. He reached out for Aahana's hand and held it close to him.

Is he going to pop the question in front of everyone? The girls had the same thought. 'I have been selected to play for the national side,' said Mansur in a shaky voice, his hands trembling. His smile widened. Aahana opened her eyes so wide that the dark eyeliner was visible. The girls looked on completely dumbstruck. 'I can't believe it, but whatever it is I think you should rush home quickly and tell your mother and sisters first before the TV stations do,' said Aahana.

Mansur looked at his coach and asked his permission. At first Bhatt looked at him sternly, and then slowly broke into a smile and began laughing. The ground reverberated with laughter. 'Go on now, but tomorrow your real test begins as you have to report to the national coach. I have only one piece of advice left for you: *Learn–unlearn–relearn and keep moving forward.* This is a first for us. I hope you can make us Kashmiris proud and that we will have more like you,' said Amir Bhatt emphatically.

Mansur nodded and raised his right hand, which blocked out the sun now with the sunlight beaming through his fingers, and slowly he closed it to form a fist and pumped it into the air. He turned around and started running.

'You…wait for me,' shouted Shaza looking at Aahana dash towards Mansur. She removed her shoes and followed suit. 'Wait for me.'

'Mansur, hold on let me catch up with you,' shouted Aahana.

'I am not slowing down,' replied Mansur, but he did slow down so that the girls could catch up. Both Mansur and Aahana started laughing as Shaza stood there panting hard, as they put their arms around each other's shoulder.

Back in the hospital Nikhil finished talking with Samir and was satisfied with what he had heard. A couple of hours of hectic discussions, questions, and cross-questions later, Nikhil and the two other CCTC agents left the hospital. Samir breathed a sigh of relief and lay back on the bed, pondering over what steps to take next.

*Ring…ring…*Samir picked up his phone to see who was calling. *Janab Aziz, the B.C.C.I selector is calling.*

'It has been done. Our bomber is inside the pit now,' said Aziz, laughing.

'Oh, my God! That's the best news I have heard all day. I did not know it would be so easy,' said Samir.

'It wasn't, but we managed to pull it off. Now no one can stop us from fulfilling our mission.'

'No, it only makes it more interesting. Mansur remains our messenger, and he will take it straight into the heart. His success will impact the Kashmir valley.'

Yes, he certainly will, and the funny thing is he won't even know about it. I am sorry to use you like this, my friend, thought Samir, feeling sheepish.

He did not mention Major Emraan of Pakistan–neither to Aziz nor to the CCTC agents. This was something he himself had to deal with, he thought as a chill went down his spine. His past had suddenly begun to catch up with him.

40 DAYS TO EVENT

Swedish Embassy,
Delhi, India,

November 1,17:05 IST

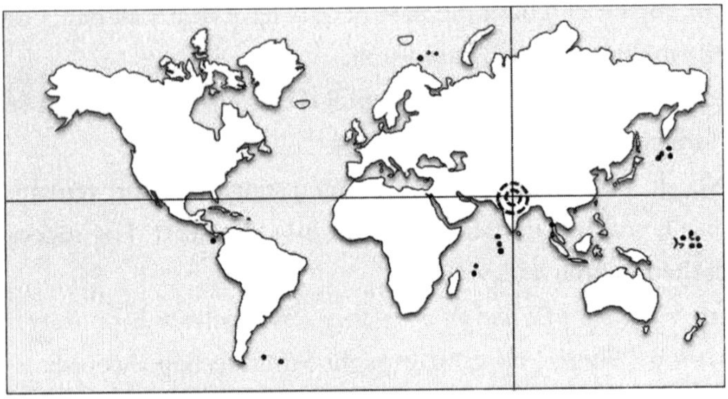

'M**a'am, it does** not make sense…for once I disagree with you. I am positive, Mansur also was their target, not only I,' said Adolf, looking into the twenty-inch screen showing a close-up, larger-than-life image of Carina's face.

Adolf was in Delhi after the Monkey Hill incident. He was initially debriefed by the CCTC agents, and later, at the request of the Swedish Embassy, allowed to go, with the assurance that any information he had would be shared with the Indian establishment. Adolf was now sitting in a fortified room in the Swedish Embassy, and was communicating with Carina. They were talking through a secured video link that was used for clandestine discussions. Back at HQ at Västergötland, Carina did not flinch at that comment. She was looking at something below the screen that Adolf could not see.

'Satellite Surveillance and other inputs from the CIA and MI-6 show that the target was either Aahana or Samir, and their names are now on the airwaves.'

'Screw the inputs. It's all wrong. I was there. They wanted to wipe us all out but their key target was Mansur,' asserted Adolf. He was alone in the room, but looked around in his mind seeking some support. He knew that Carina and the teams were targeting the wrong man. They believed that the Jihadi elements whom he and Samir had killed were trying to kidnap them, leaving alone Mansur, whom they had assumed to be a part of the Jihadi group.

'How are you so sure, Agent 4?' said Carina, addressing Adolf, now with his designated covert agent number.

'I was on the ground and they were shooting not to injure or incapacitate. Those were deadly rounds meant to kill,' said Adolf, now looking more in control. 'Mansur is clean, he is no threat!'

'Do you mean that whatever we have found out so far and the various intelligence communities with whom we are dealing are wrong?'

Adolf nodded, and Carina gave a big sigh and pouted her lips. She turned her face towards the left and nodded. Her face zoomed away. From this perspective Adolf could see that she was sitting at a desk, and then as the camera moved back he could see more people around her. The camera stopped, and he could see three other men sitting beside her.

Our intelligence team. They are also on the call.

'Í am sure you know these gentlemen,' said Carina, spreading her hands out. Adolf nodded. The other members present were the heads of surveillance and covert ops and the political attaché to the government.

'Adolf, I am going to let out something. Something sensitive which should remain with you and you alone. I hope you understand,' said Carina softly. Adolf nodded, and Carina told him about the SIC, the need for it, and how they were cooperating. Adolf listened attentively to Carina and cross-questioned occasionally to check on facts, which were duly answered by the group. His main concern was his cover, which the team assured him, had not been shared.

'So Agent 4, what you are saying is that the hundreds of brains in this operation across the Atlantic are wrong and you are right, just because your guts tell you so,' said Carina, expecting a better explanation from Adolf, ideally one based on logic.

'Let us see what we have got up to this point,' said Adolf, standing up from his off-white cushioned chair. Hands on his hips, and spreading out his black suit, he looked straight up, scratched his stubble and began walking towards one end of the room.

He raised his right hand, and pointed his index finger. 'We have a note from our dead agent Kurt, from Pakistan stating that "*Project Babylon initiated, New Safari Club and potential B.C.C.I support.*" We have a name associated with his message: Mansur. I came here to tail him, but got lucky to find his girlfriend and was able to stick with Mansur. At least long enough to understand that he is probably not a threat and not a Pakistani sympathiser.'

'So what's your point? Carina was fiddling with a paper holder resembling a miniature globe.

'It's too easy, too convenient, like I've been set up,' said Adolf, turning and walking towards the other end of the room.

'You are getting paranoid. Has the engagement shaken you?' asked the head of covert operations in a concerned voice. Carina raised her hand and told him that she would not tolerate such talk. He apologised to both of them.

'It may be a sheer coincidence,' said Carina with a shrug of her shoulders.

'Mansur is clean, there is nothing on him. The terrorists wanted to eliminate him for something else.'

'Probably, but we had another shooter. The CCTC people from Indian Intelligence found some different calibre bullets which were lodged in the head of the terrorist who was shooting at Samir at the top of…Monkey Hill. The bullet was not from Samir's Glock but from another short-range pistol.'

'Any leads on the other shooter?'

'It is assumed by the Indians that it is Special Forces stuff from Pakistan. The shot came from a distance that makes it likely the pistol was from the standard equipment issued to them. Also, no other metal casings were found apart from those from the terrorists' and Samir's guns. So we have to assume that someone from Special Forces could be directly involved and he took only one shot,' said Carina.

'Did Samir say whether he saw anyone?'

Carina shook her head 'Nothing. At least, that's what our Indian counterparts have reported.'

'Okay. The second thing we have, which may or may not be related to the case, is the '*By the rivers of Babylon*' quotes from the Bible,' said Adolf, now raising two fingers of his right hand.

'We are on it, and have been coordinating within the SIC on this one. A joint task force has been set up. We are viewing this one as an assassination attempt based on other local ground Intel in Pakistan from CIA operatives.'

'It can also be used as a recruiting propaganda by the extremists, the Islamist Jihadis.'

'Yes. We read your report regarding how they can use the genocide angle associated with the prayer as propaganda material.'

'And regarding Mansur, I will join him in Srinagar tomorrow.'

'Won't be necessary. He is coming down to Delhi to join the national cricket team for practice. Surprising rise to the national team, as if his destiny is written by God!' said Carina.

Adolf did not react at first but then gave an expression of shock 'Wow! Too soon to be true!' There was then a brief moment of silence in the group.

National cricket team…Mansur…the lion…Safari, in three months from nowhere to national cricket team. This cannot be fate or chance... Kasha–she said search for the sound for peace and I will get my destiny…the CD…Jalal…Yes.

Adolf slowly raised his head; his eyes narrowed and his mouth fell open, slowly.

'Chief, my predecessor who died…I think I know his message now, how he was killed and probably why; just give me a moment. I need to check something.'

Opening his laptop lying on the small polished teak table in front of him, Adolf powered it to life. Clicking on the folder titled *Autopsy* on the desktop screen, Adolf scanned the folder and selected a portable document format (pdf) file kept in the sea of other documents. The file opened and Adolf started reading, his eyeballs moving rapidly. Carina and rest of the SOG team could see the top of Adolf's head in front of the open laptop screen. A couple of minutes later his eyebrows rose slowly, now with a confident look, as he closed the screen shut.

'The autopsy report now makes sense. The body had gone through a zero gravity like trauma, while he was in the safe house in Islamabad; it's like nothing seen on this earth. The last package he received was a CD, from Jalal, and the same person is found on Sweden's shore killing himself and destroying the only thing in his possession, a CD.'

Carina nodded, wondering where this conversation was leading.

'Chief, it's a sonic weapon we are talking about.' He stopped for a moment with Kasha's voice ringing in his head.

Listen to the sound of the universe–the beginning and the end. To master it you need to fight your destiny.

'Adolf, where is the logic?'

Adolf was confident and smiling as things began to fall in place. Mikaela's reference to manipulating sound to create emotions like an orgasm and Kasha's urging him to search for the sound to get internal peace.

Could it be possible that the ISI or the Chinese have managed to harness the power of sound to kill—a sonic weapon?

'Chief, sound can be used for its psycho-physiological effects to create distortion of the mind and body; it can help in creating euphoria, distortion. In fact even silence is used as a torture technique. The individual feels suffocated, causing psychological trauma during an envelope of silence. And it's not necessary we need to hear it to feel it.'

'Isn't it far-fetched to think about it this way?' One of the analysts sitting besides Carina questioned Adolf's theory but a sharp disapproving look from Carina shut him up.

'I don't think so Bjorn. There is research conducted in this area and the US defence forces have created acoustic or sonic weapons which aim at incapacitating targets, but not killing them.'

'Ja! You are right Adolf, and just hold on a moment team; I need to show you something.'

Analyst Stephanie joined in supporting Adolf's theory; she swiftly moved her smooth hands on her keyboard

'There is US patent 6,017,302 filed in 2000 for "Subliminal Acoustic Manipulation of Nervous Systems," and another for an acoustic cannon way back in 1999, both positioned as non-lethal weapons for crowd control.'

She showed the patent along with the description and related diagrams. A couple of short videos of the acoustic cannon and a weapon system known as LRAD, were uploaded, as she explained its working to the group.

'See how this weapon system, LRAD, *long range acoustic device* was used by the US navy on the Somali pirates in November 2005. It lets out a piercing 150 decibels sound causing temporary blindness or nausea on the target. And not to forget American soldiers during the first Iraq war bombarded Saddam's fleeing soldiers running towards Basra with *rock* and *grunge* music. All these are psychological manipulations to break down the opponent's will.' Stephanie now sat back with a gentle smile, satisfied that she could help the discussion move forward.

'Hmmm, so there is precedence. But why would Kurt not send the message about the weapon directly? Unless he did not know such a weapon existed.'

Adolf jumped in, 'Yes Ma'am, you may be right, he did not know about the weapon, and the message he sent could be like a puzzle and someone would need to look at it like an *apophenia* technique.'

'Apophenia…WHAT!' The SOG members sitting in Sweden were common in their shock and ignorance.

'Apophenia is the experience to see patterns in meaningless data, like he wanted us to guess and link events. He could be passing a message…a distress call…with the hidden messages,' said Adolf, who had stopped strolling now and was looking directly at them.

'Remember, he specifically wanted me; he knew me as we were in the same NATO company in Afghanistan, same dinner table, for over a year. We backed each other. Kurt Edberg knew I loved puzzles and codes. He wanted me to break it!'

Carina and the others in her group looked around, surprised to hear such a far-fetched idea being put forth. Carina wanted to hear more about this theory and told Adolf to continue.

'B.C.C.I. may not be Bank of Credit and Commerce International or anything related to it,' whispered Adolf.

'What? What did you say? B.C.C.I. is not a financing institute?' Carina shifted in her chair.

'It may be. But it may also, I believe, stand for *Board of Control for Cricket in India*, basically the group that not only makes sure how the cricket structure is run in the country but also selects the national team. And it makes more sense, SAFARI–may not be an acronym but a synonym for Lion aka Mansur, which means Lion in Urdu, and what is left to us is to understand what Project Babylon is?'

This new angle piqued Carina's interest as well as that of the others in Sweden.

Adolf could be making sense, thought Carina.

Adolf spoke with an eager tone now, 'If Mansur is guilty, as you assert, then he is planning to do something deadly! And if not…he could be used to accomplish that deadly job…a host…and not the virus in this case. My counterpart was already tracking Mansur before he was taken out.'

A deathly silence enveloped the conference. The common thought echoing in their minds was that if Adolf was right then something had to be done quickly about it.

'We have a few Babylon word posts in the air. The intercepts don't make any sense right now, but the frequency has increased,' said the systems chief.

'But if I remember correctly, you said these posts were originating from Pakistan, India, Nigeria, and Greece,' said Carina.

He nodded and continued. 'It could be routed from anywhere if the digital footprints are tampered with. Only with detailed tracking can one create a map.'

'I assume you are at it.'

'Yes, we are. As we are busy with the coding exercises of the holy texts, our resources are stretched,' he said with an air of desperation. 'But I will make it happen.'

'Good. Get me something I can use in the next 48 hours…Team dismissed. I will talk to Adolf alone.'

As they left the room, many thoughts traversed Carina's mind. She was pondering whether or not she should bring Agastya into this.

Agastya may take it the wrong way if he comes to know that we have an on-going covert operation in his country, but India knows more and is hiding the information from us.

'Adolf,' she said, addressing him by his first name, 'there is something big cooking. The Chinese are also playing hardball now due to their internal political tussles. The Indians are counteracting that and building their forces around the border. The Americans want to get out of everything at some point and be everywhere at the same time. The British are stretched.'

'Do I assume I am on my own here then?' asked Adolf.

'Aren't we all?' said Carina. Adolf smiled, and winked at Carina.

Carina raised her eyebrows in surprise.

'Don't worry, I will make it happen.'

'I know you will, just make sure that you get yourself back here, safe and sound. Speaking of sound, how can you be sure a sonic weapon is involved here?'

'I understand your apprehension and sense of disbelief, but it may be a historical reference, if we think of the Bible as part of history, which can help us out with the kind of weapon we are talking about here.'

'Go on.'

'Joshua 6:5, And it shall come to pass, that when they make a long blast with the rams' horn, and when ye hear the sound of the trumpet, all the people shall shout with a great shout; and the wall of the city shall fall down flat, and the people shall ascend up every man straight before him.' Adolf recited it like a poem memorised.

'Fall of the Walls of Jericho, 1400 BC.'

'Importantly, Joshua led the attack with his people commanded to walk around the city for seven days in silence, and on the seventh day the horns were blown along with a shout from the people. And the walls came down.'

'I am surprised at your knowledge of "Christianity" now; you still registered as an "atheist"?' said Carina.

'Well…I still hold my position. Being an atheist does not mean I don't read the Bible. And to think of it, by knowing the Bible I can question its relevance. Besides, this example is from a book I read recently.'

'Which book?'

'*Anahata Nada: the Unmade Sound of the Universe*, written by a Buddhist monk with a doctorate in meta-physics, and it speaks about the power of sound in our life and the relevance of an ancient Hindu chant, "AUM" or "OM". It claims that the "great shout" before the fall of Jericho was this sacred chant.'

'Interesting. Send in the details to Stephanie, let her dig up something.' Carina saw Adolf nodding and typing on his laptop as he started sending the details, 'I hope we are not on the wrong track.'

'Time will decide.'

Time or destiny, thought Carina.

'Adolf, just do me a favour. Whatever happens, keep me posted and don't take unnecessary risks. I don't want to lose another colleague,' Carina spoke with a tone of concern as both looked at each other without showing any emotion on the face.

'So you off to Kashmir again?'

'Yes, I will, and after checking a few things I need to do some on-the-ground investigation in Dharamshala…to gather some more information on this sonic weapon.'

'Why Dharamshala?'

'It's the only place where I can find Tibetan monks and the resources which can actually answer the questions I have.'

'What questions?'

'The answer to the sound of the universe.'

38 DAYS TO EVENT

Rail line to Dharamshala,
Himachal Pradesh, India

November 3,03:50 IST

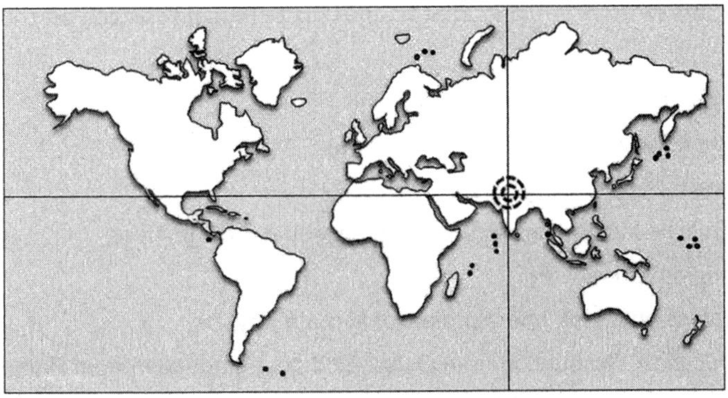

The Jammu Mail express train from Delhi to Pathankot halted with a sudden brake. Adolf, comfortably asleep in the AC compartment, was jolted awake. The train had stopped; pulling up the right sleeve of his green cardigan, he looked at his watch; 3.50 am.

Damn the driver jerking the brake so suddenly, must be a greenhorn. Got to be Jalandhar, at this time of the night...

Adolf pulled the side curtain of his small cabin window to check if he could see any station name on the platform. He ran his sleepy eyes around the platform till he saw a yellow board not so far away. It read Ludhiana.

I knew it, two hours behind schedule to reach Pathankot from here if I was lucky. Well on the bright side, at least I get some more sleep.

He pulled back the heavy embroidered curtains, adjusted himself on the bunk, and looked at the other passenger sharing the cabin. He did not move a muscle and was sleeping like a child. Adolf guessed the man must be used to this as a frequent traveller. Pulling the grey blanket only till lower chest, Adolf cherished the air conditioning chill in the cabin; it reminded him of home.

I wonder what kind of person Dr Gomin Tamang would be. He sounded OK for me to come down and meet him in person as a literary agent from Europe who wants to know more about his theories personally before trying to launch his book in

Europe. If he is able to elaborate on what he has written in his book, and answers, it will be worth the long shot coming here.

Adolf closed his eyes and visualised Dr Gomin Tamang's bald pate and cheerful face. In his mind be began to revise his bio report based on inputs from Stephanie at SOG and his personal research on the web.

Name: Dr Gomin Tamang

Age: 65 years

Status: Single

Ethnicity: Indian-Nepali origin with ancestral roots in Tibet.

Religion: Buddhism

Profession: Monk and a professor in meta-physics,

Education: Graduation from Oxford and post-graduation from Princeton.

Area of interests: Metaphysical cosmology, primarily dealing with the questions of origin, matter present and the purpose of the universe.

About his Book: *Anahata Nada: The Unmade Sound of the Universe*

- The book speaks about the "*Anahata Nada,*" the uncreated sound in the universe.
- According to his book, a primordial sound is present in the universe since the beginning, which can be written as "A-U-M".
- This sound is the prime reason harmony exists between matters.
- Usage of this primordial sound "AUM," along with mantras creates benefits to the human body.
- It speaks of how therapeutic music can be created using the same principle.

The book speaks more about the benefits of health and organs. But is the converse true…can sound kill?

Adolf dozed off with many questions in his mind that went right back to Kurt's autopsy report which spoke of systemic organ failure leading to his death.

Three hours later, bearing the cacophony of noises around him on the platform, Adolf kept his composure. The appointment with Dr Gomin Tamang was a lunch meeting fixed at two. Ample time, thought Adolf; he would first refresh himself in one of the lodges in Dharamshala. He walked along the cracked up platform undergoing repairs and headed for the exit. A few excited taxi drivers came up to him offering different rates. He politely declined indicating he would move out to the main street and decide. A colourful man with a flimsy shirt and loose pants approached him, and stuck his face before Adolf.

'Fifteen thousand rupees for two hours, place provided.'

'What?'

'You are such a rugged man, for you ten thousand…at least come and see my girls, they will make you happy between your legs.'

'Hey I think you got the wrong person, dude.'

'You don't want *nirvana?* This is the best place for it, all kinds of taste I take care…ahhh…you want a man, I can give that also.'

'Listen, whatever your name is, just take me to the destination I asked for; that will be all. Otherwise, I am picking up another driver.' Looking at the address the colourfully dressed driver's frown changed to a naughty smile.

'Ahaa! You go for personal party, lovely tandoori legs she had.'

'What are you speaking of? I think I will take another taxi.' Adolf snatched the address slip from him and turned along with his half full backpack towards another taxi, a Tavera, across the street. As he was crossing, the pimp was still shouting, 'Come back here if she does not satisfy you.' *Crazy pimp! In the land of the Dalai Lama. I wonder what he meant by tandoori legs.* Adolf talked to the driver in the other taxi, shared the address of Dr Gomin Tamang, and sat behind in the black Chevrolet Tavera. The final price negotiated for the hundred plus kilometre ride was seven thousand rupees (almost over a hundred and fifty USD) for a return trip.

Should have taken a chauffeur-driven vehicle from the embassy, but did not want to make it obvious. Besides, literary agents don't travel in embassy vehicles.

As Dharamshala approached, the scenery changed from plains to rugged ranges in the horizon. In no time, the air felt fresher, crisper and the surroundings mystical as the green quotient increased. The total journey from Pathankot to Dharamshala would take close to two hours and another hour or so to reach Dr Gomin Tamang's house, which meant he had two hours to refresh himself. So the first stop was a local hotel.

Fresh after a nice shower and heavy breakfast of Spanish omelette and a hearty bowl of Tibetan styled porridge, made of highland barley laden with dry fruits, he looked forward to interacting with the meta-physicist monk. After an hour of driving away from the town in the direction of Kotwali Bazaar in lower Dharamshala, Adolf's taxi drew up in front of Dr Tamang's house.

They were out in the open fields and tracts of green now, as the taxi reached a red coloured duplex bungalow. The driver got out and opened the small four-feet tall wrought iron gate. Adolf saw a small temple-like structure beside the bungalow on the eastern side. A stream of about thirteen Tibetan prayer wheels was in front of the temple whose entrance seemed both direct and also from the house. The bulky Tavera hammered along the uneven path bouncing the occupants along, as they moved in the opposite direction of the temple towards a couple of parked vehicles, attended by two neatly dressed drivers.

One of drivers standing beside a Tata Indica started talking excitedly with Adolf's driver. Adolf got off the car, slung his backpack behind him, and adjusted it while looking towards the magnificent bungalow and large glassy windows at the walls. His driver informed him that the other driver informed him about a lady he brought there an hour back. Adolf nodded and instructed the driver to wait for a few hours as they would be travelling back in the evening. A leopard skin cat suddenly sprang out of nowhere and ran across Adolf's path. He stopped a moment and continued walking in the same direction.

A lady here, it must be the tandoori legged lady which that pimp was referring to. Another visitor, or may be a relative, as Dr Tamang told, enough time would be given to my discussion.

Patches of sunlight pierced through the clouds and gently warmed Adolf. He walked up the stairs, towards the raised main porch and entered the house whose glass doors were already slid open. He studied the drawing room which was a mixture of old Tibetan and Nepali architecture, with brightly coloured drapes, wooden furniture and paintings. The marble floor tiles were colourful with different mosaic patterns. A couple of hammocks swung beside the door which he crossed. He was not alone; a woman stood studying a painting on the wall; one of her hands was placed gently on her hips clad in a pair of figure hugging white jeans, with a visible royal crown in black, stitched onto the back pockets, and a full sleeved black T-shirt.

It can't be she…it is!

As the feminine figure turned around, she moved her curvy waist slowly and then faced Adolf directly. Aahana!

'There is some butter tea left in the pot, and you can make yourself comfortable,' she said pointing in the direction of the red couch in front of her. A mahogany side table was placed beside the couch with a steaming blue tea kettle and couple of cups lying on it, 'Dr Tamang is with his ancestors and will join us later.'

'What are you doing here?' asked the shocked Swede.

Aahana gave a sensuous smile and said, 'Sit down; we have a lot to talk about…but first I want to know who you are…friend or foe?'

38 DAYS TO EVENT

Dharamshala,
Himachal Pradesh, India,

November 3,13:45 IST

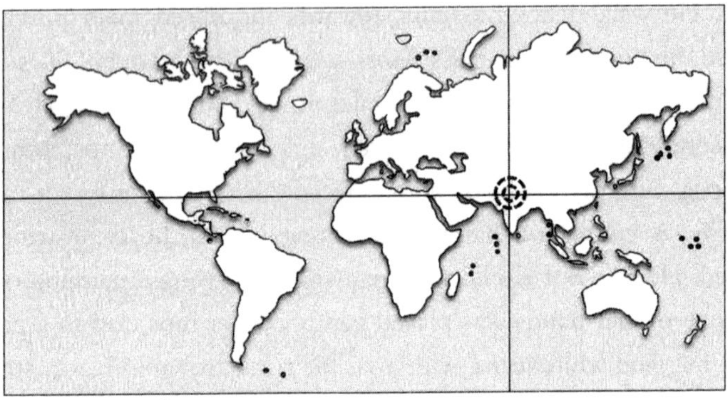

A fresh crisp breeze was blowing inside the well ventilated oval shaped drawing room. Two known faces sat facing each other, quiet but for their non verbal body language. Aahana sat comfortably with her legs crossed and a glint in her eye; Adolf sat cautiously sipping tea. Someone had to break the ice and it looked as if Adolf was more desperate for answers. Keeping the cup on the side, he leaned forward.

'So you were expecting me?'

'No, and yes.'

Adolf looked confused.

'Well, when I came here, I didn't expect you to be here, Dr Tamang told me a Swede literary agent, Adolf is coming in. So I had a sort of idea that it could be you.'

'Ok, so you know Dr Tamang?'

'Yes we had interacted in the past during my theoretical physics classes, back in Oslo; he was a visiting professor there, from Princeton.'

'Cosmic–metaphysics.'

'Yes for the class, but more off-line discussion happened on different areas of physics, theology....you name it.'

Adolf was trying to size up that a simple student-teacher interaction would not bring her here. There was something else to this visit.

'My turn now,' said Aahana sitting confidently, her arms on the arm rests. 'You lied…the terrorist who attacked us on Monkey Hill, was familiar to you, right?'

Adolf did not react suddenly at this question, just narrowed his eyes slightly, expecting Aahana to go further along her line of questioning, elaborate more.

'The bald man you killed was the same person you were staring at from the library a month back…and you were trying to find addresses of certain phone numbers.'

Adolf opened his eyes slightly wide and made a mental map of the gun stuck in his back, hidden under the jacket he was wearing.

'So Adolf, are you a friend or a foe?'

'What do you think?'

'A friend, but I have been wrong before.'

'So, you tell me more and I tell you more about me.'

Adolf had a cover story which could be verified by the authorities in India and Sweden.

'Why does it always have to be ladies first?'

Aahana looked up towards the ceiling, closed her eyes and with a slight tremble in her body, continued to speak. 'Ok, before I move ahead, just tell me if you know about Linda Ming Choy, from China.' Adolf nodded.

So she is connected to the missing mountaineers. How come we missed that link?

'I am investigating her case and also the others…which I "presume" you know,' said Adolf with a slow pace, emphasising more towards the end. They locked eyes, Aahana's brown ones against Adolf's blue.

Ok, it's time to go for gut instinct now. My back up cover story should hold good.

'Listen Aahana, I am an Interpol Police Officer,' said Adolf, removing an ID from the inner pocket of his jacket and holding it out before her, as she read it.

Adolf Silfverskiöld, Chief Inspector, Interpol, Sweden Wing

'So you are continuing your predecessor Kurt's work, about Shaksgam valley?'

She knows Kurt! Did he try to contact her?

'How do you know Kurt…what…? O.K. Aahana let's get things straight now and tell me how you have reached here…and what do you know about what is happening?'

Aahana waited for a few moments, her arms folded together and legs uncrossed as she leaned forward. Her intense look did not change, her eyes held his.

'As you must be now aware, I belong to the Nordic Rockers mountaineering club from Oslo as the climbers who were in Shaksgam valley earlier in the year.' Adolf nodded.

The more one loop closes, the more others open up.

'I was supposed to join them but could not make it. Five of us were very close and relied on each other. I hope you understand what I am trying to say.'

'Yes I do,' Adolf clasped his hands together and leaned forward.

'Something happened when they reached the site. They were supposed do some basic assimilation on the Chinese side before moving ahead for K2 and meeting up with other climbers from the Pakistan side. But when they reached the point, it wasn't the same as it was a year back when one of us had gone there scouting the place.'

'What difference did they see?'

'The site was semi flattened in some places with charred trees which still stood surprisingly strong as before.'

'That's interesting and complies with the details that we got from our satellite reconnaissance,' said Adolf calmly.

'That's the least of the worries; what was more worrisome was the presence of animal carcasses lying across, and the area was being sanitised by Chinese and Pakistani forces there.'

So there was a test conducted there.

'Adolf, they were frightened. The animals…wait!' Aahana stretched her legs to pull out her mobile from her right front pocket and flipped it open.

'There are photos, let me show you.'

Aahana pulled out the digital shots taken of the area by her dead friends' satellite phone. Adolf began to study them, zooming in and out over the touch screen. Camels' bodies were strewn across with different body parts incongruously bloated. While some had swollen heads, others had their humps or legs in disorderly shapes; in each case the eyes seemed to protrude. Birds lay dead, huddled together with their wings spread apart.

'I would like to have these photos, for my team back in France (Interpol cover) and Sweden.'

'Sure, by all means pass it on,' said Aahana, getting up and going back to the couch opposite and slumping on the soft cushions. Adolf sent the pictures to his number.

'So why weren't they stopped before by the establishment?'

'They were two weeks into the expedition and out of communication range. Details of their satellite phone were not known to many. Linda could pull a lot of strings. Her dad is the one of the biggest industrialists in China.'

Adolf listened patiently, mentally trying to put in the missing pieces. *Linda was the missing climber from the group and unaccounted for.*

'Can you reach her now?'

'No…she may be in hiding or dead, I don't know. The problem came up as they were directly taken to Rawalpindi in Pakistan, and then released in Islamabad. Nothing was done to them, just a protective escort and later released…but they were escorted by our terrorist from Monkey Hill.'

'What?'

'Yes, there are photos of him…see it as you flip ahead in the album,' said Aahana pointing towards her phone. Adolf moved his finger quickly over the touch screen, and stopped on seeing the familiar face. It looked more like Jalal having a good crop of hair.

Jalal, how does he move from China to Pakistan and to India?

'I would need to send all of these back to my team,' he requested softly. Aahana nodded.

'Thanks.'

'I recognised the person; I saw him in Dharamshala when you were looking at him but was not sure, and when you killed him back on

Monkey hill, seeing him that close was enough to convince me that they were after me; I was enquiring about the same number a month back but without results. Now I feel it could have been you also.'

Or Mansur, thought Adolf.

'Where is Kurt?'

'Kurt is dead.'

'Oh my God! May God bless his soul. How did he die?' asked Aahana in a sober tone.

'Well that's sort of classified, but it was not pleasant.'

Aahana was silent, and both looked at each other with empathetic eyes conveying it all.

'I have a few images which Kurt also shared…just a minute,' Adolf opened his backpack to remove his laptop. Aahana came behind Adolf now and they waited patiently for it to power-up.

'See these images…they are geometric shapes and other lines and boxes. Do they mean anything?'

Aahana gazed at them, her eyes lit up first as they looked familiar, but then looked closely at the images.

'You seem to recognise it.'

'Yes it looked familiar to me, as I have seen these patterns before, but I don't think it is…it can't be.'

'What?'

'Well not all five images, but I am sure of three of them; I did see them in Mansur's place.'

'Mansur's place?'

'I mean his rug, his prayer carpet-rug…but the images are in an inverse on the rug.'

'Opposite.'

'Yes, like this pentagon shaped box with three lines in the shape of flowers across are left to right at the corners on his rug.'

'And here it is right to left with a small circle in between.'

'Yes…precisely.'

'Kurt did not mention what it was?'

'Just images, we got, it may be random or common…'

'But we should not rule anything out.'

'Yes. Carpets. Interesting. Will pass that information to my team. You sure know Mansur's things well.'

Aahana smiled and walked back to settle down at her earlier place.

'Need to restructure his life one day…right.'

'Yeah…right…how soon is this restructuring?' asked Adolf in a teasing tone.

'Only after I get to know what happened to my friend Linda, and others.'

'So we hope the professor has some answers for us,' said Adolf. 'Our meeting here is sheer coincidence, and of course, getting these points across in this sudden manner. But why are you here meeting Dr Tamang?'

Adolf heard the soft bare footsteps behind him. Aahana looked up, Adolf stood up and turned. He saw an elderly, portly man, five feet five, almost bald with a single cluster of hair running across the outer periphery of his head.

'*Aum Mani Padme Hum*,' greeted Dr Gomin Tamang adjusting an orange cloak around his bare chest, and holding out his hands towards them. '*Aum Mani Padme Hum*,' Aahana replied, smiling and touching his feet as a sign of greeting. Adolf stood by and nodded his head, giving a faint smile.

'Sorry to keep you waiting, we Tamangs believe in worshipping our ancestors. It is called "Bonism," a tradition,' said the cheerful monk as he moved swiftly from one end of the hall to another.

'Some of them are happy you both are here…my ancestors that is. Especially my ancestor who fought World War I for the British Empire, seems to be most interested,' he broke into a small laughter and called for his servants to get the table ready for lunch. Adolf checked the time. 2.15 pm.

'Come…come…we have a lot to catch up,' said the monk, waving his hands to follow him.

'Yes we do,' said Adolf. They started walking with the monk speeding ahead at a steady pace.

'And regarding your statement back there…your meeting my lovely girl here as co-incidence...I don't think so.' The monk's laughter reverberated in the hallway.

'Do you think there is free will in this world, does everything happen for a reason, my children?' The monk slowed down to let the young couple catch up and put his old arms around them. Adolf had to lower himself.

'You were supposed to come here and both of you came here, no free will, only universal determinism; every random behaviour has a pattern and it's pre-destined.'

Over a hearty Tibetan lunch of meat baozi and tsampa as starters and baked meat with bean noodles cooked in the Sichuan style, Adolf introduced himself to Dr Tamang. Aahana asked him to tell the truth; after all, she too was on a mission for which she had approached Dr Tamang for help—to find out what happened to her friend Linda Choy.

Aahana told Adolf that Linda passed on more messages to her from her home in China, apart from the photograph which she shared with Adolf. She had a recording of a blank call sent by her friend just before she disappeared, but not before Linda mentioned that her body was undergoing changes, with rigor mortis setting in one leg and swelling of one of her palms.

'The call originated from Dharamshala,' she extended her hand with her mobile and showed the number to Adolf.

'It's the same number Kurt got a call from.'

'Yes we were approaching the same issue from opposite angles… and I also reached out to Dr Tamang like you. Only difference was that he was my professor when I was a student in Oslo.'

Dr Tamang did not contribute much during this discussion but listened to both sides patiently, only adding details around the food and the stories behind them. The servants came and placed silver metallic bowls with lukewarm water, with rose petals in it. They began cleaning their palms and fingers in it, and wiped it dry with the soft sunlight yellow hand towel placed besides it. As soon as the servants left, he turned his attention to his two companions.

'It's about sound and how it can be used, for good and for bad. Aahana shared the recording with me, a blank call apparently without noise, but there was noise in it; the frequency was not audible to human ears.'

Adolf's face registered his confusion. He said, 'Sorry, physics was never my strong point, unlike chemistry.'

'Hmm....but there is some biology in it, my son.' The monk snapped at the interruption. 'I like it...love being a teacher....Let's start with the basics,' he clapped his hands in excitement. Aahana gave a small giggle. Adolf did not look amused, but he smiled back.

'Humans can hear sound within certain frequencies, from the lower end at twenty hertz till the upper end of twenty thousand hertz. So the sound waves which our ears receive can be divided into three categories–infrasound, acoustic and ultrasound. What you are hearing from me right now falls within this acoustic or hearing range. For anything above the hearing limit or below, "different" rules apply, ultrasound, is the sound above our hearing range, and at the other end there is infrasound.'

'Yes I do know about infra, the sounds below our hearing capability, some animals like elephants can sense it, and tigers release it during an attack to paralyse their prey.' Adolf was brimming with confidence as the discussion inched towards familiar territory. 'And there are weapons being tested around this theory but without much success. Are you telling the call which Linda Ming Choy and the others received was a killing infrasound sound?'

'You need to have patience my son, step by step. Let's move to my study, more space for discussion there.'

Dr Tamang arose swiftly from his chair and started moving down the hallway; he had an infectious spring in his step. Aahana and Adolf duly followed him, this time keeping pace with him.

'Hmmm…it's going to rain,' they all looked out at the glass screens lining the hallway.

Dark clouds were forming, and light had begun to drop around the hills. Dr Tamang instructed his servants to switch on the lights. Climbing up the stairs to the first floor, the visitors came upon the essence of the house. If the ground floor was about furnishing and décor, the study was about both décor and design, an oval room carpeted from wall to wall. There were long Tibetan prayers flags draped on the walls.

One part of the room had a red flag with a background of snow covered mountain ranges and a lion in the foreground looking up at the sky, towards the white fiery shaped clouds challenging it. Diagonally opposite was a purple flag with the mythical bird *Garuda* flying with a serpent held in its claws as it tried to break the snake's neck with its beak. Various traditional metallic and porcelain Tibetan artefacts were placed across the room on the modularly designed oak wood shelves.

The wall shelves were stacked with books of varying sizes and colours. A blackboard on the wall divided the two shelves, and a mobile white board was kept on the side with four cushioned chairs around it. A study table in the right corner faced east with glass windows behind and in front of it. This table, despite the files, rolled up charts and paper on it was off-beat compared to the room, with a turquoise coloured twenty-seven inch Apple iMac with speakers and multiple accessories supporting it. Both visitors gazed at the magnificent machine, and were clearly impressed by what they saw.

'Its colour goes well with the background,' commented the monk, running his hand on the top of the screen.

'They have developed the art of pleasing the eyes with colour and design, or in fact pleasing the human soul.' He moved towards the whiteboard.

'So my children, if Apple can please your eyes with such designs, and there is music which relaxes your mind and soul, just imagine if someone tampers the mind with sound.'

They sat down in a triangular formation, their chairs facing one another.

'It all begins with the understanding of the primordial sound "A-U-M". There is a cosmic scheme where everything is so simple that when we put our mind and soul into it we can not only decipher it, but also find the formulae which makes it tick and control it.'

Both listened to the old monk intently, Aahana with her heart, and Adolf, his mind.

'Everything is governed by balance—positive to negative, woman to man and so on, like law. Similarly, there are laws controlling this universe which are calibrated to the minimum of minute details, so that you, I, everything in this planet and on others can exist.'

'You mean aliens?' Adolf asked.

'Maybe,' the monk guffawed. 'There is cause and effect in everything, my son, one thing always leads to another. You pull one string, a cascading impact occurs, and another event takes place.'

'I get the cause and effect part, but how does it relate to our question?' Adolf's query was laced with his irritation.

'Patience…*thaam*…slow and steady, my children. Why are we standing upright? When we jump what pulls us down?'

They both looked at each other knowing the answer, feeling embarrassed at the easy question which had no relevance, but they decided to play along.

'Gravity,' Aahana replied and Adolf nodded.

'Yes, without gravity there would be no force to pull matter together and hold to form planets or stars. In a similar way without a nucleus force, no proton or electron would be held together to form an atom. Without groups of atoms coming together, no organism, or life as we know it. If electromagnetic forces are absent, then…?'

'I get what you mean; it would result in no bonding between the various chemicals. As I told you my chemistry is not that weak,' said Adolf winking at the monk.

'Yes so like these, there are multiple rules which govern our universe. These are all finely tuned, God's own strings. Any change or distortion in this and life as we know can end.'

'A formulae as you say. Who has made it?'

'It was always there, it was for us to find out. It can only be done if we apply ourselves to it,' said Dr Tamang and continued after taking a deep breath, 'Well isn't it said in the Genesis, Bible, chapter 1, verse 27, "So God created man in his own image, in the image of God he created them; male and female he created them," so if that is true then we can do what god does.'

They stared at him.

'Manipulate and control, that's the answer you are looking at. Every atom is in a state of energy vibration, in flux. Manipulating these atoms using "*Mantras*" or sacred utterances can create a powerful force not seen before.'

'I read about these *mantras* in your book and their ability to connect with the atoms at the base level using a collaborating frequency.' said Adolf.

'Yes, you are right, my son, as the frequency of the atoms starts matching that of the *mantra*, the target atom loses its properties. The *mantra* overrides the matter which behaves in a manner the *mantra* wants it to.'

'Adolf, one of my projects during my studies in theoretical physics was sound acting like a directed energy beam to enable it to act as a levitating agent,' said Aahana as she unlocked her crossed legs and leaned forward in her chair. Adolf and Dr Tamang turned their gaze towards Aahana.

'Acoustic levitation can be achieved in laboratories. Sound has power to lift solid objects, to act like a particle beam. I will not be surprised if it can be done on the outer periphery of matter, then it is definitely possible to do it on the inside, at the molecular level.'

'Yes, you are so right, it is so good if you know physics like that and keep an open mind,' said the monk, guffawing loudly now. He cleared his throat and continued, 'Sound can be used to manipulate the air and atmosphere around; in fact Dr Nasir Raja is one of the predominant scientists and thinkers in this area. Wish we could exchange a few thoughts, but he never responds.'

Dr Nasir Raja. Maybe this old monk does have a point. There is a pattern despite the randomness in this madness. But sacred chants and primordial sound is still hard to believe.

'Dr Tamang, please enlighten me…How will this chanting impact the human body?'

Dr Tamang got up and walked swiftly to his right towards one of the wall shelves. He reached out on tiptoes for a book in the top row. Taking it over to the centre table, he opened the fifteen by twelve inch long illustrative book on the human nervous system. He started flipping the glossy pages, finally stopping at a section that had an illustrative diagram of the human nervous system on both sides of the page.

'When we study the impact of the primordial sound "*AUM*", on the human nervous system, it acts both on the sympathetic and parasympathetic areas.' The monk pointed his index finger to the left page and then the right.

'You mean the nerves which control the various internal body organs and allows for transmission of neural messages to and from the brain to the organs?' said Adolf as he gazed at the illustrations.

'Yes, the sympathetic nervous system controls most functions of the body organs, like dilation of the pupil for the eye, increasing the rate of contraction for the heart and even ejaculation for the penis.' The monk waited for a moment and continued, 'These functions are the ones which we can see and act upon in our conscious state. It also helps the body to react when it is under stress. That is the fight or flight response.'

'Yeah! I get that. When I see danger what do I do? Do I stay back and fight or do I run away?'

'Correct. The parasympathetic nervous system regulates activities of the internal organs and glands which we need or do in an unconscious state. Things like digestion, shedding tears, sexual arousal among others. The "A (aaaa)" and "U (oooo)" act on the sympathetic nervous system, and the "M (mmmm)" acts on the parasympathetic nerves."

'So chanting of "AUM" provides positive and beneficial results as it brings the mind to a stable rhythm.'

'Yes, you are right my son. But your tone suggests that you are not convinced, not yet.' He smiled.

Aahana shook her head in disapproval and looked at Adolf. 'Come on, Adolf, theoretical physicists did base some of their theories on the Vedas and non-linear ideas. An open mind here can help us find an answer.'

'Yes, but isn't space vacuum, and if my physics is right, no sound can exist in vacuum,' Adolf held his stand.

The doctor monk kept his patience and calm. 'My son, did you know that electromagnetic waves in vacuum behave in ways similar to those of sound in gas?'

Adolf nodded in agreement and referred to the idea in the monk's book. The scientist's name was Tesla, and he was associated with electromagnetic theories, with his name used as a standard unit of magnetic flux density.

'And sound is basically a pressure wave, which when it hits matter, causes resonance or vibrations to happen within that matter.' Dr Tamang slid his bare arms to both his ears and gave a toothy smile, 'sound waves of what I am talking, are hitting my ear drums inside where they oscillate and vibrate to create meaning for me.'

To their amusement, he jiggled his ear.

'The entire earth and universe consists of such vibrations of matter...stationary motion with the smallest parts of the atoms, always vibrating and spinning. When a matter is hit by a sound resonance or vibrations happen and on hitting the right frequency matter can be altered, as resonance stores enormous amount of energy not seen by us, but which can be manipulated, and the primordial sound "AUM" can help us harmonise.'

'Basically your theory holds that by manipulating this primordial chant "AUM" along with some Sanskrit *mantras* we can actually take control of another matter.'

'Give me a moment,' the smiling Buddhist monk took up a piece of chalk and drew a symbolic representation of "AUM" on the blackboard. While making the curves in the symbol the monk pressed the chalk hard to scratch on the board making a screeching noise which vibrated through the oval shaped room. Aahana and Adolf felt a discomfort. Aahana closed her eyes, turned her head to right, and Adolf grimaced, squinting his eyes.

'Oh, very sorry! Sound impacting your genes.' He apologised with a mischievous smile, turned slowly back to the board and continued writing. He wrote the words A-U-M vertically besides the symbol of "AUM" and continued writing for a few more moments as the two questioners looked on.

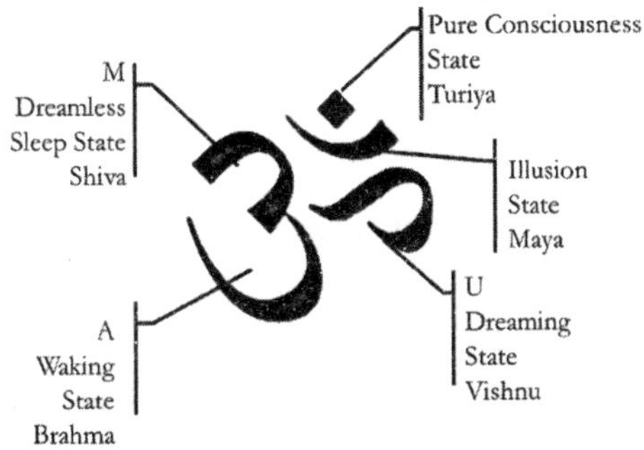

'When you look into the details of "AUM," modern science has found that it symbolises a number of different things and works in different parts of the body. While chanting the first part "A" the waking state, the resonance is felt in the abdomen which then moves into the chest when we recite the second part "U," the dreaming state. Finally, reciting the third part "M," the deep sleep state, the vibrations are felt in the head.'

He closed his eyes and began chanting "AUM" loudly. His voice vibrated across the room, its echo bounced back and forth. The chants continued and they watched the bald monk breathe in a rhythmic manner every time he finished the chant.

The acoustics of the rooms are made to enhance such vibrations, thought Adolf, feeling less sceptical.

Slowly the vibration began to resonate inside him and Aahana, almost hit them in the chest. Dr Tamang stopped chanting, opened his eyes and looked at Adolf, and he saw the changed expression in his eyes.

'I agree; it does have some impact.'

'Yes, it does Adolf; it is one of the many mysteries of the past from our ancestors which we have just begun to decipher. Thanks to theoretical physics and pioneers like Einstein and Oppenheimer, it has come into the limelight,' said Aahana, as they smiled broadly at the monk.

'In short "A" represents the conscious state, "U" represents the subconscious state and "M" represents the unconscious state. So my children, control "AUM" and control the mind, control the mind and control what the mind can do. '

'So keeping in mind what your book says, a combination of the primordial sound "AUM" and these *mantras* gives therapeutic benefits to the body.'

'Yes my son, because the *mantras* are written in Sanskrit, the divine language for Indians and Tibetans.'

'Adolf, not only Indians but mainstream scientists all around the world have recognised it as something more than a language. In fact when the American author and philosopher Henry Thoreau wanted to create the perfect language he created something similar to Sanskrit,' said Aahana.

'You mean he rediscovered it.'

'No. The tone of the language which he created was along the lines of Sanskrit. This ancient language consists of primordial sounds in different frequencies. Each of the forty nine letters is systematically created just like natural progression of sound in the human mouth.'

'Yes, my son, even NASA is thinking of using it, trying it out as a computer language.'

Adolf nodded, his eyes moist now, trying to assimilate all the information and insights. He felt droplets of water on his face. It started to drizzle outside with flashes of lightning and the rumble of thunder. Aahana rushed to close the windows at one end, and Adolf did the same on the opposite side.

It now seems more and more logical. Did Nasir, the ISI and China create a weapon based on a combination of the primordial sound and modern contemporary science? Have they used it to eliminate the witnesses one by one and also Kurt?

'Thank you sir, for all you have shared and so logically put forth in front of us,' said Adolf in a more reassured tone. He was not a heretic now. 'But, I would want to know if the converse can be true. Let me be direct, Sir. Can anyone create a weapon using this ancient knowledge, to harm the human body?'

'You are not the first to ask this and will not be the last.'

'Yes, it's nicely elaborated in your book about Jericho,' said Aahana as Adolf also nodded and added, 'That was a solid structure, what about the human body and anything in your knowledge that has been created to damage it in modern times….'

'You mean the current timeline my son, not modern time, this timeline is ancient for our future self,' said the Monk, laughing gregariously.

'Yes, sir, whatever you say,' Adolf smiled and joined his palms in obeisance as he bowed before Dr Tamang. The monk continued to laugh. The sky lit up with more lightning flashes and the rain came down heavily.

'You are fit to be my disciple. And about your question of creating a sonic weapon in the current timeline the answer is…'

A huge thunder sounded in the background. The closed windows vibrated followed by the shattering of glass. The lights went out, and Adolf felt something jump on him; as he tried to negotiate it in the darkness, he fell with a loud thud, taking down Aahana with him. Adolf moaned and Aahana let out a huge shriek.

38 DAYS TO EVENT

Dharamshala,
Himachal Pradesh, India

November 3,17:45 IST

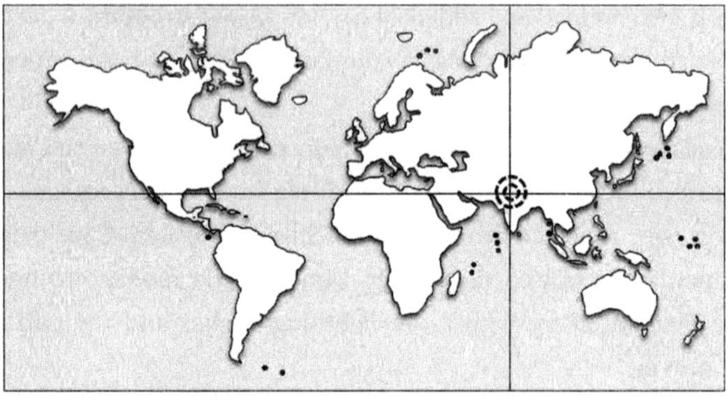

The room was pitch dark and the only sound was of two bodies as they grappled in the dark.

'Power cut, wait for a moment, the backup power will come,' as soon as Dr Tamang uttered these words, lights in the room came up and he started his hysterical laugh again.

'So there you are, come here, come here,' the leopard skin tabby cat sprung up to the monk's arms as he snuggled her, and started stroking the fur with his left hand.

'May I introduce you to my not so faithful, Lady Missy, she keeps disappearing and popping up. She jumped upon you, maybe she does not like your blonde hair,' said Dr Tamang still laughing as he observed his visitors get up from the floor and dust themselves.

'See, that's automated in your heads, you fall down, get up and then dust yourself, drilled into our minds since childhood.'

Adolf and Aahana looked at each other feeling stupid but joined in the laughter. They again sat down at their places, but with a new companion, Missy, who was now purring to full glory.

'Well that was a nice little break,' said Adolf as he got up and moved to the white board. He picked up a red marker kept in a rectangular cylindrical holder on the side rods. Using the magnetic duster, he started wiping some numbers written there. He stopped for a moment as he realised that it may be important for the monk. He turned around.

'Don't worry, I have it all here; you can clean it and write what you want.'

'Thanks. Basically, I just want to put down what we have discussed till now,' said Adolf, cleaning up the white board and opening the cap of the marker. He began writing on the white board on the left side of the board.

1. All matter in the universe is made of atoms – science
2. Each sub atomic particle vibrates and oscillates like a string -- science
3. Sound can behave as a pressure wave – science
4. Sound can lift certain objects, acting like a particle beam – science
5. Sound can be used as a weapon, both at the ultrasound (radars) and infra-sound (experimental) levels – fact
6. The sound which is existing in the universe, can be primordial in nature – part science
7. "AUM" chanting can result in mental well being – part science
8. "A – U – M" each part plays a role impacting the conscious and subconscious mind –???
9. The Sanskrit script is systematically created just like the natural progression of sounds in the human mouth – part fact
10. NASA is attempting to use Sanskrit as computer language due to its logical construction – fact
11. Mantras are uttered in Sanskrit which can impact matter and atoms –???
12. Certain theoretical physicists believe in contribution of VEDAS to modern science, and the NAZIS understood them – fact

The height of the board allowed Adolf only twelve rows of writing space. While Aahana looked on with her arms crossed, the ever smiling monk got up slowly this time, gently placed his cat over the cushioned seat and walked to the board. He took another marker from the cylindrical hold and started writing. Both looked on as the monk jotted down points with a blue marker on the right side of the whiteboard.

13. Human genome consists of over 23,000 protein coding genes – Science
14. Genes contain information or a natural program acting in a particular regulated sequence – Science
15. Alteration or disruption of genes can cause disease or alter human behaviour – Science
16. Re-sequencing and/or creation of genes done in labs – Fact

'Well what is missing here? Does God Exist?' Adolf asked, amused at the four new points. Aahana stood between the two men with opposing thought processes.

'Professor, you mean to say that our understanding for this weapon will have to reach into the realm of our genes,' she said as the monk smiled again.

'We are like a giant computer, with our genes running on automatic program, along with our brain as a micro-processor. A virus or bacteria impacts us at a physical level, but what if something attacks us at the cellular, genome level.'

'So if I read you right, what we may be talking here is a sort of sound software, impacting us at the cellular level.'

'My son, our DNA has been finely tuned like percussion music, controlling trillions of our cells to work in perfect order, harmony and balance. Alteration of genes has been a dream of many civilisations and powers.'

'That's what the Nazis also thought…and they could have been right. And right on many things.' said Adolf. The other two were silent for a moment.

Aahana was irritated, 'Come on Adolf, don't tell me you believe that shit.'

'I am trying to understand what to believe or what not to believe now; looking for options…and to be honest. All this is making sense now…such a weapon is possible. If not by this means, then by something similar or using the same principle. Professor, your book said that the walls of Jericho were bought down by the horns and the sacred "AUM" chant. If that is true, for which we are getting archaeological evidence now, this weapon may be right now in the wrong hands.'

The wily monk smiled widely, his face showing more wrinkles. 'Ahh! The book. I never said "AUM," I said the primordial chant.' The monk walked to his computer table, pulled out one of the rolled charts, and rolling it open on the centre table, he requested each of them to hold one end.

'I have painfully worked on these for many years; I believe it is true what you see, across various civilisations and across history. I can be killed for this.'

Adolf and Aahana could not believe their eyes. 'Bloody Damn It!' exclaimed Adolf, his mouth wide open. Aahana who was bending over, fell on both knees. The professor continued to speak explaining his theory around the work done on the chart. His theory: the primordial chant *Aum* was the parent to words like *Amen, Ogham* and others also.

Both listened attentively like young children. At the corner of the chart, Adolf also saw something which Kurt had drawn, *the Swastika and Star of David;* here again the *Swastika* was embedded inside the *Star of David.*

Kurt's symbols! There is more to it than all these symbols and what they represent. How is Mansur going to use this weapon? Or is it Samir?

He listened to the monk with growing admiration as he expounded his theory and the related work as evident on the chart. Missy was on the ground, her tail straight, eyes fixed on her master, her head rubbing against the monk's legs, but he did not stop speaking. Missy moved to rub her head against Adolf's legs. Outside, the rain increased in intensity, showing no signs of halting. Strong winds and thunder continued unabated, sporadically rattling the windows. It was raining here, but was dry like a bone in Kolkata, where the first test match of the India-Australia series was going to begin with Mansur playing his first international game.

37 DAYS TO EVENT

Dharamshala,
Himachal Pradesh, India

November 4,07:35 IST

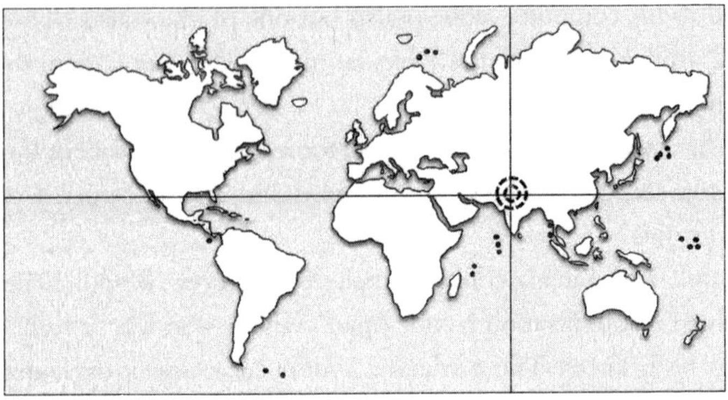

'**Best of luck** again and sorry I cannot be there. Will be reaching there tonight and will try to see if they let me meet you. Bye, Love you.' Aahana flipped close her phone after talking to Mansur for the second time this morning. Just out from the shower, her hair was still dripping wet. She pulled out a hand towel from her travel case in which she carried a single change of dress just for such an occasion.

Aahana and Adolf had spent the night at the monk's bungalow. After Dr Tamang had showed them to their respective rooms, Aahana and Adolf sat discussing the day's events, the importance of their individual searches and of Aahana and Mansur's relationship before they retired for the night. In the morning, while Adolf went for a short jog and got ready, Aahana just finished talking to Mansur now. She had already arranged her dress on the bed before going for the shower. Dropping the wet towel she started getting ready as she admired the light fog and the mountain ranges from the first floor.

Professor Tamang is right. Got to be right. I hope Adolf gets those killers–revenge for my friends. How much I miss you all! I would have been in the same situation if it had not been for my Mansur.

At the ground floor, around the breakfast table, Adolf and Dr Tamang waited for Aahana. The monk had taken Adolf for prayers inside the small temple. Adolf was less reluctant to visit a place of worship. Dr Tamang was reading the morning paper and Adolf saw the front and back pages of the newspaper which faced him. Mansur's face was on the lower half of the front page, with the headline, "Chasing the valley's dream–Kashmir's Destiny Child." Adolf had already read the same article an hour ago online. His mind begged for answers to the questions tormenting him.

Mansur had convinced Aahana not to go to Shaksgam valley because of a bad omen dream. Mansur is the key to this sonic weapon to be used, may be in a stadium. But how will he execute it…can't be infra sound all the way. There was a CD, running a particular music and then phone calls. No two patterns were the same. The delivery has to be through other means. How much is China involved in this? Is it limited to General Chan only?

'Good morning,' Aahana greeted them as she entered the room, towing her luggage behind her. Adolf looked back and waved, while Dr Tamang put down his paper and joined his palms in Namaste; she acknowledged and returned his greeting. They all sat down to breakfast, stayed away from the previous day's topic, discussing instead the India-Australia cricket match. They finished breakfast and left with their luggage, taking their time to bid farewell to the monk.

Out in the open field, Adolf and Aahana turned towards the temple where their cars were parked. Walking past the prayer wheel again, Adolf slid his hand over the golden drums and started rolling it, speaking out the words written over the twelve wheels in his mind.

Aum Mani Padme Hum…generosity, ethics, patience, diligence, renunciation, and wisdom.

Aahana did the same; praying for justice for her dead friends, success for Mansur and Adolf. Dr Tamang stood in an orange robe as he waved back at them. He called out, 'Send me the photos which you wanted to share, let me see how I can help.'

'Yes!' Adolf shouted back. 'I will, Sir, you take care.' He did a Namaste then bid farewell as they headed to Kolkata.

37 DAYS TO EVENT

Eden Gardens,
Kolkata, India

November 4,08:05 IST

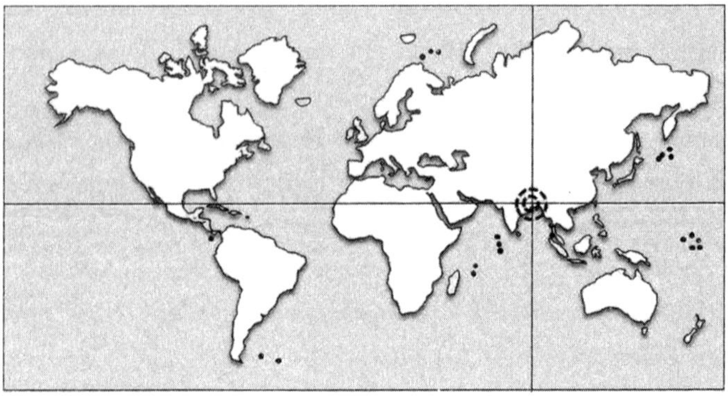

The captains of the two teams prepared for the toss. While the Australian captain, the young and cocky Ragner Gorton, was looking confident, India's Captain Sinha was in a serious mood. They exchanged the sheet that listed the playing eleven as this was the custom dating back to the origins of cricket, with the first test played over a century ago. The Indian captain did not have the playing eleven he wanted. One of the main batsmen had gone down with flu a day back so another had to step into his shoes. For the bowling choice, the coach had insisted on trying Mansur. He was worried that putting the rookie straight into the fire would be folly, but the coach insisted.

'Whose call is it?' said the match referee while holding the One Rupee coin in his hands.

Gorton indicated that the Indian captain would do the calling. Sinha called heads when the coin was flipped and heads it was. The Indian captain decided to field first, expecting to take advantage of the dew and slightly windy conditions to get some early wickets. This way he could get the Australians on the backfoot in the first session.

Both captains shook hands; Gorton still had the annoying habit of chewing gum and spitting it out in front of the opposition during the formal handshake.

Thirty minutes passed and the umpires started their march out, with the fielding side coming behind them. As they stood out in a group, Mansur was handed the blue Indian beret for making his debut. He took it from the Indian captain, feeling a shiver run down his spine as he held the cap and felt the embossed logo on top. His test cap number was also embossed on the side. For him, it was a memory to last a lifetime, and in his heart he wanted to make it count.

Once they were on the ground the captain set the field. Mansur was sent to the fine leg position. The Australian openers–Harold Hassett and Russ Deakin–walked out as Gagan Singh, India's main strike bowler, stood on the bowlers end and set the field. Sinha took his position as wicketkeeper, and he had pretty good company by his side with three slips and a gully, and an unorthodox position of deep fly slip. Mansur was already stationed at fine leg, and deep mid wicket was his only company in that area.

As the left-handed Gagan began his run up, the crowd roared in anticipation. The first ball came in and it was an out-swinger, the ball moving away after pitching on the ground. Harold went for the cut, but got a top edge and BANG, the fly slip came into reckoning. The catch was taken, the Indians jumped in the air, and Harold stood his ground. It was his first naught score in over thirty-five test matches. The fielding side went into a huddle and the captain congratulated the players on the first wicket and told them to keep the pressure in the over. The huddle broke off and Mansur returned to his position. Mansur had a spring now in his step as he felt the blood rush.

This is going to be easy. Just keep the line and attack. I can do it…when my chance comes.

The game continued. Mansur was told to warm up and that he would be coming to bowl in the nineteenth over. India had taken three more wickets up to that time, with Australia reeling at 75/4. Australia's captain, Ragner Gorton was batting with a score of only two runs off thirty balls. Mansur was given the task to attack him. Once Gorton was gone, India could actually clean up the rest by teatime. At least that was the plan.

Mansur took a deep breath as he discussed the field position with Gagan. The captain had given Gagan his instructions, and he would assist in helping the bowlers set the field. It was decided to attack Gorton's legs for an LBW. The plan was to attack with short stuff and push him back and then go for the dipping ball to get his wicket. The field was changed to a 4-5 now favouring the leg side. Two fielders were positioned for the hook shot and two more for close-in catches on the leg side.

As Mansur and Gagan were placing the field, Gorton's batting partner, Edmund Whitlam, started walking towards them, then he turned around when he was close to them. The mind game had started—it was *the rookie versus the perception specialist.* Gorton had made a comment once that '*perception is reality.*'

'Just bowl as you did in the nets,' said Gagan.

Mansur nodded and started to take his mark at the run-up. His first international ball in test cricket. With the whole world watching. Srinagar and Kashmir would be glued to their TV sets. His family huddled around the television in his home to see him bowl. Samir watched from Delhi as he bowled to the Australian captain.

Allah! this is it.

Taking a deep breath and closing his eyes, he tried to regain his focus. He began his run up, building up speed and running straight onto the pitch. Mansur jumped and put in a short one, with his head down and eyes up, trained on the batsman.

'No ball!' shouted the umpire.

The ball hit the pitch and rose not as expected. Gorton rocked back and pulled the ball on the leg side. Six runs from the bat and one run from the *no ball.*

Mansur stopped and looked down. The commentary team eyed the slow motion replay and commented that it was a marginal call at best. They felt it was tough luck for a rookie to have a no-ball call in his first international ball. Mansur had to realise that all was not hunky dory on the international circuit. The media was divided in its opinion on giving such a raw aged man a chance to play in this league. A lot of bad press had followed the selection, with several questions being asked on the logic behind his inclusion. The majority opinion did not favour him despite Mansur's impressive record-breaking show in the two first class games he played. One headline even read, 'Geriatric Quickie to Rescue India.' Whether or not the pun was intentional, these news stories did compel Mansur to question his right to play at the national level.

Mansur began bowling again, pitched on off side and Bang! Four runs! Next ball on legs, Gorton flicked it for two runs. A straight drive, cover drive followed with a couple of runs again on each delivery. The last two balls were pitched in short, and Gorton defended them for dot balls without scoring. Mansur's first over in his debut cost him seventeen runs. He stood dejected, walking with his head down. Gagan ran to him and threw an arm across his shoulder to pacify him.

'Mansur, don't worry, my first over in my debut went for fifteen. It's normal…nerves,' explained Gagan in a soothing tone. 'I then took two wickets in my second over…you will get your man eventually.'

Another over passed in which eight runs were scored, and Mansur was given the ball for his second over. Whitlam was facing him now, and he took a single off the first ball to give the strike to Gorton. The next five balls were dispatched around the grounds. This over cost India twenty-nine runs.

The rookie had given away forty-six runs in two overs.

Gorton had a smirk on his face as he started his verbal volley at Mansur, telling him to go back and get some experience.

Mansur was devastated as he stood frozen. Australia had moved to 131/4 in 21 overs. The game had turned and the run rate rocketed up. With six to seven overs more to be bowled before lunch time, the Indian captain decided to employ defensive tactics. The next period of six overs before lunch brought in another thirty runs. Australia closed at 161/4 in 27 overs, an aggressive score.

The TV commentator asserted that the game was in Australia's favour with both batsmen being set. The turning point of the game came with Mansur's over. One of the commentators even said that it would be a long time before Mansur got to bowl again. His comments were prophetic as the next over of Mansur came only after forty overs had been bowled. He was now used by the captain only as a change bowler to give his other bowler a break.

At the end of play on the first day, Australia was on top at 350/6 and Gorton still was not out and batting on a magnificent 140 runs. Mansur had bowled six overs out of the ninety of the fielding side. He had given away seventy-four runs, and his heart was broken.

Fifteen hundred kilometres away, Samir sat in a hotel room in Delhi, watching the game. He forcefully stubbed out his cigarette in the ashtray; his plan to use Mansur was going to fail if he was dropped from the playing eleven. The package was not delivered, and Mansur had to do it in the field. Aziz would surely get fired and his cause would be lost.

I need to move in and turn a few things on my own. Samir picked up the hotel phone and called the receptionist.

'I would need to book a flight to Kolkata as soon as possible. Can you make the arrangements?'

Janab Aziz is now in Kolkata. I will talk to him in person and make sure Mansur stays on the team. The timing is not right for him to be out now.

Samir opened the cupboard and started to set aside clothing for the trip. *Buzz...Buzz*! Samir's mobile phone, which was in vibrating mode, started moving on the table beside his laptop. He picked up the phone. 'Yes, sir. Yes sir, I understand...the line is secured now,' said Samir, pushing a rubber button on the side of his mobile meant for encrypting the line of communication, which would avoid monitoring of the call.

'Crystal clear, sir, I will not do that now.'

'Yes, I was thinking about it...but will not do it now.'

'Okay, sir, agreed. I will come to the coordinates for the meeting.'

'Yes sir...I understand. It will be delivered.'

Samir put down the phone. His superior had just ordered him to stay put in Delhi.

Damn mind reader he is, but he has ensured that the package will be delivered on time. Nothing seems to be working...and Janab has to take care...China also, a WAR is coming!

Cygnus Times

Inside

How can you make money in the stock market without your husband knowing?

Liquid water and metallic remains found in Mars

Page3 News: New movie of Khan has a successful weekend release, and he signs a $100 million Hollywood deal.

THE PEOPLE'S NEWS THAT MATTERS

Aussie Kangaroos Make PAPAD of India paper Tigers

Saloni Sex Scandal Still Rocks India

New Delhi: Both houses of Parliament were rocked yet again by the opposition demanding clarifications and explanations from the PMO to come clean on the rumours that Saloni, a personal assistant in the Home Ministry was sexually exploited. An audio had surfaced which is being investigated by the police. There are inputs from unconfirmed sources that a large amount of money is associated with Saloni.

Chinese Troops Build-Up Continues Along Border

PTI News, New Delhi: There are more specialised Chinese units moving into positions across India's north-east border and Ladakh region. The Chinese government maintains it is temporary movement for an internal exercise.

Kolkata: India suffered a humiliating defeat against Australia, in the first test match of the series. The defeat, an inning and 53 runs, has brought back haunting memories of the past. India resumed at 22-1 on the fifth day, still 181 runs behind Australia's mammoth 510/7 first innings score. It looked as if the second wicket century stand between the old warhorses would give India a draw, but once they got out in consecutive overs the rest of the team collapsed at 150 with just 20 runs added and the post-tea session still left.

This was the very ground on which Sourav Ganguly's team India halted the great Australian team. More is left to be desired while watching this poppadum show by the current Indian team, who series after series have surely lost direction after the 2011 world cup victory. One of the biggest questions is: What is the geriatric Mansur Haider doing in the team?

His conceding over a hundred runs in the first innings and getting only three overs to bowl in the second one, it is clear how much confidence the captain has on Mansur.

Tiger vs. Dragon	India	China
Army Personnel	1.3 Mio	1.7 Mio
Air Force Planes	1500+	3000+
Naval Crafts	170+	550+

21 DAYS TO EVENT

Oval Office, White House,
Washington DC, USA,

November 20,17:05 EST

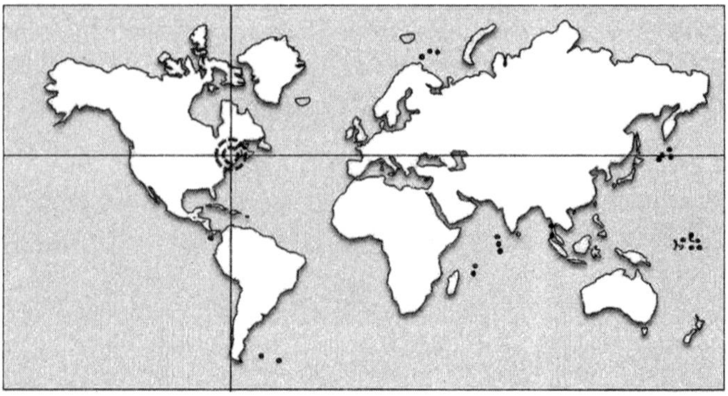

Three hours into the meeting, the members of the United States War Council were still discussing hypothetical situations and scenarios for steps to be taken if war broke out between China and India. Apart from the U.S. President there were twelve attendees physically present, supported by another five members from across the globe participating via video conference. The group had considered various scenarios and was in agreement that some level of skirmishes would occur in the coming weeks.

'Our objective is to negate any engagement by both sides,' said the Secretary of Defence, looking around the group for approval. The group nodded in unison.

'President, Sir, we will try to minimise any losses and reel in both parties. We are all well aware of whose side we are on in this, but we cannot show it openly,' said the Secretary of State.

'Further, we will be providing Intel to India on the movement and see if we have to bolster their capabilities to counter the Chinese,' said the Secretary of Defence.

'That's all fine, but can anyone explain to me why the HELL, despite our efforts in educating them and briefing them on the situation, they are withdrawing their primary forces from the border and placing them some thirty kilometres behind?' The President took in the whole group assembled before him.

Yitzhak Herzog, fresh from his India trip, spoke up.

'Sir, the fact is that they know something about *Shaksgam Valley* weapon testing, and the UFOs which showed up across India. No matter how much they deny it, we should not rule out that angle. Maybe they know about the weapon and will use it on the Chinese,' said Herzog. The President puckered his lips and glanced at the U.S. Ambassador to India with a look of disappointment.

'Enough...We have given that story far too much attention already and have lost both men and material investigating the matter. I even revived "Project Blue Book", because of this. We found nothing. If anything is there we shall see it. Period!'

Thirty more minutes of discussion had gone in before the President leaned forward in his chair to say, 'I have met the Indian Prime Minister and closely interacted with him. There is some other reason for this movement of forces, and sitting here, we can only speculate. So it's time we stop talking and start doing something.'

There was a pause before he continued. 'My plan of action would be this: Check with our sources within Indian armed forces, diplomatic circles, and other personnel on why this action was taken. Convince them that build-up near the border is the best way to hold back the Chinese.' The President continued, 'I want one of the *Carrier Strike Groups* to immediately move into the Indian Ocean. Try to organise something...a humanitarian operation, a battle exercise...anything. In a worst case scenario, if war breaks out, we would need to take our civilians out, otherwise this may serve as a deterrent to the Chinese.'

'Our response time to reach the Indian Ocean will be around two weeks. We can use CSG-9 with the *USS Abraham Lincoln,*' said the Chairman of the Joint Chiefs, who also was an Admiral.

'And...' the U.S. President turned towards the video conference link and began addressing the attendees. 'I want to keep the Pakistanis in good humour, so keep a check on what they are up to, Mr Ambassador.' The U.S. Ambassador to Pakistan nodded.

The discussion reached its conclusion with the final notes being taken. The group dispersed and only the Director of the CIA stayed behind. The President went and sat behind his desk.

'Thank you for the updates on Mansur. Have we learnt anything new?' asked the President.

'Nothing. He is playing Cricket and he is not good at it,' he paused for a moment, removed a page marked "Above Top Secret" and placed it before the President. 'We are following a theory that he may be a bomber and have alerted India's anti-terror unit. They promise to keep an eye on him but dismiss the talk despite the fact that there was some shooting incident involving Jihadis and probable Pakistani elements near the Line of Control on the India-Pakistan border.'

'Yes, the Monkey Hill Incident…I got the briefing on that one. We are in observation mode only, and I believe you have the men on the ground watching him, right?' the President enquired.

The CIA chief nodded.

'I did not want to discuss this with the others, but I want General Pervez to be taken out if necessary,' said the President.

The CIA chief wetted his lip and spoke, 'I think I just have the man for that job. His name is Colonel Eccleston. He has some options developed; we will run it through you later. Then you can pick an option…just like Osama's, Abbottabad raid.'

'Not that kind. This time no capture, only kill. Keep me updated.' The President shook hands with the CIA chief and he walked out of the Oval office.

CABLE: US EMBASSY BEIJING TO SECRETARY OF DEFENCE

VZCZCXYZO6824
DE RUEHBJ #0678 0170912
ZNY SSSSS ZZH
P 030912Z Nov 21
FM EMBASSY BEIJING
RUEHHK/AMCONSUL HONG KONG 3910
INFO RUEHOO/CHINA POSTS COLLECTIVE
RUEHIL/AMEMBASSY ISLAMABAD PRIORITY 2159
RUEHBUL/AMEMBASSY KABUL PRIORITY 3346
RUEHNE/AMEMBASSY NEW DELHI PRIORITY 0129
RUEAIIA/CIA WASHDC PRIORITY
RUEKJCS/JOINT STAFF WASHINGTON DC PRIORITY
RUEKJCS/SECDEF WASHINGTON DC PRIORITY
RHEHNSC/NSC WASHDC PRIORITY
Wednesday, 21November, 09:12
S E C R E T SECTION 01 OF 01 BEIJING 000024
SIPDIS
EO 12958 DECL: 10/03/2062
TAGS CH, IN, PM, PARM, SKV
SUBJECT: REPORT ON ACTIVITIES OF VICE CHAIRMAN
F THE CENTRAL MILITARY COMMISSION GENERAL ZENG CHAN
Classified By: Political Minister Counsellor J.Wang

1. (S) Summary: General Zeng Chan is showing political ambitions and making changes in the command structure of both internal and external security apparatus. End summary.

2. (S) Vice Chairman of Central Military Commission (CMC), General Zeng Chan's views on US are quite clear, mandating his people to have views like the book "The China Dream" and other similar lines of thoughts. He is making pledges to his troops to convert China into the world number one by overtaking US. This is causing friction between him and certain sections of the politburo.

3. (S) His current strategy is India centric with plans to carry out more infrastructure projects inside

Pakistan Occupied Kashmir. His recent announcement of more investment in Gwadar port in Baluchistan also is primary in this direction to take more control, thus securing oil supply and giving PLA's Navy an additional dock.

4. (S) He travelled to military garrisons in Chengdu and Lanzhou regions for inspection of the group Armies (13th, 14th, 21st and 47th). Both these regions border Kashmir and India's North-East region. The Tibetan 52nd and 53rd Mountain Brigades at Chengdu received special attention with creation of more oxygen enriched barracks near the border with India involving the use of plants to generate additional oxygen. This was done to help the mountain brigades and other PLA army units to fight altitude diseases.

5. (S) His close aide Senior Colonel Meng Quansheng, was deputed to the Chengdu military region, from Hong Kong garrison. He is designated to handle border troops directly at Arunachal (disputed) border with India. He also appointed another close aide Senior Colonel Xu Wanquan to head the People's Armed Police. More such appointments are expected at other levels.

6. (S) He also met with Nobel Laureate Dr Nasir Raja at the Pakistan's Consulate General at Chengdu.

COMMENT

7. (S) With control of Second Artillery Corps (strategic missile force - including nuclear ballistics) by CMC, this trend is dangerous. Postings of his trusted officers into front-line positions across India and at para-military levels indicate that he may want to initiate some action. Increasing the level of budgetary allocation in the internal security shows they are expecting a situation of internal disturbance.

With China to table a bill on Kashmir on Dec 11th, more posturing on the border is expected. It has been one month since General Pervez Hussein has met with General Chan, but his meeting with Pakistani scientist Dr Nasir Raja can be an alternative bridge.

Taking into account the last report shared about General Chan, which had his views on matching up to United States Pacific Command by encouraging PLA Navy's submarine fleets to explore the Pacific, our view is to see all these incidents showcasing a potential military coup.

20 DAYS TO EVENT

Flight back to Pakistan, Somewhere above Chinese Airspace near Kashmir

November 21,11:15 CET

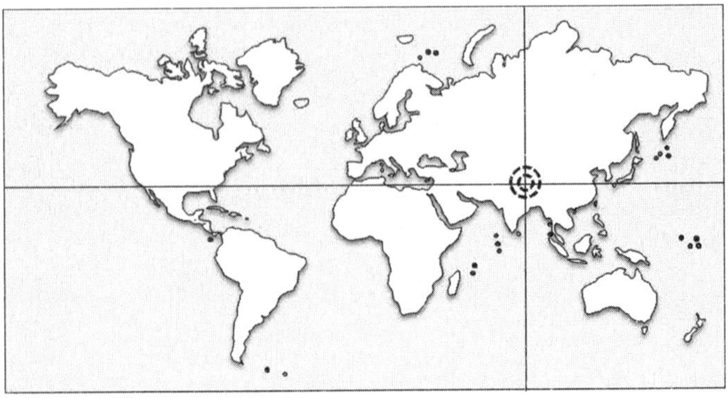

Tearing through the Himalayan sky at Mach 0.89 (954 km/hour) was Boeing's Dreamliner 787-9 Jet, a new jewel in the crown of Air China. The Himalayan tract hundreds of miles below was as serene as it was a thousand years ago. Sitting in the private bedroom suite 1G of the first class section was Dr Nasir. He was in China, where he was attending an international physicist's conference at Chengdu. The conference was a cover for his real agenda, the meeting with General Chan and his team of scientists.

Despite their help till date, including proposing tabling of a Kashmir specific bill for independence at the United Nations, Dr Nasir did not share all his knowledge on his secret weapon. He just released pockets of incoherent information which would not make sense even to the brightest scientist in the subject of theoretical physics. He applied the same rule in Pakistan also, he trusted no one around him.

General Pervez Musa Hussein says he fights for Kashmir. General Chan says he is sympathetic to the Kashmir cause. No one fights for Kashmir. The west, the east are the same. The Pakistanis, the Indians and the Chinese are all hypocrites.

Walking out of his private suite, he headed towards the library and recreation lounge. One of the smartly dressed hostesses in a single piece short red tunic came very close to him and asked if he needed help. He took a whiff of her perfume and politely turned down her offer for help. He continued his slow walk towards the exclusive centre but not before taking in the dark stocking she wore through which her bright yellow skin shone through alluringly.

General Chan still has his cronies around me. First it was the massage girls he sent to my room every night in Beijing and Chengdu, and now this cute lady popping up now and then. How does it matter to me? He still does not get it.

As he glanced at the serene photos and abstract paintings along the aisles, the scientist felt an opposite emotion inside him. He had seen persecution come not only to himself but also to the ones he respected.

Both my mentors were prosecuted. Dr Mohammad Salam, by the Pakistanis, because he was an Ahmediyya Muslim; they even went to the extent of declaring him a non-Muslim.

And Robert Oppenheimer. After all he did for the United States, he had to go through a period of humiliation for being declared a communist sympathiser.

Good that I managed to get all his work even after his untimely death. If he had not started researching the power of Vedas, and Biblical weapon used to bring down the walls of Jericho the ancient power would not be within my grasp.

The scientist took in a deep breath.

The Chinese think they are smart, trying to chisel out their own world. They have cheated my own brothers by occupying part of my land in Kashmir. Walking in Shaksgam valley for my experiment after the incident was so breathtaking, as I walked the land of my ancestors the first time.

No one deserves a life of order and peace. Chaos should be all around, and it will come when I strike out all their leaders at one go…and the song 'By the River of Babylon', by Mikaela Wallander group will cause the sonic disruption to kill all listeners. Poor Mikaela will play her last song, it will start with the cricket team.

Reaching the lounge, he looked at the neatly displayed magazines on the wall. The *Time* magazine cover story was about "Bikini Wars," how China destroyed Brazil's domestic bikini industry. He sat down, as another smartly dressed hostess offered him a mixed juice tonic in a dazzling crystal glass. He took the glass and sipped the bitter grinded juices. In his mind there was also one more name, which Pervez had mentioned recently.

My fellow Kashmiri Mansur is now in the team…it will be sad to kill him but it has to be, unfortunately done. No more mistakes now, like I did in Oslo leaving my Bible with some frequencies in the rental car. Naah…no one will understand, By the rivers of Babylon.

20 DAYS TO EVENT

Stockholm-Arlanda International Airport
Stockholm, Sweden

November 21,11:15 CET

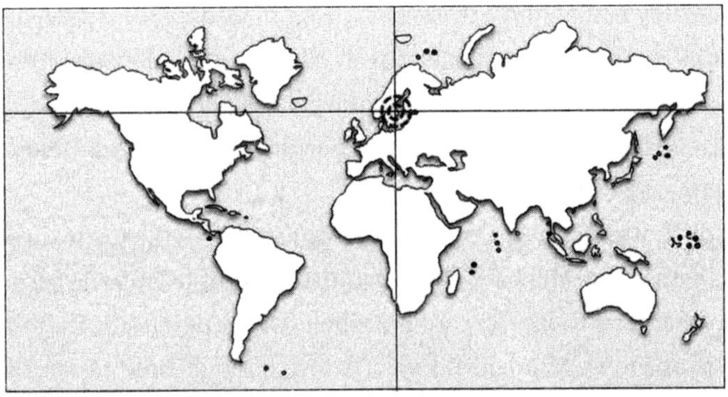

'**Cabin Crew, please** take your seats for take-off. "*Kabinpersonal, ta era platser för start.*"'

The Scandinavian Airlines captain made the announcement before the Airbus 330 started taxiing down the runway towards its eleven-hour journey to India's sin city, Mumbai.

'I love take offs, the pressure is irresistible, does the hots for me inside,' said the blonde air-hostess.

'Ja! Speaking of hots, seat number 4A is hot with a capital H,' said her brunette colleague as they strapped their belts for lift-off.

'Oh really, let me take a look, once we are free from this bondage.'

The mega jumbo plane continued its ascent towards the sky, climbing over 30,000 feet in less than fifteen minutes. The lights brightened and as they reached cruising altitude, the "fasten seat belt" sign was switched off. The blonde, five feet eight inches tall air hostess unstrapped the buckles from her waist, and gently helped the strap to slide through her dark blue jacket. She got up, adjusted her skirt and picked up the intercom to make an announcement to the passengers informing that they were free to move about and could switch on their electronic devices. Other standard messages were also passed on, before she locked the intercom and turned around to her colleague.

'That's that! Next stop, "Get 4A" within visual range.' The blue curtain from the airhostess's cabin area was parted slightly, and she moved her gaze quickly to seat 4A. Sitting relaxed, stretching out his leg was a well built man in a black suit. She checked the passenger roster and read his name, *Adolf Silfverskiöld.* She turned to her colleague with a glint in her eyes. 'He is mine!' 'I will take his row.' She opened one of the racks, took out a medium sized purple velvet bag, pulled out a heart shaped perfume bottle and sprayed perfume on her neck. 'Now lady, let's start with what we are good at.'

Adolf was back from a weeklong meeting with Carina and the SOG team. Even the CIA chief had dropped in to provide his inputs and they agreed to liaison more on the covert operation. An hour and half stoppage at Munich did give Adolf enough time to stretch out his legs. With a long flight now, he thought it would be a good time to catch up on reading. He pulled out Dr Tamang's book, "*Anahata Nada: The Unmade Sound of the Universe*" and was beginning to settle back when his concentration was disrupted by a sensuous voice near his ear.

'Hot towel or cold towel for you sir?' Adolf took in the blond look and the familiar name on her name tag and smiled back.

'Cold towel please.'

Adolf took the scented cold towel, pressed it on his face with a mild pressure and then moved it around his neck.

The air-hostesses in the meanwhile walked around the other passengers and offered them the cold towel, collected it and returned to their galley area. They brought out the first set of refreshments–for the passengers. Adolf received extra attention again from the tall, blonde airhostess. Adolf responded more and chatted slightly more each time. Two hours into the flight she walked back once more towards seat 4A.

'I hope all is well,' she said as she bent over him conscientiously, her face just a feet away from his. He saw her blue eyes, nodded gently and smiled back.

'I hope you don't mind my talking like this. I saw your name on the roster, Mr Silfverskiöld. I don't meet many of us on this flight.'

'Yes, Miss Ann Silfverskiöld, read your name on the tag,' he smiled in return. 'We may be related…'

'Ahh! You are very observant. Hope you were watching the tag only,' she whispered back. Adolf laughed softly.

They started talking softly in Swedish, Ann Silfverskiöld continued to flirt, flashing her eyes and adjusting her hair around her face. Adolf could see the Prussian blue ear rings, shaped like a half moon on her ears, and also feel the fragrance of her perfume build up around as she put her hand on the chair back and then on her knees. They continued to make small talk about their background and Ann asked if he would like to see Mumbai. Adolf pointed to his ring finger with its gold ring and puckered his lips with a slight smile. Ann's face registered a slight disappointment but she quickly hid it and continued talking. She rose after a few moments.

'*Bra träffa dig* Adolf, hope you enjoy the rest of our flight. And I didn't see you using our AVOD system. It has the latest entertainment channels, movies and music.'

'Ahh…it's book reading for me,' he said, showing the book cover to Ann. She looked at it, twisted her slender neck gently and read the cover page. Her eyebrows rose and she bent over again.

'I know this book, the author says something about universal sound, *nada* or something.'

'Wow…I am impressed! You have interests in this area.'

'Naaa…not me, someone else whom I met a few months back had books from this author. I just peeked and asked him about it…I thought it was about Raphael Nadal…but he said *nada* meant something else around sound.'

'Oh interesting!'

'What was more interesting was that he closed the book and did not bring it out during the rest of the flight, like it was porn or something… is it porn?'

'I assure you it is not *porr*,' said Adolf in a lower tone.

Ann giggled, covering her lips with the first three fingers of her right hand. She apologised.

'It's ok, tell me more about the person, which flight?'

'Not one, four. I was with the Pakistani doctor on three flights around…I think June-July and one in October…all in the Dubai-Frankfurt sector, but he was travelling to Oslo.'

'You sure?'

'Yup! Can't forget that artistic looking, wheatish face; in the second flight he was with another man, bald and clean shaven like a blob of meat, both stopped talking whenever I was around and acted as-if they did not know each other.'

'That is suspicious, didn't you report it?' *Blob clean shaven head…Jalal.*

'I sort of did to my local enforcement person on flight…but that artistic chiselled face guy was a Dr Nasir Raja and a frequent flyer. Always either first or business class on our star alliance network of airlines…so we did not look further into the matter, did not probe further.'

Nasir Raja could be the guy who rented the car in an alias, where the Bible was found with Babylon passage highlighted, thought Adolf.

'Do you know the other person's name?'

The experienced air-hostess was now slightly surprised at Adolf's interest. She started speaking in Swedish again at a lower pitch, asking why was he interested. Adolf had his answer ready. *Interpol!* He opened a couple of his suit buttons to show his metallic badge. Ann was more impressed but she didn't remember the exact name and was willing to help out with more, once they landed in Mumbai.

'It is my first time in Mumbai, I can use some company to show me around the place,' said Adolf. Ann shook her head giving a naughty smile.

'What about that lady?' She indicated the ring on his finger. 'Well, I will still be wearing it…we can move around as friends, right?'

Ann nodded, straightened her hair and gave a slight wink to Adolf as she walked away. *Dr Nasir Raja in-flight to Oslo, the bald man can be Jalal also, going to Oslo...reading Dr Tamang's book...it's all falling into place...the target may be Oslo…but where does Mansur fit in?*

20 DAYS TO EVENT

Hotel Maurya,
Delhi, India

November 21,17:05 IST

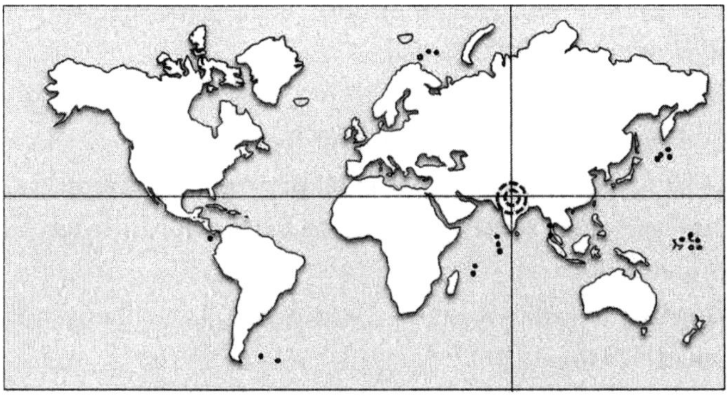

Mansur was sitting quietly in the upper lobby of the hotel. Samir and Aahana were with him. It had been a devastating two weeks for him. The team had lost two games in a row and was down 2-0 in the series. In the first game Mansur had conceded over a hundred runs in the first innings with a double-digit run rate and bowled just three overs in the second innings. Mansur was dropped and did not play the second game. The third test match would start on November 22, and Mansur was this time included in the list of the first twelve. He was now bowling fast and furiously at the nets.

I would have to go back to Srinagar if I fail again, back to the drudgery of old life. The dream is now only sour, but there is still hope, and people still believe in me.

He raised his head and looked into Aahana's brown eyes.

'I really don't understand how you two can still say that I am ready to play tomorrow.'

'Really, Mansur, I am surprised that you are still doubting your potential,' said Aahana sternly. 'This isn't the Mansur I know, the person who never lost hope and rescued me last year.'

'She is right. Even I had given up, but you pushed on and moved ahead alone,' said Samir.

'Mansur…' Aahana spoke softly as she drew closer to him. She knelt before him and looked up into his eyes. He wanted to embrace her, but as usual, controlled the urge.

'This is not the way I want you to end this. It's only a game. You told me once that you were here for the love of the game, and you don't get scared of what you love,' she said.

'But…this is different.'

'You get hit once and you lose your focus?'

'I just can't stop thinking about all of you…about mother, Zoon, Sana, and my father's memories. All the expectations…It just adds to the tension.'

'Don't try to justify your fears,' said Aahana in an unusually strong, stern, matronly tone.

Mansur looked her directly in the eye. He had never heard Aahana speak to him like this.

'Listen, Mansur, it's true we all have expectations from you. Your sisters, your mother, Samir, I…but remember, always remember that we have expectations because we believe in you. And you can only help yourself if *you* believe in *yourself*.'

Samir nodded and sat beside Mansur. Putting his hand on Mansur's shoulder, he said, 'Do you remember the two words you always say… the two magic words?'

Aahana smiled. 'Mansur, my dear…*What if*…What If you get up now and tell the coach that you are ready. What if…you go out and succeed?'

Mansur raised himself, remembering what he had forgotten.

'You are special, and we all love you. We all have great expectations from you, and it is these expectations which will help you fulfil your potential. It does not need to end this way. If it has to finish here, make sure you give it your best shot. Leave no reasons; otherwise it will haunt you forever.'

Mansur looked intensely determined. 'I am not a coward.'

'I never said that. But if you need to leave, make sure you have done all you can do within your power. I for one know you haven't even touched a bit of it till now. So many people are looking up to you. Your family, your friends, your locality in Srinagar. In fact, the whole of Kashmir is looking up to you.' Aahana held Mansur's hands, 'So many people cannot be wrong. Remember the Oracle,' she whispered.

Mansur's eyes widened as he had never said anything about her to Aahana.

'I talked to your sister. She told me. She also told me that no matter what happens they all love you and always will.'

Saying this Aahana started whistling her song, "Blue Skies," and sang some of the words.

Mansur's eyes lit up. He remembered the note the Oracle had given him that read, "*Fight your Destiny, Build Hope and Make it Happen.*"

'I have to go and meet the Coach,' he stood up suddenly.

Aahana and Samir also stood. With a sudden surge of energy Mansur embraced Aahana. She was surprised at first but then put her arms around him. Samir's smile widened.

18 DAYS TO EVENT

Feroz Shah Kotla Stadium,
Delhi, India

November 23,09:28 IST

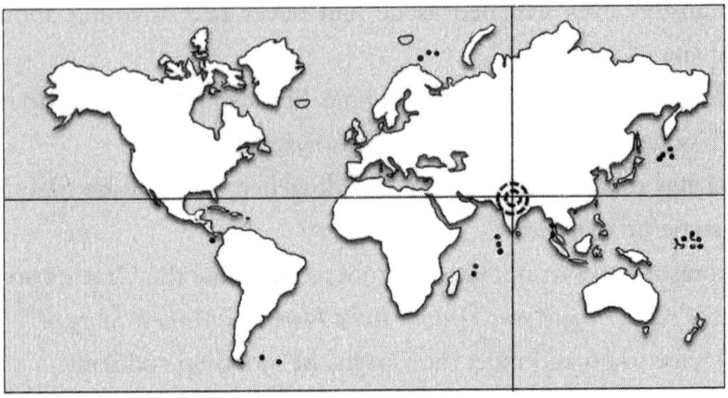

Second day of the third test India-Australia Test Match

Scores:

Australia 1st Inning: 490/4

'Say, Chappy, what a run feast yesterday. Gorton's team fell short of the record by only four runs. Breaking the 1910 record of Australia against South Africa would have been another feather for Gorton's rumbling Kangaroos.'

'Yes, the highest score for any team scored on day one. It is good that such old records still stand. This way we can remember the old greats.'

'Agreed, Gorton is shaping up well, and he has ended up at the same score Clem Hill ended on that day at 191. The only difference is that Gorton is still not-out and should comfortably get his fifth double century today.'

'What can the Indian team do this morning, Chappy?'

'Pray…'

The second morning of the game was about to begin, with just two minutes before the start of the day's proceedings. It was slightly windy, and a definite chill had set in Delhi. The Indians had taken their fielding positions and the two Aussie batsmen were at the crease.

Gorton was going to take the first ball of the day. He marked the crease again on the off-stump, asking the umpire if the position of his bat was unidirectional to the wicket. The umpire nodded, and he did his customary twirl of the bat as he marked the spot. Gorton was ready, and he was amused to see who was going to bowl to him.

Mansur stood at the Stadium End of the bowling crease, ready to begin his run up as soon as he got the umpire's instruction. Mansur had mixed feelings as he stood there with the cherry in his hand.

Bad day yesterday, nine overs only and giving away more than fifty runs, Ya Allah! Give me the strength to do justice to the confidence shown in me by my captain.

The captain had visited him the previous night and told him that he would be the opening bowler. He sat and discussed his plan to get not only Gorton out, but to ensure that the entire Australian team was out before lunch. It was a good two-way discussion, with both talking like equals. They agreed on the plan and discussed the field setting. As part of the plan, Mansur had done a couple of mock runs to the wicket without delivering the ball while Gorton took his stance.

The mind games had started.

The umpire signalled for the day's proceedings to start, and the crowd roared as Mansur ran to deliver the ball. The delivery was a short pitched one with a slight effort in order to generate a pull shot, and a pull shot came. The result was four runs. The commentator again started talking about how Mansur was not ready to play in the international arena and that he should go back to basics. Mansur took the ball from the fielder and went back for his run up.

Why are they persisting with this man? He just does not learn, thought Gorton as he got ready to face the second ball.

Mansur closed his eyes and started his run and increased his pace significantly as he neared the crease. He gave a long jump before delivery and released the ball with his arm outstretched. The ball release was quick, and it started dipping with a swing towards the onside. It pitched and then changed its direction towards the offside. Mansur's eyes did not leave the ball as he watched it travel. Gorton, who was expecting an in-swinging dipping delivery, had taken a leg glance position to turn the ball on the leg side. His eyes had a glimpse of the ball changing direction after pitching, but he had already committed to a leg glance and his head and body moved in that direction.

Shit! I am in trouble.

The ball moved from the middle stump direction at pitching to dislodge his off-stump. There was a brief pause. Mansur ran towards Gorton, got down on one knee and with his fists pumping the air, and face tilted upwards, he shouted his heart out.

'Allahhhhh!'

The place erupted. Gorton froze. As the fielders poured in, it dawned on him that he was out. He started walking out in a huff. Banging the bat on the ground, he picked it up and walked out, mouthing a few words to Mansur. Mansur wanted to react, but kept quiet and simply pointed towards the dressing room.

It was Mansur's first international wicket. He had pulled out a stunner of a delivery to get an in-form batsman out. The commentators also praised the delivery but were quick to add that it would take more than Gorton's wicket to stop the Australian victory march.

15 DAYS TO EVENT

Feroz Shah Kotla Stadium,
Delhi, India

November 26,09:30 IST

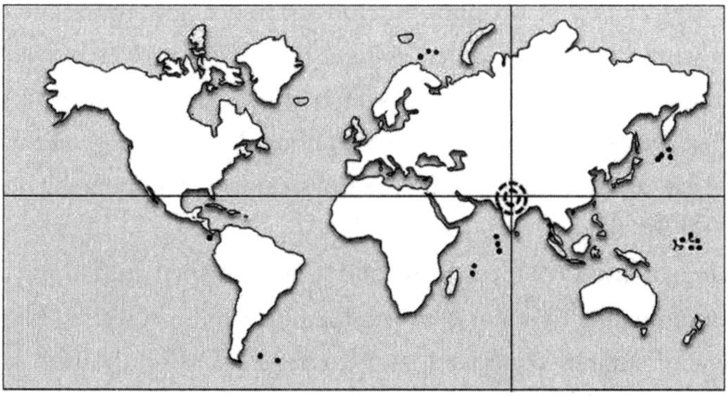

Fifth day of the third test India-Australia Test Match

Scores:

Australia 1st Innings: 550/ all out

India 1st Innings: 220/ all out

India 2nd Innings: 300/ 9 (following on)

Lagging by thirty runs at the beginning of the day, the last pair was trying to extend their runs and had so far survived sixty minutes of barrage and volleys of both balls and words from the opposition. Mansur did a good job shielding Gagan from the bowlers by taking the strike most of the time and Gagan did his bit by surviving the few balls he faced. India scored only twenty runs in one hour and the opposition was getting frustrated.

Gorton maintained an attacking field with a packed off-side with seven fielders. The idea was simple: barge in short stuff for Mansur to pull, defend or take the ball on the body. It was *bodyline* revisited, and the spectators and players in the dressing room noticed how the fielders were being positioned. The line of attack from the bowler was now the off-stump instead of the leg, with the intent of the ball rising up towards the batsman quickly.

Reid moved in to bowl to Mansur. The first ball zipped past his nose, the second ball rose close to the body, and Mansur opted for evasive action, bent backwards and got out of the way. The third ball hit him on the helmet, and the catch was taken. The Aussies gave a mock shout and closed in on him. Gorton offered a few more altercating words with a couple of others joining him. The umpires moved in to calm things down. Gorton wanted the batsmen to lose their focus which they had held strong for more than an hour. *Mental disintegration* was the term used, and it meant getting the opposition down mentally both on field and off field.

Mansur tried to focus hard and Gagan helped him along at his end, emboldened by Mansur taking the blows and protecting him. The barrage of attacks continued, and a couple of overs passed by with five more runs being scored. India was now just five runs away from making Australia bat again, and some seventy overs were left in the day. It was shaping up to be a long period. As Mansur evaded yet another ball, Gorton was growing impatient, and the whole world could see his facial expression changing to one of frustration. Gorton came close to Mansur and placed himself at *silly point* fielding position. The mental disintegration tactics continued.

Gorton was smiling now. *It's only a matter of time.*

As one more over passed, Gorton came close to the two players who were now having a mid pitch talk.

'Guys, come on, try hitting out. You will get some runs.'

Mansur and Gagan went back to their respective creases with Mansur facing a new over. The first ball hit Mansur on the pads and the ball was outside the line. When the Aussies appealed for LBW, the umpire took a hard look and turned it down. A collective tone of disgust rose from the fielders. Gorton went to Mansur.

'You are out, why don't you walk?'

'Go back. The next ball will go over your head,' Mansur retorted, breaking his silence.

'Yes...yes, over my head, but I still don't get it. Why have you been selected?'

Mansur felt a rush of adrenalin through his body, and he squinted at Gorton.

The bowler was ready now, and Gorton once again positioned himself close by. The next ball was a play and miss, with the keeper collecting the ball. Mansur could feel the pressure build on him.

*Why am I here, what am I doing? I need to fight…I need to succeed…*I need to *make things happen.*

'Hey, I wanted to ask you something. Are you an Indian or a Paki? Whose side are you on?' snapped Gorton.

Mansur was now enraged. He was here to play cricket and hadn't expected such tone or language. He wanted to take a swipe at Gorton's head with his bat, but resisted.

'I am here for the game, Gorton…just for the game,' he replied in a loud and clear voice. There was an audible snigger among all the close-in fielders.

'Yeah...mate, but you still don't know whose side you are playing for,' said Gorton. Mansur was now livid as he moved in with an aggressive posture towards Gorton. Gorton was unfazed and did not budge from his position. Gorton winked and chewed his gum more vigorously. Mansur was breathing heavily now, almost panting, and needed to vent his pent up anger.

A red bird with a blue breast swooped down just when Mansur raised his left hand; it landed on Mansur's bat, which was placed near his shoulder, and began to tweet. On hearing the sound, Mansur stopped. He slowly moved the bat away from his shoulder, and the bird kept on singing, its small head moving around as it continued its music. Mansur looked on with awe, the musical notes exerting a calming effect on him. The umpire called him to start playing. A smile slowly crossed Mansur's lips, and he began laughing loudly as the bird flitted from the bat to his shoulder before finally flying away.

The fielders, the umpire, and Gagan could not understand what was so funny. But to Mansur it was clear: he had received yet another sign; the Oracle had found another way to reach out to him. He recalled the words she had whispered in his ear.

'You will hear the music from the air, a bird will come and sing at your shoulder...then remember what is written in the paper.' Her signs keep coming up. *This is my moment and this is my day.*

There were three balls left in the over and twelve more before lunch break was called. Mansur was now determined to follow the Oracle's instruction–swing his hands...as he had to fight his destiny to build hope and make it happen.

The next day, standing near the Amar Jawan Jyoti, Samir Ansari was waiting to meet *Janab*. While waiting he read an editorial cut out from a newspaper which summarised India's victory over Australia and Mansur's breathtaking performance with the bat and ball.

Cygnus Times

Tuesday, November 27

Baramulla Bomber Destroys Australia

From the blog of Suraj: www.princecalledsourav.com

The Indian cricket team did not turn the table on the Australian, they virtually threw it at them. The victory of Eden Garden back in 2001 was sweet, but this was sweeter.

Back then the Captain sat down without moving from his place during the historic partnership, this time all players did not move when Mansur was batting. Mansur along with Gagan, helped India get a 55 run lead, and later both of them blew the Aussie batting line-up under twelve overs.

In the end it would be said India won by eight runs, but the way India won would ensure that more followers come into the longer version of the game. And in Kashmir it was no different, as in Mansur's home town in Baramulla , they cheered for every wicket he took with calls of 'Ihsan Allah' reverberating across the Valley also.

Mansur took seven wickets, and each of the seven wickets was well crafted. Mansur and Gagan worked like a pack of wolves, hunting down the batsmen. The Aussie captain, Gorton was dumbstruck and at loss of words in the presentation ceremony. I don't blame him. After all who would have thought?

The next game in Mumbai is going to be interesting now. Let us see if the Aussies can get beyond the trauma that was inflicted, as they have to again face a pace barrage and the country Mansur bombs.

What a find Mansur Haider has been. His name means invincible lion, but I will call him the Baramulla Bomber. Not only India should be proud of what he has achieved but the world should be happy seeing the birth of real pace bowling India. There will be more Mansur's in Kashmir, and every common man should get his due now.

Samir smiled, he knew now the plan was working.

Janab was right. It has started, and this will lead to an internal implosion of a positive kind. And he gave the right name–BARAMULLA BOMBER. I wonder how did Janab get that idea to name him like that. But it is good, Mansur is blowing away the Aussies. Aha, Janab is here...now we need to focus on the December attack. Still no idea where the attack is going to be set?

11 DAYS TO EVENT

Oslo Spektrum,
Oslo, Norway

November 30,14:15 CET

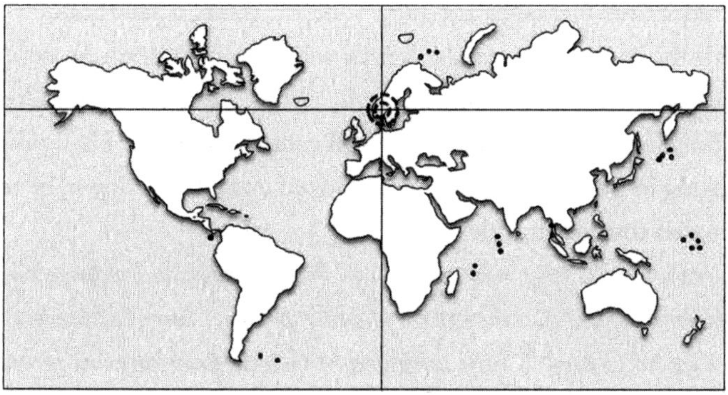

'**Dr Nasir walked** in long strides on the wet stone pavement, his gloved hand clasped across his blue overcoat, trying to protect himself from the cold air. A red scarf covered his bowed head as he watched his feet move across hexagonal blocks of the pavement. Sniffling due to the cold, he was strolling back to his hotel, the *Clarion Royal Christiania,* where he had been a regular guest in the recent past.

As he passed the Central Station, he thought about the day. Since morning he had been at the Oslo Spektrum conducting experiments for the D-Day where he would unleash a modified version of the Shaksgam Valley weapon. Oslo Spektrum, the famous arena for various functions, would hold a concert on the evening of December 11, the Nobel Peace Prize Concert.

The world will see their leaders perish a slow and painful death and no one will know what to do but…I need to find a way to be immune myself in order to execute it.

He raised his head slightly to see some faces smiling at him, and he smiled back gently. He was again lost in his thoughts as he reached the gates of his hotel.

Three versions of the weapon, but still have to get the correct frequency to match the hall vibrations, to make the attack successful. But…Lord Shiva has been merciful, his 'damru' *creating the primordial sound A-U-M and guiding me to find the divine frequency.*

As he collected his keys, he was greeted by a couple of smartly dressed hotel staff sitting across the reception. Wishing them back he enquired about messages for him. One of them, a tall blonde turned towards the computer screen to check and shook her head. As he left the polished wooden framework, he noticed the other East Asian looking receptionist picking up the phone and calling someone. He could hear her talking in Mandarin as he slowly moved away. Head down, he smiled and moved towards the elevator.

General Chan's spies here too, General Pervez's maniacal benchmen staying in my adjacent room. At least the ISI has told who they are…every Chinese looks a spy to me. General Chan feels I am using ancient Chinese knowledge and he has every right to the results from my use of it.

Dr Nasir pushed the blue elevator button and waited patiently for the cylindrical glass elevator to arrive. He loosened his scarf and scratched his neck gently, rotating his head in a circular motion.

General Pervez and Chan will never appreciate the power of the Vedas. They don't understand. It's not about religion but knowledge. After all, the Vedas were given directly by the Gods.

The lift halted at his floor, and he stepped out to the Curacao blue mosaic carpeted hallway. He felt for his electronic key which he had slipped inside his overcoat pocket earlier. He inserted the key inside the steel coloured contraption and entered his room. He took out a crumpled package from an internal pocket of his coat. He slipped open the other corner of the white coloured wooden closet and placed his shoes. The electronic safe was in front of him; he tapped in the four digit code and took out his laptop. He walked towards the study table and placed the laptop and the crumpled package side by side on the wooden surface.

He then moved towards the small kitchen to prepare tea. He came back to the table, switched on his laptop and entered the numeric password. As the laptop powered on, he had a few sips of the tea and opened the crumpled package and took out a rectangular, elongated metal object in a bubble wrap which he carefully laid down on the table; he removed a memory chip attached to the black object. The rectangular object was illuminated with a few LED lights and a couple of digital screens that showed up numbers in hertz. Dr Nasir inserted the software and while it ran, he continued drinking his green tea.

Non believers don't trust the power of the Vedas. Given by the gods word by word, knowledge of it can make one all powerful. My teacher Oppenheimer only scratched the surface; I managed to go deep enough to control some elements. Forty-nine varieties of fire! And we humans have discovered only a few of them. I have mastered the power of sound from fire.

Dr Nasir noticed that the light in the rectangular object beside the laptop had stopped flickering. Sitting in front of his laptop now, he tapped on the screen at an icon shaped like fire but green in colour. The screen colour changed to fluorescent green and a set of menu buttons came up. He tapped the menu button titled *Giza.*

The mysterious Giza pyramid has the most beneficial and relaxing frequency known to humans 6.8 hertz. No one knows the reason for this frequency but this is the frequency which causes the alpha state in the mind, making it calm. I am going to use this system against the brain itself with the help of this creation of mine... the alpha wave frequency modulator.

Dr Nasir now held the rectangular shaped object in front of his eye, marvelling at his own creation. The *alpha wave frequency modulator* was created with an ability to modulate frequencies within a closed environment. It was able to disrupt the alpha wave pattern of the brain and frequencies of other human organs. The mechanism of action was to be carried out in two ways. The first one was to create an effect of oxygen toxicity within the human anatomical system. If carbon-dioxide and other gases can be harmful to the human body, so can be oxygen in large quantities. During a spaceflight, high oxygen concentrations contribute to damage across multiple body systems. Similarly, the *alpha wave frequency modulator* creates an environment where a cell starts to call for more oxygen supply. In response the brain and respiratory system start to pull in more oxygen in a multiplier effect and the damage starts to set in.

The alpha wave frequency modulator not only impacted the brain but also the central nervous system to control the nerves of the body. Dr Nasir tapped in a few icons and started calibrating the data which the modulator memory chip had recorded in the Oslo Spektrum. He began to calculate the impact of acoustics and vibrations in the hall for the impact to take place. A multicolour diagram came up on the screen, which looked like multiple strands tagged together. The strands were blue, green, yellow and red. The 3-dimensional diagram was that of the Sonic Hedgehog (SHH) signalling molecule.

The SHH is responsible in patterning of the central nervous system during vertebral development, during the stage of a growing embryo. The pathway which Dr Nasir was disturbing was the Indian Hedgehog (IHH) protein and was trying to influence the second wave of attacks after the brain was hit.

Using a silver colour electronic pen in his right hand Dr Nasir was tapping and turning the strands around and typing on the numbers pad. The strands tightened and loosened as the scientist was trying to adjust the shape.

By manipulating this signalling protein he aimed for patterning the central nervous system. The body would be hit first with convulsions followed by difficulty in breathing and pain within the chest, and then alterations to the eyes and vision. This will finally end in unconsciousness and death to the group of subjects.

The modulator was to be placed in one of the thirteen private corporate boxes; which was a secluded section in the hall, the corporate was Zrotriya Ltd. The advantage of these private boxes is that each has a separate VIP entrance with an independent elevator, and a clear view of the stage, proceedings and the hall.

The challenge was to customise a grand scale so that most of the expected 6000-7000 guests of the evening were impacted at the same time. The only way Dr Nasir would be able to take control of the situation would be by being present at the location and continuously fine-tuning the alpha wave frequency modulator to ensure maximum impact on the victims. In order for that to happen, multiple factors had to be taken into consideration. To understand the acoustics of the hall Dr Nasir clicked another icon which showed a rotating 3-D image of the Oslo Spektrum hall. He adjusted his square shaped spectacles and used the electronic pen to mark spots. A mathematical equation followed each mark of the spot duly noted by the scientist as he wrote it down on a paper pad.

The mathematical algorithm based formulae took into consideration not only the design of the hall, but also the resonance produced by the print fragments on walls created by artist Rolf Nesch. Dr Nasir had travelled around the world to access the areas where Rolf Nesch contribution was present to take readings and calibrate the impact of the algorithm.

The music playing at the particular moment of the attack would also have to be considered since the frequencies emanating from the musicians would have an impact on the listeners. To tackle this Dr Nasir attended earlier musical functions held in the hall like the A-ha's farewell tour and the peace prize concerts. An on-field experiment being conducted in 2009, almost gave way. Dr Nasir had to stop one of the first experiments done in Norway in Nordmøre near Oslo, on Dec 9, 2009. The disruptions in the atmosphere caused the blue Norway Spiral phenomenon, a day before the US President Obama got his Nobel Peace Prize award.

He felt a tingling sensation as his mobile vibrated inside his trousers pockets. He took out his smart phone, frowning at the caller's name.

What does he want now? He only brings troublesome news.

'Hello!'

'Salam Walekum Janab,' came the reply from the other side.

'You can tell General sahib, that all is well and under control. Operation Babylon is on…'

'Janab, I have not called for this…,' the caller interrupted rudely.

'What has happened?'

'He is here?'

'Who is here?'

'The Swedish CIA agent, Adolf.'

'Here means?'

'Here in Oslo, he entered the Spektrum hall after you left.'

'What? I thought your brother had taken care of him?'

There was a silence at the other end, as the caller started breathing heavily, clearly agitated.

'I am sorry, I forgot,' replied back Dr Nasir in an apologetic tone.

'It's ok, even I keep forgetting my twin brother was killed in Monkey Hill in Kashmir.'

'OK…we need to deal with him but ensure that we take control of things.'

'I want to finish him off.'

'No Jalal! No. I understand how you feel about Altaf's death but we need to wait.'

'What…but…'

'We first need to know how much he knows.'

There was a grunt of disapproval from Jalal.

'Do you see him?'

'Yes I can, and it looks like he is waiting for someone, checking his watch regularly…wait he is making a call.'

'Don't do anything till I come there…I have a solution to take him down without any trouble…just listen and follow my instructions.'

Jalal listened intently as Dr Nasir spoke and a curt smile appeared on his face.

11 DAYS TO EVENT

Oslo Spektrum,
Oslo, Norway

November 30,16:15 CET

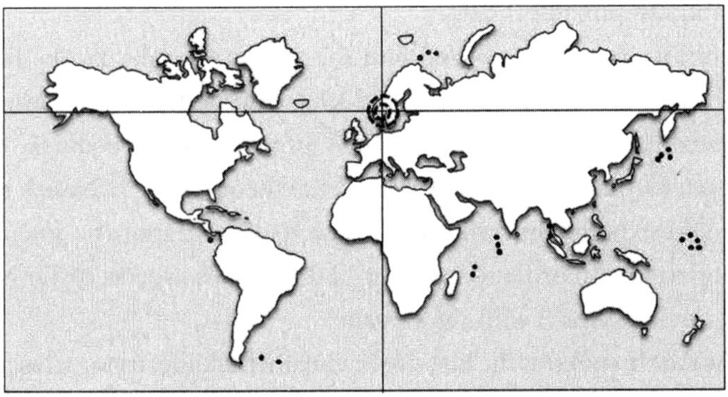

Adolf stood outside the gates of Oslo Spektrum, slowly scanning the area.

What was Dr Nasir doing in this place?

Ann Silfverskiöld's feedback about him had helped him piece together previous inputs along with the SOG team. The SOG team created a travel map on Dr Nasir and the places he had visited over the last five years, also concentrating on the places where he had stayed for any specific duration. They tried to identify patterns in the travel, but they were either sponsored trips for lectures and conferences, or tourism related visits to museums, architectural marvels, music shows and historical sites. As a Nobel laureate he was invited to the Nobel ceremonies both in Stockholm and Oslo. They were at a dead end.

As soon it became clearer that they were on a wild goose chase, the consensus was reached not to tail Dr Nasir. Orders came in from Carina's superiors in the government and also from the US and UK governments. CIA and MI-7 were both instructed to drop this line of investigation and concentrate on General Pervez's movements and the new threat emerging from jihadist movements getting traction in Egypt, Libya, Yemen and Sudan.

Adolf was alone in not falling in line with this decision. He conveyed the same to Carina, who would rein him in officially but personally she would not stop him if he was on to something he knew. His help would be curtailed and he would have to rely on unofficial channels–Aahana, Ann and Dr Tamang.

He asked Aahana to send him the photos and details she had of the Shaksgam valley expedition and keep him updated on Mansur. He requested Ann to get any travel related information she could lay hands on about Dr Nasir. Adolf worked on the theory that Dr Nasir's recent work and experiments will be the key to any weapon he intends to develop to use. In order to understand the various aspects of Dr Nasir's work, he discussed it with Dr Tamang.

As Adolf stared at the massive Spektrum building, trying to ascertain if this was the place where it would all end, he heard his mobile buzz. *Dr Tamang! Finally he has called…some answers.*

He flicked open his mobile and sat down on one of the benches in the garden.

'Hello Doctor.'

'Hello my son…how have you been?'

'So far not so good. I need more help to understand Dr Nasir's recent work in String theory and related studies.'

'Well I did go through what you sent and did some research on my own.'

'Do you have answers to my questions?'

'I think I can give a direction on what you seek.'

'So you have an idea on how this weapon will work?'

'Not an idea, but a rationale on why such a weapon can work…and you would have to remember what else I discussed in our last meeting.'

'Yes very much…'

'Everything in life moves in rhythm and with a sense of balance…it's like something happening in cycles again and again without disruption. And guess where is it directed from?'

Adolf was silent, pondering on what to answer but remembered Dr Tamang's lecture on nature's effect on humans and animals.

'Nature's rhythms.'

'Yes.'

'But how is Dr Nasir's work related to it…I don't get it?'

'Step by step my son, patience. Let's take a woman's monthly period for example, it has its natural cycle every month and changes as the woman ages, right?'

'Yes.'

'Well, did you know menstrual cycles between two close women, like those of female roommates actually get synchronised over a period of time.'

'What?'

'A sense of equilibrium has to be maintained…learn the nature and know how God makes things work.'

'Yes, I get the picture on gaining equilibrium between systems. However Dr Nasir's work around string theory and sound is for gaining an energy source. Are you telling me that this force can actually disrupt the balance around systems?'

'Yes the sense of equilibrium exists between elements–humans, animals and even plants. All of us are moving in rhythm, between each other, without even knowing what impact they can create. When such disruption occurs the body tries to regain balance. Take jet lag as an example, where our body is trying to cope with a change in equilibrium between a current time and location. To tackle this disruption, our body needs to make adjustments.'

'Ohh…I get it! Dr Nasir's work may intend to disrupt this balance quickly.'

'Yes, exactly. To understand this better there are two things you need to understand–resonance and entrainment.'

'I know what resonance means, you have explained that to me… resonance is the frequency at which the object vibrates under natural circumstance, without anything altering it…right?'

'Yes right you do remember…good.'

'Yes and I remember the tuning fork experiment that you showed me that morning in your house…both objects cooperated with each other.'

During his visit to Dharamshala, Dr Tamang had shown a tuning fork experiment where he took two tuning forks and kept them close to each other. He struck one of them and it started vibrating. The second tuning fork which was not hit also started vibrating due to the sound of its neighbouring tuning fork. After a period both started vibrating similarly and a balance was created.

Dr Tamang continued, 'So resonance allows one body to meet and match the natural vibration of another in a passive way. But… entrainment, on the other hand, is active, and not within one's control.'

'Does it mean that both are opposites, like something at different ends of a spectrum?'

'Yes, to put it simply, you can term it that way, as with entrainment the natural oscillatory patterns or vibrations of one object are replaced with another set of oscillatory patterns.'

'A different vibration…but the question is Dr Tamang, can it be manipulated or controlled, and if so how?'

'Of course it can be manipulated, we do it every day of our life to others, knowingly or unknowingly…in love and in sex.' Dr Tamang gave a short burst of laughter.

'It is done via brain waves in our everyday life…the waves tend to oscillate in a synchronous manner when we feel comfortable. Like when we talk to loved ones, or in a professor to student scenario, or a physician to patient, all of them entrain each other. And the best example is priests and preachers' connection with their congregation.'

'If I put things simply, in layman's words, can I say it's a messaging and feedback mechanism?'

'Yes and it is known as bio-feedback. Our brain constantly works on our body to maintain this rhythm, and people who practice yoga achieve this in the appropriate way…the brain, the heart and respiration process is connected. You slow down one, the other gets impacted and vice-versa.'

'So brain waves are the key to controlling the events.'

'Yes…but may I also add that this is currently theory and all practical experiments are only at the periphery right now.'

'You mean it is highly improbable but not impossible.'

'Yes, my son…and music is the best way to reach out to a wide audience. So my guess would be check on Concert halls where music can be used to manipulate the frequencies of the body.'

'Thank you doctor, it has been a really fruitful discussion.'

'Well you know where to reach me whenever you have doubts…but I will be out of touch for sometime.'

'Why? Are you travelling somewhere?'

'Yes going to Tibet, have to visit someone near Lhasa in connection with my current research. But do send me a message and I will get back as and when I can.'

'Sure will do thanks,' said Adolf with great appreciation in his tone.

Adolf slid the phone inside his pocket and looked around the few people around the garden involved in different activities. Just then, a striking woman, a veritable *femme fatale,* entered the garden. She looked like someone straight out of the books, with a mini bouffant hairstyle, her broad forehead and high cheekbones visible despite the dark shades she wore. Many eyes were on her as she walked in wearing a knee-length black skirt and a purple high-collared top beneath a small black jacket. As Adolf gazed at her, he realised that she was walking directly towards him, and he recognised her. It was Ann Silfverskiöld.

'Hi…you are really hard to catch.'

'What are you doing here?' Adolf's disapproval was clear in his voice.

'Don't get annoyed, I know you must be thinking I may be stalking you, but I don't know…something inside just wants to be close to you, help you out.'

Adolf did not mind her help as he was here due to her. But he did not want Ann to be around as she could be a distraction to the investigation. He didn't want to share any information.

'Well, you know I told you that I am working on a sensitive case and we should not meet directly…'

'Yes I know!' she cut him short giving him a light hug and a peck on the cheek. Adolf responded similarly and saw Ann's smile change to concern.

'I am sorry but had no choice; Dr Nasir is not here alone.'

From a distance across some trees Jalal watched them chat, waiting to give Dr Nasir and the other colleagues some time to get to the rendezvous point before his action started.

'Ann, I am moved by your concern. But I cannot put your life in jeopardy'

'Yes, I understand Adolf.'

'No, I don't think you understand the gravi…,' Adolf stopped as he saw a figure watching them, and ducked behind a tree when Adolf gazed at him. He held Ann by the shoulders and looked directly into her eyes.

'Were you followed?'

'No…I don't know, I don't think so, why?' said Ann, as she turned around to see where Adolf was watching. The figure looked out again at them and turned around and started walking away. Adolf moved in his direction telling Ann to wait there. But she refused and began following him. Adolf did not bother now as he increased his pace towards the figure, whose cap blew away, revealing his bald head. The figure bolted out quickly. Adolf and Ann paced up, and Adolf looked at Ann, surprised that she was keeping up with him. They went out in the open lane and saw the figure slow down, and look at them directly as they closed on him. He turned into an alley-way between a row of buildings.

It may be a trap, but got to catch up with him, thought Adolf.

Ahead of Adolf, Jalal moved slowly in the alley-way towards a dead end…He stopped and turned around to see Adolf and Ann inside the alley as they walked towards him slowly. Adolf halted on seeing Jalal and held Ann by her hand.

Jalal! But I killed him on Monkey Hill.

Adolf took out his service handgun, a *SIG P229,* clasped it tightly with both hands and pointed it at Jalal. He heard a shriek from Ann and turned his head around, still pointing the gun towards Jalal. He saw Ann stop and raise her right arm and place it on the wall for support. She looked at him and held her stomach. Adolf felt his heart beat faster; his throat starting to parch and feet begin to wobble.

Something is wrong. Kurt! It's the weapon...this is the weapon...

Adolf sensed that they had been incapacitated by a sonic weapon and saw three figures emerge behind Ann. One of them looked like Dr Nasir.

Jalal closed in slowly behind on Adolf. Adolf swivelled around and hit Jalal with his left elbow, pushing him to the wall. Ann got the cue and kicked out at one of the men behind her just as Adolf caught another with both hands and pushed him to the wall. A tall bearded man in the front lunged forward and hit Ann on the head. Ann was slow to react and fell down. Adolf saw this and tried to use his head to ram the guy, but felt too weak for a charge. His legs were trembling.

Adolf collapsed, but did not lose complete consciousness. As he struggled he found himself dragged along the ground. He saw Ann lying motionless, being left behind.

'You...you killed my twin brother in Kashmir,' said Jalal coming close to Adolf.

Adolf tried to focus. He was incapacitated by Dr Nasir's miniature sonic weapon. Adolf could make out only a few words now.

'What to do with him Doctor?'

'Do not take him to Pakistan; we need to know what he knows. Take him to India. I will arrange it, and we can then set him up as a terrorist operative who blew up the cricket team. This way we can keep the Indian government in tangle with the western world.'

'Isn't that risky...final test match...Mumbai...need to test... weapon need to wipe out...need to test...very important...weapon.'

'I'll take...and hide him.'

Mumbai stadium is also the target...Samir is going to use Mansur for the operation, thought Adolf before losing consciousness.

7 DAYS TO EVENT

**Wankhede Stadium,
Mumbai, India**

December 4, 18:35 IST

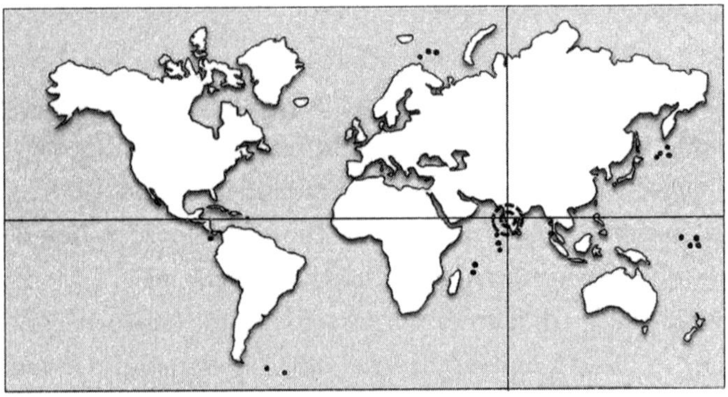

It was the end of the third day of play and India had an overall lead of 240 runs with 5 second-innings wickets in hand. It was a great overall team performance after having conceded a 60-run lead to the Australians. Mansur was now in the thick of things, taking seven wickets while bowling in the first innings, and scoring an invaluable fifty while batting.

The Aussies were not able to face many of his balls and took evasive action. They decided that assuming defensive stance against him would be best until they settled on a suitable strategy for attack. The Australian media started questioning Mansur's bowling technique and the speed he generated, indicating that he may have a suspect action. One commentator also started making noises about his polydactylism, trying to a make a point that having two thumbs on his bowling hand gave him an advantage in variation. It was a battle among the media allocating space for him, with on-air channels, print, and web media covering him in detail. His village in Baramulla was in the spotlight, so were his family and the city of Srinagar. Needless to say, Mansur had become a hero for India and the voice of Kashmir. His was the story of an under-achiever turning into a hero, and he had been tagged *the bomber from Baramulla* as his deliveries would jump and explode in the batsman's face.

With two more days left, India's effort in the game was not over yet. In order to win, the team had to put in a big score and take all of Australia's wickets before the end of the test match. If that happened India would square the series and Mansur would definitely be not only the man of the match but also the man of the series. India may have found its first fast bowler who could bowl at a speed of more than 155 km/hr.

Malini Basu from Newsgate was in the media centre along with her team. She was trying to get some exclusive bytes from Mansur. She regretted her earlier decision not to cover him during the local games, a couple of months back. At the time she thought the potential sex scandal with Saloni and the Prime Minister would be the bigger breaking story.

Both the Indian and Australian captains were in attendance, answering questions from the media. While Mansur was the flavour and theme of the conference, there was a question put to Gorton by Malini asking his opinion on the travel advisory posted by their government warning their citizens not to travel to India as a result of the rising tensions between India and China. To this Gorton replied candidly, 'We are here for cricket, and sports can build bridges and remove the divide. Running away has never been part of our plan, and we are confident that diplomacy will find a solution.'

The conference ended on that note, and both Captains got up. Watching them from close quarters and filming the proceedings was Salim Bhakth from Pakistan's *Associated Press*—at least that's what his credentials indicated. But he had another name—Jalal, one of Brigadier Pervez's special ops team members and an ardent supporter of Jihad against India and Western countries. The original Salim Bhakth had been murdered when he arrived in India. Jalal handled the anti-India operation. Four of his core members had been wiped out by Mansur and his friends during the *Monkey Hill* incident in Kashmir. Jalal's objective then was to bring down Mansur, but now it was too late to think about that. Any action taken on Mansur alone would have serious repercussions, but if both teams were attacked and Mansur was killed, no one would know the actual target.

Mansur was lucky to have Adolf by his side the last time. Now with Adolf out of the way, he will be totally alone and we will have a free rein.

However Jalal missed out on one crucial piece of information. JJ, aka Jay, Malini's trusted friend and cameraman, knew Salim Bhakth of Pakistan's *Associated Press*. They had never met formally but had developed a good professional relationship over cyber space, sharing technical info and details. During his meeting earlier in the day Jay had his doubts when Salim did not recognise him. Now Jalal had to tie down this loose end tonight and take care of JJ and strike on December 5.

A double strike and the actual reason would be buried. Once we sacrifice ourselves we will set in motion the world's destruction.

Sitting in his apartment, the Home Minister's face bore a serious expression. He held the phone with his right hand and took down notes as he carried on his telephonic conversation. 'Yes I understand Carina, you know you can trust me...utmost secrecy, it will be between us.' He listened in some more. 'His name is Adolf Silfverskiöld, and you believe he is in India. Yes, that will be fine, send in the last trajectory location, and don't worry I will put my best and most trusted man on the job…he is capable of getting things done. I will discreetly enquire about that without your name or your agency's name coming up…This is between old friends.'

'Thank you, and hope you are working on Intel we gave on a possible strike in Wankhede Stadium.'

'Yes we are Carina, that's why I am here…to control things on ground level.'

They exchanged a few more words before closing the call. Agastya went to the home screen of his Nokia phone and tapped an app to make the line a standard secure line.

The Americans never reach out, they must have put their other assets on the job. So many expatriates working now…not surprising some of them may be covert operatives…unlike masquerading as tourists and doing plane watching in Mumbai. Will speak to Ansari…he may have some idea on Adolf.

Agastya was unaware of Adolf's presence a few kilometres away, chained in a shanty dwelling within Dharavi, which was a hidden terror cell.

These terrorists must be having state backing. Jalal wants to know something from me otherwise he would have killed me. Bringing me to India, don't get it? May be Dr Tamang was right…everything is connected. Let me meditate.

'AaaUuuMmmAaaUuuMmm'

'AaaaaaaaUuuMmmAaaaaaaaUuuMmm'

'Ah…Mennnnnn'

'Ahhhhh…Men'

'AaaUuuMmmAaaUuuMmm'…

Adolf was meditating in tandem both "AMEN" and "AUM" as the sacred utterance whenever he was left alone in the room. The vibrations from the chants helped him concentrate and calm his mind.

Dr Tamang was right with regards to the scared primordial sound "AUM" and its descendent "AMEN." It does have power…Mikaela.

He adjusted his chain to reach his right hand and turned the gold ring. He grimaced in pain at this daily torture.

I was never supposed to be in this case, Kurt selected me. I was in Dharamshala which I should have never revisited, if it had not been for Dr Tamang's book which I picked up unintentionally…I should have never been in this position…if I am pushed into this corner, there must be a power which will pull me out. Mansur is not the vehicle for the bomb…these people want to kill him, not protect him.

Adolf had heard some more of the conversation; from his limited knowledge of Hindi and Urdu, he could make out that Mansur was targeted for a kill and not to carry out an operation.

Thousands of miles away, Mikaela knelt before a statue of Jesus. She prayed for Adolf's success and for the lord to keep a watchful eye on them.

He does not believe you exist, but that does not make him wrong…forgive him. I believe you and trust you and he loves and trusts me…please protect us.

6 DAYS TO EVENT

Wankhede Stadium,
Mumbai, India

December 5,13:20 IST

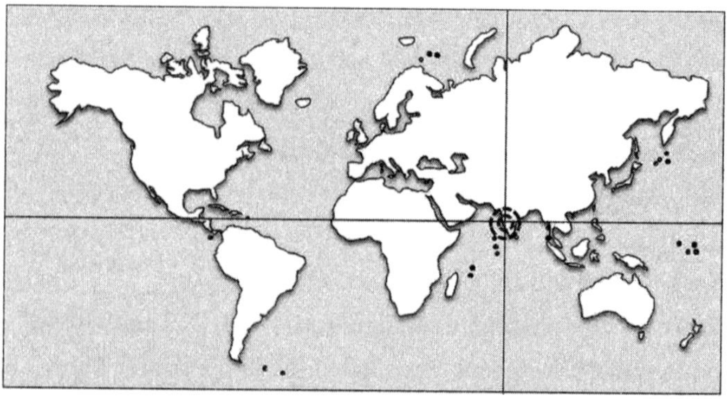

By **lunch time** on the fourth day of play, Australia had set a target of 335 runs to win in five sessions. The Indian team managed to score 400 runs before being bundled out, thus establishing a lead of 334 runs. The atmosphere was tense. While most of the spectators were engaged in the game, JJ followed Jalal aka Salim. He wanted to confront him and prove to Malini that he was right about something being amiss. Jalal knew JJ was following him, and felt that would be the best way to take care of him as he and his men could corner him.

JJ followed Jalal into the parking lot. JJ called out to Jalal to stop; Jalal quickened his pace around the parking lot maze. JJ, who was not a natural athlete, had to jog to catch up with him. As he crossed between two SUVs parked side by side, he tripped and fell. A sharp pain shot through his legs; looking down he saw he was bleeding.

I have been shot. These men are killers.

He gained his voice and was going to call for help when a couple of well built men jumped on him. While one of them covered JJ's mouth and held back his hands, the other held his legs. They carried him into the van. The most JJ could do was emit a muffled sound, which was drowned out by the noise from the stadium as the post lunch session began.

'Do we kill him now?' one of the men asked Jalal who was sitting in the driver's seat lighting a cigarette.

'No, let him see what we are doing, and then we can take him out piece by piece, then we will take care of his dusky lady companion,' said Jalal, puffing away.

JJ's eyes were wide with fear and his heart was pounding. Just then he heard his phone ring.

Malini's ringtone.

One of the burly figures picked it up and passed it on to Jalal, who looked at the flashing readout: 'Malls'. He extended his hand with the phone towards JJ.

'Take it, keep it in speaker mode, and say that you are going out and will be back later. No funny business,' Jalal threatened.

JJ took the phone and answered it.

'JJ, where the hell are you?'

'I am outside the stadium, needed to go somewhere. Will contact you later.'

'What? How can you go? This is crazy.'

'Hey, Malls, you know me. Don't worry... *Trust me, I am a Mumbaiwala.*'

JJ had played a gambit, and hoped Malini did not reply or ask him anything.

'Okay, keep me posted. Bye.'

'Sure...bye,' JJ shut the phone.

Malini knew something was wrong. JJ was from Delhi and always prided himself on the fact he was a *Delhiwala.*

Mumbaiwala...something is wrong. Is it him chasing Salim?

Malini jumped, rushing out of the room to find a quiet place where she could connect to her Delhi office for more information on Salim Bhakth. Samir was standing around the corner and watched Malini rush out of the media room.

'What happened? You look worried?' said Samir with a sense of authority.

'I think something has happened to my colleague, JJ,' Malini was frantic.

'Why, what happened? You need help?'

Malini had no idea what to do. She was confused and needed to take control of her emotions. She knew Samir and also the fact that he had strong contacts.

'I need info from gate security,' said Malini quickly to Samir.

They rushed down and found a security person on the stairway. Samir asked for directions to the security control room. The constable hesitated, but Samir took him aside, away from Malini; she saw him flash a small leather cover that the constable held and say something quietly to him. Minutes later, he returned and told her the control room was on the floor below theirs.

'What did you do?' she asked him as they rushed down. Malini clutched her handbag tightly.

'I gave him a Gandhi,' said Samir.

'What?'

'Tipped him Rs.500.' They reached the outside of the control room and were stopped by security. Malini flashed her press credentials and said she had a security issue to discuss. The inspector was hesitant at first, but a CCTC officer who was standing behind told him to let them through. As they crossed, Samir and the CCTC officer nodded to each other.

As they entered the room the officers sitting inside were taken aback on seeing the two of them. The CCTC officer who followed them in said it was okay, as he had let them in. Malini started blurting out what she knew and said she felt something wrong. She requested to see the security camera footage.

'Miss Malini, this is highly inappropriate. We have tight security. Nothing happened,' growled an officer sitting in the room.

'Look at the footage and verify,' said the CCTC officer.

The officer made a face, a disgruntled noise and instructed two of his men to examine the footage of the last thirty minutes, even as he made a call to the main gate to confirm if any media person or anyone else had walked out.

'What's that?' said Samir, pointing at one of the screens.

They saw the footage of JJ walking in the car park and two guys suddenly rushing towards him before they moved out of the frame. The time shown on the screen was 13:20.

'What's the next camera showing?' said Samir.

'We don't have anything else in that zone,' said the officer.

'A blind spot! You call this security?' fumed Samir. The CCTC officer told him to cool down as they all looked at the other footage.

'We need men near that area,' said the CCTC officer, and he instructed someone on his walkie-talkie to move to the parking area. The officer told a couple of armed police constables to accompany him. Malini and Samir went along, too. As they reached the ground they saw more armed constables scanning the area in pairs. All seemed normal, with a few civilians moving around looking surprised to see gun-toting police around.

Malini was requested by the CCTC officer to stay back, but she was adamant, 'No chance mister!'

'Sanjay, Sanjay Pal Uppal,' said the officer, completing the sentence with his name.

Samir told them to hurry and start looking for out of the ordinary movements or something that did not fit the picture.

Jalal, who was sitting inside the van, saw the movement of police from the car's side-view mirrors. He instructed the other men inside to keep quiet and not make any noise. 'Make sure he is quiet.' he said.

Jalal got out of the van, locked the door, and walked out without turning and looking at any of the security personnel. One of the officers close to him enquired who he was, to which he replied he was Salim Bhakth, and showed the press ID card. Malini, who was three parking lanes away, saw Jalal showing his card to the officer. She went hysterical, and began shouting and pointing towards Jalal, who saw her.

Jalal twisted the dial of his watch, which released a pointed steel blade, and he struck the officer standing close by on the neck. Blood gushed out as the officer fell, clutching his jugular vein. Jalal snatched his victim's Tavor assault rifle. Samir and Sanjay dashed forward, both taking out their Glock 17C pistols, and tried to take aim at Jalal. Jalal rushed out into the open towards another parked car, not wanting to expose the van and thus the plan. He ran, avoiding the fire from Samir and Sanjay, who were now moving in tandem in a synchronised motion, two by two, taking cover, using the cars as shields.

Finding himself surrounded from all four sides, Jalal hoped that his men in the van would now get out and save themselves. But they did not move and the van stood still.

Jerks…People like them bring shame to Allah.

Samir and Sanjay charged forward with cover fire provided by the other security personnel. As the bullets whizzed past, Jalal was slowly surrounded. Samir and Sanjay nodded at each other, and Samir went on one knee and took aim. Sanjay changed his angle of attack, running towards the target, and lay down as he got close. Now left with no avenue of escape, Jalal charged towards the security personnel who were firing. He was shot in the legs by Samir but he was hit in the head and body with a volley coming from those around him.

Samir ran towards the fallen terrorist and checked to see if he was alive. Finding him dead, Samir lost his temper and told the security personnel how they should maintain restraint in order to take terrorists alive. Sanjay mentioned the van from which the suspect had exited. The security personnel ran towards the van and surrounded it, maintaining a distance and hoping that it was not rigged. Sanjay went close to the van and instructed two more officers to cover him from behind. As he opened the van all three had guns positioned inside. They saw two men holding guns and one man lying on the floor of the van.

Both sides shouted at each other to keep down the guns. The men inside the van were more confused and scared now. They put down their guns and kept their hands on their heads as they came out of the van and knelt down. The security personnel took hold of their hands and put them on the ground. Sanjay went inside the van and turned the fallen body over. It was JJ. He was dead.

Malini, who had been watching the action from afar, now ran towards the van. Seeing the body, she collapsed and fainted.

'Get the medics here,' Samir called out.

A couple of local police personnel looked puzzled and surprised to hear Samir passing orders, but they complied. More local police arrived on site, including the senior officer who was at the control room. 'Please move aside, we are taking charge here,' he said, ordering his men to take control of the prisoners.

'No, you don't,' said Samir, displaying the same leather cover he had shown to the security person earlier. The senior officer took one look at the cover, stepped back and saluted Samir. The leather cover with the CCTC card identified him as *Major Samir Ansari, Special Officer CCTC, 'Anti Terror' Cell.*

5 DAYS TO EVENT

Home Ministry Office
Delhi, India

December 6, 11:10 IST

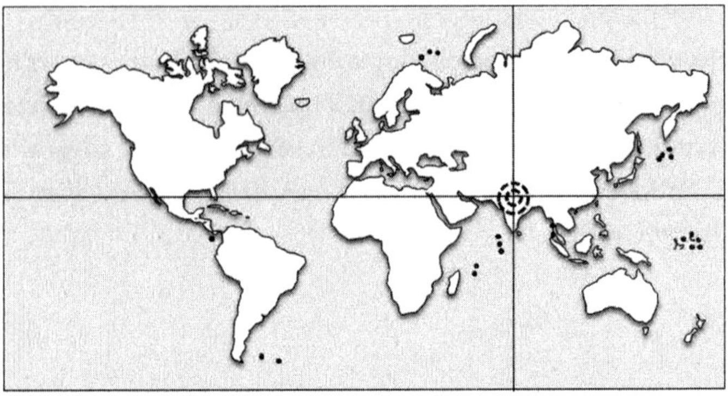

Agastya was in Delhi within his ministry's premises, six floors underground. He was maintaining a constant vigil on two fronts—the situation at the Mumbai game, after the shootout and the seemingly potential battlefront with China in the east in Tawang. Things were going as per plan on both fronts.

The CCTC team along with officials of the Home Ministry was in the thick of things preparing a case against the Pakistan government. The shooting incident in Mumbai did create a stir but the Australian cricket team in its never-say-die attitude persisted, wanting the game to go on and stayed back. CCTC senior officer, Samir Ansari, gave his report after interrogating the terrorists. The captured terrorists gave away their plan and mentioned a Pakistani army commander being involved. An initial interrogation had uncovered little information, and it was expected they were only pawns, with the king still alive and kicking. But there were a few surprises springing up, like finding Adolf, who was then escorted to the Swedish Embassy.

'Sir, we have the Defence Minister on the digital video link,' said one of the military aides to Agastya. Putting down the blue-brown diary in which he was making notes, Agastya stood up, stretched his legs, and shook his head to relax his neck. It had been a long night and he'd had only two hours of restless sleep. He walked next door into the room of the strategic nuclear bunker, one of five built in Delhi.

'How are you, sir?' said Agastya, looking at the large screen and seeing the Minister in battle fatigues.

'As you can see, I am just one of the guys here. Just a couple of stars short,' said Abhimanyu, smiling and pointing towards his olive green jacket.

'Sir there is no doubt about the satellite pictures, even the Americans, Russians, and the British have confirmed it,' Agastya spoke in a sombre tone. The surveillance photos were courtesy India's space program which had got its military wing two years back—DIPAC (Defence Imagery Processing and Analysis Centre).The pictures they were now viewing were of the Chinese military build-up on the eastern front of India's border around Arunachal Pradesh. China's *string of pearls* strategy had been completed and they were making their next move: border confrontation with India!

General Kashyapa continued to smile.

'Sir, even though I know how you'll respond I must insist that you move away from the frontline,' said Agastya in a concerned voice.

'There is a time for talk and there is a time for action. This is the time for action, and my being here ensures a reason for the tactics we intend to pull off,' said the battle-hardened veteran, stroking his silver-white French beard.

Agastya knew he could not dissuade him from making his last stand there. The primary mission of Abhimanyu had been to remove the historical Tibetan scrolls, *Thangka,* and other commentaries. Now with one of the potential key scrolls for the *Shaksgam Valley Vimana* (UFO) link safely out, Agastya wanted to ensure that the Chinese did not cross the border and cause more trouble.

Politics and Army should never get together. I hope the current Chinese Premier prevails, and takes down General Chan in time.

'So how is the story of our boy in Mumbai?' asked Abhimanyu, smiling.

'Everything is under control...post lunch session, final day Australia at 174 runs for five wickets. They need 161 more off 55 overs. Mansur will clean them up.'

'Good. Samir agreed and followed our plan. It's still not over. We need to use Mansur for a few days and by the blessings of our Guardians ancestors we will succeed…amen.'

'Amin you mean,' replied back the Home Minister.

'Hahaha…yes they are all the same. I need to get to the front now. Wait for my message…and Agastya, remember that the good thing is that he has delivered it again,' said General Abhimanyu, smiling from the screen.

5 DAYS TO EVENT

Tawang Border along China
Arunachal Pradesh, India

December 6,15:10 IST

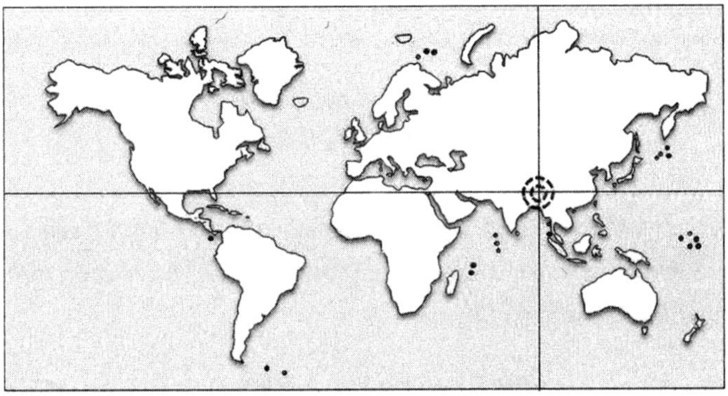

Defence Minister Abhimanyu Kashyapa reviewed the troop positions and communicated with the commanding officer of frontline forces and central command back in Delhi. Being part of the old guard, Abhimanyu informed one and all that he would be able to improve the morale of the troops from ground zero. This theory was meant for public consumption only; his real job was to ensure that the manuscripts from the Buddhist library in the Tawang region were removed safely from the conflict zone.

These manuscripts are now safe in Nalanda. They not only speak of our past, but also are a key to understand why the Vimanas (UFOs) returned post the Shaksgam Valley explosion. Now to see to it that the Chinese are not able to enter and reclaim Indian Territory again. We lost the 62 war, but this time, with Operation Vajra in place, the shock value would be enough to stop the Chinese.

Abhimanyu Kashyapa was now travelling to the frontline borders on the newly constructed highway. He passed a signboard that indicated

Lhasa 480 kms

Beijing 4100 kms

This may be the day I atone for my sins of 1962.

Opening his diary, he saw an old photograph taken in 1963 during his visit to Kohima in Nagaland. It showed him standing in front of the memorial of the 2nd British Division, XXXIII *Corps (British India),* which fought against the invading Japanese forces, where his father died. The memorial had an engraved epitaph that read:

"When You Go Home, Tell Them of Us and Say,
For Their Tomorrow, We Gave Our Today"

How true this verse is for every soldier of any country. Father, if only I had the chance to know you better. The time is approaching. I will not meet up with you in heaven till I redeem myself of my sins.

Two hours later, he was sitting inside the field CO's camp to oversee the operation from the ground. The camp was not like the old primitive hut he had seen during the 1962 conflict. Fifty years earlier most of the dwellings of soldiers near the front had walls matted with bamboo. Then it was primitive under the cold conditions. Moreover, due to the absence of proper road network and usable helipads, transportation of frontline supplies was by ponies and porters. The administration had been more active in this area over the last few years and created a network of ALGs (Advanced Landing Grounds), helipads, roads, and usable tracks that gave tanks and armoured carriers easy access. This scenic region was now an active military zone, and the civilian population was completely relocated to safer areas.

The Indian army had based only two brigades totalling around 10,000 men, but they were highly mobile. They had been given the following objectives:

i. Defend the front against any aggression without pushing forward across the McMahon line.
ii. Evacuate all civilians and non-combatants.

iii. Pull back to the designated secondary defence line if overwhelming force is encountered across the border.

The estimated Chinese forces across the border entailed three combat divisions. It was a disadvantage in the ratio of five to one. But Kashyapa had formulated a bold plan, '*Operation Vajra,*' where the end objective was to eradicate the threat and totally annihilate all offensive forces if they crossed within a specified zone of the demarcated borders within India, via a tactical nuclear strike.

A Captain entered the room where the CO and Defence Minister were reviewing the maps. He saluted them and moved towards the table where the map was spread. The Captain had just led a forward *recce* twenty kilometres from the FEBA, *Forward Edge of Battle Area,* to check if the Chinese forces had made any movement.

'Our recce is over; the enemy is on the move. They are moving their infantry ahead and we shall be face to face in the next hour or so,' said the young captain eagerly as he looked forward to a confrontation.

The CO reviewed the position the captain indicated. He remarked that the Chinese artillery was in a held back position for forward range attacks.

'If they are not pushing the artillery in, it means they are not backing their troops for more penetration and looking for skirmishes,' said the CO.

'True, and they don't have any gunships or other airborne assets near the strike zone as per our surveillance and the satellite recon we have received from the Russians,' said Abhimanyu, who sat with his right hand on his head as he studied the map.

When and how the move would come. Diplomacy is still open and international back channels are working overtime to diffuse the situation.

Abhimanyu got up, smiled at the men in the room, and said, 'Gentlemen, it's time to speak to the troops.'

They all nodded. The CO took the helmet from the table, put it on, and instructed the young captain to get his troops ready to meet with the Defence Minister.

All three walked out of the makeshift forward command centre. The evening was now fast approaching and the natural light swiftly fading. But the night sky was going to light up soon. While the CO and the young captain were thinking of how best to hold back the potential invasion, Abhimanyu was thinking about the mistake of running away from the battle and getting captured, that he made forty years ago.

I will NOT run away this time.

Though physically in the camp, his mind was elsewhere. He could hear, "*Bol Bajrang Bali Ki Jai*," which meant Victory to Lord Hanuman. This was the war cry of his *Rajput* infantry regiment.

He remembered how the coordinated shelling had transpired in October. Calls were made to stop the enemy, but without proper coordination between the different divisions, the 2nd Rajput based at Num Chuk stood no chance. He ran away leaving his men stranded. It was then that a shell exploded near him, knocking him unconscious. The next thing he remembered was waking up in a convoy that was headed to what was to become his new residence—the P.O.W. camp.

Days turned to weeks, and weeks into months. The Chinese said that the war had ended and China was withdrawing from all captured areas as they did not consider India an enemy. Their reaction was due only to the belligerent nature of the central government of India.

Thousands of years of friendship and you attacked us, is what his Chinese captors kept telling him, to make him feel guilty.

A few months later he was released and taken into protective custody by Indian Army officials who wanted to make sure he had not been brainwashed by the enemy. Two more months of observation and therapy ensured that he was okay, and he was released to his regiment. Abhimanyu Kashyapa felt ashamed that he had had to face such indignity, as his family had established a tradition of serving in the armed forces for well over five generations.

Thanks to Lord Shiva, who gave me strength to survive and helped me guide the Rathore family, and oversee the Haider family secretly in Srinagar. The secret of the Guardians has finally passed into the Rathore family last October in Nalanda. Agastya now knows the truth about the Guardians and our own Operation Babylon to save Kashmir is at the most important stage. Mansur will deliver!

CCTC INTEL TRANSMISSION:

LOCATION: DELHI HQ TO HOME MINISTERY

6th December, 17.00 IST

China's entry into Tawang area repulsed.
83 causalities reported.
Two more skirmishes reported along border: Dibang Valley (Arunachal Pradesh) and Nakpolatok (Sikkim)

6th December, 17.21 IST

Defence Minister General Kashyapa injured in attack.

Airlifted from forward base in Tawang towards Kolkata,
Details awaited on injuries.

6th December, 17.30 IST

Skirmishes in control, 18 casualties reported from Nakpoltok front only.

Firing halted on all posts. Ceasefire called out.

6th December, 17.42 IST

China's Politburo Chairman to counter renegade General Chan. Cause for that action status unknown.

Next step is counter China's bill in Kashmir.

From the cricket blog

www.princecalledSourav.com

All of us need a reminder!!!!

Someone once said, 'It is not over till the last ball is bowled or the last wicket taken'. How true that was. No matter how much cricket has progressed in the last century, with the new technologies and increasing power game, there still is no sight like a yorker length ball uprooting the stumps. And then watch the pacer's expression and eyes being followed by his teammates, opponents, and the entire audience. This happened five times yesterday…and by the looks of it, this will occur many more times in the future. The good thing: India is on the right side now.

Mansur Haider, the 'invincible lion,' the pacer from Baramulla, Kashmir, was making the opposition Australian batsman hop and skip with his balls on the pitch, which looked like a minefield. Australia had no answer to Mansur's deliveries. Singlehandedly he turned the match on its head, taking five wickets in the last session of play in the four overs he got. It looked like an Australian victory till the first wicket he got, when it looked like India could come back before the momentum swung back to the Australians, who were getting the runs. But then things changed, with Mansur knocking down the Australian captain with a screecher of a bouncer, and then unloading a barrage of short stuff in such a way that fear ran high among the batsmen. It was not that the wickets fell and India won the game, it was the way in which it was taken. Complete domination by one man, Mansur, blowing the opposition away. Such was his domination that the Australian captain shook hands with him in the post match conference and was seen speaking to him as if he considered him a peer.

On the other side of the Indian border there are reports of skirmishes between Indian and Chinese forces, and in time we will know more details. War like in Kargil in 1999, calamity like Tsunami in 2004, terrorism like the 26/11 Mumbai in 2008—these have united India in the past, but cricket is the one game which can cut across the nation and bind people together. This Indian cricket team in this series has done just that. Following its disappointing play since the 2011 World Cup, this young team has now matured. All kudos to the captain, the coach, and the selectors aside, it would not have happened if someone had not given them a sniff of victory and the belief it could be done. Mansur rose to the occasion and the team rallied around him. He has reminded us of something important…something we forgot…He reminded us what each one of us can become.

Sometimes we all need a reminder to get our life moving forward again. Sometimes we all need someone to give us that reminder.

But overall we need to remind ourselves that if we don't take that first step, we will never move ahead. So let's all start today towards our goal. Mansur has not only answered India's call for a fast bowler, he has answered Kashmir's call for a hero. And no matter what happens now… victory or defeat…Mansur Haider has become the Baramulla Bomber.

On other news, China may table a bill on Kashmir in upcoming UN session in New York. This is adding salt to our wounds, with some reports coming in that Indian and Chinese armies indulged in border skirmishes along the Tawang border where the Defence Minister was visiting. Both governments deny any incidents of firing, it is strange that the Defence Minister of India is now in a hospital with burns and a senior PLA officer, General Chan killed in a freak accident in Beijing.

T-MINUS 5.0 HOURS TO EVENT

General Assembly Hall, United Nations
New York, USA

December 11,08:30 EST

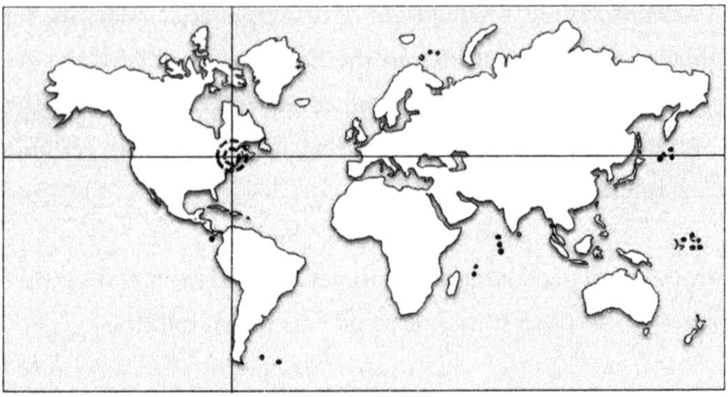

A**n emergency session** of the United Nations had been convened for an important discussion. It was a platform for the three parties, China, Pakistan and India, to talk with each other. The aim was to establish a resolution to end the conflict between China and India on the eastern front. Senior political leaders representing nations were in attendance.

General Pervez Musa Hussein, sitting in his army fatigues, scanned the different delegates sitting at the Assembly. His cold, grey, wrinkled eyes stopped when he saw the Indian delegates sitting a few benches away to his right.

Damn the Indians, damn the bloody Defence Minister. Who would have thought he would sacrifice himself! A deviation, but my plan still stands. I will play the Kashmir card. My Chinese counterpart will launch another engagement, this time in Beijing, bringing the government down. The Americans and Russians will be too shocked to react, after the terror strike that will occur shortly. A new world order of the pure will rise.

Pervez gave a curt smirk that did not go unnoticed by Agastya who gave him a stern look as their eyes met.

The proceedings started. The Secretary General opened the discussion with a welcome address on the importance of the day, with the two nations coming out in the open to declare peace. The Chinese delegation was called upon to offer their side of the story. The Chinese Interior Minister walked up towards the dais located precisely at the centre in front of the hall. In his speech he gave details of how an aforementioned military exercise had turned into an intrusion. He also emphasised that they had reacted to intercepts received by their forward units that Indian army units had moved into Tibet. They did mention that the intelligence had come from Pakistan ISI and the Chinese central military command decided to ignore it, but the front line commander insisted on following the specific threat.

Delegates present at the meeting were surprised. They had never heard any Chinese diplomat speaking in such a defensive tone. The Pakistani delegates felt uncomfortable listening to the Chinese Interior Minister's speech. When it was over, all eyes turned towards the Indian delegates to approach centre stage. The Indian delegates simply watched the goings on. Agastya remained calm and took out his cell phone and punched buttons. He spoke a few words and finished the call with a smile.

Pervez, this is your last day at centre stage. One stroke and it will all be over. You are making a big mistake.

Agastya had just called Samir, who was in a room adjacent to the main conference room. He had told him to come into the hall with his special guest.

Samir switched off his phone and put it inside the jacket of his dark suit. Looking around the room, he started walking towards a maroon-coloured plush sofa where his special guest was seated—Mansur, the Baramulla Bomber.

He touched Mansur lightly on the shoulder, 'It's time.'

Mansur and Aahana hugged each other briefly, then followed Samir out of the room towards the main UN assembly hall.

Back in the assembly hall, General Pervez had already started his speech. He opened with the usual rhetoric on how India was manipulating the system and overlooking the main issue. He called upon the world community to recognise Kashmir as an independent country, otherwise there would be chaos, not only in the region but also around the world. Pervez finished his speech by talking about how the local Kashmiris never got a chance to be in the forefront of any activity and even now many Indian Muslims were being marginalised. He ended his rant and walked down the podium. Agastya stood and strode to the podium as if nothing had happened. Their eyes met and held for an instant as they passed, as if questioning each other's existence.

Pervez's mobile phone was vibrating in silent mode, but in the heat of the moment, he didn't bother to look at the instrument. Little did he know that at that very moment, US Special Forces along with a small section of select Pakistan Special Forces were zeroing in on high value targets across different Pakistani cities. To make matters worse, his Chinese counterpart, General Chan, was dead in an accident. The synchronised action was possibly due to the quiet engagement between the different intelligence groups of these nations pressurised by the US, the UK, and Russia. Pervez's cronies were trying to get in touch with him for orders on how to tackle the sudden action being taken by the authorities. His presence in the UN was the only way to break the chain of command and keep him out of active engagement in Pakistan. This would effectively end all resistance among the soldiers who were considering a mutiny.

Agastya stood and surveyed the sea of faces looking at him, fully aware the session was being broadcast live and the world audience was watching. Taking a deep breath, he smiled, showing his dimple. He did not carry any papers, and it was widely expected that he would make an impromptu speech. But he had other things in mind, like speaking for a few minutes before handing over the podium to a surprise speaker.

As Agastya started his speech, Samir and the others entered the hallway and were guided to where the Indian delegates were sitting. All eyes were focused on Agastya. The Pakistani delegates sat quietly, but Pervez was animated, shocked to see Mansur in the hallway. What was he doing here!

No, it can't be...something is not right here.

Pervez looked towards the podium. Agastya was smiling.

'Dear friends, colleagues, and fellow citizens, I stand in front of you today, not to give my view of the supposedly grave situation here but to tell you a story. A story about hope, about life, and most importantly, about freedom…I know you may be wondering how this is connected to the discussion here.'

He paused. A long pregnant pause.

'Some say I am a great writer, but to be a great writer I need to be a great reader and the more you read, the more you feel empty. One of my favourite authors is Ayn Rand, and to quote her on this occasion will suffice as my message for the afternoon. She once said, and I quote, "*The spread of evil is the symptom of a vacuum. Whenever evil wins, it is only by default: by the moral failure of those who evade the fact that there can be no compromise on basic principles.*" The evil here is our fear inside, the fear to resist and challenge what is wrong. When this fear keeps growing, evil will slowly take over good and we all will be prisoners of this evil. And…it will not matter which religion you follow or what your beliefs are!'

The assembly hall was silent, the anticipation palpable. It was the first time they had heard India use such strong language in the UN assembly.

'Religion and belief are just words, but they have a great many meanings and interpretations for different people. It's like one man's freedom fighter is another man's terrorist.' Agastya was now looking directly where Pervez was sitting. 'Isn't that right, Pervez?' Agastya smiled and Pervez looked dumbstruck.

What the fuck is he doing? Pervez was red-faced.

Many members were shocked at this approach by Agastya. The American ambassador looked across at his British and Russian counterparts and tried to get some kind of non-verbal gesture to understand what was happening. The Russian and British ambassadors gave a faint smile, nodded, and said something to their assistants, who then got up and left their seats.

'Pervez, there are people like you who feel that by shouting a few threatening words, and then using religion as a tool to manipulate emotions, you can blackmail the world. But I stand here to tell you and people like you that we Indians are an ancient race. A race that not only values its own culture, but also respects every other culture. We do not need lectures on it. If your way of thinking was right, then why aren't you the most prosperous country on the planet? Why aren't your people the happiest people on Earth?'

Agastya signalled for Mansur to come forward. Mansur approached the podium and in a moment stood next to Agastya.

'I will continue, but first I want to introduce you to someone special. The man standing next to me has made our country believe once again that region, religion and ethnicity does not decide one's success. Six months back Mansur Haider was just a normal club player and now he has united not only our country with his victory but also brought together the *heaven on earth* Kashmir closer to us.' He inclined his head towards Mansur. 'He wants to pass on a message, a message which he has taught all of us back home...that a common man can rise, and when he rises the whole world can only watch.' Saying this, Agastya stepped back and left the podium to Mansur.

Mansur stood and his gaze swept across the hall.

God, is this what I was told about by Abbu? The whole world will hear you, he said, and then peace will be a possibility.

He cleared his throat as he felt a lump build up inside. 'I do not know why am I standing here or even sure of what I am speaking of. Also I do not know why any one of you esteemed members would want to listen to what I have to say.' Mansur took a deep breath and looked at Aahana, who was smiling at him. He smiled back. 'The honourable minister met me in person to tell me he would need me here not to support what he was saying, but to speak my mind, to say what I think of the madness that surrounds me and to tell my story.' Agastya, who was standing behind him, nodded.

'I am standing here not as a representative of Kashmir or India, but as a human being. I am going to speak here about two things which every human being cherishes...one is freedom and two is the human spirit.' Mansur held up one, then two fingers of his right hand. The giant screen flashed a close-up of his hand and everyone saw the six fingers on his right hand. A couple of Indian delegates fidgeted in their seats at the mention of the word 'freedom,' but continued to give Mansur their attention. As he spoke, a few UN police entered the hall, quite unusual, for they were normally stationed outside.

'*Azadi*, or freedom, do I want it? Yes, I do. Will it help me? Yes, it will. To think of it, what is life without freedom? I am here asking all of you for a free Kashmir.'

A loud gasp reverberated across the hall and died down immediately. The Indian delegates stood up, and only Aahana and Samir remained sitting. Back at the podium Agastya raised his head but looked away immediately, as if nothing had happened. Pervez smiled at this surprise opportunity. But it was short lived, and a frown crossed his face when he heard the next line from Mansur.

'But I want more than that. I want freedom for the people of Tamil Nadu, Karnataka, Bihar, Maharashtra, and every other state of India. I want freedom from hatred. I want freedom of the human spirit.' Hearing this, the Indian delegates calmed down.

'My father used to tell me a poem. It was by one of India's greatest poets, Harivansh Rai Bachchan. It was titled *Agneepath,* which means 'Path of Fire'. This poem speaks about the human spirit and the trial by fire the protagonist had to undergo without support. The poem has no English rendition, but if translated it would go something like this:

The obstacles may be large like a strong Oak tree
It may be tall and strong
Leaves and support may be there
But never request for help
You have to walk on the path of fire, the path of fire to succeed

You will never tire, you will never stop to rest
You will not turn around
Take this oath, this oath, take this oath,
You have to walk on the path of fire, the path of fire to succeed

The view is magnificent
How man has moved ahead
With sacrifice of tears, sweat and blood
Body is torn apart, Body is tired
You have to walk on the path of fire, the path of fire to succeed
Keep moving forward on the path of fire, the path of fire.

And it is in the name of the human spirit that I demand freedom from all of you. You all hold responsible positions and everyone in your country looks up to you. As a human being I am asking for my freedom. Help us. Support us because we, the common men, are trying to reach our destination peacefully.'

Pin drop silence. Pervez had heard enough. He got up but his colleagues told him to sit down.

'I was never given a chance; I had to take my chance. I heard from someone that one needs to work hard and the universe would start conspiring to help you. But then the contrary is also true. There are those forces in the universe that try to keep you down, try to see to it that you do not succeed, and it was the same with me. But someone told me the following line, which helped me, and I am sure it will help you.'

People around the hall were now listening attentively.

'Fight your destiny, build hope and make it happen, because you don't know which forces of the universe will come into play. That's all I want to say. I hope the message has reached some of you and you can help your common man.'

The hall stood up as one and clapped. Four members from the UN police were now positioned next to the Pakistani delegates. Pervez got up to leave, but a burly officer held him and whispered into his ear, 'Sir, can you walk out with us, calmly?' Pervez could not comprehend the situation. The other Pakistani delegates sat shell-shocked and utterly silent.

Agastya walked up to the podium and shook hands with Mansur. He was told he would have to address the member countries again.

'Friends, thanks for the reception you gave Mansur. We all need our common man to rise and win. With each victory, all of us will win. But I want to remind you of something else. Something we have forgotten'.

Mansur walked back towards his seating area to Aahana. Agastya spoke in a serious tone.

'We stand here representing humanity, the best and worst of humanity. Humanity. This one word unites us and yet, at the same time, it differentiates us. We are differentiated by the borders which we have created for our security, by the national anthems which we have adopted to buoy our national identity, by the races being used as a weapon to symbolise the idea of superior or inferior beings. I am here not to build these differentiations but to speak about our calling. Our calling is to fulfil our dreams. When we are born, it is our parents who dream for us, and as we grow into maturity we start dreaming of what we are supposed to do…but somewhere along the way we kill this dream.'

Agastya gave a long pause as he looked around the assembly hall. He took a deep breath, closing his eyes. He opened his eyes and looked in the direction of Mansur.

'We need not fear people like him. Not because he dreams while sleeping, but because he dreams when his eyes are open, and such people can change things in the most unexpected ways. Mansur dreamt of playing one day, not only for himself but also for the memories of his father, for his family, his state, and this dream when fulfilled brought joy not only to him but also to the entire nation. It's not about winning or losing, it is about pursuing what you believe in and seeing it through to the end.

'And what happens if we all start dreaming with our eyes open? We will all say together, "This is not my end, this is not how I want to finish. I am better than this. We all are better than this!" And it is in this "we" that we will have to find our common goals, our reason for existing on this planet and the road to fulfil our common dreams, our calling. Thomas Edison once said, and I quote, "If we did the things we are capable of, we would astound ourselves." But what are we capable of?'

He paused once again and looked around the hall and at the roof; pointing towards the roof he continued.

'We dreamt of reaching the stars, and we did it, we dreamt of stepping on the moon, and we did it, we dreamt of reaching out to another planet, and we did it. If we can do such magnificent things why can't we remove our differences here, here back at home?' His voice boomed as he brought his hand down.

'If we don't join together now, we will be lost in the sands of time, fail to take our destined place in the universe. Humanity deserves better and it is up to us to deliver it. Remember if we have the capability to dream as individuals and fulfil our goals then why not dream as one, for humanity's sake? Think of the things we can achieve by working together. Think of the changes we can bring about, perhaps not in our lifetime, but in our children's future and their children's future. This will not happen overnight. It may take months or even years, but we need to make a start and stay committed to see that what we start we carry through to the end. I do not know what the future holds, but I can know about the past and control the present, and it is in this knowledge we can make our future worth living. *Amen, Amin, Aum and Ogham.*'

The whole hall applauded in appreciation. The Chinese UN delegation did not put forth the Kashmir bill, and the session was closed. The delegates started leaving. Pervez was worried due to this development which he had not accounted for.

Nasir will still go through with the plan...I better get back to Pakistan by tomorrow to get things to roll on.

A tall blonde figure sat down beside Samir. 'Adolf! Good to see you!' said Samir happily. Adolf smiled. 'It's not over. Pervez is still alive, and we need to move quickly to avert his plan.'

'What is it?'

'Let's go somewhere we can talk.'

Agastya, Mansur, and Aahana joined the group. Adolf rose and shook hands with them and gave a mini salute to Agastya, who was pleasantly surprised.

'Sir, we need you to join us.'

'Where? Why?'

'Sir, Carina will be arriving soon, and we need to meet up in the *Cobbler* later. We need your help in preventing a sure-shot potential assassination attempt. And yes, one more thing before I forget. Does anyone have experience in sky diving and parachute jumps?'

Samir's hand shot up, but all eyes turned towards Aahana as her hand was also up. 'Twenty-two thousand feet is my personal best and a lot of BASE jumping.' All eyes around her popped with surprise. 'And I am not leaving you all alone on this,' she said.

'Wow, you are something,' said a surprised Adolf. Aahana smiled back, lifting her eyebrows.

'So what is it? Building, bridge…?' Samir asked but Aahana interrupted him.

'Cliffs and mountains around Norway.'

'Norway! Well!' Carina had overhead the conversation and joined the group from behind. 'Talk about coincidences. Join me in the Cobbler Room soon. We don't have time to waste,' she said gravely to the group.

T-MINUS 4 HOURS TO EVENT

Cobbler Room, United Nations,
New York, USA

December 11,09:30 EST

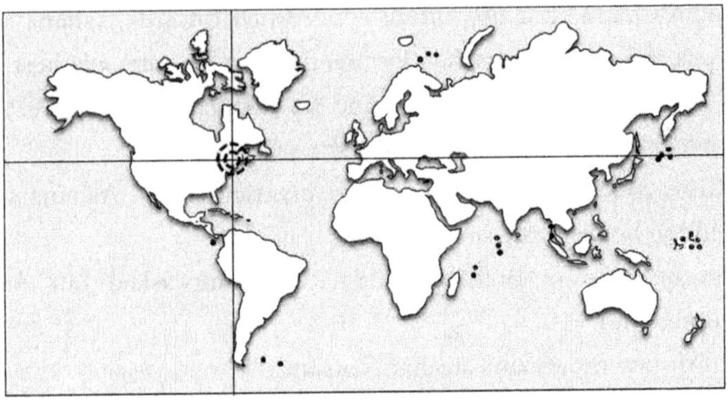

'**So why is** this room called the cobbler room? Not like I see any shoes around?' asked Aahana as she looked at the medium sized conference room with an oval table at the centre.

'There is a history to it; and I will entertain you with it till our chiefs come.' said Adolf.

Aahana and Mansur were happy to see Adolf. They hugged each other and Aahana gently pressed his hand.

'Good to have you back,' said Samir.

'Yes, lots of confusion to sort out,' said Adolf looking at the group and moving his arm around indicating them to sit down, 'And Aahana to answer your question, the Cobbler room is a sort of room akin to a dead zone for communication devices and bug free. None of your devices will be working here.'

Aahana and Samir checked their phones and saw no coverage.

'And the room came up after the infamous 1960 Khrushchev shoe hammering incident, which freaked out both NATO and US that a nuclear war would follow. Senior US, British, and Soviet officials had to jointly negotiate here in this very room to calm down their respective representatives. Since then the room had been used on many occasions when leaders wanted to meet in secret.'

The cushioned door opened again and Carina, Agastya and a couple of other men and a woman entered the room. Adolf recognised two of them as his colleagues from SOG, analysts Stephanie and Bjorn. The third man, wearing a US army uniform, extended his hand towards him.

'Good Evening, I am Colonel Eccleston, from Pentagon. I shall be the touchpoint for your group and CIA, Whitehouse…you name it.'

Adolf shook hands and also saluted him, which was acknowledged by the Colonel, 'OK, and I am sure you know all of us.'

He nodded as Carina and Agastya also sat on seats next to each other.

'Thank you all for joining us, and I am sure you will have questions regarding why you are here in this room, it's not that we don't bring in civilians here, but times are such.'

Aahana and Mansur nodded, figuring that they were the sort of non-military, non-political civilians here.

'As Stephanie and Bjorn will set up the presentation I will brief you on what we know,' Carina looked at the faces around the table.

'We now know that General Pervez is planning a potential military coup along with his Chinese counterpart.'

'A sort of double coup in the two countries,' said Agastya.

'Yes, and this information was passed on to the Chinese Premier by the US President, who had then taken action in the last forty-eight hours and you can see the result, on China not pushing ahead on the Kashmir agenda.'

'The skirmish at our east border with China could not be avoided, but the escalation was halted…unfortunately our Defence Minister is fighting for his life now due to injuries sustained.'

Carina and others nodded sympathetically.

'Adolf getting captured was a blessing in disguise, as we were only able to put in pieces of this puzzle after Stephanie and Bjorn got in touch with him…right Adolf.'

'Yes we did know the location, but now we are sure…it is the Oslo Spektrum concert, today December the 11th. And the weapon being used is sonic in nature.'

The group looked at the screen now as Stephanie and Bjorn informed the group that the set was done and they would begin.

Both SOG analysts gave a brief on the codes they received from Kurt and inputs from Adolf, Aahana and Colonel Eccleston. The use of sonic weapon as weapon had been discussed and Kurt's Intel message of *River of Babylon* came up.

'We know the weapon kills the human body and organs, and for a sonic weapon to be activated sound has to be manipulated. The last act of today's show in Oslo Spektrum is 'By the River of Babylon,' so we are currently assuming that this is where the weapon will be activated.'

That's Mikaela song for today! Adolf shifted in his seat

'The target will be winners of the Nobel prizes, especially the Peace Prize winners, the *First Spouses Group* comprising the spouses of the US and Russian Presidents and Prime Minister of UK, India, Canada and Australia.'

'Their group is involved with social causes. Why target them?'

'It's not they but their husbands who will also be attending the ceremony. With the plan of military action later by China, it will add to the confusion when leading nations will not have their leaders or if their spouses are killed it will leave them emotionally compromised.'

'The bogie man for the strike is suspected to be Pakistan's scientist, Dr Nasir, and the weapon will be something similar to that tested in Shaksgam Valley.'

'Why can't we take General Pervez down?' Samir asked.

'The Pakistani civilian leadership will not act, they are scared of any action against Pervez and his military.'

'The other option is to engineer a coup in the Military to take Pervez down, or do the mangoes operations again, said Colonel Eccleston. Carina raised her hand to indicate him to stop.

'We will consider other options later but first we need to understand how to disarm the weapon. Please continue, Stephanie.'

'Thank you Carina. Kurt sent a lot of messages but we were not able to piece them together, but inputs from Aahana, Adolf, and Colonel Eccleston brought out some interesting thoughts on how the weapon can be stopped...Bjorn will show you how,' She stood aside for her colleague to take over the presentation.

Bjorn removed the sonic weapon presentation and opened a folder containing images and double clicked on the first one, and then put it on screen-show.

'What you see on the screen now will be something I want you to keep in mind.'

The group saw images–geometric, floral, and other patterns. Mansur slowly moved in his chair and stared at the images more intently.

'Yes Mansur, some of these designs may look familiar, from your rug or carpet on which you pray,' said Bjorn.

'I don't get it,' said Mansur, looking confused and looking around the table for answers.

'We had these images taken not from your carpet, but two of them from Kurt's mails and the last pictures he sent from the wall...it did not make sense at first. But when Adolf mentioned just yesterday that Aahana thought these images are from Mansur's carpet it started to make sense.'

'Each carpet is created on a design which is unique and visualised by its weaver. This creation is done on a coded script which is understood only by weavers and carpet designers.'

'You mean like it's another language of its own?' asked Samir.

'Yes, like a software...own code, own system and own secrets.... It is called the Talim.'

'The what?' Samir was confused.

'Talim, or to put it simply, a coded pattern guide unique to Kashmir, but handed over from ancient Persia, current Iran.'

'I know a little of its history.'

'Ok, and it reached India via the Mughal Empire.'

'So I have an old carpet containing some sort of secret code,' Mansur was astonished.

'Well it is ancient and handed down to the family through generations, so it does have antique value and may also have some hidden message.'

'So in short you are saying the Haider family carpet in Mansur's possession has a design for this sonic weapon.' Samir walked up close to the presentation screen to see the images close by.

'Not entirely, it may have something related to it…the design on the carpet and the scanned Buddhist scroll printouts taken from Dr Nasir's system and our ex-agent Kurt's mails have some similarity.'

'It's a long shot.'

'Life is a long shot…and who knows there are no co-incidences. What say?'

'Let's take our chances.'

'See, there are floral patterns which may be regular, but the geometric ones are what I am interested in.'

'So how do you plan to use it?'

'To map the design which Mansur will help creating from his carpet, then work on the way to develop it to the Talim anguage for which we will have an expert join us in a couple of hours.'

'And then?' asked Aahana

'Hope for the best…need to see what comes out, but by then you and this group will be in Oslo, inside the hall and we will have the antidote for the weapon.'

Aahana, Mansur and Samir looked towards Carina and Agastya. Carina stood up. 'Yes three of you will be travelling with an international set of commandos led by Adolf. Mansur, we would need you to remember all you can of your carpet, draw the images and pass it on. Aahana we believe your knowledge in quantum physics and sonic area can be useful, and Samir you will be needed to work alongside Adolf and your Home Minister.'

'Sir, anything I am not appraised of?'

'Yes Samir, we will be going into the zone, I have taken the responsibility to bring out the dignitaries, and also see if the weapon is working or not.'

'How?'

'Well a device has been prepared to read if my heart, lungs, and iris are oscillating in the right frequency. Once the weapon is activated these organs will start vibrating in a different frequency, and that will be our signal we have failed and need to evacuate.'

'So Sir, if the vibrations increase it's a sign to dash off,' asked Samir with concern in his eyes. Agastya nodded.

'And to show the group how a Talim looks, see the screen now,' said Bjorn as he clicked on an image and the scanned paper with Talim language came up.

'These signs look like an old angelic language, older then Hebrew,' whispered Colonel Eccleston to Carina. She nodded.

'Yes! We are just starting to know the secret. We are just beginning to connect the dots, my fellow Guardian,' whispered Carina as the Colonel smiled back and nodded in agreement.

T-MINUS 1 HOUR TO EVENT

Somewhere in Nordic Region Airspace

December 11,18:30 CET

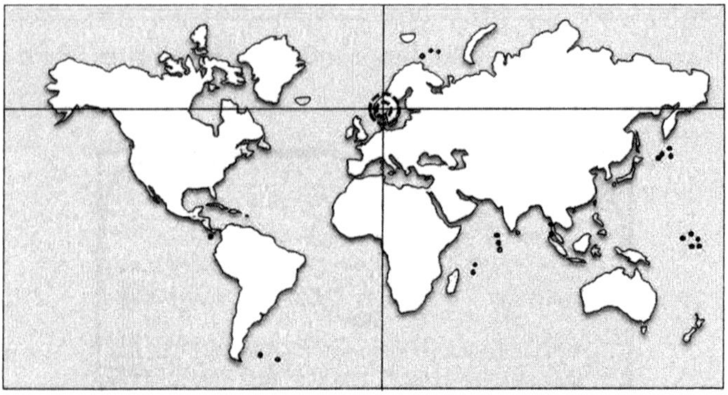

The B-X004 long-range bomber was cruising at over fifty thousand feet above sea level. This aircraft was an advanced version of the C-130 Hercules, which was normally used for the stealth operation. It was developed as part of a secret military program between the American and British forces.

Inside, there was a five-member elite commando unit and a team of civilians. Their objective was to drop down unnoticed, directly on the Norwegian king's palace in Oslo where the Nobel Peace Prize Ceremony was taking place.

A tall, suited up commando from Poland turned to his team leader. 'Tell me why we cannot inform the Norwegian authorities on the ground about the situation before we go in.'

'We don't want to cause panic on the ground by calling in right now. We need to catch the suspect and close the loop,' replied Adolf, who was leading the operation along with Colonel Eccleston, the aide of their new-found Indian partners.

Adolf saw Mansur drawing the images and sending across to the SOG analysts. The Talim code was prepared and sent but was making no sense. Adolf scribbled it as the few came in.

Mikaela, your song is the key to this…you will know something I am sure.

A few miles away and hundreds of feet below, Mikaela was getting ready for her group performance. This was supposed to be the last act before the state dinner. The show featured musicians from various countries. The idea was to get a few common notes across in a harmonious way to showcase the unity of the world and music's power to foster peace.

'So your boyfriend said he would be joining you.'

Mikaela looked at her colleague in the ladies' room mirror as they applied themselves to their make-up.

'Knowing him, he will make a subtle entry, like sitting in the audience silently or waiting outside.'

In the corporate box, watching the show from above was Dr Nasir Abiad Raja.

Allah, please forgive me, but there is no other way. I need to spill blood to bring justice to the holy land.

There was a buzz on the door; he walked to the door slightly surprised. He was not expecting anyone. When the door opened he smiled to see familiar faces from the scientific community greeting him.

'Well, won't you let us in?'

'Well, there are better places to be than here, my friends.'

'Like where?'

'There is another row of corporate boxes which has a better view, let's go there.'

They all moved out; nobody noticed Dr Nasir using a remote activated switch. He had just activated the sonic weapon.

'By the Rivers of Babylon' is the last song of the show…till then I think it's time to catch up on old memories. That will be the only thing left in less than an hour.

'T**eam! Get ready**, five minutes to drop zone,' shouted Colonel Eccleston at the team, which was now breathing in fresh oxygen in preparation for the jump. They had been awaiting go-time for over thirty minutes now.

The four-member international commando team stood up in an instant. Adolf and Samir were already strapped up and standing. Adolf would lead the forces on the ground level, while the veteran Colonel would monitor the proceedings from the air.

While Agastya and Mansur would be jumping with assistance by having partners accompanying them to ground, Aahana would be making the jump on her own.

It was to be a typical military precision jump known as HALO, which stood for *high altitude and low opening*. It was a free-fall jump in which the parachute opened up late after a long free-fall through the sky.

The height for their current jump was forty thousand feet, and the gear was the best in the class suited for this operation. Each jumper wore customised polypropylene knit undergarments to keep the body warm. This was needed to avoid frostbite.

Two commandos jumped first. It would be their job to get in touch with the ground team, which had initiated contact with the relevant security forces on the ground. Samir would be next to go down, and he would take Mansur along with him.

'Don't worry, it will be a cakewalk,' yelled Samir as a deafening noise sounded on the plane.

'It's not me, it's Aahana. Are you sure she'll be fine?'

Aahana came forward and hugged Mansur and pressed her lips tightly against his. 'This will keep you afloat, and don't worry about me.' She smiled and pinched his cheeks. Dazed, Mansur said nothing.

'It's time, lover-boy,' shouted Samir. He and Mansur jumped, and Aahana looked on as they faded from view.

'Lady, if you were a guy I would have said that you have some balls!' yelled Adolf, raising his voice to be heard above the surrounding noise of the military jet and gusty wind thousands of metres above the ground.

'Darling, we do have balls. The difference is that ours are a bit closer to our head, so they work better,' shouted Aahana as she winked at him, put on her oxygen mask, and jumped off the bomber plane, but not before chanting a sacred set of words "*Aum Mani Padme Hum*" in her mind.

Adolf watched her rapidly drop out of sight, her skydiving form perfect.

Lucky guy Mansur, to have a girl like her. Mikaela should try this sometime.

Next to exit the bomber military jet was the Polish commando with the Indian Home Minister Agastya strapped to him. Finally it would be Adolf's turn to jump, accompanied by the British commando who completed the team.

Agastya took out his mobile phone and looked longingly at a photo of himself and his wife Vitasta. He glanced back at his Polish partner who was ready to take him down. Placing his mobile back in the zipper pocket, adjusting his gloves again, and putting on the oxygen mask, he prepared to make the jump as the bomber plane flew in a curve around the designated drop zone. As they took flight, he could feel the instant rush of blood.

Agastya felt the cold wind assault his face. His mind was a battlefield raging with questions:

'GOD*! Here we are on the way down to* DESTROY the ANCIENT VEDIC weapon tested at the SHAKSGAM VALLEY *and I am feeling that I am too old for this stuff. And to think of it, I would not be here if there had been no Partition or if the first war with Pakistan had not been stopped in 1948. If Lal Bahadur Shastri had not died in Tashkent or if Indira Gandhi had stuck to her decision and rolled into the western part of Pakistan during the 1971 war, WE would not have been in this grave situation. IF only there was a chance to roll back TIME and change the past. When could have we changed it? Could it be it back in 1947 on the 2nd of November or July when Gods power was unleashed!*

Nine bodies were now hurtling downwards in a synchronised fashion. Five of them were moving like darts towards ground level, Oslo, and the other four were using the wind for resistance and balancing the fall. The flaps of the spider suits were stretched and well spread out now.

30,000 feet…

20,000 feet…

10,000 feet…

'Parachutes!' shouted Adolf through the common mike as he pulled his parachute cord.

More parachutes blew open, and in a moment the sky was filled with several open chutes. The time to land at the drop zone was mere moments away. The airspace was cleared for them to land, and with the high-level authorisation coming just fifteen minutes earlier, no one apart from the two ground teams knew what was happening. They could see the parachutes and its carrier more clearly now. As the first two commandos landed, they disengaged their chutes and rushed towards the two-member ground team, which was dressed in special military fatigues like them.

'Updates?' The Japanese commando asked his ground colleague, his tone low. 'Dr Nasir is in, but we have no idea about the bomb.'

'What do you mean no idea?'

'The area is clean and has been sanitised two times already. Our men are everywhere, but…'

The ground team stopped their explanation as they saw a chute with a feminine figure landing, and when the helmet was removed they could see Aahana's hair billowing in the gusty wind.

'She is with us.'

'Yes, Carina told us to also expect a few civilians.'

Adolf and the others landed. Letting go of their chutes, they converged around the ground team. Agastya's face was flushed red due to the jump. Mansur approached Aahana. They hugged each other and exchanged a few words.

'Team, we all know what we have to do,' said Adolf, looking towards Agastya.

Agastya nodded, and the team dispersed into four groups. While three of the commandos were there as snipers to take down the suspected bomb carrier, the Russian commando along with Agastya and the ground team needed to reach the Indian and American delegates to make sure they were protected. Mansur and Aahana were to mingle with the crowd and try to get a sense of what was happening. Adolf and Samir would reach out to the internal security apparatus and look on via cameras, surveying the area for suspects and passing the information on to the team.

Adolf harboured a vague description and had an idea of how the carrier would be used.

'By the rivers of Babylon, the carrier will strike through the mind'...a sonic weapon using the ancient Sanskrit Mantras will be used. Music is the key...Mikaela is playing...oh my God! She loves music and it has brought me close to her and here now...Kasha...can't be that right. It must be somewhere in the Orchestra...but have to be sure before I raise the issue.

T-MINUS 45 MINUTES TO EVENT

Oslo Spektrum, Oslo, Norway

December 11,18:45 CET

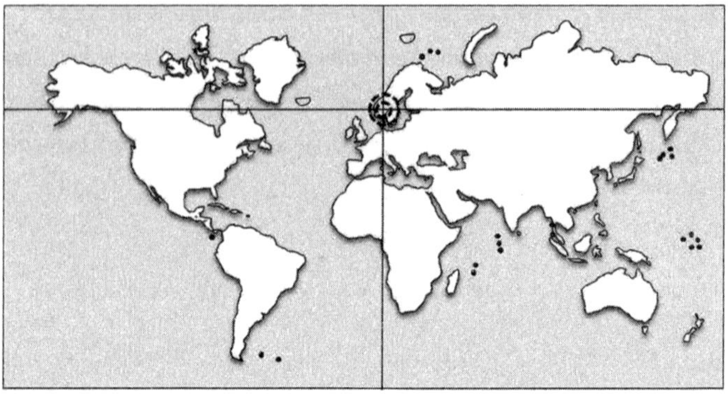

Agastya mingled with the Indian invitees, and it had all the appearances of a homecoming. Avoiding the recommendation he got from Carina, he still briefed the Indian Prime Minister Aditya Khurana on the situation and how he had gotten there.

'Funny—to think of why we are all here and how a terror attack here might destroy the soul and spirit of what it stands for,' said Khurana in a sombre tone, thinking how the concept of peace that the Nobel prize stood for would be shattered by the attack.

'Excuse us...excuse us.' A commotion was being created by two tall figures running across the hall and up the stairs. Agastya saw Adolf and Samir rush upstairs, and surmised that they had found something or made a breakthrough.

So it's happening now. I have to get the PM and Mansur to safety. Where is Mansur?

Agastya tried to make sense of the crowd. It was confusing as most of those present looked similar in their black jacket suits.

Back on the first floor, Samir was just following Adolf's cue. He was trying to catch up with him as Adolf was running like one possessed. Adolf removed the internal communicator and squeezed the black button.

'Team, this is leader. We have an *Omega* situation, I repeat, the situation is *Omega.'* They entered the upper hallway on the third floor. As they turned the corner he could see the members of the orchestra walking down a staircase at the other end.

'Well, Adolf…what now?'

Adolf's eyes were frantically searching for Mikaela. The orchestra was getting ready making preparation to play in the concert.

'There she is!' Adolf pointed towards Mikaela, dressed in a half-draped white gown and a small dark teal satin blouse. 'Mikaela! Mikaela!'

On seeing Adolf shout, Samir started shouting the same, albeit in a different pronunciation.

Mikaela turned around to see Adolf all rushing towards her. She was pleasantly surprised as she had not expected him to come and had assumed he would miss her performance.

'So you were almost late again,' she said, rushing forward and hugging him tightly. Adolf embraced her, but pushed her back a little.

'We need to talk. I need to ask you something.'

'Didn't you find the right time to bang in like this?' Would he choose this moment to ask her to marry him?

'Ahh well!' Adolf was a little tongue-tied, at a loss for how to handle the situation.

'Ahem! Excuse me, ma'am,' interrupted Samir, bowing his head to her. 'I am Samir, Adolf's colleague, in a sense. I think we need your help on something.'

Mikaela was surprised at what she heard. She had thought that the stranger was there for something else. She regarded Adolf with disdain.

'I think we will have time for that, I just need five minutes so that you can hear me out,' pleaded Adolf, holding both his hands mid air before Mikaela's face, signalling surrender.

'I hope you have a good explanation for this.' She entered an empty room nearby and signalled for them to follow.

'Oh, I am sure he has…and this time it's international,' mocked Samir, who was trying to get some fun out of the situation that Adolf had landed himself in.

Adolf explained the situation. He summarised how they had come to be there and the potential danger faced by all of them.

'Think, think clearly, dear. There must be something.' Adolf was insistent.

'I understand the situation and the need to question whether anything is out of the ordinary, but how do I fit in?'

I've been wondering the same thing for the last fifteen minutes, thought Samir.

Adolf recalled that Mikaela had mentioned in one of her earlier emails that one of the troupes would be playing a modern version of the prayer 'By the Rivers of Babylon.' Samir felt it was a long shot, but by the way things were going, even a one in a million chance should not be discarded. Adolf was following his gut instinct to *leap first, look later.* It always worked for him. He emphasised to her about the prayer 'By the rivers of Babylon.'

'There is something,' said Mikaela, raising her tone substantially. 'I don't know if it's that important, but judging by the sound of the music, some notes were missing during the last practice session.'

Samir and Adolf looked at each other and Samir shrugged his shoulders, indicating that he did not get it. Adolf squeezed Mikaela's hands more tightly. 'Do you mean, someone in the group is not playing right?'

She nodded, and tried to break free. Adolf released her and agitatedly paced the room.

'My dear, you would need to point out where the missing music is coming from.'

Samir was a little confused in the beginning but started getting the hang of Adolf's hunch.

'So Mikaela you will need to listen to your troupe playing the music and identify the instrument.'

'Tell me more Adolf. We are due in the next few minutes. I may know about something you have missed about this music or the sonic issue.'

Adolf elaborated on their finding of certain signs by converting Mansur's carpet geometric shapes back into carpet language Talim. Mikaela's eyes lit up as she listened to Adolf.

'Adolf I know a bit of this design craft…learnt it from a Turkish musician who was into carpets. Can I see it?'

Adolf showed her the sketches of the notes which were prepared during the flight.

'It is not complete Mikaela, we got it done as much we could. Any linkages to music you can decipher?'

'Yes…'

'Yes! Good!…Go on.' 'Well, I know that while preparing the carpet, the instructions are given by the two weavers at opposite ends which then sounds like a song.'

'So one would need to know how the different signs sound.'

'Yes…and…'

'No Adolf I don't know how to read this, but I think I recognise a few of them and know how they sound…'

'Wait, my team is trying to contact me.'

Adolf tapped his communicator device in his ear and listened to his caller.

'If Dr Nasir was on the corporate floor we need to know which one of the boxes he was in.'

'Search the floor! Go room by room…royal guest or no royal guest in those rooms.'

Adolf looked towards Mikaela as she was twisting her head to read the paper in his hand with the Talim script. He gave her the paper and continued talking.

'Yes! You have my permission. Find him and arrest him, Noble Prize winner or not,' instructed Adolf and continued, 'Don't shoot him even if he resists…we need him alive to know where the weapon is.'

And to know how it functions, too valuable a target to kill.

'Adolf, why don't I make notes of this Talim script and see if I can make sense out of it.'

'That's a good idea, but the better idea's to keep it with you….,' said Samir, looking at Adolf for approval.

'Yes he is right, anything out of the ordinary you can see?'

Adolf was again interrupted by an incoming message.

'Team leader.'

'You are positive. Ok, I am on the way.'

Adolf turned his head swiftly towards the row of corporate boxes above his head, and pulled Samir close.

'Samir, one of the corporate boxes has the something which may be the weapon, and Dr Nasir was there. Aahana and Mansur are there already…corporate box belongs to Zrotriya.'

'And Dr Nasir?'

'No sign of him for now, but we are scanning the perimeters.'

Adolf turned towards Mikaela, kissed her gently, and patted her head. 'I think we have it under control…you go on to the show.'

Both darted outside as Mikaela watched them disappear. The covert operatives moved towards the direction of the exclusive elevator leading to the corporate boxes. The security present there checked their credentials and exchanged a few words with them.

'We need to split up and take up two action points.'

'I had the same thought…the home minster is already sitting in the crowd with the Indian delegates.'

'Yes, you reach the minister; see if his body organs' frequency vibration has noted any changes. One thing on our side is that this will not be instant but a build up.'

'Yes I know, and also the vibrations move towards the higher frequency, thus disrupting the balance.'

'Any change…dart him out and sound the alarm…Mikaela will stop.'

They shook hands and Adolf stepped inside the elevator, their determined eyes gazing at each other as the shiny steel doors of the elevator closed softly. As the elevator climbed gently an announcement was made by the two hosts of the evening.

'Dear patrons and guests, it has been a great show till now…but we are saving our best for the last.'

'Yes Hugh, and it gives us great pleasure to introduce our final group for the evening, an orchestra comprising of musicians not only from our Nordic regions but also around the east and the west.'

'And we have an array of string instruments playing in this group from *Nyckelharpa* from Sweden, *Veena* from India, *Pipa* from China and *Charango* from Argentina. A truly United Nations of string music,' said the male host who then did an air guitar jig, moving both his hands like playing a virtual guitar. The audience broke into spontaneous laughter.

'Well these string instruments are ancient and each has a history of its own. Take the *Veena* from India for example, the variant played here is the called the *Rudra-Veena* and *Rudra* is another name for the Indian God of destruction, Lord Shiva.'

'Aha…but that's just one part….Hugh. It is said the twenty-four frets in the *Veenas* impact the twenty-four segments in our spinal cord, which impacts the body *chakras* controlling our physical and mental well-being.'

'Spine chilling information,' said Hugh as he mimicked a shiver.

The audience again broke into laughter, this time the vibration was accompanied by an echo.

'I think we should not take up more time, so playing, 'By the Rivers of Babylon' as a "faith pop" with 'dashes of rap and techno music from the group led by Mikaela Wallander.'

Hearing her name Adolf looked towards the stage from the top and saw the various musicians come up on stage and introduce themselves. He turned back towards the assembled group now. 'Well I think we don't have much time…if our guess is right then this is the song where the sonic weapon will get activated.'

'Well I think it is already activated,' said Aahana, pointing towards a hexagon shaped metallic casing box.

Adolf stared at the object as a couple of bomb disposal unit members entered and started removing some of their gadgets. They took out an electronic device shaped like a hand-held hammer with a digital reading of numbers. They knelt and moved the device across the box and began punching the circular buttons of the electronic console, trying to match readings from the box. They nodded at each other after a few seconds, and one of them looked towards Adolf.

'Sir we need to open this, power surge is seen here…I think we inform the show to be cancelled and clear out this room.'

Adolf tapped a button of his ear piece to give further instructions.

'Team leader to all assets, start…ahhhhh,' Adolf gave a shriek and fell. Mansur held him as he fell, but he also began grimacing. Aahana and the other officers present inside the room also fell on the floor and began trembling. Adolf looked at his colleagues falling; grinding his teeth he tried to get up but fell back.

It is the same thing…he is back!

Adolf turned his body towards the door and saw a man in a navy blue suit walk in slowly. In his hand was a red oval shaped device with an aperture in between where two fingers met.

'So my friend…I should have listened to Jalal and killed you…two times now. You are becoming a nasty habit,' a thundering voice boomed.

The new visitor bent towards his victims. The struggling group saw the bearded man; Adolf spoke up with great effort. 'Dr Nasir… we know….'

'I can't hear you,' said Dr Nasir, showing his ears blocked with a green protective disc, 'You will be dead soon. All of you, instead of destroying the device, you want to decode it…you are all greedy. Don't have the courage to stop, but does not matter, all of you will be dead soon.'

T-MINUS 5 MINUTES TO EVENT

Oslo Spektrum, Oslo, Norway

December 11,19:25 CET

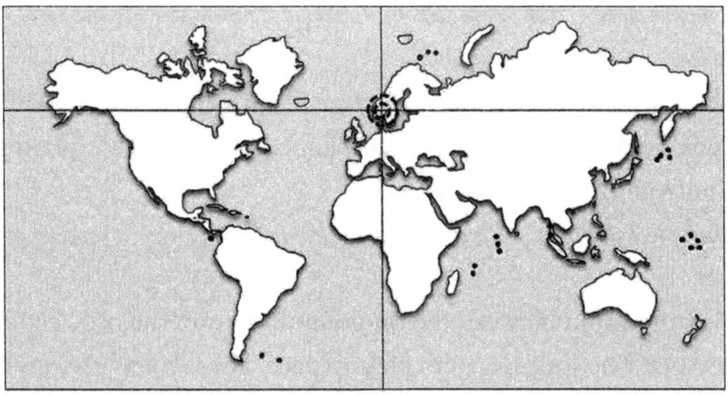

Samir sat next to Agastya and looked at the digital frequency reader attached to his wrist for the umpteenth time, his gaze shifting from the frequency reader to the spectators around and back to the frequency reader.

Heart ok, lungs ok, and iris ok.

'Tense moments. How am I holding up?'

'Very well Sir, everything is within normal parameters, but…'

'Yes the orchestra is yet to start…and after it starts if the weapon is activated we will get a chance to catch Dr Nasir in action.'

'We have got the location of the weapon now, but Dr Nasir is not around.'

'No other updates from Adolf.'

'The bomb squad is there trying to assess if they can defuse it,' Samir stopped as the crowd began clapping

He looked down at the frequency reader again. *Heart ok, lungs ok, and iris ok.* He turned his gaze towards the stage.

Mikaela stood at the centre of her twenty strong orchestra with her *Nyckelharpa* held gently in her hands. She began the first recitation a few seconds before the orchestra joined her. A rendition of gentle flute and harp strings began to fill the hall. The build up of the music increased, and then three singers took a step forward towards the standing microphone. 'By the Rivers of Babylon…' the singers started the first words of the prayer song.

Got to disrupt the song as minimum as possible, if Adolf believes the weapon to be sonic in nature then usage will be disrupted if the notes are not right or new ones added.

Mikaela looked at the piece of paper on which Adolf had scribbled the signs from the Talim. She had clipped it along with her musical notes in front of her in a stand.

Music to kill music…I just recognise a few in this Talim*; it may be do ra ra la thi thi…*

Her mind split between the on-going show and the page clipped in front of her. The song began to pick up pace. Mikaela was concentrating on the music, and deliberately began to miss notes from her recitation.

The violinist standing next glanced towards her and raised his eyebrows noting a change in the symphony. Mikaela responded with a slight smile and a gentle nod. He counteracted the change of Mikaela's notes by adjusting his own music. The violinist moved his second and third fingers across different areas of the string and loosened his hold by raising his chin slightly. A variation had begun unknown to the spectators in the hall and corporate boxes.

Dr Nasir watched from above, holding his hand out, still feeding his victims a sonic blast from the short-distance device.

Why have the people not started feeling uncomfortable? It should have started now. It's not working…

As Dr Nasir's face begin to flush with rage, he moved closer to the two officers of the bomb squad and pressed one of the three buttons on the device. As soon as he released his finger of the white button, the already struggling two officers began to shriek, but their voice got muted with the orchestra music. Convulsions started and their bodies started swaying wildly, blood began to ooze from their eyelids and mouths.

Adolf sensed an opportunity and looked towards Mansur who was closest to Dr Nasir.

Go for it Mansur!

'Subhaan Allah, Alhamdo lillah, Allaho Akbar.'

Mansur lunged forward, swinging his arms towards Dr Nasir and managed to push him towards Adolf. Dr Nasir stumbled at the sudden jerk and lost his footing. He fell but balanced himself by using his hands to stop the fall. But the hand held sonic device was separated and fell towards Aahana. Adolf leapt towards him and jumped over Dr Nasir. Mansur also joined in, and though weak, they managed to pin down Dr Nasir. Adolf used his elbows and hit Dr Nasir on the head to knock him out cold. The three intertwined bodies now began to disperse as Mansur and Adolf got up slowly.

Bang!

'No...Aahana, No!' shouted Adolf.

Bang! Bang! Bang! Bang! Bang!

Aahana in a swift move used the hand-held gun of the dead officers and fired at the hand-held sonic device destroying it and turned towards the bigger sonic device, pumping bullets into it. She dropped the gun as smoke came out from its nozzle, and walked towards Mansur.

'Why Aahana? Why?'

'Adolf, no one has the right to have such powers,' said Aahana coldly.

Adolf, Aahana and Mansur moved towards the windows, still slightly dazed, looking towards the Orchestra. And then it happened...

The music reached a crescendo with the notes starting to peak; the end was approaching. The different musicians in the orchestra were turning the sound around in increasing tempo for the grand finale, the closing.

Samir was now standing next to Agastya and again requested him to move out. Agastya reacted in a stone-deaf manner as he concentrated on the music.

'Sit down, Samir, and enjoy the music.'

What the hell is he doing? Has he gone nuts...but nothing has happened!

'Don't worry, Samir, I know the tension in your mind,' he said, looking at Samir with a reassuring smile. 'Nothing is going to happen... this is beautiful.'

The music roared for one final time and then closed down.

For a moment there was silence, which seemed to last for hours, and then the entire hall stood up.

The applause and cheering was deafening. The various dignitaries were looking at one another and smiling. The Iranian delegates and American delegates moved towards each other and started shaking hands and exchanging words. The Israeli ambassador, who had also been invited, moved towards a couple of invited Arab delegates and started talking.

Something had happened in the hall, with people feeling gentler, more open, and approachable.

Agastya closed his eyes and breathed a sigh of relief.

Yes, it worked. Another piece of the puzzle has fallen into place. They were right…it is the universal language. But we were lucky, the impact has been the opposite, otherwise the side effects would have showed on all of us like it did on Kurt and the mountaineers.

He put his hand on Samir's shoulder; Samir stood dazed from the music. He looked at Adolf, who was now holding Mikaela's hand, and also saw Mansur holding Aahana's hand. For a moment it was as though they were connected, understanding each other and able to read each other's thoughts. It was like they were all one, and not separate beings.

Agastya's mobile phone started vibrating. He saw Carina's name flashing on the screen. He flipped open the phone.

'Hello, Augi.'

'Yes, dear.'

'So you wrapped up things, but our discussion is still incomplete.'

'Yes I know.'

'And Leolus, am I right to assume you know more than what you told me…especially around Shaksgam valley, and the UFOs?'

Agastya remembered the discussions which they had in the few moments before boarding the flight.

Carina, a Guardian herself, wore the Gemini family ring and told me the story which only a Guardian member would know.

'Ha-ha…' Agastya chuckled.

'So we need to meet.'

'You know where to get me. I will be in the same place day after tomorrow, 6:00 p.m.'

'Okay, I will be there. I heard you made some changes to the place.'

'Come and see it for yourself. At least for any patriotic Indian it is an awe-inspiring sight.'

'Okay, Augi. But I will also want an answer to my earlier question… in or out of the order?'

'I will have one, don't worry.'

They ended the call, and Agastya moved towards Mansur, who was standing with Samir, Adolf, and Mikaela. He shook Mansur's hand and gave him a soft hug. He told Aahana that she was a lucky girl.

'I don't think so, Mr Home Minister. It is he who is lucky,' quipped Aahana.

They all laughed. Adolf still had one doubt in his mind.

Why the hell was Mansur involved in all this in the first place…where did he fit in the scheme of things?

Hundreds of miles away in Stockholm, Carina arrived in her office after catching another flight from New York. She was preparing to travel to India the next day.

She looked up at the grand painting depicting the inquisition conducted by the Catholic Church in 1616 with Pope Paul V as head of the papacy.

Galileo changed the world with his heliocentricity theory and we will do so again. The time has come to bring Leolus in. He is ready, and it's Jaipur once again. What a perfect place to sort out the jumble. Agastya had fooled everyone. B.C.C.I. and Saloni, the sex scandal, my foot. He was playing us all along…like a true Guardian.

Cygnus Times

Inside

How to open a Swiss bank account officially

Mysterious signal picked up from Andromeda galaxy

Black money and UFO sighting! Is there any connection? Indian scientists baffled as new photographic proof available

THE PEOPLE'S NEWS THAT MATTERS

Is It A Case of Exploding Mangoes Again?

More Tributes flow for Late General Kashyapa

New Delhi: More tributes from around the world are coming in for the late Indian Defence Minister General Abhimanyu Kashyapa. He breathed his last two days back, at New Delhi. He was being treated for multiple burn wounds which he had sustained during an accident in the Tawang region. Indian Home Minister Agastya Rathore released the following one-liner on hearing of his death. 'Though no more, his name will not only be enshrined, but embedded in a similar way along with greats like Sardar Patel, Indira Gandhi and Chanakya who wanted to see a united India...a strong India.'

Islamabad: A plane carrying Pakistan's next ISI chief General Pervez Musa Hussein and two senior officers of the Pakistan Air-Force crashed in the eastern part of Pakistan after suspected engine failure. Also killed in the crash was the new American military attaché to Pakistan, Colonel Rutherford Zachary Eccleston.

The Embraer Phenom 100 VIP jet on the way to Islamabad had crashed in less than ten minutes after takeoff from Bahawalpur, 60 miles west of the Indian border. Ironically this was the same location where Pakistan's President Mohammad Zia ul-Haq, had mysteriously crashed along with 28 people, including US Ambassador to Pakistan.

Rumours of a military coup are gaining ground, but are currently being denied by the civilian government. More details are awaited.

2 DAYS POST EVENT

Jantar Mantar, Jaipur
Rajasthan, India

December 13,18:00 IST

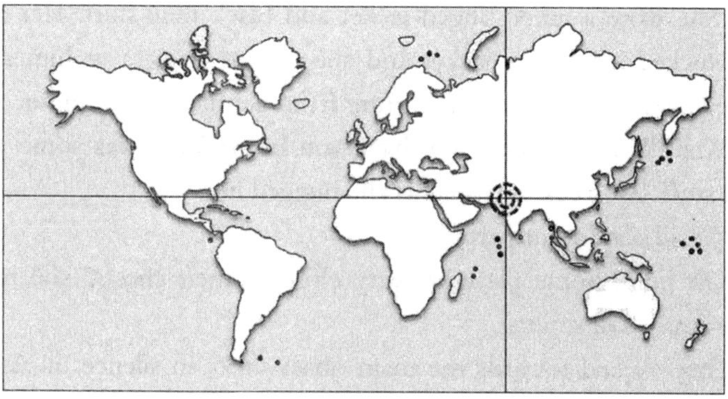

As he waited for Carina to enter the new layout made at the Jantar Mantar, Agastya stood near the Ram Yantra. They had met there a couple of months earlier, but since then some changes had been made near the structure. A new structure had gone up in the area adjoining the historical site. It was on a raised circular platform. More than two thousand national flags were planted on this platform and were flapping away in the cold evening wind. The large number of flags was reminiscent of the U.S. freedom zone.

Some people started moving out of the complex as the place was closing down for the day. As Agastya waited, he looked at the setting sun.

Our ancestors were so right. Hundreds of years ago they knew the positions of the stars and measured them with remarkable accuracy...and we have almost forgotten their contributions. To think about it, Carina was right, in a way, in studying archaeoastronomy--the study of how our ancient ancestors perceived and studied stars and the universe.

A gust of wind blew suddenly. Agastya closed his eyes and with his head down walked slowly towards the protection of some bordering trees. The flags were flapping to their full glory as he walked past them.

Tears welled up at the corners of his eyes. Agastya always grew emotional at this place, which was the brainchild of the late Defence

Minister and his uncle Abhimanyu who expired from wounds sustained in the skirmishes at Tawang.

'Agastya!'

Agastya turned his head and saw Carina walking slowly towards him. She wore a green-tinged jacket and black mini-skirt. Her hands were tucked inside her jacket and she looked straight at him as she flashed a gleaming smile, a departure from her usual demeanour.

'Well! Well! Agastya, how have you been? That was some pretty good stuff last week,' she said as she hugged him.

'We all played our parts.'

'Oh right! Some played it very close to their chests,' she replied sarcastically, still smiling.

They walked towards the main observatory in silence till Agastya spoke up.

'What do you mean, Cary, *close to the chest*?'

Carina came a little closer to him and put her lips close to his ear.

'S…A…L…O…N…I, *Saloni*. Strike one,' she whispered softly. 'The personal assistant was present only as a budget code for operation "Mansur Haider" or your project Babylon.'

Agastya straightened up. He looked at Carina closely and saw her eyes teasing him.

'B.C.C.I. *Project Babylon Operational, New Safari Syndicate Involved…Potential BCCI Support*…a wrong BCCI. Strike two,' she spoke with confidence, noticing Agastya's expression change from being clueless to that of a slight smile of knowingness. His dimple appeared through his beard.

'Ha-ha-ha-ha…'

Carina could not help but smile on seeing Agastya laugh with such abandon.

'So no strike three, dear? And what's this Leolus stuff?'

'Well, I want to hear from you first…and Leolus, if you explain to me, then I will tell you the important message I have for you.'

'It's simple, Carina. It's about destiny, about manipulating the universe to save a nation,' replied Agastya, toning down his voice. They were inside the main complex, walking towards the Ram Yantra.

'Cary, my people are an emotional lot. We think with our hearts and not with our minds. We suffer a lot of pain, unhappiness, issues, and differences. Somehow we manage to pull ourselves together and move ahead. A 6000-year-old civilisation does not deserve such treatment. Something better is needed, and this can happen only in a united country that will follow and believe in someone…a hero.'

Carina adjusted her hair and slowly turned towards Agastya. There was a moment of silence as they tried to size each other up.

'Okay, I will go over everything in detail. I trust that you already know the big picture and will fill you in on the rest,' said Agastya, getting down on the ground and lying back facing the sky. Carina sat down beside him.

'There will always be confusion within an intelligence circle on interpretation of various intercepts, and in this case we utilised Pervez's plan against him.'

'That I know, and you seriously managed to keep us people guessing. You sure did. We were on the wrong path altogether, and had I not met you face to face in New York at the UN, I wouldn't have known.'

'You mean…'

'Yes, you slipped up there when you said the potential strike may not take place, and your face seemed to tell more than you seemed to be saying,' said Carina now with confidence. 'My first thought was that you would definitely know about the Shaksgam incident which you have done such a good job of covering up…'

Agastya smiled once again.

'And that made me think that there was more to all of this. And then I checked Samir's calls to Delhi.'

'You intercepted his calls?'

'Like you said to the American Ambassador to India, *'We are all listening to each other.'* Also I got a hint that Saloni was not a lady or a sex scandal but an acronym for a budget code…a few Saloni messages had some numbers associated.'

Agastya silently watched Carina working on her hypothesis and, to his amazement, moving in the right direction.

'And then things started to fall in place...' A flash of lightning lit the sky followed by the roar of thunder. They looked up instantly. Seeing the grey clouds in the evening sky, they surmised it would rain soon. Agastya now sat up and pointed towards where the twelve Zodiac instruments were placed. Carina nodded and both stood up and started walking towards it.

'So in short I knew B.C.C.I. in the message was the organisation running the cricket operations and S.A.L.O.N.I is actually a budget code and the Safari Syndicate. It was not a cabal of the intelligence community but an odd group of politicians cobbled together to make fit what they see.'

'I am proud of you. Despite all the precautions I took, you have come close to decoding the biggest manipulation that we have accomplished in the country…now my turn.'

Agastya explained the need for creating unity in the country and how things were getting worse, with problems both at external and internal levels. With the ever-growing internal security threat and the rising tensions at the border with Pakistan and China, India was not safe. The threat perception was further compounded by the post recessionary after-effects. To every problem there was a solution, and with problems as big as the Kashmir issue, the solution had to be a drastic one. The solution was S.A.L.O.N.I., in which an entire system was manipulated to create a hero from Kashmir.

'The chosen hero was Mansur Haider, the bowler who could bowl at a tear-away pace and uproot any batsman with the cricket ball using them like bombs, your *Baramulla Bomber*.'

'You wanted to give Kashmiris a hero, a hero they could identify and empathise with,' said Carina in a gritty tone.

'It's more than that. I wanted a hero for the country, a person whom the whole of India could follow and love. Somehow things went smoothly and mostly as per plan.' Carina gazed at Agastya for some time and shook her head.

'Carina, war is in our blood. We are animals. It is the rules of society that keep us under control…Social Rules. We should fight as if it is the only language we understand. But the world has changed now. This is the only way forward. Manipulate at every level for the greater good.'

A few moments of silence passed between them. In his mind Agastya thought of how the plan had worked to perfection, despite a few hiccups. But in the end it was successful.

'You know, come to think of it, you are right in a way…in fact, you are one hundred percent correct. You did the right thing, and it does not surprise me—your ancestors did it before you did, and you just perfected the art on a minor scale.'

Looking at her, he gave a calm look as if he was expecting what she was going to share.

'Why do I think you know what I am going to talk about…the Moors Convention, the Guardians from the Royal Lineage.'

His face grew more serious, his eyes focusing intently on her.

'It does not exist anymore,' said Agastya in a low tone.

'It always has and always will, and we have acted mostly independently. It is just in the recent past that we have started joining forces to bring the convention back to life.'

'What do you mean bring it back to life?'

'Your family was a part of it, and someone from your lineage did visit the last meeting that the convocation had as a group, during the wedding of King George VI on 26 April 1923 in London.' Carina came close to Agastya. 'They brought a big silver jug with holy water in it,' she whispered. 'The water was from the holy river Ganga and from the secret river Sarasvati.'

'How do you know the Sarasvati part…'

'We were all in it together—it passes from generation to generation! Your name is Agastya Harshvardhan Rathore, royal lineage from the ancient *Suryavanshi* clan in *Bharat-Varsh,* or India as we know it now.'

A cold breeze passed through as both looked up at the twilight sky.

'And my name is Carina Leijonhufvud, which you must know through genealogy is from a noble family. I belong to the lineage of the royal family from the ancient Nordic region that has been handed the secret of the convocation.'

'I knew something was there in the royalty line but never thought of asking.'

'It happens…and we were watching you…waiting for you to join in.'

Both stood still; Agastya brushed his short beard with his left hand.

'And what exactly were you waiting for?'

'To see if you really had the guts to do what you did with Mansur. But you mastered the art, confused all of us. Mansur's messages across the border, dummy codes, making the Pakistanis think Mansur was not on their side, making the Americans think Mansur is perhaps against them. In a sense we were all observing him for different reasons and, in a way, protecting him.'

Agastya raised his hands and shrugged his shoulders.

'You all fell for it, but to do something right we need to manipulate the popular vote.'

'Yes, and we know you are ready. After World War II our network got broken, with imperial lines across various nations being destroyed. We have now managed to regroup, and together we can actually do good!'

'Good…but *good* is specific. I am thinking for my nation. The convocation principles got destroyed with the great betrayal of World War II.'

'Yes, I know, but we have the chance to amend it all and forgive our sins. The Jews and millions of those innocent souls who died during the war will forgive us.'

'Our family is the family of the lion.'

'Yes. Leolus, from the constellation Leo, my lineage stands for the constellation Gemini, and we have four others with us—Capricorn, Sagittarius, Taurus, and Scorpio.'

'Only six... where are the other six? We need twelve to hold any round table convention of the guardians.'

'Yes, we need the other six, and we need to find them fast as we fear the rise of Ophiuchus.'

'The thirteenth zodiac carrier…I thought the whole lineage was vanquished, had been routed.'

Carina shook her head with a serious expression on her face, and held Agastya's arms.

'We think he has come back, and the UFO's reported in Shaksgam valley earlier which you and your people have covered up so nicely is probably related to it. Isn't that so?'

'Not that I am aware of. But I will not share now what happened there. Maybe in time'.

Not so soon, dear. We ourselves are yet to understand it, and I have lost the most precious thing I had.

'But we know, Agastya, we know…your wife Vitasta died because of it.…the flying triangular objects were also seen over Srinagar, Kottayam, Nalanda and some more smaller towns.'

Agastya's face flushed as memories of his wife flashed through his mind, advancing to the ill-fated day when she disappeared.

'She is not dead, just lost…and once we understand the phenomenon I will get her back! But on initial assessment we believe that Dr Nasir's testing of the sonic weapon in the valley brought them there...they can be termed as *vimanas* which are explained in our ancient texts,' said Agastya hurriedly, not able to hide his emotions.

So then this part is also true…

'Carina, if I come into the order I need to be sure if the Guardians are going to do it for the right reason this time?'

'Yes, we are, and as you said earlier…for proper social rule we need order. And we are the ones who have the opportunity to bring order into the world and protect it…and together we will also look into this UFO or *vimana* phenomenon as you call it.'

Agastya's head was bowed as they continued walking. He began to review what he knew of ancient history.

Galileo was one of the members of the Guardian order, and he found something and was ready to make the world know until the Vatican shut him down during the inquisition. What did he see and what did he know that made the Church so scared of him? Archaeoastronomy…Jantar Mantar was built and we thought we could find something, but could not…Why is this happening now?

'How are we supposed to go about it?' asked Agastya.

'Well, believe it or not, Mansur may be the key, and we need to handle Professor Kaul.'

'He is just an old archaeologist. How is Mansur the key?'

'Not just any archaeologist, he is also an archaeo-astronomist, and an Indologist who also worked with United Nations Office for Outer Space Affairs (UNOOSA). This complicates our task. He is closing in on things. Especially the ancient metallic tablets and the records. And Mansur…well, his bloodline carries a secret. He will try to find out more about his family now, after all he now knows his carpet held an old secret.'

'Yes, but Professor Kaul is a civilian on a quest, we cannot just bump him off. Why not let him find the truth, we do owe it to the world…humanity should know. We ourselves don't know the entire story of our origin.'

'Remember one thing, Agastya: There is a power there somewhere and it is watching us, and for his sake we need to bring stability around the world…and stability means control over information. Our job is to keep humanity moving till we come face to face with the truth.'

'Is someone really out there, Carina?'

'Not out there, up there. Someone up there is looking at us from the skies. God? Alien? I don't know. But there is something up there and we are just fulfilling our destiny and roles assigned to us, like this was all supposed to happen,' said Carina, pointing towards the sky.

Both looked into the sky now and saw stars shining brightly. They smiled and hugged each other lightly.

'Augi, in the end it's all about destiny. Fighting it…'

'Yes, you are right, and she was right, too.'

'Who?'

Agastya smiled and looked up at the brilliant night sky stretching overhead, as far as the eye could see..

The old coffee reader Kasha from Srinagar– 'Fight your destiny, build hope and make it happen,' because you don't know which forces of the universe are conspiring against you. But which force is controlling us?

Epilogue

In pace, ut sapiens, aptarit idonea bello

In peace, like a wise man,
he appropriately prepares for war

407 DAYS TO EVENT

Farmhouse, Nalanda, near Patna,
Bihar, India

October 31,20:30 IST

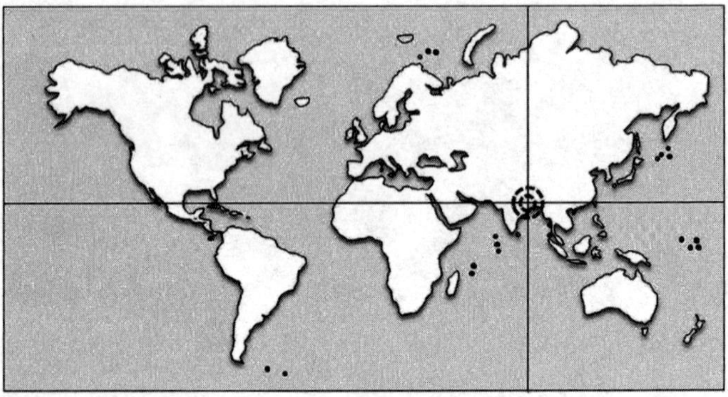

'**You are sure** this plan is going to work, Sir? Fixing up the Indian Cricket team so Mansur Haider can play in it?'

'Yes Samir, I am sure. If we are able to make the situation favourable for Mansur Haider and manipulate his activities under controlled circumstances, it is possible. Anyway, haven't we worked on Mansur for the last five years, ensuring he gets the necessary practice, directly or indirectly?'

'Yes Sir, we have, but I did not know the exact reason till then. I'll follow the orders as planned,' Major Samir Ansari conceded.

'But what would happen if things go out of control or not as planned?' Captain Sanjay Pal Uppal was not convinced as yet.

'We will have to improvise. Remember, team, there are only perceptions and illusions in life; anything can be manipulated.' The Indian Home Minster's voice boomed across the room.

He had just devised a bold plan to solve the Kashmir *issue.* The plan was a mixture of appeasement, stringent, affirmative and manipulative action. The appeasement and stringent action was on-going since India's independence from the British, the affirmative and manipulative action was something new being tried. Funding was done though indirect routes to famous film directors like Khan, Chopra and Johar to develop films on Kashmir based topics like romance, comedy and family, nothing related to terrorism. More local talent was being given affirmative action to mainstream India. A mixing of cultures was in the process. The *Mansur Haider* case would be of manipulation.

Agastya looked towards the four CCTC officers, three from the Special Forces wing of the Indian Army. Captain Sanjay Pal Uppal, Captain Sunil Kochar and Major Nikhil Srivastava were listed in the armed forces; the fourth, Samir Ansari, was a ghost. Samir trained under the Indian Army and served in operations in the North East, but he was not enlisted. All four were handpicked by the Defence Minister General Abhimanyu Kashyapa, who was also present at the presentation in this farmhouse.

'Sir, how do you protect the identity of Mansur and our activities?' Captain Sanjay's voice held his anxiety.

'We all know Pakistan has an operation underway called Project Babylon.'

All three nodded, with the Defence Minister still not showing any expression.

'We will use their operation name "Babylon." Hence whenever we communicate with this name Pakistanis will think we are discussing their plan.'

'Sir, isn't there a risk that they may put two and two together and retaliate?' asked Samir.

'I don't get it,' said Agastya.

'Sir, for example if we talk about Mansur as our candidate they may interpret it like Mansur is someone we are using against them; that can put his life in jeopardy.'

That's what I would want, both ways we can win then, thought Agastya.

'That's a chance I am willing to take.'

The three officers and Samir saluted and left the room.

'Collateral damage?' asked General Kashyapa.

'It depends on how you look at it, Dead or Alive, Mansur is going to be made a hero; it does not matter. The nation is important.'

'My God! You have grown! Your grandfather would have been proud.'

'I did not know him; he died in England badly burnt. If it was not for you I wonder who would have guided me till here…to reach this pinnacle.'

Precisely Agastya, but there are more things that need to be done and this time for humanity or whatever we have left of it.

'I haven't been entirely honest with you on your grandfather's death,' said Abhimanyu Kashyapa. 'Sit down now, this will take some time. I have some history to share with you…history related to your ancestors. Somehow I felt this was an opportune moment, so I brought this along.'

Agastya sat down as he saw the patriarch remove a medium sized metallic box from a case he had brought along. He removed a red, old cloth bound book.

The cover-page of the book had two signs–one of them was the *Swastika* which was embedded inside the *Star of David.* There were twelve circles drawn in different parts of the *Star of David,* and a white circle in the centre. General Abhimanyu Kashyapa now sat across the short table and placed the book in front of Agastya Harshvardhan Rathore.

'This book is titled–"CHOS SKYONG", which meant Protector or Guardians in Tibetan. You are the protector of the Suryavanshi clan…from the constellation Leo.'

Notes: FACT OR FICTION

DEPARTMENTS, AGENCIES, AND ACRONYMS

Central Counter Terrorist Command (CCTC): India's Central Government Anti-Terrorist Organisation, operates under the Home Ministry. Developed from officers and resources from RAW, IB and Special forces, it has a tie up with various international sympathetic spy agencies across different governments.

Fact (in part): The Home Ministry has proposed to create a new centralised unit that reports directly to the Home Ministry.
http://www.satp.org/satporgtp/countries/india/document/papers/09dec25pib.htm

Bank of Credit and Commerce International (BCCI): A Pakistani merchant bank formed in 1972. The bank allegedly had the blessing of CIA director George H.W. Bush (later to become the 43rd President of United States). The bank was said to be used for worldwide money-laundering activities and converting black money into white. At one time it was the fastest growing international bank, with *Time* magazine describing it as 'a global intelligence operation and a Mafia-like enforcement squad.' The bank was closed down in 1991.

Fact: Even after having been closed down and even after an investigation, many of its functions still are not understood.
http://www.fas.org/irp/congress/1992_rpt/bcci/
http://www.nytimes.com/1993/05/02/books/the-worst-of-all-possible-banks.html
http://en.wikipedia.org/wiki/Bank_of_Credit_and_Commerce_International

Swedish Neutrality and wiki-leak cable, 09STOCKHOLM552: According to the Wiki-Leak cable, Sweden may no longer be neutral in conflicts and can take sides. The title of the cable was: NEW SWEDISH DEFENSE PRIORITIES: SWEDEN PUTS NEUTRALITY IN THE DUSTBIN OF HISTORY

Fact: True
http://www.cablegatesearch.net/cable.php?id=09STOCKHOLM552

Special Operation Force: Special military units with licence to kill used in special combat role and sometimes used for espionage. It's SAS in UK, Delta Force in US, GROM in Poland. In India – MARCOS, NSG (Used against terrorists of 2008 attacks in Mumbai), Garud, Para Commandos (1971 war against Pakistan, Kargil, 1999)

Sweden has its own version *Operationsgruppen,* but they are into intelligence also. Also known as SOG, it was formed in 2011 with consolidation of two special ops units, Special Protection Group (SSG) and the Special Reconnaissance Group (SIG).

(Trivia note: The unit was called *Särskilda Skydds Intelligens Gruppen* or SSIG in Baramulla Bomber first draft, as new name was not decided for the merger in 2009/10)

Fact: True
http://sofrep.com/8314/swedish-sof-the-sarskilda-operationsgruppen/
http://www.militaryphotos.net/forums/showthread.php?124558-S%E4rskilda-skyddsgruppen-(SSG)-Official-Release

EVENTS

Tunguska Event: An explosion which occurred on June 30th 1908, in Russia. The explosion occurred near Podkamennaya Tunguska River. The blast is estimated to be about 5.0 on the Richter scale. 80 million trees were estimated to be destroyed over 2,150 square kilometres (830 sq mi) area. Speculations are many on why the explosion occurred, from a bursting of a meteor or comet mid air, to black hole, anti matter, aliens war to even the scientist, Tesla conducting an experiment.

Fact: True
http://en.wikipedia.org/wiki/Tunguska_event
http://science.nasa.gov/science-news/science-at-nasa/2008/30jun_tunguska/

Safari Club: A pact formed in 1976 by an international group of intelligence agencies, including France, Egypt, Saudi Arabia, Morocco, and Iran, to share information and conduct covert operations. The CIA allegedly was also involved in its formation to compensate for the loss of freedom of activity due to measures taken by the U.S. Congress after the Watergate scandal.

Fact: Various reports indicate that this was established to fight communism and its spread. It may be still active in some form (intelligence agencies and objectives may have changed).
http://stevenjohnhibbs.wordpress.com/2010/09/05/cia-drug-running-terrorists-the-imperial-anatomy-of-al-qaeda/ http://www.historycommons.org/entity.jsp?entity=safari_club_1

Farkhor Air Base: a Tajik military base that has had a 25-bed hospital since 2001 to treat Afghan Northern Alliance (opponents of the Taliban) members.

Fact: Existence of medical facilities present; some reports indicate that it will be turned into a base with fighter planes.

http://www.indianexpress.com/news/tajik-air-base-is-ready-gives-india-its-first-footprint-in-strategic-central-asia/24207/
http://en.wikipedia.org/wiki/Farkhor_Air_Base

Saint Joseph's Franciscan Convent Massacre: Occurred around October 26, 1947, in Baramulla, Kashmir, India when invading tribesman from Pakistan looted, plundered, and raped the town, reducing the population by more than tenfold.

Fact: Reported in the *New York Times* by Robert Trumbull, November 10, 1947.
http://www.un.int/india/ind29.pdf

Shaksgam Valley: Region in Kashmir that is part of the 5,800 km Trans-Karakoram Tract. It is a highly inhospitable region, with many high mountain ranges. Most of the valley was part of the Kingdom of Shigar, located inside Pakistan-Controlled Kashmir (POK), till 1963, when Pakistan gave up its claim and ceded administration of the area to China. India claims the land as part of the unified state of Jammu and Kashmir. The Siachen Glacier runs along one edge of the valley, where the Indian military maintains a presence due to its strategic nature.

Fact: True
http://www.telegraphindia.com/1061120/asp/opinion/story_7023564.asp
http://en.wikipedia.org/wiki/Trans-Karakoram_Tract
http://www.hinduonnet.com/thehindu/thscrip/print.l?file=20061020001608500.htm&date=fl2320/&prd=fline&

SCIENCE

Archaeoastronomy: A study of how the ancient human race studied and understood the stars, universe and phenomenon in the sky. This science can be seen across different cultures and timelines from the earliest of times. The Mayans, Sumerians, Babylonians, Egyptians and many civilisations had an active system of astrological study and their knowledge on star systems are very accurate when compared with the current era. In Jaipur (India), Jantar Mantar is one such example of a site where archaeoastronomy was studied. Other examples are Stonehenge (England), El Castillo, Chichen Itza (Mexico).

Fact: True
http://en.wikipedia.org/wiki/Archaeoastronomy

A-U-M as the Primordial Sound: Aum is a Vedic sound of Sanskrit origin. As per Puranic literature, Aum is the sound present during creation of the universe, hence primordial in nature. It is said to be the originator sound for everything we hear.

Fact: Open to interpretation, more details in website (when completed)
http://en.wikipedia.org/wiki/Om
http://www.spiritsound.com/aum.html

ABOUT SVASTIK TRILOGY

Svastik trilogy is a series of three books – Yes!

The books are connected – Yes!

Do I need to read them one after another – No!

Surprised!

Well, Svastik trilogy is a series of three books – *Eka*, the first part is the Baramulla Bomber; *Dvitiya*, the second part is titled, The Consultant. And the third part (*Tritiya*) is yet to be titled. The books are connected with a question. The question of what is the power behind the creation of the Universe and human origins.

The main protagonists of the first two books are different but both stories run parallel during the same period. The main protagonists in the first two books are searching for an answer. And the third book connects them together. So anyone can enter the series either reading the first book first or the second book first. But both books need to be read before the third book. And each book will answer specific questions.

And what are the other questions? Well they are the following:

- *How was the universe created?*
- *What is the power of the supernatural force in the universe?*
- *What is relation of archaeoastronomy to us now?*
- *Are there secret societies controlling and manipulating the world activities?*
- *Is everything pre-destined or can we control our future?*

ACKNOWLEDGMENTS

The question: How did I begin? — 'By Accident'
The question: How was the journey till now? — 'Painful'
The question: Was it worth it? — 'Time will tell…but, we don't actually exist! Do we?'

Baramulla Bomber is because of many people, incidents and experience I have gained over the last 36 years in my current time-line. The story was forming since 2005, but I started writing the first words on 29th September 2009 in Srinagar, Kashmir. This trip was done when I was in heavy debt and going through a huge mental battle to survive.

Why was that necessary? Well because I believed in the story so much, and after a catalyst hit me, I did not want to postpone it.

Since then many people have come and helped me, guided me, criticised me but most important motivated me to keep on going. I am mentioning a few names, but if I missed any name out…apologies, and I will await your smashing emails and calls.

First I want to thank my family, my parents and my sisters (especially my twin sister) and their families. I am indebted to them for the support, love and care they have provided without prejudice and judgment.

My friend Naveen Khurana for making me smile and see the calmer side of life. Ashish Kochar, for being there and discussing everything under the sun. Aekloveya Shyam for helping me in my critical time of personal need.

Thank you, Devesh, Anand, Kari, Rishi, Srikanth, Arjun, Vishal, Simran, Meenakshi, Asha, Yulia.

To Prerna Mitra, thank you for starting the writing dream with me ten years back, on our–*Sari in the Boardroom* article.

To my schools and institutes and my bosses for allowing me grow and thrive.

To my team and colleagues, for working along with me and supporting me with their hard work.

Thank you, Hemant Galagali for giving me valuable feedback and continuous inputs during the horrid rewriting days. Thank you Shraddha Majalkar for giving me an initial feedback.

To Ashish Malik, Anupama Sensharma, Naveen Khurana, Shweta Sharma for reading the initial drafts, finishing it and giving me feedback.

To Anuradha Goyal for motivating me with a few words each time we talked.

To Dola, thanks for the help along with other members of my alma matter. Thank you to the teams of IIM Kozhikode and MICA who supported specific projects related to Baramulla Bomber.

To my entire editing team who over the last two years at different times have supported me and improved the Queen's English for me.

To my roomies over the years: Amit (5 of them), Rajesh, Sahil, Sanchit, Karan, Avinish for having patience with me.

To Jyoti Kumari, thanks for all the help and guidance.

To Niyogi Books for accepting me into their esteemed family.

To Gita Rajan, for the tireless effort to smoothen the book, and keeping the author spirit in me alive in the final days.

To Shiny Das, for lending me an ear (or ears, not sure ☺)

Thanks to the team of Shawshank Redemption for making a film which helped me escape (like Andy Dufresne) from my own personal prison.

To the character Rocky (Sylvester Stallone), whose motto of going one more round, motivated me to have that *eye of the tiger* and keep moving forward.

To all science fiction movies and serials which kept my imagination alive and kicking – chief among them *Star Trek*, *Star War* and *Back to the Future* series, and Carl Sagan's *Cosmos* documentary.

To Dada (Sourav Ganguly), for the fighting spirit he has shown over the years.

To Amitabh Bachchan, for entertaining us and making me laugh and cry over the years.

To MJ – May you rest in peace now.

To Amish (Shiva Trilogy) and King Hopper Kartik (Horn OK Series) for writing on subjects they believed in, making the market believe that such subjects can work in India.

To multiple authors who had written to me and urged me not to lose hope and keep moving forward.

I would also like to thank my future wife (wherever she is), who will have to have a lot of patience dealing with my idiosyncrasies.

Finally to my readers, thank you for giving me a chance to entertain you.

And to my critiques…live long and prosper!

OTHER ACKNOWLEDGMENTS

Initial Critique and Structural Editor: Sucharita Dutta-Asane.
Other Editorial Support: Bharati Mahadevan, Amulya Kulkarni, Shiva Sihag and Karl Monger.
Critique and Initial Support: Kaniskha Gupta, Writer's Side.
Manuscript Critique: Hemant Galagali.
Images and Illustrations: Design-Flyover, Muralidhara HM and Shruti Ravi.
Cover Page: Damonza.
Big Thank You: Anuradha Goyal & Dola Halder.

SOCIAL MEDIA DETAILS

Twitter Handle: @clarkprasad

Facebook page: Author Page:
http://www.facebook.com/#!/pages/Clark-Prasad-The-Official-Fanpage/188104207902785

Web Site: www.clarkprasad.com

SPECIAL ACKNOWLEDGMENT

A special acknowledgement to the most important group of people of whom I heard a lot of stories since childhood – the Indian Armed Forces, of which both my parents (Captain (Dr.) J. Prasad, AMC and Lt. S. Prasad, MNS) were members. Thank you for all your sacrifices. I always remind myself that for my future you all have sacrificed your today.

Standing here, my father in front of a WWII memorial

July 1969, Kohima, Nagaland, India

The words engraved there

"When you go home tell them of us and say for your tomorrow we gave our today"

SVASTIK TRILOGY

Will Return in

The Consultant: Shopno Paradox

Paranormal Espionage Thriller

How do you stop an assassination which
has been committed by you in the past!

Join the hunt with
Naveen David Talpade…to search out the secret of
Black Money, and NWO!

Preview of Svastik – Dvitiya

Turn Page

SCHUTZ-STAFFEL FIRST STEPS

Hooghly River, Calcutta
Bengal, British India

July 1st,1939,13:13 Calcutta

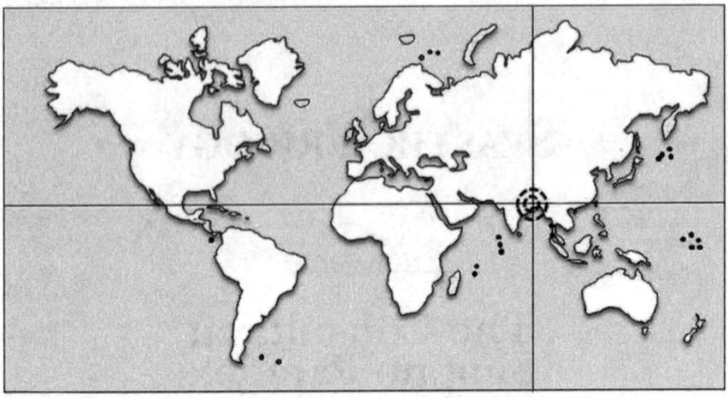

The gentle humming sound from the boat was matched by the squawking crows flying close to a boat crossing the Hooghly. Some crows tried to land on the sail of the steam-powered river boat but were shooed away by a couple of the boat's occupants. The five occupants who had rented the boat for the crossing were going back into the city after a long and incredulous journey from Tibet.

The enveloping silence did not have a calming impact on the group leader, German zoologist and SS officer Ernst Schäfer. He looked on at the ongoing construction of a bridge across this great river of the Bengal, which was nearing completion. Schäfer pondered on the incomplete mission entrusted to him from the Nazi high command.

The Führer and my Schutz-Staffel commander will be disappointed. We have not done our work; the conquest of the planet should not be started now.

The boat rocked hard as the sail caught wind, shaking the occupants on the boat. Some wooden boxes and leather cases fell and scattered in the centre of the boat. Schäfer called out to one of his men to ensure the cargo they were carrying was kept in order. The cargo included photographs, head casts and measurements of people. Animal specimens like Tibetan dogs, wolves, foxes, birds were also sent back earlier to Nazi Germany, along with seeds of different varieties of crops.

Schäfer walked towards one of the scattered suitcases, picked it up and adjusted it along with the other luggage. It had a robe of the Dalai Lama himself and some gold coins personally handed to him by His Holiness himself.

Himmler will not be happy. We did not get the metallic tablets. It's not in Lhasa but thousands of miles away in Shaksgam Valley.

Back in Berlin, in Nazi Germany, alone in his chamber was the commanding officer *Reichsführer* of the SS, Heinrich Luipold Himmler. Just back from the fourth anniversary ceremony of the Nazi research unit, *Ahnenerbe* which was developed to study the forefathers or origins of the Aryan race, he was going through a report sent from Tibet.

My men may not have got the metallic tablets from Tibet but young Heinrich Harrer will reach Nanga Parbat in Kashmir soon and then travel to the Shaksgam Valley. Hopefully then the tablets to guide us next will be there.

On his table a silver Swastika, hooked cross was engraved, and Himmler ran his hand across it feeling the cold metal against his skin. He closed his eyes and got up slowly, taking a deep breath. Opening his eyes he walked slowly to the window. Looking though the glasses he could see a regiment of his SS troops marching on the lane below.

The Swastika for the world and Hakenkreutz for us, the power of the Gods are with us. Knowing ancient India has guided me till now. Getting the SS, modelled on the ancient Hindu warrior sage Kashyapa was a great idea from her, it is working perfectly. She may be actually right, know the Vedas and know the start and end of the universe, she said.

Himmler took a deep breath again and released it slowly.

We need to find more about CHOS SKYONG, the Guardians. First let me read these mystical poems.

He opened a small leather bound red book, next to a bible. The leather bound book was with inscriptions translated into German from Sanskrit.

Karmanye Vadhikaraste, Ma phaleshou kada chana,
Ma Karma Phala Hetur Bhurmatey Sangostva Akarmani

THE SEARCH RESTARTS

Natural History Museum
London, United Kingdom

December 11,11:30 GMT

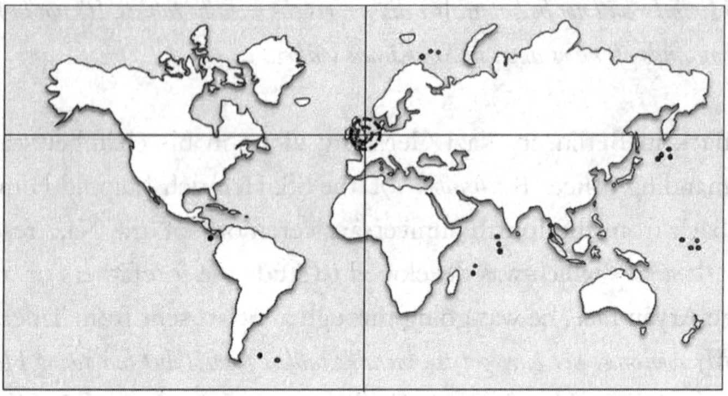

'**Professor...Professor Kaul**...Pro—Ouchhhh!' The caller tripped and was on the floor. The professor's assistant, Roberto, looked up at his boss, who reached out his hand to him.

Roberto spoke before he could stand up, 'You were right! There is a link to the artefact collected in Skeleton Lake, in Roopkund, and the ones taken from Lima Museum.'

The professor grinned toothily.

'And the skeletons...I tested some samples and...they are vibrating at a different frequency then a normal human skeleton.'

'I know...That's why we are leaving right away for India.'

'What! And the preparations...the instruments.' Roberto was dusting off his coat, and he saw the professor give a thumbs-up sign.

'Ahhh...Carla, it's her again. She has done it.'

'Right! Let us find more about *CHOS SKYONG*, and why the Nazis, especially Himmler, was so obsessed with Tibet and Vedic period of India. And the first step has already been taken, I have this person, who calls himself the "Consultant" and he claims he has details of the ancient metallic tablets and also the records!'

Roberto's eyes widened

Tablets yes, but the records of the universe! It cannot be true.

About the author

Clark Prasad, alter ego of Suraj Prasad, could be called a mixed citizen. Born in a leap year (year of Rocky, All the President's Men, Omen, Hera Pheri and Kalicharan) in Lagos, Nigeria he lived most of his life in New Delhi and had his education in Lagos, Delhi, Mangalore, and Kozhikode.

A pharmacist with a management degree, Baramulla Bomber is his first book. His first education on the mysteries of the universe came via Carl Sagan's *Cosmos*, and since then he never looked back on reading, watching and discussing about the universe. He grew up during the cold war days with BBC radio was one of his mysterious companions as a kid, when his father played the news regularly everyday. World War II news and documentaries on CIA-KGB tussle kept him engaged. As a kid he wanted to be an archaeologist or an astronaut, but fate had its own road and he got involved with Mr Carbon aka Chemistry. Currently he is a healthcare management consultant.

Aside of writing, travelling and hiking, he is deeply involved in alumni related activities for his Alma Mater.

Clark's favourite authors are Robin Cook, Jeffery Archer, Robert Ludlum, Frederick Forsyth and Tom Clancy. Books like *The Odessa File, Patriot Games, Coma, Not a Penny More not a Penny Less*, and of course *Da-Vinci Code* are some of his favourites.

He is based at Bengaluru, Planet Earth.